# DARK PRESENCE

# DARK PRESENCE

*A Paranormal Thriller*

*by John Turiano*

ISBN: 978-1-7342196-9-2

Cover Art by www.miblart.com

For updates on the latest book releases and promotions subscribe to the mailing list at:  jturiano.com/author.htm

*Special thanks to Sue, who gets all the first drafts and is my greatest critic. And to Steve for his edits, invaluable insight, and suggestions, helping make the book the best it can be. Also, thanks to all the readers and reviewers, for without them I do not think I would have the will to continue writing.*

# PROLOGUE

HAVE YOU EVER RECOGNIZED SOMEONE YOU DON'T WANT TO SEE? You could be shopping, dining, or at some other public place. Sometimes you turn and look away before being noticed. Other times, they stare back and you freeze, not knowing how to react. Do you look away, acting nonchalant, or give them a nod of recognition? That just happened to Marie. She was returning to her car when she spotted him. She panicked for a split second before turning away, but it was too late, for he had caught her glance.

She walked away quickly, keeping her back to the man, all the while drawing a mental image from her brief glimpse: He wore a black baseball cap pulled down low over his brow, a thick mop of curly, brown locks poked out from the hat. It had been many years and she couldn't be certain it was him, that is, if not for the eyes, they were a dead giveaway. For he had returned her look with a cold, evil stare. If you look closely enough, the eyes are truly a window to the soul, and this one was dark. This man was scary, and pardon the overused cliché, seeing him sent a chill up her spine. She hurried back to her car and drove off.

# PART ONE - GATHERING GLOOM

# CHAPTER 1

IT WAS A STRANGE REQUEST AT SUCH A LATE HOUR, but she did not want to disappoint her best friend. So she slipped on a lightweight jacket and left the comfort of her cozy apartment. The smell of wet grass and sweet elderberry filled the air as she trudged along the sidewalk. Crickets chirped in harmony while a swarm of June bugs danced around a buzzing street lamp. She started her Kia Forte sedan and drove off to her late night rendezvous.

Marie was having second thoughts as she pulled into the barren parking lot in back. There were just two cars and neither of them resembled her friend's red Subaru. There had to be an explanation. Perhaps Kimbra was stranded without a ride, for she gave no details in the text. Regardless of the reason, Marie abandoned the safety of her car and hurried off to the busy street a short distance away. She rounded the corner and approached the front entrance.

Tony's was a local pub they frequented together, it was dark and nearly empty as she entered and searched for her friend. Two men were seated at the bar and a young couple occupied a nearby table, but there was no sign of Kimbra. She took a seat at a secluded booth in back and placed a call which went immediately to voicemail. She closed the connection and was typing another text when a tired looking waitress appeared. It was awkward sitting alone at a bar at such a late hour, Marie decided a drink would help calm her nerves and ordered a glass of white wine. She looked around, checked the time, and tried to give the appearance of waiting to meet someone, which she was. Mercifully, her drink arrived shortly, she took a sip and waited...

Two glasses of wine later Marie got up and left. Not sure whether to be angry or worried, she hurried back to her car, locked the door, and again checked her phone. All her texts and voice messages were unanswered. She considered stopping at her friend's apartment to settle the matter right then and there. Kimbra had been having problems lately and could be in trouble. On the other hand, she was prone to dramatic outbursts, and it was very late. There could be a logical explanation: she could have misplaced her phone, or it could have a dead battery, or any number of other reasons why she didn't show up. Better to resolve the matter another time. Marie drew in a deep breath, started the car, and drove away.

She pulled into her parking lot tired and cranky, got out and slammed the car door shut. The sound echoed back from the darkness. It was quiet now, the sprinklers were off, there was only the chatter of a lone cricket to break the silence. The flickering glow from a lonely television set stood out, dimly lighting a single window on the dark brick exterior. A slight headache was fermenting as Marie entered the main door and plodded up the stairs, fumbling for her keys. She could have sworn she left a light on as she entered the darkened apartment and flicked the light switch on. But her surroundings remained black.

Strange, the power was on in the building. Probably a tripped circuit breaker, she thought. As her eyes slowly adjusted to the darkness, the LED clock on the microwave became visible, glowing out the late hour in a bright green.

That meant there was power in the kitchen, must be a burnt light bulb she reasoned.

Deeper into the apartment she ventured. Someone suddenly grabbed her from behind! The feel of cold steel pressed against her throat, producing a sharp pain.

"Not a sound," a male voice commanded.

The grip around her chest was smothering as she was dragged into the kitchen.

"What do you want? I have money," she struggled to speak as a blade pressed deeper into her throat, breaking the skin. A warm sensation ran down her neck, staining her beige blouse red.

"Never mind that. You have been a royal pain in the ass. You could have ruined everything."

A shadowy, green figure reflected back from the microwave glass door. The voice was vaguely familiar, a voice from the past.

"Wait, I know you, don't..."

Before she could finish her sentence the knife plunged deep into her throat, severing a carotid artery. Blood spurted as the knife ran across her windpipe. The man released his grip and Marie dropped to the floor, choking on her blood as she slowly bled out. Her vision was cloudy, the scene surreal, as if this was happening to someone else. Consciousness slowly faded. The last image her brain registered was a dark red puddle of blood spreading out over the white ceramic tile floor.

# CHAPTER 2

LIFE CAN BE CRUEL, FEELING LIKE IT'S SOMEHOW ALIVE AND OUT TO GET YOU. Like when you wake up with an uneasy feeling that something is wrong. You can't quite put your finger on it, but you're somehow out of sync with the rest of the world. Most days are fine... then you get a reminder out of nowhere that something isn't right. Sometimes it's subtle, like a passing thought, a familiar smell, or a vague sensation of déjà vu. Other times it's a cold slap in the face, like today.

Kimbra's dark brown eyes were glued to the cherry wood casket. Was she somehow responsible for Marie's death? Kimbra had a way of drawing those closest to her into her world, into her drama. Her life was a mess and Marie was always there to lend an ear. They were *best friends forever* since sixth grade, and unlike a lot of other *BFFs* they remained close. There was one major fallout though, over a boy, but they managed to get beyond that. Their friendship had survived all that life threw at it, that was until now.

The pain of guilt weighed heavily on Kimbra as she stared vacantly at the coffin. Who killed Marie and why? Marie did not have an enemy in the world, yet someone had gotten into her apartment and brutally murdered her. If it was robbery they had little to gain, Marie was far from rich. Kimbra looked out at the mourners with an uneasy feeling gnawing away at her gut.

"Let us pray," the priest called out, startling Kimbra from her thoughts.

She looked upwards, as if some answer could be found in the heavens above. High aloft, puffy, gray clouds drifted lazily by. Back on solid ground, Marie's parents dabbed at their tears, her brother, Christopher, stood nearby with glazed eyes fixed downward. Tears welled up in Kimbra's eyes. How did it come to this? How could this happen? Her mind drifted off in a daydream.

It was a warm and sunny day, typical for Northern California, except that it would now be marked forever as the day before Marie's death. The two were seated at an outdoor cafe.

"I think I'm being watched," Kimbra explained.

"Watched! What makes you think that?" Marie asked.

"I don't know. I mean, I can't explain it, it's just a feeling I've been having. But I'm pretty sure someone has been in my apartment."

"What? Are you serious?"

Marie took a gulp from her drink and set it down, listening intently.

"I can't be certain, but things have been moved around. Little things, but unless I'm going mad, they have been moved."

"You don't think it's the landlord or repairman, do you?" Marie suggested.

"I don't know... I guess it could be."

"Have you asked?"

"No."

"Well, that's creepy. You should check. There's probably a good explanation. Could be you're just on edge. How has work been? Are you stressing out there?"

"Work is a little strange but not super stressful."

"*Strange*, how do you mean? You're not doing anything illegal, are you?"

"No, no. The tests I'm administering are a bit odd, but nothing illegal."

Marie knew Kimbra was working under a government contract and the work was confidential. The two sipped their drinks as three guys passed by. Marie rolled her eyes, finding one of them particularly attractive.

"What about Mick?" Marie mentioned out of the blue.

"Mick! Wait, you don't think he could be involved with any of this stuff do you?"

"I don't know. I'm just throwing it out there. I know you were in love with him, but he was a real creep," Marie added.

"I *thought* I was in love with him. Anyway, that was a long time ago. No, it couldn't be Mick."

The sermon was finished, everyone rose from their seats. Marie's parents and brother each placed a white lily on the casket. The other mourners followed suit, creating a bouquet of lilies. Pulleys creaked as the casket was lowered deep into the pit. The crowd dispersed, each individual filing into their respective vehicles before driving off. Marie remained behind with the other departed souls, her life snuffed out before it had barely begun.

The gathering at the Sadowski's following the funeral was brutal. What do you say to your best friend's parents, knowing no parent should experience the loss of a child? Kimbra went through the motions, expressing her condolences and reminiscing on happier times. But truth be told, she was anxious to leave and mourn in private. She ducked out as soon as possible.

By the time she arrived home, Kimbra was exhausted. She tossed her purse and keys on the kitchen table, plopped down on the sofa, and kicked off her shoes. Her eyes scanned the sterile looking, one-bedroom apartment with its white walls and kitchen cabinets. She did her best to warm it up with a dark sofa and earth colored accents, but a lot of good that did now. She buried her head in her hands and sobbed. She could not get her mind off Marie and the senseless murder. How could it happen? Out of nowhere she sensed a presence, someone was watching. She looked out at two bright blue eyes staring back at her. A gray and white cat brushed up against her leg, as if sensing her pain. The cat purred as Kimbra picked him up and gently stroked his ears.

"Just you and me now Smokey," she whispered while gazing out the window.

The sun was shining bright, birds were chirping. The world outside continued merrily along, unconcerned in the least that Marie was gone and Kimbra's life was falling apart. The air conditioner hummed out an intoxicating tune, the clock on the wall slowed to a crawl. She had an urge to call Marie but quickly caught herself. Instead, she set

Smokey aside and roamed into the galley kitchen to pour a glass of wine. Returning with the glass and bottle, she sunk into the plush sofa, resting her feet on the coffee table. Smokey cuddled up alongside her as thoughts spilled into her consciousness.

Marie had asked, and now Kimbra wondered, could Mick be involved in some way? Mick was her first love. Kimbra never felt loved as a child and it felt good to be wanted. So when Mick came along, she overlooked his faults, and there were many. Though she could not see it at the time, the breakup was inevitable. Suddenly the phone rang, startling her back to the present. It was her sister, Gina.

"Kimbra, I'm so sorry I couldn't make it to the funeral."

"That's all right."

"Did Mom show up?"

"No, are you kidding? She's too busy with her own shit to give a crap."

Although never diagnosed, their mother had violent mood swings. Heather divorced their father, Reece, when Kimbra was three. Many men came in and out of Heather's life but one in particular came to mind. Cody, was a two-bit musician that lived with them when Kimbra was in high school. His relationship with Heather was rocky and the fights were monumental: they were physical, loud, and frightening. Kimbra hated Cody and resented her mother for the little attention given to her and Gina.

"Well, can't say that surprises me," Gina said. "I'm really sorry. Marie was a good friend. How are you doing?"

"I don't know, I'm a mess. There's so much shit going on right now and I don't know what to do."

Kimbra told Gina what little she knew about Marie's murder and the strange feelings she was having. She and Gina didn't talk much but when they did, it was comforting. They had endured a lot together growing up, the kind of stuff you never forget. The two sisters would forever share that bond.

"I'm sorry. Sounds like you're dealing with a lot."

There was a silence as quiet as the hundreds of miles separating the two. Gina finally broke the lull.

"Did you call Grandma and Grandpa?"

"No."

"I can tell them if you want," Gina offered.

"No, I should call Grandma..."

"Hey, remember the times Marie came to Grandma and Grandpa's for the summer?" Gina asked.

"Of course."

"You two were so close. Did you know I was jealous of that?"

"What? No, you got along great with Marie. You were both outgoing and athletic, always beating me at stuff. I was the fat girl."

"Maybe, but she was *your* best friend. And you weren't fat!"

Kimbra had to laugh at that. She *was* chunky, but she never thought about her sister being jealous of her friendship with Marie.

"She was the best friend you could ask for," Kimbra lamented.

The tears began to flow, Kimbra was about to break down.

"I'm sorry. I didn't mean to bring up old memories so soon," Gina offered.

"No, that's fine. I'm glad you shared that with me."

Kimbra blew her nose with a tissue and continued. "So, how are things in Colorado? How are you and Greg doing?"

Gina and Greg were doing fine. Kimbra was happy for her sister but in all honesty, also a little jealous. She looked up to Gina, who did her best to include her younger sister when they were kids, but it was tough keeping up with her. Gina was slim, outgoing, and comfortable with boys, while Kimbra was none of those things. And now, Gina had moved on and started a new life, while Kimbra was stuck in the past, still trying to figure things out. Everything around her was spinning out of control.

She ended the call wishing to be alone with her sadness, but had one more task to fulfill. It had been a while since they last spoke and she felt guilty.

"Hi, Grandma."

"Kimbra, I'm so glad you called. I was just thinking about you, wondering how you are doing since you broke up with Carter and moved."

All that now seemed like light years ago with the events unfolding over the last week.

"Thanks, I'm doing fine."

"That's great honey, I knew you would. How is the job going?"

Kimbra kept it short, explaining the job briefly before telling her grandmother about Marie.

"That's terrible! Oh, dear, I'm so sorry. Marie was such a good friend. I remember the summers you two spent with us."

Kimbra fought back the tears and finished her drink.

"We can talk about it another time if you want."

"Thank you. Maybe some other time," Kimbra agreed.

"Kimbra, I know it's difficult to see right now, but when life closes one door, it always opens another. You can never replace a friend like Marie, but you *will* get through this."

Her grandmother held a special place in Kimbra's heart, she always seemed to know the right thing to say. They finished their conversation, leaving Kimbra once again alone with her thoughts. She poured another glass of wine and got up to play some music. The soulful voice of Van Morrison soothed her soul, the alcohol helped deaden the pain.

# CHAPTER 3

KIMBRA WOKE WITH A SPLITTING HEADACHE and squinted at the window. Soft light splashed through frilly curtains, but the hangover made it feel harsh. She trudged into the bathroom, brushed chocolate-brown hair from her eyes, and stared into the mirror. Her large brown eyes were narrow and red as she ran a finger along her cheeks. Were those bags under her eyes? The last few days had certainly taken their toll on her mental and physical well being. She sighed, then filled a glass of water and washed down two pain killers.

A short while later she was sitting on the back terrace with a hot mug of coffee cradled in her hands. Her head clearing a bit, all that remained was a mild buzz from the alcohol consumed the night before. The funeral had been emotionally exhausting, it was Saturday, and what she needed was a long hike to sort things out. Only when the pot of coffee was drained to the last drop did she muster the energy to get started. A breakfast of fried eggs and toast gave her strength, a hot shower left her feeling invigorated. She dressed, fed Smokey, and was headed for the door when the buzzer rang. A burly man in a gray sports jacket and white button-down shirt stood outside her door. He stood five feet, ten inches, with a slight paunch. The shaved head made him appear younger than his late fifties, Kimbra thought.

"Miss Evans, I'm sorry to bother you but I'd like to ask you a few questions."

Kimbra stood frozen in the doorway.

"Anthony Rizzo from Fremont PD. We talked briefly after your friend's death."

"Oh, yes. Of course. I'm sorry," Kimbra tried to recover from her brief loss of memory.

She opened the door and offered him a seat at the kitchen table. His eyes darted around the place before he took a seat. Kimbra felt her heart rate go up, a cop's presence in your apartment would make anyone nervous.

"Can I get you something?" Kimbra offered. "I can make another pot of coffee or a single cup?"

After convincing him it was no bother, he accepted her offer.

"Got any cream?" he asked.

The best Kimbra could do was milk. She watched his coffee change color from dark brown to a creamy tan as he poured in a generous amount of milk.

Rizzo caught her staring. "Acid reflux. With all the coffee I drink, a little creamer helps tone it down."

"So, what is this about?" Kimbra asked, ignoring his dietary issues.

"In light of recent developments in the investigation, I have a few questions, if you don't mind."

"Recent developments?"

"You mentioned your phone was lost the day of Marie's murder."

"I noticed it missing that night and reported it lost the next day," she explained.

"We went through Marie's phone records and a text was made that night inviting her to Tony's Bar and Grill."

Kimbra sat on the edge of her seat.

"Do you know who texted her?"

Rizzo took a sip of coffee before delivering the shocking news.

"The text was from your phone."

"From *my phone*!"

Kimbra's heart seized up, her mind went off in a flurry of thoughts. All her suspicions were confirmed. She *was* somehow responsible for Marie's death. But how? Who could have used her phone and how did they get it?

Rizzo's mouth moved, but she barely heard a word.

"Marie placed several texts to your phone, but none of them were returned."

When did she last have her phone? She thought she brought it home that night, leaving it on the nightstand when she took a bath. She panicked, immediately thinking someone had been in her apartment like she told Marie the day before. But there had to be a logical explanation. Maybe she was wrong and dropped it when she got out of the car or misplaced it somewhere else. She checked everywhere...

"Miss Evans!" Rizzo spoke loudly.

Kimbra snapped out of her thoughts. "Yes, I'm sorry. What did you say?"

"Can you think of anyone who would want to harm Marie?"

"No."

"A boyfriend, coworker, someone who may hold a grudge?"

"No, not really."

"An old acquaintance, someone she mentioned in passing? Anyone you can think of."

That got Kimbra thinking, Marie had mentioned Mick as a potential stalker.

"There was an old high school boyfriend of mine. He and Marie never got along. He would never do anything like this though."

Rizzo pulled a notepad and pen from a jacket pocket.

"What's his name?"

"Mick, Mick Donnelly. But he wouldn't do this. Besides, we broke up in high school. That was a long time ago."

"That's all right, it's worth checking out. I don't want to leave any stone unturned. When was the last time you spoke to Marie?"

Kimbra could feel the tears welling up, "I told you about that last time."

"I know. If you could just go over it again. You were under a lot of stress, maybe something new will come to mind."

Kimbra stirred in her seat, staring into her mug of coffee. The black liquid was swirling like a tropical storm.

"Miss Evans!"

Kimbra nearly jumped out of her seat, her nerves on high alert, her mind struggling to make some sense of it all.

"Sorry. Well, like I said earlier, the last time we got together was a couple of weeks ago, the day before..."

"I'm sorry, this must be difficult for you, but it may help with the investigation."

Kimbra nodded.

"How were Marie's spirits?"

Kimbra took a moment to compose herself.

"She seemed fine. That's just it, there is no explanation for this!"

Rizzo seemed uncomfortable pushing it any further. He extracted a roll of antacid tablets from his pocket, popped one in his mouth, and rose from his chair.

"If you think of anything else, please don't hesitate to call."

Rizzo placed his card on the table and left. Kimbra sat there in a stupor.

A short time later Kimbra took a gulp of water, marveling at the rolling grasslands and chaparral from her vantage point above the valley. She encountered a few hikers along the way but the trail was mostly quiet. Grateful for the solitude, she settled on a nearby rock and took several deep breaths, letting the sun warm her face. The fresh air and quiet helped her mind unwind, her thoughts soon turned to the past.

The year was 2008, Christmas was a week away and lost in the chaos. Kimbra's mother and her second husband, Tim, just moved to California. Kimbra was yanked out of school in the middle of sixth grade. She didn't have a lot of friends and she wasn't very popular, but at least in Oregon she was in a familiar school. Kimbra was devastated at the prospect of starting over and being alone. She stared down at her desk, wishing the year would evaporate away and she would no longer be *the new kid*. She was doing her best invisibility act when the teacher drew attention to her.

"Kimbra, I don't expect you to know everything, and I won't count tomorrow's test grade in you final average. Just do the best you can."

Kimbra's face turned a bright shade of crimson as all eyes in the room locked on her. Two girls shared a smirk, she wondered if it was at her expense. Oh God, please help me get through this day she prayed to herself. She quickly looked around to acknowledge everyone and dropped her head down low.

Lunchtime could not have come soon enough. Not wanting to be different, Kimbra stood in line studying the various items placed on her classmate's trays. The main course was popcorn chicken, which was really ball-like chicken tenders, or pasta with tomato sauce. Most of the kids were selecting the chicken, so she did the same. A salad, apple, and carton of milk rounded out her tray. She exited the line and froze, the reality of her being totally alone hit home. Not a single friend to sit with, she was a social misfit. The noise was making her dizzy. Someone passing by bumped into her and she stepped aside. Searching for a place to hide, she spotted a table in back with several empty seats, a small refuge in a sea of teenagers. Gripping her tray tightly, she shuffled in that direction, right by the girls in her class with the smirk. They stared as she passed, then turned to gossip. She plopped down, grateful for the several empty seats between her and the nearest person, and stared down at her food. She tried to look busy as she picked at her popcorn chicken.

When she felt nobody was looking, Kimbra gazed up and scanned the room. Someone was staring at her, she quickly looked away. Popping another bit of chicken into her mouth, she formed a mental picture of the girl. Shoulder-length, chestnut-brown hair rested on a turquoise blouse. Kimbra looked up again to see the girl's dark brown eyes still locked her way. The girl waved. Kimbra looked around to make sure it was her she was waving at, then returned a slight hand gesture. The girl smiled, got up with tray in hand and approached. Oh, no, Kimbra thought to herself.

"Hi, I'm Marie!"

Kimbra returned a faint, "Hi."

"Mind if I sit here?"

"No," Kimbra blurted out in shock.

Marie sat down and took a gulp of milk. "I'm in your math class, I sit in back. I saw you get on the bus this morning."

"You live in my neighborhood?" Kimbra asked.

That's how they first met. Marie lived several houses down and the two quickly became best friends. Kimbra would frequently escape her chaotic home, spending time in the calm that was Marie's house. It was that, or find a quiet place outdoors to hide. They remained best friends all the way through high school. That was, until Kimbra met Mick.

# CHAPTER 4

**October, 2011**

KIMBRA COULD BARELY HOLD HER EYES OPEN. Mr. Maxwell was rambling on about Romeo and Juliet. It was so difficult to make any sense of, she couldn't understand why anyone would like it. It was bad enough that her life was a tragedy, now she had to read one. Her day was off to a horrible start and she was exhausted. She was up all night listening to her mom and Cody argue, then she almost missed the bus, which would have been dreadful. Asking Cody for a ride was the last thing she wanted to do. Although dead tired, she somehow found the energy to get out of the house and make it to the bus stop on time.

Kimbra raised her head slightly, lifting her eyes towards the clock. 7:55 AM. Ugh, why did school have to start so early? She would never make it to lunch. She glanced around the room, spotting a few familiar faces, but being a freshman in a school of 1,700 teenagers guaranteed there were would be plenty of new students. She plopped her head back down and drifted off to sleep.

By the time lunch period arrived, the morning classes were lingering in Kimbra's memory like a bad dream. Lunch was early on her schedule and she was rarely hungry. Still, she was eager to trade the classroom and crowded hallways for the disorienting din of the cafeteria chatter. She filled her tray, exited the line, and worked her way to the back of the room. She sat down next to Marie and let out a sigh. An empty seat separated them from a group of older girls gossiping. In many ways high school was no different than middle school.

"Having a bad day? You look beat," Marie said.

"Thanks!"

"Sorry, but you look exhausted. What's going on?"

"I didn't get any sleep last night. Mom and Cody were at it all night," Kimbra explained.

"That sucks. What are they arguing about now?"

"You know, I don't even care anymore. I just wanna get the hell out of that house."

"You can always stay at my house you know," Marie offered.

"I know. Thanks, but I'll get through it. It's just a lot harder now with Gina gone."

"Well, I'm always here for you."

"I know. Thanks Marie."

It was a conversation spoken before, there was a lot arguing at the Evans' house and it sometimes got physical. Kimbra used to share the misery with her sister, but Gina had graduated and moved out. Just then someone dropped a tray, disturbing the natural order of the lunchroom. For a brief moment the noise stopped, followed by a few mean spirited laughs. Marie and Kimbra shared a smirk, and the chatter resumed. Yeah, high school was a lot like middle school. Kimbra could not wait to graduate and leave Oakdale behind.

"Hey, don't look now but there's a guy staring at you," Marie whispered.

"What, where?" Kimbra asked as she turned her head.

"To your left. The guy with the jeans, white tee, and dark hair doing a James Dean impression."

"What are you talking about? He's not looking at me."

"Yes he is..."

A boy taking an interest in Kimbra was a new experience. When she was younger, she had been a little on the chunky side, *baby fat* her grandma said. But then came adolescence and along with it she grew in height and slimmed down. Boys began to take notice, but she was still self-conscious about her body and uncomfortable with boys. Kimbra spotted the guy and quickly turned back to Marie.

"He's in my English class. His locker is near mine."

"Well, he seems pretty interested in you."

With the school day done, Kimbra found herself glued to her locker wondering what to do. Marie had a dentist appointment and that left Kimbra with nowhere to go. She dreaded going home early. Her mom would be getting home soon and God only knew where Cody would be. Maybe there was some extra-curricular activity she could join or sit-in on. Anything to avoid being home alone with Cody. She was contemplating her options when a voice startled her.

"Lost in thought?"

She turned to face mysterious brown eyes peeking out from a thick mop of dark roast coffee colored hair. It was the boy who caught her attention in the cafeteria. She wasn't sure before, but now that she had a second look, she thought he was cute. He had a boyish look and piercing eyes.

"Kimbra, right?"

Taken by surprise and not really comfortable talking with boys, she hesitated before finally blurting out, "Yes, that's me." The words sounded lame the minute they left her lips.

"I'm Mick. I'm in your English class. Nice to meet you," he said extending a hand.

She reached out and he returned a light handshake. He held it briefly until their eyes met, then gently let go.

"So what do you think of Maxwell?" he asked.

"Oh, he's all right I guess."

"Yeah, I heard he was pretty cool. You're a freshman aren't you?"

"Yes."

"I'm a junior. Got behind in English so I'm taking Maxwell's course. You heading out?"

"I guess. I mean I was just thinking what to do."

"Oh, well hey I can give you a ride. I got nothing going on. We could grab a bite to eat if you want, or hang out."

Kimbra rocked back on her heels, uncertain what to say.

"C'mon, it'll be fun."

His eyes peered at her through locks of hair, a slight smile formed at the corners of his mouth.

"All right, sure. Why not," she finally agreed.

The two walked down the hallway side-by-side, around the corner and out the front door. The sun was blazing and the air hot as Mick fished out a pair of stylish sunglasses and they proceeded to the student parking lot. He stopped in front of a black motorcycle.

"Here we are," he announced with an air of pride.

"I thought you had a car," Kimbra said, trying not to sound surprised.

"I have a beat up pickup truck I'm working on, but this is my preferred mode of transportation."

Kimbra took a step back as he unlocked two helmets and offered her one.

"What's the matter? Have you ridden a bike before?" he asked.

"No... not really."

"Well, it's nothing to be afraid of. Perfectly safe. I'll take it slow if you want."

A group of students passed as Mick continued to hold out the helmet. Kimbra hesitated, then stepped forward and accepted the heavy head gear. She pulled her long, dark hair back and squeezed it on. He adjusted the chin strap, latched it, and tugged on the helmet. His eyes met hers as a smile formed around his mouth, Kimbra could not stop herself from mimicking his expression.

"It's supposed to be a snug fit," he explained before putting on his helmet and mounting the bike.

"Hop on!" he said.

Kimbra studied the highly polished chrome engine strapped to a black frame with two wheels. It did not look *safe* to her, but she did not want to disappoint Mick. She took a deep breath and climbed on, her arms dangling in the air.

"You can hold onto the seat, or wrap your arms around my waist," he suggested.

Kimbra grabbed tightly onto the seat as Mick lifted the kick-stand. He engaged the choke, held in the clutch, and started the bike. The engine sputtered a bit before coming to life. The noise was deafening as Mick revved the engine.

"Are you ready?" he yelled out looking back.

Kimbra nodded and away they went, winding their way through the parking lot. It felt awkward at first, but she quickly learned to shift her weight with each turn. When Mick turned onto the road and picked up speed, she wrapped her arms around his waist to steady herself. Buildings flashed by and the wind caressed her face. She could hardly believe she was on the back of a motorcycle with a boy she just met.

"Where are we going?" she yelled out over the roar of the engine.

"How about an ice cream?"

"Sure. That sounds great!"

The wind tousled her hair and slapped at her blouse as they took to the highway. Kimbra let go of her fear, letting her worries fly off with the wind. She was living in the moment, carefree, exhilarated, and oblivious to any of the crap going on at home. After ice cream, they went to a quiet park and laid on the cool grass overlooking a river. Mick pulled out a joint and held it up as an offering.

"Oh, no thanks," Kimbra said.

"Have you tried it before?"

"No, not really."

"C'mon, it's such a beautiful day," Mick prodded.

"I will. Just not today."

"Okay, no pressure. Mind if I do?"

"No, that's fine."

Kimbra was not against a little weed, she just wasn't willing to try it that day. Her first encounter with Mick was a once-in-a-lifetime experience, one that she would remember forever, and she didn't want to spoil it. They talked a bit, mostly about Mick, and enjoyed the silence in between. It never felt awkward and the afternoon drifted along like a soft summer breeze. It wasn't long before the munchies kicked in for Mick and they left to get a burger and fries. Before she knew it, the sun was setting. She was sad it was over and depressed at the thought of returning to the madness she called home.

It was dark by the time Mick dropped her off.

"Thanks, I had a great time," she said, climbing down from the motorcycle.

"Me too."

Kimbra gave him a kiss on the cheek and headed up the sidewalk. She glanced back and Mick returned a smile.

She opened the door to a darkened house. The glow from the television lit up the living room. Cody got up from his seat, her mom was nowhere in sight.

"Where have you been? You're mother has been worried sick!" he scolded her.

"I'm sorry, I was out with a friend."

Kimbra headed up the stairs to her room ignoring his stare. She had little respect for Cody and was in no mood for his shit. She was laying on her bed with earbuds in place when her mother swung open the door.

"Where have you been?" she demanded.

Kimbra removed the earbuds and shot back an inquisitive look.

"I said, where have you been?" her mother repeated.

"Out with a friend."

"And you couldn't call?"

"Sorry, we lost track of time," Kimbra apologized.

It wasn't like they had a regular time for dinner or anything. Her mother was often busy showing houses. Meals were last minute, many nights Kimbra took care of herself. If Cody was there, she would leave or try to avoid him. He was creepy and had made more than one advance on her sister.

"Who were you with?"

"You don't know him."

"Did you eat?" her mother asked.

"We grabbed a bite earlier."

Her mother stood there tapping her foot. Finally she spoke.

"All right. Next time call."

"I will."

That was it. Her mother left and closed the door. She was too preoccupied with other matters to worry about Kimbra.

# CHAPTER 5

THE EARLY MORNING SUN WAS HEATING UP, not a single cloud in the sky as the dark sedan passed a row mobile homes. Car ports covered with corrugated metal accented some of the structures. Front yards consisted of a narrow patch of dried grass with a metal storage bin on some. Rizzo turned the car down a side street. Weathered wooden fences separated the tightly packed structures on tiny lots, the occasional air conditioning unit poked its head out of a window. Rizzo took another right, pulled over and got out of his late model Crown Victoria sedan. He dug a finger into his collar, loosened it a bit, and approached the tin roof covered entrance. He stepped onto the stoop and knocked on the door, a dog barked several units down. There was no answer and he pounded harder, aggravating the dog and neighbors even more. Finally, he heard a rustling inside, and a hushed voice.

"All right, just a God damned minute, will ya!"

The door creaked open revealing a short, stocky man in his late twenties. A pot belly protruded through his dingy white muscle shirt. Thick, unkempt brown hair flopped down over his forehead.

"Who the hell are you?" he blurted out.

Rizzo flashed his badge and identified himself, a neighbor several units down stuck his head out.

"I'd like to ask you a few questions."

"What's this about?"

"It's regarding Marie Sadowski," Rizzo explained.

The man's face froze momentarily.

"Are you aware she was murdered?" Rizzo asked.

"Yeah, I saw that in the news. What's this got to do with me?"

"I'm interviewing people she knew and your name came up."

"You got a search warrant?"

"Do I need one? We can do this down at the station if you prefer."

Donnelly looked down the street at his nosy neighbor and shot an annoyed look in his direction.

"All right, c'mon in. But make it quick, I gotta leave for work soon."

Rizzo studied the cluttered quarters as he moved towards the kitchen table. A bow was leaning against the bedroom door along with a fishing rod and tackle box. Next to those on an end table, was a box of .30-06 caliber ammunition, gloves, and a large hunting knife.

"You hunt much?" he asked.

"A little. So what of it?"

"Just curious."

"Is that what you wanted to ask me? Cause if that's all you got, I have to get going."

"Sure, I'll get to the point. Were you close to Marie Sadowski?"

"No."

"But you knew her."

"Not really."

"Weren't you classmates at Oakdale High School?"

"Yeah, but we didn't hang out."

"When was the last time you saw her?"

"I don't know. Had to be in high school."

Donnelly looked a bit uneasy, he was rocking on his heels.

"What were you doing on the evening of June 1st, the night of Ms. Sadowski's murder?"

"I don't remember."

"Think hard, it might save you a lot of trouble."

Donnelly's left eye twitched slightly, "Yeah, I think that's the night I tied one on with my brother."

"You're sure?" Rizzo asked.

"Pretty sure."

Back at the police station, Rizzo was mulling over some papers with a cup of coffee and a roll of antacid tablets on his desk.

"How's the investigation going?" a fellow detective asked.

"I've got a suspect with a history of abuse with women. He has a two-year old child and has been ordered to pay child support, not your model citizen. I have a witness who states the suspect knew the victim in high school, and he did not get along with her."

Liz Montero, rolled her chair over to Rizzo's desk.

"High school? How many years ago was that?"

"Eight or more, but it establishes a pattern. I noticed a hunting knife in his trailer. Could match the wounds on the victim."

"That's pretty thin," Liz said.

"The same witness thinks someone is breaking into her apartment and moving things."

"That's weird. You think they're related?"

"It's possible. The witness and this guy dated in high school. The victim was her best friend."

"Now that's interesting. Do you suspect a love triangle?" Liz asked.

"It's possible."

"Interesting, but it's razor thin."

"I know. He's got an alibi that I have to check out, but what I really need is a search warrant."

# CHAPTER 6

THE BENEFITS FROM SATURDAY'S HIKE were short-lived, Kimbra was emotionally drained. Waves of isolation and despair would wash over her. When she wasn't busy, her mood would plummet. It was Monday, a day she would normally dread, but this day she hoped the daily work routine would keep her mind off Marie's murder and the fact that her phone was involved.

The visit from Detective Rizzo was fresh on her mind as she drove past a two-story office building situated in San José, the heart of Silicon Valley. The front entrance had an impressive portico rising two-thirds the height of the building. Dark tinted windows stood out against a sleek white exterior. The modern, thirty-thousand square foot structure made her feel she was part of something bigger, something important. She turned the corner and parked in the rear lot.

At the employee entrance she swiped her card and passed through the turnstile. Hoping to avoid any conversations, she nodded at a few familiar faces along the way and proceeded directly to her cubicle. She sat down and sighed, a picture caught her eye. The photo of her and Marie, taken at an amusement park, reminded her of a day she would cherish. It was a care free day, like the times they spent together before life got so complicated. It was a brief break from the trials and tribulations of middle school, a day now part of her distant past. With Marie gone, all that remained was a hole in her heart.

Kimbra's thoughts drifted to Mick. He was her first love and like a drug, the affection he turned her way was intoxicating. She was quickly sucked into his world. It was wild and scary, but also exhilarating. Maybe it was the alcohol and drugs, maybe it was a deep-seated desire to rebel against the world, or just a desire to be loved, but she went along willingly. Marie did not approve and at that time, Kimbra could not understood the resentment. Kimbra foolishly suspected the reason was jealousy. She tried to include Marie, even setting up a double date with one of Mick's friends, but Marie refused. Kimbra was spending so much time with Mick, she hardly noticed it at first, but she and Marie drifted apart. She recalled the last big fight when Marie cornered her in the school hallway.

"What do you want?" Kimbra's tone was mean.

"Nothing. Can we talk?"

"Sure, as long as it's not about Mick," Kimbra replied coldly.

The two girls were leaving school. Unlike earlier times, they were worlds apart. Marie tried to break the icy awkwardness.

"How's your Mom doing?

"How should I know? I hardly see her."

There was an uncomfortable silence. Kimbra suspected Marie wanted to apologize or at least reconcile their differences, but she was too stubborn to open up and give her a chance.

"Don't get angry but there's something I think you should know," Marie finally spoke.

Kimbra could feel her anger well up, the hair stood up on the back of her neck.

"What? What is it?" she snapped.

"I saw Mick with another girl."

"So. So what!"

"He's been seeing her for a while."

Kimbra lashed out at Marie.

"You're just jealous! Leave me and Mick alone."

"No, that's not it at all! Why would I be jealous?"

Kimbra turned and ran off.

They never spoke again until after the breakup with Mick, and Kimbra felt terrible just thinking about it. A knock on the metal frame of her cubicle startled her. An attractive Asian man in an expensive suit greeted her. His hair was dark and wavy, his perfect teeth were white as snow.

"Good morning. Just wanted to check and see how you're doing."

Kimbra was uncomfortable discussing her personal life with anyone, least of all her boss. Death of a close friend was the reason given for the time off, so he knew, and it surely wasn't his fault.

"I'm fine, thanks," she said.

"Well, glad to see you're back. Keep me posted on the next round of tests."

"Sure, I will do that."

When she first applied for the job, she was surprised to see the owner, Dr. Fang Wu, at the interview. She had seen him speak at San Francisco State University and he remembered her, at least that's what he said. Kimbra was later offered an entry level position administering psychological tests. Being a psych major, it was right up her alley and she was anxious to put some distance between herself and her ex boyfriend, Carter. Quantum Thunder was an up-and-coming company doing groundbreaking research in paranormal phenomena. Kimbra checked the time and closed her laptop. She grabbed a white lab coat hanging in the corner and rushed off with a manila folder in hand.

The test subject was seated at a metal table when she arrived. A video camera mounted in the upper corner peered down at them.

"Good morning. My name is Kimbra Evans, I'll be administering your tests today."

His name was Chad Addison, a college student at San José State University. His soft face was framed with a light growth of beard and soft brown hair to match. They were looking for people with exceptional extra-sensory skills and Chad had shown unusual abilities in the pre-screening. Kimbra sat down across from him and pulled out a stack of twenty-five white cards with simple black shapes on them. She showed him the five distinct shapes.

"Are we doing that test again?" he asked.

"Sorry, but I have to confirm the earlier results. Do you mind?"

"No, it's fine."

Chad's bright blue eyes widened as they focused on Kimbra. The corners of his mouth raised slightly, making Kimbra feel a little flattered. Was he flirting with her?

"Okay, if you can just relax and take a deep breath..."

"I'm familiar with the test," he said cutting her off.

Kimbra held up the first card with a plus sign facing her and concentrated on it.

"It's a plus sign," he reported confidently.

Kimbra recorded the answer and held up another card.

This time he paused a few seconds before answering, "Squiggly lines."

Next, she held up a square which he answered correctly.

"You can't see it can you?"

"No, not really, but I kind of see it in my mind," he explained.

After holding up several more cards Kimbra finished the test. There were twenty-five cards in the deck and five unique cards. Getting them right 20% of the time was the expected result, anything above that could indicate some psychic ability. Chad's score of 49% was off the chart.

Kimbra pulled another set of cards from her lab coat and showed them to Chad. She typed at the computer, shuffled the deck and held up a card with a drawing of a giraffe facing her.

"Seems like the same test but with different cards," he said.

"Not really, this is a test to measure temporal displacement."

"Temporal displacement?"

Kimbra attempted to explain.

"We're looking for the ability to predict a card shown *before*, or *after*, the one you are shown. Some researchers believe that could indicate a displacement of time, a precognition of a future event or a different timeline."

Chad nodded, Kimbra wasn't sure he completely understood the concept. When the test was completed he asked how he did.

"I don't really know at this time," Kimbra said. "The computer will calculate the results."

That was only half true. She could tell by a quick glance that Chad's results were exceptional. There would be more tests, but she wondered where it would lead. She knew they were looking for a number of candidates for the *Next Level*. What that meant, she had no idea.

# CHAPTER 7

**October, 2012**

KIMBRA LAY AWAKE IN BED, propped up with several pillows. She was listening to the newest album from Sleeping With Sirens when her bedroom door swung open and in walked Cody. There he was with his hippy dippy mullet hair-do and creepy goatee. His thin lips were moving but nothing came out. Kimbra removed one earbud and spoke.

"What the hell, can't you knock?"

"I did. You didn't hear me."

"Yeah, 'cause I'm listening to music. What?"

"Your mother will be out late at a real estate course. Just wanted to see if you were hungry."

"No thanks, I'm fine."

Kimbra stuffed the earbud back in as Cody moved forward and sat next to her on the bed. He looked out the window like a lost puppy, then turned his stare her way. She pulled out the earbud again.

"What? What do you want?"

He hesitated, as if something was bothering him. He was always arguing with her mother, maybe he was splitting. That would be good news.

"I just wanted to see how you're doing with school and all," he said. "We never get a chance to talk you know, you and I."

"Well, I'm fine."

"That's good... Listen if that friend of yours ever gives you a hard time, you know you can always talk to me."

"Okay..." Kimbra put the earbud back in and turned up the music.

Cody scrunched over and brushed her hair softly to one side.

Kimbra sat up straight and ripped out both earbuds.

"I'm fine, really! You can go now. I want to be left alone."

Cody moved his arm over her legs, placing his hand on the other side of the bed, facing her squarely.

"You know you're such a beautiful girl. I wouldn't want any young man taking advantage of you."

He caressed her cheek and moved closer, so close she could smell the reek of his cigarette breath. Kimbra's heart raced, beads of sweat formed on her forehead. Cody had made advances on her sister and Kimbra was prepared for this, at least she thought so. She pulled her knees up, swung her feet past his arm and bolted out of the bed.

"What are you doing, I asked you to leave. Get out!"

Cody got up slowly and faced her.

"Get out!" Kimbra repeated as she stood by the door.

He moved slowly toward her.

"There's no need to get upset, I didn't mean any harm. I was just trying to help."

"Yeah well, get out!"

Cody drifted into the hall. Kimbra slammed the door shut and locked it, then frantically dialed Mick. One ring... two rings. She waited anxiously as it went to voicemail.

"Mick, call me right away! I really need to talk to you, now." Next she quickly typed out a message.

call me now!!! really need to talk to u!

She had to get out. Kimbra grabbed her purse and jacket before storming out of her bedroom, quickly moving down the stairs and towards the front door.

"Where are you going?" Cody called out from the kitchen.

"Going out!" she yelled back before slamming the door shut behind her.

It was twilight, the last hint of sunlight was below the horizon when she stepped onto the sidewalk. No reply from Mick. He was at band practice and probably didn't hear his phone. She moved briskly along, not knowing where to go, what to do. She only knew she had to put some distance between her and home. She hated Cody, hated her mother for being so selfish and stupid with her choices in men. Gina was lucky to get out of the house when she did. Kimbra had two more years to endure before she could get the hell out. She popped in her earbuds and blasted a favorite hard rock song: Been to Hell by Hollywood Undead. It was loud, angry, and fit her mood. Lights were popping on in homes along the street, she wondered what kind of lives existed inside. Were any of them as crazy as hers?

She drifted aimlessly along and before she knew it, she had reached Marie's house. Kimbra always felt safe at the Sadowskis, it was a haven from her crazy world, a harbor of refuge. She wished she could share her problems with Marie, but that ship had sailed. Marie would never speak with her again. She pulled up her collar and moved on.

The playground was dark and deserted. Tired of the music, Kimbra took the earbuds out. A single cricket was chirping, probably as lonely as Kimbra on that cool fall night. She sat on a swing, looking up at the stars, pondering her place in the universe. When she was down and out, she would sometimes write. Her doctor suggested it in middle school. She had been impulsively scratching herself, *self-injury disorder* they called it, and anyway, the writing helped and she liked it. Short stories, poems, random thoughts. It helped pass the time and deadened the pain. Just then, a cool breeze blew in, making her shiver. She rolled up her collar and pulled out her phone. She began typing. Moments later she finished a short poem she had been working on. She called this one Lost:

> *Empty streets, covered in darkness*
> *Warm, cozy homes, their lights cast a glow*
> *Outside I wander, a shadow, a ghost*
> *Like a cold winter breeze, with nowhere to go*

As the time dragged on, her eyes grew heavy. It was after ten when Kimbra's phone lit up and buzzed. It was Mick.

"What's up? Is something wrong?"

"Yeah, I'm really stressing out."

"What's going on?"

Kimbra sighed and wiped away a tear.

"Just the usual shit storm at home. This time it was Cody."

"What happened?"

Kimbra tried being open and honest with Mick, it's just that he sometimes didn't seem to care. Still, it was comforting to spill her guts to someone, and Mick was all she had.

"He tried to make a pass at me."

"What! That creep. Does your mom know?"

"No, she wouldn't care."

"You don't know that. You should tell her."

"Mick, I told you he pulled the same shit with my sister! Gina told Mom and nothing happened. Mom didn't believe her. Either that or she just didn't care."

"So, what are you gonna do?"

"I don't know. Can you pick me up?"

"Sure. I'll be right there."

She waited for Mick, wondering what the future would bring. Mick was graduating in the spring, that is, if he passed English. What would happen then? She feared he would grow tired of her and move on. There were rumors of another girl and for now, she pushed those thoughts aside. Mick was the only one who showed her any love and she was not willing to give up on that so easily. Only one thing was certain, she had to get out of her house.

# CHAPTER 8

NOW THAT I HAVE A KEY, I CAN COME AND GO AS I PLEASE. Picking the lock my first time was easy. Finding a spare key hanging on the wall was a stroke of luck, taking an impression and making a duplicate was a no-brainer after that. Kimbra is at work, so I have all the time I want. Her apartment is small, but the open design makes it feel larger. She's done a good job decorating, I like that. The walls are a drab off-white, but she's spruced it up with a warm earth tone sofa, an area rug, and dark wooden accent tables. I remove a tiny device from a large plant in the corner and examine it closely. Crappy thing failed. I carefully attach a new tiny microphone at the base of the thick plant. Next, I attach a tiny camera to the base of the large screen television and take a step back. Perfect, it's barely noticeable and should capture the entire living area as well as some of the kitchen. Now, I will have eyes *and* ears on my subject.

What's this? Out of the corner of my eye I notice a gray blur. Scared the shit out of me, but of course, it's her cat.

"Here kitty, kitty," I coax the creature to approach as I get down to his level. I remain still, holding out my hand slowly. Acting coolly, the cat just sits there and scratches his ear.

"Here kitty," I repeat.

The cat stands and approaches me slowly. I remain motionless, and let it sniff my hand. Only when the cat rubs against my hand do I reciprocate and scratch its head. So unsuspecting, so trusting, I can't help but think how easy it would be to crush its little skull. I never considered myself a dog or a cat person, but I had liked my grandmother's cat. This one seems friendly enough, kinda reminds me of Shadow. Ah, but I'm getting distracted, I have work to do.

I move to the bathroom, nicely accented with burgundy towels, gray and burgundy throw rugs, and a burgundy toilet cover. The tub has, you guessed it, a burgundy shower curtain. I could put a camera in here, but I don't need to see her on the crapper. That's not my thing. I pick up her toothbrush and open my mouth. I hesitate for a moment, then lick it quickly and put it back.

My heart rate increases as I move to the bedroom and plop down on the soft bed. I like the abundance of pillows and the soft and satiny comforter, it smells amazing. Someday I will share this bed with Kimbra. It will be different this time, she is nothing like Lisa. But, I have to be patient if this is going to work. I get up and examine the room. The walk-in closet is stuffed to the max. A jewelry box on the dresser, that's interesting. Next to that is a picture of Kimbra and her high school friend, Marie. I wince at the thought of how Marie could have ruined everything. A small container with earrings and other small objects catches my eye, I move the dainty objects around ever so slightly. Not enough to arouse any undue alarm, just enough to establish my control over this domain. There's a small aloe plant on the nightstand. I attach another camera there. Perfect, my work is done.

The cat appears in the doorway and stops as if awaiting my approval, before jumping onto the bed. I continue exploring and opening drawers. I run my hands through soft sweaters and leggings, disturbing the placement ever so slightly. Socks and undergarments are in another drawer. A scented lavender pillow. I am drawn to a pair of satin black panties and a lacy black bra, running them through my fingers and smelling them. I shouldn't. Not yet at least, I don't want to overplay my hand. Ahh, the hell with it. Sometimes, I just can't resist my compulsions. Besides, I deserve a reward for my patience and hard work. I stuff them both in my pocket and leave.

# CHAPTER 9

TWO WEEKS PASSED SINCE MARIE'S DEATH. Kimbra had not shared her grief with any co-workers. It wasn't healthy, but she preferred to grieve alone. She stepped into the shower, hoping to wash away her heartache. She lingered in the relaxing water, letting her thoughts melt away, until it was late. Now she rushed to get dressed. Ripping a drawer open she noticed something was missing. Where were they? She rifled through the laundry but they were nowhere to be found. She had not worn the black bra and panties in a week or more. They should be in the dresser drawer, but they were gone.

She started to panic, wondering what else could be missing. Her eyes moved to the dresser, noticing a small dish containing earrings. A tiny dust free area on the dresser indicated it had been moved recently. She imagined someone in her apartment, rifling through her belongings. She opened each drawer, carefully examining the contents and their arrangement. Taking a step back, she looked around the room taking note of the contents and their position; the lamp, her book, a container of hand cream. Was her mind playing tricks with her, or was the book moved?

Kimbra dressed in a hurry and took a quick inventory of the entire apartment. Smokey followed her from room to room, sensing something was wrong. Nothing else seemed out of place. She filled the cat's dish with moist food, grabbed her purse and hustled out the door, happy to be free of the apartment where she no longer felt safe.

Fumbling for her phone, she placed a call while scurrying along the sidewalk. Detective Rizzo answered as she hopped in the car.

"Detective, this is Kimbra Evans. I'm sorry to bother you, but I don't know what to do."

"What's wrong?"

"I'm not sure I mentioned this before, but I think someone has been in my apartment. Items have been moved around. Today I noticed a few items missing."

"What items?"

"Some personal items... clothing."

"Are you certain? Could be you just misplaced them, clothes get lost all the time."

"I'm certain."

Rizzo cleared his throat. Kimbra got the impression he wasn't taking it seriously.

"You think someone has been in your apartment?"

"Yes."

"Could it be someone you know, or the landlord? Does anyone else have a key?" he asked.

"No. I checked with the landlord and he said he was not in my apartment. I'm the only one, other than the landlord, that has a key. Wait, Tammy has a key," Kimbra mentioned it almost as an afterthought.

"Who's Tammy?"

"She lives across the hall. She looks after my cat when I'm away."

"Would she have any reason to be in your apartment?"

"No."

"Why don't you check with her? See if she could have lost the key or something."

"I will. Detective, I'm really starting to worry."

"Have you filed a police report?"

"No. You're the first person I'm mentioning this to, other than the landlord... and Marie."

"Do you think this could be related in any way to Marie's death?"

The question hit Kimbra like a punch to the gut. Could it be? Was it Mick?

"I don't know."

"Okay, listen, I'll look into it. In the meantime, I suggest you have your locks changed."

Kimbra arrived at work late and frazzled. To top it off, Trent called in sick and she had to take over his workload for the day. She was seated at a table in Test Room A. A woman in her fifties with fiery red hair and sympathetic brown eyes, sat across from Kimbra. Lines on her face suggested a wisdom that seemed to belie her age. It was strange, but something about her was familiar. Kimbra studied the contents of the manila folder in her hands. The woman's name, Christina Sullivan, and a photo were provided. Missing, was a case history along with personal data typically provided with other subjects.

"Good morning. My name is Kimbra. I'll be filling in for Trent today."

"Good morning dear. How is Trent feeling?" the woman asked in a soothing voice.

"I'm not really sure."

Kimbra gazed down and quickly ran through the test procedure outlined in the folder, a box sat nearby on the table.

"There are several objects in this box that I will ask you to examine," Kimbra explained.

"You seem a bit worried," the woman commented.

Kimbra let out a sigh and brushed a lock of hair from her eyes. She had an uneasy feeling, as if the woman was reading her mind.

"You have no idea."

Or did she? The woman's eyes indicated otherwise. She reached out and gently touched Kimbra's arm. A warm sensation rushed through Kimbra's body, her head buzzed and she felt dizzy, as if she were just given a mild sedative. She was relaxed, as if in a trance. It seemed as if an eternity passed before the woman looked up, let go of Kimbra's arm, and jerked back in her seat. The warm feeling faded quickly, leaving behind only cold and darkness.

"What just happened?" Kimbra asked.

"I'm sorry dear. I shouldn't have..."

"Shouldn't have what?"

"Nothing. It was nothing."

Kimbra studied the woman who looked a bit rattled.

"You saw something, didn't you?"

The woman was silent.

"Please, you have to tell me!"

The woman remained silent.

"It was something terrible, wasn't it?"

Silence.

"Christina! Please tell me."

The woman's voice was raspy, as if she didn't want anyone to hear.

"You have to understand, time is fluid. What I see... I don't always know if it's from the past or yet to occur. What I saw was dark and shadowy, it wasn't clear."

"But you saw something," Kimbra egged her on. "What did you see?"

The woman was troubled, as if it caused her pain to relive the vision.

"I witnessed a murder!"

"Was it a woman? My friend was killed two weeks ago."

"It was a woman. I'm sorry, but I really shouldn't say anything more."

Kimbra was reaching a breaking point.

"Why? Why can't you tell me?"

"I'm sorry, I have to leave," Christina exclaimed as she got up and left.

Kimbra sat there dumbfounded. Then she sprang up and bolted out the door. Down the hall, she rounded the corner and leapt up the stairs. She bypassed the secretary and headed straight to his office. It took all her control to resist pounding on the door. Instead she knocked. Thank God he was there. Still short of breath she entered the office, shutting the door behind her. Dr. Fang Wu was seated at a large desk. His figure was silhouetted in front of a bank of smoked glass windows overlooking a serene setting in the rear of the building, complete with park benches and shady trees. He straightened up with a surprised look.

"Kimbra, what is it? Please, take a seat."

Still upright, she tried to compose herself.

"I just left Test Room A with Christina Sullivan. She had a vision of Marie's murder."

"A vision? What makes you think it was Marie?"

"She touched my arm, and she saw a woman being murdered!"

"I'm sorry you had to experience that, but Ms. Sullivan has had premonitions and visions of numerous murders."

"Why wasn't I given more information on Christina?"

"Christina has moved on to the Next Level phase of our research. You're filling in for Trent today, and you don't have the security clearance for that information. Please, take a seat."

Kimbra paced before finally deciding to take a seat.

"So what is the Next Level?"

"That area of our research requires Secret level clearance. I believe the necessary paperwork is being processed for you."

"How long will that take?"

"It can take several weeks, or more."

"Can you tell me more about the program?"

Fang glanced out at the beautiful sunny day outside, his leather office chair creaked as he swiveled back to face Kimbra. He was ruggedly good looking with dark, wavy hair and high cheekbones, a permanent furrow crossed his brow.

"The Next Level deals with enhanced telepathy through brain chemistry. I can provide you *all* the details as soon as your security clearance is approved."

It would be futile to ask for more before her clearance was approved. She left his office feeling empty, yearning to learn more about the Next Level program and Christina.


The work day done, Kimbra was anxious to do some research on Christina, but she had something to do first. She knocked on the door across the hall from her apartment. A woman in her fifties answered the door.

"Hi Kimbra. How are you doing?"

"I'm fine, thanks. Hey, I just wanted to ask if you heard anyone in my apartment during the day the last couple of weeks."

"No. Why, is something wrong?"

The door closed to a crack as a cat approached. Tammy was a hair stylist with two cats and a girlfriend with commitment issues. She also had a propensity towards drama and Kimbra did not want to worry her.

"Nothing, just checking. You still have my key don't you?"

"Yes, of course. I can check if you want."

"No, no, that's all right."

"You sure? I can check," Tammy offered as Kimbra turned to leave.

"No, thanks Tammy. It's fine."

Kimbra checked every room in her apartment for any sign of an intruder. Once satisfied that nothing had been disturbed from earlier that morning, she sat on the sofa with her laptop computer and a glass of wine. Smokey was cuddled up at her side as she typed *Christina Sullivan* in the search bar.

There were seventeen million results! Not very helpful. She added *California* to the search string, which narrowed it to eight million. Sullivan was such a common name and she had nothing else to go on. She took another sip of wine and added *premonition*. That narrowed it to 654,000 results. On a hunch she added *murders solved* which narrowed it to 450,000. Now she removed everything else and wrapped *murders solved* and *Christina Sullivan* in double quotes. There were now 4 results. Three of the four links mentioned a Christina Sullivan along with murders solved. The first article from the Oregonian, a daily newspaper in Portland, mentioned a murder solved with the help of a psychic. The second link mentioned another murder in Oregon solved with her help. The third article mentioned how Christina helped solve a string of murders across Oregon and Washington. Kimbra took a sip of wine and stroked Smokey's ears. She vaguely recalled a few of the murders from her time living in Oregon. But who was the person in Christina's vision? Was it Mick?

"What do you think Smokey?" she asked her furry companion. "Christina may have some answers. We have to find out more."

# CHAPTER 10

IT WAS THREE WEEKS TO THE DAY SINCE MARIE'S DEATH. Kimbra was heading out the door when her phone rang, it was Rizzo.

"Miss Evans, I have good news."

Kimbra stopped cold, half-way to her car and held her breath.

"We arrested Mick Donnelly last night and are charging him with the murder of Marie," Rizzo reported. "I already informed her parents and you were next on my list."

Kimbra bent over to catch her breath. She was anxious for them to find the killer, but how could it be Mick? She hadn't seen him in seven years.

"How do you know... I mean are you sure?" she asked.

"We received an anonymous tip. He was seen leaving the scene of the crime. The witness claimed he followed Mick to his home and watched him bury something nearby. We searched his place and obtained a murder weapon and other physical evidence, including your phone."

"My phone!"

So it was Mick who stole her phone. He was the one breaking into her apartment.

"He used your phone to lure Marie away long enough for him to break into her apartment and wait for her to return."

Kimbra was in shock, she began to feel nauseous.

"Forensics is still working it, but it's a solid case."

"But why? Why would he do that?"

"You had a relationship with him, how did Marie fit into that?"

"She never approved."

"That could be it. Never underestimate a jilted lover."

"Sure, but that was so long ago."

"Revenge can be a powerful motivator," Rizzo suggested.

That got Kimbra thinking, Mick tried to get back together with her after they broke up. Marie was dead set against it. Maybe he held a grudge.

"Miss Evans?"

"Yes, I'm sorry."

"We're not done with the investigation by any means. He's denying it, but that's what they all say. Once we build the case and the evidence mounts, they usually open up. I just wanted let you know we arrested someone."

"Thank you. You will let me know of any developments?"

"Of course. Enjoy the rest of your day. This is good news."


The rest of the morning at work was a blur. Kimbra evaluated several new candidates while Chad was promoted to the Next Level. She was dying to know exactly what that meant. Hopefully her security clearance would be approved soon and Fang would reveal the details. She hoped to see Christina again as well, maybe she could shed some light on the murder. Detective Rizzo suggested Mick held a grudge against Marie. That only confirmed Kimbra's involvement. Guilt-stricken, she desperately needed someone to talk to. She instinctively thought of Carter, but they weren't talking. There was always Gina, but she had dumped on her too much lately. Totally frustrated, she decided to go out for lunch, take a short walk, and hopefully clear her mind.

She stepped out into a blazing June sun, grateful for the light blouse and sunglasses. A short walk later, she was greeted with a blast of cool air inside the deli. Beads of perspiration on her body gave her a chill as she placed her order at the counter and waited. When the food arrived she was happy to find a quiet table in the shade in the outdoor dining area. She was half-way through her wrap, enjoying the solitude, when a man approached catching her attention. He stopped at her table and froze. Kimbra glanced up from her meal.

"Kimbra? Kimbra Evans?"

He had a sparse brown beard and thick curly hair. His eyes were a mysterious dark brown.

"I'm sorry, have we met?"

"I went to Oakdale High School. You were in a couple classes of mine."

"I'm sorry, it's been a while..." Kimbra struggled to recall a name for the face.

"Daniel. Daniel Visser."

There was an awkward silence. Kimbra was hoping for some peace and quiet and here she was running into an old high school classmate that she did not recognize.

"You were in my ninth grade English class, also my twelfth grade Psych class if I remember correctly."

Kimbra could not place him.

"You were good friends with Marie Sadowski," he added.

"Oh yes, I remember now," Kimbra lied.

His eyebrows drooped, "I'm sorry, I shouldn't have mentioned Marie. I'm so sorry for your loss."

"Thank you."

Another moment of awkward silence.

"You haven't changed much. I recognized you right away," he said in an apparent attempt to lighten the mood.

Kimbra took a quick glance around. There were several empty tables.

"I'm sorry, I didn't mean to interrupt. I just wanted to say hi," he explained. "You have a great day."

As he turned, Kimbra felt a hint of guilt. She didn't want to be rude, and maybe a little chitchat with someone would lift her spirits.

"Wait! Would you like to join me?" she blurted out.

"No, no I don't want to disturb you," he said turning back.

Kimbra shot him a disarming smile and focused on his eyes. He stood his ground, his eyes returning her gaze.

"You're not disturbing me. Besides, I could use someone to talk to. That is, unless you're meeting someone."

"Well, all right, and no, I'm not meeting anyone."

He set his tray down and looked around before asking, "Do you come here often?"

"Not really. I don't get out much."

He took a bite of his sandwich and looked around.

"Do you?" Kimbra asked.

"Do I what?" he uttered after gulping down a mouthful of food accenting a prominent Adams's apple.

"Come here often?"

"Oh, yeah I guess. I have an office around the corner."

"That's convenient. What do you do... that is if you don't mind my asking?"

"A little bit of everything. Private investigations and security research."

"That sounds interesting," Kimbra commented. "How did you get into that?"

"It's a long story and not terribly interesting. I'd much rather talk about you. What have you been doing since high school, if you don't mind *my* asking?"

Kimbra was not comfortable discussing work or her personal problems with anyone, let alone a stranger. Then again, she could use someone to talk to, and he seemed nice enough. Besides she had asked him to join her. She caught herself fixated on his eyes, they were hypnotic.

"It's all right if you don't want to talk about it," he offered.

She lost track of time. Did he notice her staring? She quickly responded.

"I work down the street, at Quantum Thunder."

Daniel paused mid-bite to speak. "Isn't that the modern two-story with the smoked glass windows and huge entrance?"

"Yes, that's it."

"I always wondered what they do in there."

"Me too," Kimbra announced without thinking.

Daniel looked up, his expression anticipating an explanation.

"I mean, they do government research. I'm working as a psychometrist."

"A psychometrist.... That means you administer psychological and neuropsychological tests, right?"

"Yes! Most people would not know that."

"Well, it's my business to investigate people and what they do. Where did you get your degree? I assume you have a bachelor's or master's."

"I earned a Bachelor of Arts in Psychology from San Francisco State University."

Kimbra was warming up to Daniel. He was intelligent and interesting. She wanted to ask him more about how he got into private investigations, but she was running late.

"I'm sorry, I have to get back to work," she said. "I really enjoyed our conversation."

"I did as well," he said getting up to see her off. "Maybe we can continue it sometime. I mean, I don't want to be pushy. Maybe we'll cross paths again, seeing as I work right around the corner."

Kimbra grabbed her purse, half expecting him to ask for her number. He did not.

"That sounds wonderful. Nice meeting you, Daniel." She couldn't believe she just used the word *wonderful*.

"It was nice reconnecting with you as well."

Daniel said he worked around the corner, but she never got the name of his business. Back at the office she Googled his name and checked his profile on social media. There were a lot of pictures of him, several with an attractive woman. There was also mention of his business, Magellan Research. It all seemed legit. She enjoyed her conversation with him and hoped to run into him again. She decided she would have to go out to lunch more often, especially that restaurant.

That night Kimbra felt a little safer in her apartment now that Mick was in custody. Smokey was cuddled up next to her on the sofa as Nora Jones sang a soft, jazzy tune on the stereo. Kimbra reflected on the day as she sipped a drink. She was trying to understand why Mick would do such a horrible thing. He wasn't the best person. He was a cheat, a liar, and self-centered. He had a quick temper, but he was not a killer. Or was he? How could you really know? He was heavily into drugs. Maybe that spiraled out of control. But why Marie? Could he have held a grudge all those years? Kimbra was struggling to make sense of it and needed a break.

"You know what Smokey? I need another drink."

She filled her empty glass with vodka, soda, ice, and a splash of lime juice. She was stirring the mixture when she got an idea. She yanked her high school yearbook off a bookshelf and returned to the couch. Thumbing through the senior pictures, she stopped at the last names starting with *V*. Now she flipped the pages slowly until she found it. The face and beard were thinner, the hair much longer. She went through the entire yearbook searching for more pictures of him. Daniel Visser wasn't in any clubs and didn't play any sports, but she did find one other picture of him. He was seated on a window sill in the stairwell with a pretty girl with long dark hair. Kimbra did not recognize either of them. That was understandable, Oakdale was a big school and most students stuck to their cliques. Just then her phone rang startling her. It was Carter. She was not in the mood but seeing as she had ignored two earlier voice messages, she picked up.

"Kimbra, hi. I've been trying to reach you."

"Sorry, I've been dealing with a lot lately."

"I know. I'm sorry about Marie."

Carter attended the funeral and tried talking with Kimbra then, but she brushed him off.

"I heard they charged your old boyfriend. You mentioned he wasn't the nicest guy, but holy shit, murder! What happened?"

News of the arrest traveled quickly, Kimbra thought.

"Carter, I don't know and it's driving me crazy just thinking about it. Sorry, but I don't want to talk about it now."

"All right, I understand. Listen, the reason I'm calling is my trial is coming up soon and it would really help if you would appear as a character witness. Could you do that for me, Kimbra?"

Kimbra sighed before replying, "I don't know, Carter. I'm dealing with a lot of shit right now."

"You do believe me don't you? I never downloaded those pictures onto my computer. I don't know how they got there. Someone targeted me."

"Why? Why would anyone do that Carter?"

"I don't know. I must have pissed someone off. All I know is I didn't do that. I'm not into child pornography, that's disgusting. You have to believe me!"

Kimbra had heard all this before. Carter was desperate and she wanted to believe him, but like a lot of things lately, it just didn't make any sense.

"All right I can appear, but there's not anything I can tell them."

"That's fine. Just having you there would be a huge boost for me. Thank you."

"Of course."

"Do you think we could get together sometime? Lunch, dinner, anything. I miss you, Kimbra."

Kimbra's dark brown eyes grew misty. She missed Carter too. She had loved him, or thought she did. They had a history. But lately she wasn't sure he was the one, and with the doubt over the arrest and all...

"We had some good times together you know," he said.

He was right. The time they spent together at SF State were some of her best years. College life provided them a warm and cozy cocoon, sheltered from all the crap going on in the world. It was a special time, but those days were gone. It's ending was inevitable. She had to leave the cocoon, spread her wings and take her chances in the real world. And look how that turned out.

"I know we did, Carter. I know."

# CHAPTER 11

October, 2016

KIMBRA WAS TURNING HER LIFE AROUND. She moved out of Oakdale, leaving her mother and that deadbeat molester Cody behind. It wasn't easy, but she did it. Getting financial aid and student loans was a daunting task, especially without any assistance from her mother. Gina had already navigated the process and was a big help along with Kimbra's high school counselor. By the time her second year at San Francisco State University rolled around, she was feeling pretty good about herself.

Sunlight splashed over the high-rise student housing buildings. Decorative trees in the courtyard sparkled in brilliant shades of yellow and orange. Kimbra sat with a sandwich and a second year psych book in her hands. She traded her first year dormitory-style residence for the modern off-campus housing, sharing a two-bedroom, fully furnished suite with her first year roommate, Lindsey.

As far as boys were concerned, Kimbra was emotionally spent and kept to herself her first year. But this was a new year, a new location, and a fresh start. She decided to reinvent herself and be open to new experiences. So when a guy in her Sociology class approached her, she was in a much better place.

"Excuse me, Kimbra right?"

"Yes..."

"I missed SOC 105 yesterday. Did I miss anything important?"

"No, not really."

"Oh, I'm Carter by the way," he introduced himself with a soft handshake.

He had a stocky build, square face, and thick wavy hair. He was dressed in chinos, an expensive polo shirt, and brown suede Derby shoes.

"Are you a Psych Major?" he asked noting the book she was reading.

"Yes, and you?"

"Oh, English. Not sure what I'll do with it though. Dad would prefer I become a lawyer."

"And what do you want to do?" Kimbra asked, not sure if the question was appropriate or not given they just met, but then he started the conversation.

Carter pushed dark framed glasses up his nose, "I would like to write."

"That sounds interesting. What kind of writing?"

"Novels, though I don't suppose that would pay the bills. What about you?"

Now he was getting personal, but he seemed nice enough and Kimbra was intrigued.

"I'm still figuring that out. But I am interested in child and abnormal psych."

Two flashy girls in short skirts and preppy tops strolled by and greeted Carter by name. Kimbra felt out of place in her jeans and canvas sneakers. Carter returned their greeting and turned his attention back to Kimbra.

"I've seen you here before. Do you live nearby?" he asked.

"I'm on the third floor."

"Small world, or should I say campus. I'm on the sixth."

Kimbra began seeing more of Carter over the next month. Her mention of a non-existent boyfriend back home kept the relationship at a comfortable distance. She was seeing someone her senior year in high school, but that ended quickly after graduation. But Carter persisted, and Kimbra was growing fond of him. She needed stability and normalcy in her life and he seemed to fit that role. Carter was intelligent, thoughtful, and came from a well-to-do family. He had lots of friends and was focused on his school work and career. So, with winter approaching fast, the temps cooled down and their relationship heated up. After Christmas break, Kimbra moved in with Carter.

It was a comfortable and stable relationship, something Kimbra yearned for with all the chaos back home. The two enjoyed a storybook romance at college knowing it would not last forever. Before they knew it, graduation was approaching and it was time to make a life-changing decision.

"Have you decided what you want to do after graduation?" Carter asked.

Kimbra had been struggling with that question.

"I don't know. I would like to get my masters, but that's not possible. I can't afford it."

"We can look for an apartment in LA. I've got a lead on a job there and I'm sure you could find something there, save a little for your masters."

Moving back home to Oakdale was not an option Kimbra wanted to consider, but moving in with Carter permanently sounded like a big step and she wasn't sure she was ready for that. She considered moving to Colorado, near her sister, but if she did that she would lose Carter. They had a nice relationship and she wasn't ready to throw that away.

"That sounds nice. Can I think about it a little more?" Kimbra asked.

"Of course."

Graduation came and went, and the couple moved to Los Angeles where they rented a small two-bedroom apartment together. It was close to Carter's parents who helped him get a job at a small publication company. Carter worked remotely several days a week. The time saved commuting allowed him to work part-time on his novel. His father, a partner at a large law firm, wanted Carter to become a lawyer and join the firm, but he permitted his son the indulgence of writing. Kimbra got a job as a substance abuse counselor. Life was good, life was normal, and she had gotten out from under that cloud of despair. Her life was moving in a positive direction, or so she thought.

Then it happened. They say all good things must come to an end, and it did. It happened abruptly this time. Kimbra was at work when her phone rang.

"Carter, what is it? I'm kind of busy."

There was a murmur of background noise over the line.

"I'm sorry, but something has happened."

Kimbra began to worry, thinking the worst. Was he injured, sick?

"What is it? Are you all right?"

"Not really. I've been arrested."

"What! What are you talking about? You're kidding, right?"

"No. I can't believe it. Kimbra, I've been charged with possession of child pornography."

It's funny how the world around you freezes in moments like that. It's as if you're watching events unfold to another person, like watching a movie. Kimbra began to doubt she ever really knew him. Her chaotic life had surged back in an instant, and it flipped her out. Carter was released on bail, but their relationship was never the same. She felt bad about that, you know, not standing behind her man, not supporting him in his time of need. But, at the time she was feeling trapped in a situation spiraling out of control. Kimbra applied for a job in San José and left Carter.

# CHAPTER 12

KIMBRA SAT IN THE CUSHY CHAIR, EAGERLY LISTENING. Her security clearance had been approved and Fang was explaining the Next Level research program.

"In 2014 the Office of Naval Research embarked on a four-year, $3.85 million research program to explore the phenomena it called premonition and intuition, or *Spidey sense*, as it was referred to back then. The program grew out of field reports of soldiers using intuition to predict and avoid disasters. They accumulated reams of data, but were unable to come up with a scientific explanation. Since then, there have been many investigations on the phenomena. Some of them held up to rigorous scientific scrutiny only to be later refuted."

Fang's leather chair squeaked as he shifted his position. Warm sunlight filtered through tinted windows and onto the documents in his hand.

"Our research began with an interest in telepathy. As you are aware, telepathy is the ability to transmit words, emotions, or images from one person's mind to another without the use of any known sensory channels or physical interaction. If we could communicate telepathically, it would give our military a huge advantage. We took a new approach, concentrating on quantum energy and its possible role in telepathy. If you think of thought as pure energy, like an electro-magnetic wave, transmitting thoughts from one person to another can cover great distances. When you include quantum entanglement, it could happen instantaneously. If we could better understand the mechanics behind it, it would open a world of possibilities. But enough of that, let me show you."

Fang rose from his chair and led Kimbra out his office, down the hall and into an elevator. He inserted a key card and pressed the button labeled *B*.

"Oh, I almost forgot. Here's your key card. It'll give you access to the basement and other secure areas."

The elevator descended and stopped with a jolt. The doors opened, revealing a waiting area with chairs and a main desk.

"This is our reception area," Fang explained. "The service elevator leads to another area, but this is where you'll enter."

He introduced her to the receptionist and opened a door with his key card. Kimbra followed him down a white hallway lined with closed secure access doors.

"Part of our research involves human intelligence and its origin. If we can unlock its origin, perhaps we can accelerate its evolution."

Fang swiped his card at a door and they entered a large room filled with cages of mice and larger mammals, mostly monkeys. He approached a man in a lab coat and introduced him as Dr. Stanwix. He had dark hair and glasses, and was standing over a maze with a mouse inside.

"Doctor, would you mind giving us a brief explanation on the origins of intelligence and what we're doing here?" Fang asked the man.

"Of course. Yes, well at some point a huge jump up the evolutionary tree occurred. A mutation is believed to be responsible for a vast increase in the number of neurons in the human brain. We discovered several indicators of this including the NOTCH2NL gene family found only in humans. We are increasing intelligence here by artificially expressing a similar sequence in mice."

Stanwix picked up the white mouse and held it gently as it wriggled its whiskers, examining the world from its new perch.

"This is Algernon."

"From the book?" Kimbra asked.

"Yes, that's correct," Stanwix replied.

The book, *Flowers for Algernon* by Daniel Keyes had a mouse with the same name in it. It's the fictional story of a mentally challenged man, named Charlie, who has his intelligence increased through a science experiment. Were they able to do that now?

"Algernon is somewhat of a celebrity here," Fang explained. "He has been a remarkable success story and has given us a line of descendants to work with."

"This is a new maze for Algernon," Stanwix explained as he gently placed the mouse at the beginning of the maze and started his stopwatch.

The furry, little critter immediately set about its task: solve the complicated labyrinth and win the prize, a chunk of cheese. He scampered about, pausing only once or twice before he completed the maze in short order.

Stanwix stopped his watch. "Nineteen seconds," he announced. "Not his record, but pretty darn good."

"He didn't make one mistake. How is that possible?" Kimbra asked.

"Algernon's neural count has been increased by a factor of ten," Stanwix explained.

Kimbra suspected there was something else going on. It was either an incredible scientific breakthrough, or a scam.

"But there's more to it than intelligence and increased neural count, isn't there?" she asked.

"Yes, there is," Fang agreed.

"Thank you doctor," Fang interrupted. "Kimbra, let's talk."

Fang left the lab as Kimbra followed, anticipating an answer to her question. Once back in Fang's office, he replied.

"So, yes, there's more to it than an increased neural count, there's something going on we don't completely understand. We may have discovered a *psychic gene* if you will, enabling a connection with the universe around us."

"A psychic gene," Kimbra repeated.

"How is it that Algernon seems to know the path of a maze he has never seen before? Is it intuition, remote viewing, or something else? One possible explanation could be a quantum connection with *spillover* energy from another dimension. Some physicists believe time flows in both directions, allowing people to sense things that have not yet happened. A hidden dimension, or the ability to traverse time, could both be explained with quantum physics. Whatever is going on, we have opened the door with our research."

"That's incredible!"

"It is, but there is so much to do before any of this can be proven. And for that, we need to test higher forms of life. We began human trials several months ago."

"That's the Next Level?"

"Yes. We are artificially expressing the NOTCH2NL genes in exceptionally gifted people. Those with high emotional intelligence and paranormal abilities."

"People like Chad and Christina?"

"Yes."

"But what about risks? Are there any side-effects?"

"We are closely monitoring that and there are safety protocols we follow, the government is involved in every step of our research. So, I don't need to stress enough the importance of keeping this secret."

"Yes, of course," she agreed.

Kimbra left her meeting with Fang, having more questions than answers.


That afternoon Kimbra sat at her desk reviewing the information on the Next Level research Fang had provided. She skimmed over the scientific jargon, concentrating on the summaries. Apparently there were structures in each cell called *microtubules* that were believed to play a role in quantum computing and could explain consciousness itself. Fang mentioned telepathy could be thought of as an energy transfer and their research was digging deeper into that.

Apparently, at the quantum level, the definitions of space and time become murky. An atom can exist in two separate locations at the same time. You could theoretically send a message anywhere in the universe in an instant. It was fascinating, but most of it way over her head. Kimbra's area of interest was psychology, she was not a physicist or a molecular biologist.

By the end of the day her body was hungry and her brain exhausted. She stopped at a local market to pick up a few items for dinner: fresh veggies to roast and put over pasta. As she approached the wine aisle she spotted a familiar face. She was hoping to run into him again, and here he was.

"Hi Daniel."

"Kimbra. How have you been?"

"I'm hanging in there. I see you like wine," she commented.

"I do. Also a nice beer as well," he said. "Tonight feels like a wine night though, if you know what I mean."

"Oh, I understand completely. I'm here to replenish my stock."

"That's one of my favorites," Kimbra pointed to the bottle Daniel was examining. It wasn't the expensive brand Carter preferred, but on Kimbra's budget it was a nice compromise.

"Well, we have at least one thing in common then, don't we?"

Kimbra picked up two bottles for herself. "I guess we do. Hey, I wanted to tell you I'm glad you stopped by the other day at the deli. I apologize if I wasn't in the best of moods."

"No need to apologize, I enjoyed our talk. Oh, I wanted to tell you I'm so sorry to hear about your friend Marie."

"Thanks. It's been rough."

"I heard they arrested Mick. Weren't you seeing each other in high school?"

"We were. That seems like ages ago."

"Well, if you ever want to talk... I mean about anything. I'm an excellent listener," he offered.

"I'd like that."

They exchanged phone numbers and agreed to get together soon. Kimbra decided if he didn't call soon, she would call him. She needed someone to talk to, and he said he was a good listener.

# CHAPTER 13

THE ONE HOUR FLIGHT TO LOS ANGELES took two and a half hours, a mechanical issue was given as the reason for the delay. Kimbra sat on the witness stand, duly sworn in and ready to do her part. Carter's wealthy parents retained the best legal counsel for their son, though they did NOT select an attorney from the firm and they did NOT attend the trial. That would prove too embarrassing for them. They wished to keep the trial as quiet as possible, as if the whole matter could be easily swept under the carpet. The defense attorney, Spencer Langmore, was a distinguished looking gentleman with wispy gray hair and a neatly trimmed goatee to match. He addressed the witness in a peaceful tone. His voice had a calming effect on the room as if this would be a pleasant experience.

"Miss Evans, how long have you known the defendant?"

Kimbra wore a navy blue pantsuit with a lightly patterned blouse. Langmore's staff had provided a video instructing her on how to be the perfect character witness. How to act, what to wear, what to say. She sat respectfully with ankles crossed and hands folded on her lap.

"I've known Carter for seven years."

Langmore looked around the room, as if to exaggerate the number.

"In all that time, has the defendant ever displayed any sign of behavior that you would question, did he have a temper, did he lie, cheat, kick the cat? Anything that would lead you to question his character?"

A soft smile formed on Kimbra's face. "No. Carter would not harm a fly. He was kind, gentle, and thoughtful."

Langmore turned to face the jury, paused, and resumed the questioning.

"Miss Evans, can you describe your relationship with the defendant?"

"We dated in college and eventually shared an apartment there. After graduation we moved to Los Angeles where we lived together until recently."

Kimbra had been coached on how to handle their current living situation. Langmore did not want the prosecution bringing it up first.

"You said *until recently*. Can you expound on that?"

Kimbra cleared her throat. "Yes, well I received a job offer out of town. We decided it would be best for both of us if I accepted the position."

"And are you still seeing each other?"

"We are not."

"Why is that?"

"We were drifting apart and decided we needed some space."

"Did the charges against Carter have anything to do with your separation?"

That was a tough one. Thankfully they had covered it earlier.

"It may have precipitated things, but like I said, we were drifting apart."

"I understand. Back to your relationship, I assume it was romantic?"

"It was."

"I'm sorry to have to ask this, but did you have a healthy sex life?"

Kimbra cleared her throat and kept the answer brief, "Yes."

"Was there anything you noticed in his conduct that someone may consider out of the ordinary?"

"There was nothing abnormal about our relationship. We were in love and we were exclusive."

"Did you notice any perverted behavior or strange attraction to minors on Carter's part?"

"Absolutely not."

"No further questions your Honor."

Langmore sat and the district attorney rose for cross-examination. Shaply dressed and in his mid-forties, Gerard Becker was a little too slick for Kimbra's liking. He approached the witness stand like a cat about to pounce on its prey.

"Miss Evans, how did you react when you found out about the charges?"

"I was shocked."

"Why was that?"

"Because it was out of character."

"I see," Becker said in a condescending tone. "You stated earlier that you had a *healthy* sex life. How would you define that?"

"Normal. It was a normal sex life," she blurted out.

"What's normal to you, could be considered perverted to others. Did he take pleasure in any out of the ordinary behavior?"

"Out of the ordinary?"

"Did he ask you to dress up, wear a wig, act differently? Was there any sadomasochism, bondage, or other unusual behavior outside the parameters most would consider normal? I think you know what I mean."

"No! Of course not."

Becker fired off the questions in rapid succession. Kimbra was warned he would try to rile her and they were right. Her anger was welling up, she was losing her composure.

"Miss Evans, did Carter have any secrets he kept from you?"

"How would I know?" Kimbra's tone came across as angry.

"Of course, how would you? Did you keep any secrets from Carter?"

"Secrets?" she asked.

"Yes. Surely the two of you did not share everything. Perhaps an embarrassing moment from your childhood, or a call from an old boyfriend. We all have certain things we are reluctant to share with our loved ones?"

"I guess."

"Do you think it's possible he had some secrets he kept from you?"

"Again, how would I know?"

"Well, let's say something you found out, or something he revealed later."

Beads of perspiration formed on Kimbra's brow and underarms. She stirred uncomfortably in her seat.

"Not that I can recall."

"All right Miss Evans, just one more question. Had Carter ever surprised you before?"

Kimbra was not liking this man. He was smug and condescending.

"How do you mean?" she asked.

"I mean did he ever do anything out of the blue? Surprise you with flowers? Laugh inappropriately? Do something unexpected?"

Kimbra was anxious, feeling on the defensive, her heart was pounding.

"I guess..." she reluctantly admitted.

"Of course. People can, and do surprise us. And when they do, it can seem totally *out of character*."

Becker turned his attention to the jury.

"We've all heard stories of neighbors, friends, and even wives of serial killers who had no idea of what they were capable of."

Becker turned to face Kimbra again.

"We don't really know what goes on in the minds of others, do we?"

Kimbra wasn't sure if the question was for her or rhetorical.

"No further questions your Honor."

Becker was done and Kimbra was dismissed before she could muster another word.


On the flight home Kimbra played back the day in her head. She thought her testimony went as well as expected. She felt sorry for Carter. He continued to deny the charges. Perhaps the prosecutor was right on one point: how well can you really know someone? If Carter was lying, then he was sick and needed help. Whatever the outcome, she wished him the best. Carter had always treated her kindly and showed no signs of any abnormal behavior. Though she didn't feel the same way romantically, she was still fond of him.

The plane touched down in San José and Kimbra rushed out the terminal. Caught in rush hour traffic, it was well after eight when she finally reached her apartment. Stressed and exhausted from the long day, she put together a quick salad, ate, and was looking forward to kicking back in the living room before going to bed. She was changing into her pajamas when she sensed someone watching. Noticing the drapes were open, she shut them quickly, stepped to the side and peeked out a small opening in the drapes. Someone was out back, looking up!

She rushed out the bedroom and into the living room to get a better view from the sliding glass door. There was too much reflection from the kitchen lights, so she opened the door and quietly stepped out onto the balcony. A soft summer breeze brushed her hair, the trees rustled, as she looked out over the darkened courtyard. As her eyes adjusted to the darkness, objects slowly appeared out of nowhere, like a black-and-white photo coming into focus. A shadow, or something, quickly moved right to left across her field of view, disappearing in an instant! She leaned over the rail to see if it was still out there, but saw nothing. Was it still out there, lurking in the shadows? Her eyes strained, struggling to discern more detail out of the night. Suddenly, something moved to her right, illuminated by the ambient light. But wait, it was too small to be a person. It was a cat, or fox, or a raccoon.

She turned her eyes back to where the person was last seen and waited, studying the area intensely. She stood there frozen, wondering if someone was looking back, studying her. She remained there until a shiver broke her concentration. It was a warm summer night, yet she was chilled. Now she wondered, was her mind playing tricks on her?

Back in the safety of the living room she poured herself a glass of wine and tried to relax. Her mind conjured up what she saw through the bedroom window earlier. A dark figure of average height and build, staring up at her. He wore a black baseball cap and a dark outfit. She was focusing on the face, darkened by the shadow of the hat, when the phone rang, scaring her half to death.

"Hi, Kimbra. This is Daniel... Daniel Visser."

She expected the interruption to be annoying, but instead found his voice soothing.

"Daniel, how are you doing?"

"I've had better days. How about you?"

It felt like he had just read her mind.

"You have no idea," she said.

"Hey, we discussed getting together last time we met at the market. I just wanted to see if you were still interested."

# CHAPTER 14

THE TWO SAT IN SILENCE, the din of conversation and tinkling of dinnerware in the background. Scents of lemongrass, garlic, and spices filled the air. Kimbra took a sip of her Tom Kha Gai soup, a strange mixture of chicken and coconut: rich and creamy yet tangy and salty.

"Mmm, Daniel, this is delicious."

"I'm glad you like it."

This was a new experience for Kimbra, she and Carter never went to Thai restaurants. Daniel had picked her up, and she was uncomfortable with this being a date. After all, they had only recently met. She barely knew him in high school, and they did not hang out in any of the same circles. Still, it seemed like they made a connection and since Marie's death she could use someone, other than Gina, that she could confide in. But she was not ready for a relationship and did not want to give him the wrong impression.

"So how are things going?" he asked. "Sounded like you were having a bad day when we last talked."

"Oh, I was. I've had a rough time since Marie's death."

"It must be tough."

"I really miss her..." Kimbra drifted off in thought. Her eyes moistened.

Daniel reached across the table and touched her hand gently.

"I'm sorry. If there's anything I can do."

Kimbra patted his hand and slowly pulled away.

"Thank you. It's just something I have to deal with."

She went back to her soup, and the two ate in silence. When they finished, the waiter came by to remove their empty bowls.

"Is there something else bothering you?" Daniel asked.

"Yeah, I guess there is."

"Do you want to talk about it? Might help to get it off your shoulders."

Kimbra looked deep into his dark brown eyes. He seemed genuinely concerned and sincere with the offer.

"I guess. There's just so much."

"I'm all ears," he prodded.

The waiter came by and delivered the main course. Impeccable timing Kimbra thought. She looked down at her pad khee-mao, also called drunken noodles.

"Looks delicious."

"I hope you like it."

Kimbra took a bite of the spicy stir-fried noodle dish, showing her approval with a smile. She chased it with a sip of a light, crisp, beer and continued.

"I don't think I mentioned my boyfriend, or actually ex-boyfriend. Carter, and I had a parting of ways recently."

"No, you didn't mention that."

"It's difficult to talk about and it was kind of a shock."

Daniel remained silent, listening intently.

"He was arrested for possession of child pornography," she blurted out.

"I see. That must have been a shock," he said.

"He denies it. Says he has no idea how that got on his computer."

"It's possible," Daniel offered. "There are plenty of hacks and malicious viruses out there."

"I know, but he was just convicted, and I'm not sure I can trust him."

Carter was sentenced to three months in jail and given a hefty fine. It took the jury only four hours to find him guilty.

"Well, that must be difficult. Are you still talking?"

"No. Not really."

Kimbra took a hearty sip of her drink. It was a relief telling someone about Carter. Daniel remained silent as they ate. For some odd reason, it wasn't overly awkward.

"There's more," she said later when her stomach was full and the alcohol had kicked in. She wasn't sure how he would react, he would probably think she was crazy, but what the hell.

"I'm sorry?" Daniel returned a quizzical look.

"There's more I haven't told you. I've had a strange feeling that someone has been stalking me."

"What makes you say that?"

"I think someone has been in my apartment. A few personal items are missing and things have been moved around."

Daniel's dark eyes widened, studying her intensely. His jaw dropped, ever so slightly.

"That's terrible. Who would do that?"

"Mick. I mean he stole my phone, but why do creepy stuff like take my clothes and move things?"

Daniel was speechless for the moment. Finally, he came up with the words.

"You think you know someone, but they can change."

"I know. Mick's in jail now, but I still feel like I'm being watched."

"You think someone else is breaking into your apartment?"

Kimbra was beyond frustrated, she was afraid.

"I don't know. I'm not sure of anything anymore!"

"Okay, so what about Carter? Could he be angry over the break-up?"

"I don't think so. It would be totally out of character for Carter to do something like that."

"Well, you never know. Love can drive people to do crazy things."

"I suppose. Anyway, it's driving me crazy. Marie's murder was so senseless, and now the creepy feelings I'm having. I have a terrible feeling they are somehow connected."

Daniel was silent. A weird tenant that Kimbra ran into from time to time came to mind.

"Maybe it's someone living in my complex?" she suggested. "There's this guy that stares at me, never says anything, just stares at me."

"Do you know his name?"

"No. I think he lives downstairs, I can check the mailboxes."

Daniel pushed his plate aside and leaned towards Kimbra.

"Look, what happened to Marie, it's tragic. I'm so sorry it happened, but you are under a lot of stress. It could be your mind playing tricks on you, you're scared. Who wouldn't be? Mick was in your apartment, he stole your phone, but he's in jail now."

Daniel leaned back in his chair and looked around the dining area. Kimbra was feeling she had laid too much on his shoulders.

"I know, you're probably right... But hey, all we've done is talk about me. What about you? What's your story?" she asked trying to change the subject.

"My story?" he asked.

"Yes."

The waiter returned, asking if they wanted coffee or dessert. They opted for coffee. Kimbra waited for a response from Daniel.

"Not sure if you know this, but I don't like talking about myself much," he admitted.

"C'mon, I just shared my crazy life story and I don't know anything about you."

"All right, what do you want to know?"

"I don't know. Tell me about your mother, father, any siblings?"

The waiter returned with two hot coffees. They both took theirs black.

"Okay, no brother or sister. I never knew my father. My mother moved out when I was seven."

"I'm sorry to hear that," Kimbra said.

"Nothing to be sorry about. I moved in with my grandmother. School was difficult for me, I was pretty shy."

"You, shy?"

"Hard to believe, right," Daniel explained with a smirk. "But really, I didn't like school much."

"Me neither," Kimbra admitted. "What did you do after that?"

"I joined the Army."

"The Army."

"I needed to get away. Thought the Army was a good way to see the world."

"Was it?"

"I got away all right. Didn't see much of the world, but I did get to see a lot of Afghanistan."

Daniel took a sip of coffee and looked off as if deep in thought. Kimbra waited for him to elaborate on Afghanistan. He did not.

"Anyway, I finished my tour and returned home. Shortly later my grandmother died. I went to Sacramento State and got a degree in criminal justice. I got pretty good with computers there and got my first job as an intelligence analyst in Oakland. A few years later I struck out on my own and started my investigation business."

"That's amazing. What's the name of your business?"

Kimbra already knew this but didn't want to sound like she had looked him up.

"Magellan Research."

"What made you choose San José?"

"I saw an ad for a private investigator who was selling his business."

"It must be exciting work."

"Sometimes, though not as exciting as you might think. Not the exciting stuff you see on television or the movies. I do a lot of research on the internet."

Kimbra was thinking he could help with Marie's murder, maybe shed some light on a motive, but she was reluctant to ask. She wasn't comfortable asking for help, after all they were just getting to know each other. Perhaps another time.

Daniel pulled up in front of Kimbra's apartment complex, the engine still running. Dim lights lit the way down a sidewalk bordered by well manicured shrubs.

"Thank you for dinner, I had a great time," she said.

"You're welcome. I enjoyed it as well."

Their eyes locked for an awkward moment. Kimbra reached for the door handle as Daniel moved closer. She turned her head in his direction, then she panicked and quickly looked away.

"I can walk you to your apartment," he offered.

"Thanks, but I'm fine. It's a short walk."

They said goodnight and the moment was over. Kimbra got out and headed down the walkway, resisting the urge to look back. Only when she reached the entrance to her apartment building, did she steal a glance back. Daniel's car was still there, no doubt making sure she got inside safely.

# CHAPTER 15

NESTLED IN A CORNER OF THE BASEMENT WAS A DIMLY LIT ROOM. Chad and Christina sat facing each other, a tall partition between them blocked their view of each other. A monitor screen was placed in front of each of them. They were each fitted with head gear, not unlike that worn by wrestlers, but lighter weight and with a bundle of wires running out the back. Dr. Stanwix, the molecular biologist, sat in the back of the room. Kimbra was seated at a terminal next to Stanwix, she presented a brief orientation to the test subjects.

"The head devices you have on contain computer chips targeting specific regions of your brain we believe are responsible for telepathic activity. The goal of this experiment is to initiate a successful telepathic connection and capture and measure those signals."

Stanwix was working feverishly at his terminal with his back to the wall. The backs of multiple monitors hid his face from the test subjects. Network cables ran along the floor from Stanwix's station climbing up to the test subjects' head gear.

"Miss Evans, you can begin when ready," Stanwix announced.

Kimbra sat in front of a monitor with a split screen. Each section set to display the output sent to one of the test subjects.

"Okay, I'm ready. For the first experiment Christina will be the sender and Chad will be the receiver. I'm going to display several images on Christina's screen and give her time to concentrate and send each image telepathically to Chad. Are you ready?"

They both acknowledged they were ready.

"I'll let you know before I display each image. I have to warn you, some of the images are quite graphic. They were chosen because images that elicit a strong emotional response are the most likely to be transferred telepathically. Here is the first image."

A black-and-white photo of a park bench in winter flashed up on Kimbra's and Christina's monitors. Both subjects, sender and receiver, concentrated intently. Chad's brow tightened. Moments later he responded.

"Cold and dark. I'm not getting a clear picture, but that's what I feel."

"Okay, good. Next image," Kimbra announced.

Another black-and-white image appeared, this time a man's face horribly burned and disfigured.

Chad jerked back in his seat and reported, "Again dark. But this time... a man... his face... is grossly deformed!"

Kimbra continued displaying the disturbing images which got more graphic and colorful as they progressed. She could see Stanwix's face glowing from the displays in front of him. He looked to be thoroughly engrossed with the data. The last image was actually a video. It was a perverted sexual act in full color.

"That's the end of the images," Kimbra sighed. "I apologize for their graphic nature, but I explained earlier why they were selected."

"We're getting a lot of useful data," Stanwix announced. "Give me a minute before we begin the second test."

Kimbra tapped her foot nervously. She could tell Chad and Christina were anxious as well.

"Mind if I light up?" Christina asked pulling out a pack of cigarettes.

"I'm sorry, that's not allowed," Kimbra answered.

Christina put the pack away and stirred in her seat. Chad's fingers tapped away on his desk like a woodpecker. He appeared to be lost without his phone. Phones and electronic devices were not allowed in the basement.

"We want you to be comfortable, but we can't introduce any chemicals into your brains. That could skew the data," Kimbra explained.

The test subjects anxiously waited for the second test. Finally, Stanwix announced he was ready.

"We'll do the same thing, except this time Chad will be the sender. The images will be similar in nature but different. Are we ready?" Kimbra asked.

Christina sat upright and drew in a deep breath.

"First image," Kimbra announced. A black-and-white image popped up on her screen and Chad's. It was a swan in a dark pond. Chad concentrated on sending the image.

Christina closed her eyes, her face went blank as she concentrated on receiving a signal.

"It's soft, feathery... a bird, perhaps an egret or swan," she described what her mind was envisioning.

Kimbra announced the next image. Another black-and-white, this time a horrific scene of a car accident. Christina focused again for a brief moment, then suddenly jumped back in her seat and appeared to be in a trance.

"Christina, are you all right?" Kimbra called out.

Hearing no response, Kimbra stood up to get a better view. Christina bolted up out of her chair, scaring the daylights out of Kimbra.

"What happened?" Kimbra asked.

Christina looked around the room appearing to be disoriented, then shook her head.

"Christina, are you all right?"

"It was horrible," Christina began to sob.

Kimbra put her arm gently around Christina's shoulders and guided her to her chair.

"Why don't you sit down."

Christina sat and spoke through her sobs.

"There were burnt bodies, hundreds of them, and body parts everywhere, strewn all over a field!"

"That was not the image sent to Chad," Kimbra explained, as Stanwix and Chad joined them.

Christina was shaking.

"Christina, what did you see?" Stanwix asked.

Christina stopped sobbing long enough to blurt out, " The broken remains of a large jet. The smell was horrible, the stench of burning flesh and jet fuel. It was a plane crash!"

The experiment was over. Chad left. Christina was given a mild sedative and left twenty minutes later, after she calmed down. Kimbra was cleaning up the test room when Dr. Stanwix grabbed his things and got up to leave.

"Doctor, what happened? Chad was shown a picture of a car accident. One person, one car."

"She appears to have had a vision, possibly stimulated by the images. There is a lot of data I have to study."

"What exactly are you looking for?" Kimbra asked.

"That's a very good question," Stanwix said clutching his laptop. "We're looking for proof of a mechanism for sending telepathic signals. We suspect it is coming from quantum vibrations in the microtubules of the neurons. But finding a signal in the vibrations is like searching for the proverbial needle in the haystack. I suspect it's there, we just need to find it and decode it."

Stanwix pushed his glasses up his nose and left. Kimbra finished cleaning up and rushed back to her cubicle. She scoured the internet for recent plane crashes. Christina had described a large jet airliner with hundreds of passengers. The last large airliner crash was an Air India Express in 2020. 152 of the 160 passengers were killed. Was Christina's vision an actual crash, a premonition, or a vivid hallucination brought on by the drugs?

That got Kimbra thinking. In explaining Algernon's ability to solve the maze, Fang had suggested a quantum connection and a *spillover* of energy from another dimension allowing the mouse to somehow solve the maze. Christina had some kind of connection to past or future events. Kimbra wondered again if she could help her find a reason for Marie's murder. She looked around to see if anyone was watching and opened the personnel directory, searching for Christina Sullivan. Now that she had access to Next Level data, she could see all the data on the test subjects. Knowing full well she was not supposed to contact them, she jotted down Christina's phone number and address. What she would do with that, she wasn't sure.

# CHAPTER 16

THE NEXT MORNING BROUGHT WITH IT, GRIM NEWS. Kimbra sat at the kitchen table, lost in thought as the television droned on in the background. Between the annoying advertisements and weather predictions, something caught her attention. She gasped as she put down her coffee. A man with jet black hair and a sour look was speaking. It was his words that pulled her in, like a vortex sucking in everything around it.

The Boeing 747 went down early this morning in a remote field outside of Pittsburgh. Wreckage is strewn across a 2-mile swath of wooded land. Fire and rescue teams have been on the scene since shortly before dawn. There were 237 passengers on board, no survivors have been reported as of the latest reports. The cause of the disaster is under investigation.

The announcer went on to explain there had not been a crash in the US with more passengers since a TWA airbus went down on November 12, 2001, crashing into a neighborhood in Queens, NY. All 265 people on board and 5 people on the ground were killed that day. Just two days earlier, Christina had experienced a vision of a plane crash. Now it had come true! Was the premonition related to the Next

Level program or just another of Christina's visions? Whatever was going on, this woman could be the key to shedding some light on Marie's murder. Kimbra had to find out more.

She was on edge and late for work when Smokey sauntered in for his breakfast. She fed the cat and rushed off to shower. Getting dressed, she again had the strange feeling she was being watched. Getting that feeling out in public is unsettling, having the same feeling at home is terrifying. It was nothing tangible, nothing she could prove, but she somehow felt violated. Her nerves were frayed as she left her apartment.

Stuck in the middle of rush hour traffic, Kimbra's phone rang and she fumbled to answer it. A horn blared, scaring her half to death as she swerved to avoid a collision. Lost in the commotion, the phone dinged as the call went to voicemail. Not wanting a repeat of the near accident, she caught her breath and decided to check it later. Just as well, as she was not ready to handle any additional bad news at the moment.

Arriving late at her cubicle, she set down her purse and checked her voicemail. Just as she feared, it was another setback.

"Miss Evans, this is detective Rizzo. I wanted to let you know, Mick Donnelly was released on bail last night. The judge felt he was not a flight risk or a danger to others and he managed to post bail. He will be under close supervision though and will be wearing an electronic monitoring device at all times. If you have any questions or concerns don't hesitate to call."

Wow, her day just got worse. Kimbra spent the next thirty minutes going over data from the latest experiment before her phone rang again. It was her boss, and he requested to see her right away. She suspected it had something to do with Christina and her suspicions were confirmed immediately in his office.

"Have you heard about the plane crash this morning?" Fang asked.

"Oh my gosh, yes! It's horrible... and she saw it coming."

"It would seem so. She was terribly distraught about it and has dropped out of the program."

"I can understand that. Do you think her vision was related to the program, I mean did we cause it?"

"Cause a premonition? I don't think so, but there's no way to be certain. She has had visions before. Did you know she helped solve a string of murders in Oregon and Washington years ago?"

"No, I did not," Kimbra lied, not wanting him to know she had investigated a test subject.

"So, it could have nothing to do with the program. Anyway, it's tragic and she is out."

Fang was quiet, he seemed to be in a reflective mood. Kimbra sensed something else was bothering him. She sat down, giving him time. She wasn't sure if he even realized she was still there.

"I think we're at a cross-roads," he said almost to himself.

"How do you mean?"

"I think we're onto something big. We could be on the verge of identifying a mechanism for telepathy as well as the moment of consciousness."

"The moment of consciousness?"

Fang's attention was off somewhere else. It was not like him to be distracted from their conversation. Kimbra was about to repeat the question when he spoke.

"It's complicated. We are measuring quantum computations inside the brain. That information, stored as quantum bits or qubits, could represent various states that are capable of referring information both forward and backward in what we perceive as time, enabling our perception of real-time consciousness."

Kimbra was having a difficult time processing that. "Forward and backward in time?" she asked.

"Time is really a construct that our brain uses to make sense of the world around us. Real time consciousness can't be explained with conventional methods. If you measure it down to the millisecond, by the time a signal is received, sent to the brain, and processed, the event has already occurred. For example, in order for a professional tennis player to return a volley, they have to swing before the ball is ever served. How is that possible?"

"I don't know," Kimbra said.

"Only with quantum superposition can we begin to understand it. Think of Schrödinger's cat."

Kimbra was familiar with Schrödinger's cat, a thought experiment where a hypothetical cat in a box is considered both alive and dead until you look inside.

"The cat exists in two states until it is observed. The state is determined by the observation. This has been proven in the lab. Quantum physics could offer an explanation, but is that occurring in the brain? Stanwix believes we are about to prove that."

It sounded fascinating, but Kimbra wondered what would they do with that knowledge. Telepathy could be a dangerous tool. And God only knew what the government could do messing with our perception of time, as Fang had said.

"Anyway, I wanted to let you know our higher level tests will be on hold until we identify another qualified candidate to replace Christina."


That night Kimbra was troubled. The plane crash, the premonition, and the talk of *quantum perception of time* was frightening. She sat on the couch curled up in a ball with Smokey at her side when she felt a presence. She couldn't describe the feeling, but she was not alone. A hot flash washed over her when, *creak*, a sound shot out of the bedroom. She froze, held her breath, and listened intently. The wind rustled outside, making it difficult to hone in on the bedroom. Her heart pounded, a lump formed in her throat when she heard it again. A creak, like a footstep on a loose floorboard. She reached for her phone and got up slowly, as quietly as humanly possible and worked her way to the kitchen. Smokey hopped off the sofa and followed her.

A knife sat firmly in a block of wood on the counter, she pulled it out, holding it in a defensive position. She took two steps towards the bedroom when another sound stopped her cold. A scraping sound coming from the back of the apartment. She waited... Then it came again, and she knew. It was the sound of a branch scraping against the outside of the building. She continued towards the bedroom, inching her way until she reached the darkened doorway. Something had moved in there, but how could that be? She had been through every room in the small apartment. No one could have possibly gotten in, or did they? Maybe they were hiding, waiting for her to get home. Her mind quickly ran through potential places to hide: under the bed, in the closet, behind a door. Was there access to an attic, an access panel or something? She didn't know. Just then, Smokey brushed past her and into the bedroom. She drew in a deep breath and somehow mustered the courage to reach in quickly and turn on the light.

The bedroom was empty, except for Smokey, who had jumped on the bed. Kimbra returned to the living room feeling a bit silly. She wondered, was her mind playing tricks with her? But she was certain she heard the creak of a floorboard. Horrific thoughts popped into her head. Was someone messing with her mind, using telepathy on her right now? Were they reading her mind, watching her every move? She imagined how terrifying Christina's premonition must have been and decided on her next course of action. She knew she wasn't supposed to, but she dialed the number anyway and bit her lip. One ring... two... three. Maybe she wouldn't pick up. It was probably just as well. Then she picked up.

"Hello?"

Kimbra froze.

"Hello?"

Kimbra cleared her throat. "I'm sorry. This is Kimbra Evans... from Quantum Thunder."

"Oh, yes. What is it?"

"I'm sorry to bother you..."

"What is it dear?"

"I'm sorry. Your vision, I mean premonition... it must have been horrible."

"Yes, well I've had them before. I'm just devastated with the size and scope of this one, and that I couldn't do anything about it. I tried to identify the airline, a flight number, anything..."

Christina's voice trailed off before she spoke again.

"Anyway, they would not have believed me. They never do. I realize how crazy it would have sounded, but I should have tried something."

There was a silence over the phone, Kimbra did not know what to say.

"Is there anything else, Miss Evans?"

"Oh, please call me Kimbra."

"Of course."

Kimbra bit her lip and continued, "Something has been troubling me. I'm anxious most of the day and can't sleep. I can't explain it but I have this feeling I'm being watched."

"How is it you think I can help?"

"I'm not sure, but the vision you had of my friend's murder..."

"I can't be certain that's what it was," Christina cut her off.

"I know. But it came when you touched me. I think it was Marie's murder and that it's connected to my being watched."

"You do?"

"I do."

# CHAPTER 17

BEAMS OF LIGHT BROKE THE TWILIGHT AS A RED SUBARU VEERED DOWN A WINDING DIRT ROAD. The property was nestled on six acres of secluded woods northeast of Sacramento. Kimbra parked in front of a pair of large ash trees, a short gravel walkway led to a beautiful log cabin home. A pair of dormers peeked out from the roof like twinkling eyes. Two porch lights illuminated a covered porch running the length of the house and wrapping around one side. The front door had a large frosted window surrounded by two sidelights, to the left was a metal welcome sign with a bear on it. Kimbra rang the doorbell and waited. Moments later the door swung open. A woman with fiery red hair greeted her with a warm smile.

"Come in. I hope you didn't have any trouble finding the place."

"No, not really," Kimbra lied, too embarrassed to admit she made several wrong turns on the way there.

She stepped into an awe inspiring open space with cathedral ceilings, dormers, and skylights above. The floor was a beautifully finished oak. The stone fireplace provided a cozy, yet spacious feel. The kitchen was adorned with modern appliances and knotty pine cabinets. The style was traditional but elegant. Christina offered her a seat in the living area. Kimbra sat on a sofa as Christina settled into a comfy chair.

"Can I get you something to drink? Coffee, tea... or perhaps something a bit stronger?" Christina offered.

"Coffee would be great, thank you."

Kimbra drove straight from work. It was a three hour drive from San José and she was tired. The coffee would provide a much needed boost. Two cats sauntered into the living area as Christina was making the coffee.

"Don't mind them. They're quite friendly, once they get to know you."

"Oh, I love cats," Kimbra admitted. "I have one named Smokey. What are their names?"

"The gray one is Mulder and the black and white is Scully."

Kimbra had to laugh to herself at the reference to the main characters, Fox Mulder and Dana Scully, in the dark, sci-fi television series, X-Files.

"I love your home," Kimbra commented.

"Thanks. I can give you a tour while the coffee's brewing, if you're interested."

"I would love that."

Christina took her through the 1,800 square foot, three-bedroom and two bath house. The walls throughout the house were covered in knotty pine, the ceilings had the same covering with large rough-cut wooden beams for supports. The floors were finished in hardwood, with the exception of the bathroom and master bedroom, which had tile and carpeting respectively. It was Kimbra's dream house. When the tour finished, they returned to the kitchen and filled two mugs with steaming hot coffee.

"We can sit on the porch if you want," Christina suggested.

"That would be great."

They exited through a sliding glass door and onto a covered deck on the side of the house. A covered hot tub was perched on an attached open deck overlooking the woods. They each sat on a wicker chair with a soft cushion. After a brief discussion about the property, Christina got to the reason for the visit.

"So you think the vision I had of a murder is related to your feelings of being watched?"

Kimbra nodded.

"But they arrested someone for the murder, an ex-boyfriend of yours, right?"

"Yes. I just got word the other day he has been released on bail."

"I see," Christina said between sips of coffee. "What makes you think your feelings of being watched are related to the murder of your friend?"

That was the million dollar question. "I don't know," Kimbra sighed.

"Where is it specifically that you feel you are being watched?"

"Everywhere. When I'm home alone, when I'm out in public, sometimes at work."

"Any specific time of day?"

Kimbra shook her head. Christina set her coffee down and held out her hands.

"Let's see if we can find out more."

Kimbra set her coffee down, reached out, and their hands met. Christina inhaled and exhaled slowly. Not sure how to respond, Kimbra looked down in a reverent manner and closed her eyes. She wondered how her life had come to this, sitting with a clairvoyant in the middle of nowhere, seeking answers from the beyond. A clock in Kimbra's brain ticked off the seconds as she concentrated on her breathing. She cracked her eyes open to sneak a look at Christina, whose eyes were closed in deep concentration.

Snap! Kimbra turned her head to a sound in the darkened woods, the crack of a branch, the movement of something. She listened intently, eyes wide open, scanning about for the source of the disturbance... but she detected only darkness. Must have been a small animal, a raccoon or possum she reasoned. She turned her attention back to Christina and closed her eyes. The wisp of a moist summer night's breeze kissed her cheeks, that's when it happened. Like a wave washing over you, Kimbra felt a warm sensation and opened her eyes. Christina's grip tightened and her eyelids fluttered. She rocked sideways, ever so slightly, like she had lost her balance. Kimbra closed her eyes again and concentrated.

"Do you have a burgundy, brown and cream area rug in the living room?" Christina's voice echoed from an unknown place.

"Yes," Kimbra answered, not entirely sure she was heard.

"A painting above the sofa, a beach scene with two wooden chairs and a blue umbrella. Is that yours?"

"Yes."

Christina's grip tightened again. "There's someone in your apartment!"

Kimbra instinctively jerked away but Christina's grip held tight.

"Whoever it is, they are moving about. The nearby plant. A round device is placed there. Possibly a microphone."

Kimbra remained silent, not wanting to break the trance.

"Something is being attached to the bottom of the television. Another device, maybe a camera?"

The anticipation was killing Kimbra. Still, she remained silent.

"The stalker is in your bedroom now. Another camera is placed... on an aloe plant. Now they're going through your drawers... A pair of black undergarments is being taken."

Kimbra's eyes opened a crack. Christina's eyes moved back and forth under her eyelids. Kimbra jumped when they suddenly opened wide. The grip was broken.

"Who was it? Did you see who it was?"

Christina drew in a deep breath and exhaled slowly. "No. The vision was through the eyes of the intruder."

"But someone was there, or is there now! Is someone there now?" Kimbra was frantic.

"I can't be certain, but I believe this has already taken place."

"I knew it! Someone has been in my apartment! What should I do?" Kimbra shouted.

Christina took another deep breath and let it out slowly. The whole experience seemed to have drained her physically.

"You're sure that's your apartment?"

"Yes! Yes it's my apartment."

"You should call the police. But what will you say? You can't very well tell them a friend saw this in a vision."

"I mentioned this to Detective Rizzo before. I don't think he really believed me, but maybe he can help."

Kimbra pulled out her phone but Christina stopped her. "You won't get any reception here. Use my land line."

Kimbra hurried to the kitchen with Christina at her heels and picked up the phone in the kitchen. It was late, but he did say to call anytime. Sure enough, he picked up.

"Rizzo," a gruff voice spoke.

"Detective, this is Kimbra Evans. I hate to bother you at this hour, but someone has bugged my apartment."

"Okay, take it slow. What have you found?"

There it was. Kimbra didn't see any way around the question.

"I'm at a friend's house. She saw someone in my apartment!"

Rizzo pressed for the details and Kimbra explained everything, including how Christina had solved a string of murders, helping law enforcement. She didn't think he thought it was credible.

"Did you have your locks changed like we discussed earlier?"

"Yes."

"Do you think Mick could be involved with this?" he asked.

"Yes. I mean, I'm not sure."

"Okay, I can stop by in an hour or so. How does that sound?"

Kimbra explained she was three hours away, Christina had a suggestion.

"Honey, you can't drive home now. Besides, you don't want to stay there tonight. Why don't you stay here?"

Kimbra cupped her hand over the phone. "Are you sure? I don't want to impose."

"Nonsense, don't be silly. You can sleep in the spare bedroom."

"Miss Evans?" Rizzo called out. "Are you there?"

Kimbra whispered a "thank you" to Christina and answered her phone.

"Yes, I'm here. I'm going to spend the night at my friend's."

"That sounds like a good idea. I'll stop by tomorrow morning then."


Kimbra sank into the soft sofa with a brandy, Mulder jumped up and nestled next to her.

"He likes you," Christina commented on the gray cat.

"I guess so. Thanks for letting me spend the night here."

"Oh, it's no bother. I couldn't let you go home with bugs in your apartment. I hope they catch whoever did this."

"Me too."

The two women sat, sipping their brandy. Kimbra was feeling safe and starting to relax, if that was possible.

"Christina, they gave you a drug to enhance your abilities."

"Yes."

"What does it do? I mean what effect has it had on you?" Kimbra asked.

Christina swirled her brandy around in the snifter glass, letting the aroma out, and thought it through.

"At first I thought the drug enhanced my abilities. But now... I'm not so sure. Something else is going on, I can feel it. I feel different, more alive, more in tune with the world around me, if that makes any sense. My visions used to be murky, and always occurred in the past. Now, they're crisp, more defined. And then there's the plane crash. I never had a premonition before. Time doesn't feel so constant anymore. It's hard to explain, but it seems like time is shifting, or at least my perception of it. And here's the strangest thing, it's crazy and I don't have any solid basis for it, but I think that given time, I may be able to control it."

# CHAPTER 18

**Two days earlier**

THE WORDS PLAY OUT OVER MY LAPTOP SPEAKER.

Kimbra: *"I'm sorry. Your vision, I mean premonition... it must have been horrible."*

A silence follows as the person on the other end speaks. I cannot make out the words.

Kimbra: *"Oh, please call me Kimbra."*
Unknown caller: Pause.
Kimbra: *"Something has been troubling me. I'm anxious most of the day and can't sleep. I can't explain it but I have the feeling I am being watched."*
Unknown caller: Pause
Kimbra: *"I'm not sure... but the vision you had of my friend's murder..."*

What! What does this person she is talking to know?

Kimbra: *"I know. But it came when you touched me. I think it was Marie's murder and that it's connected to my being watched."*

Does this person know what I did? How is that possible? I turn up the volume, straining to hear something, anything of what is being spoken on the other end. Ahh, but it's useless, I can't make out a word.

Kimbra: *"I do."*
Unknown caller: Pause.
Kimbra: *"Can we meet sometime, anywhere you like?"*
Unknown caller: Long pause.
Kimbra: *"Great! That's 29 Mountain View Road?"*
Unknown caller: Pause.
Kimbra: *"Thank you so much. I'll drive out right after work on Friday."*

Kimbra is clearly rattled about something. What does this person know? I have to find out before they ruin my plans.

*   *   *

Friday arrives and I rush out early, giving myself plenty of time. It's a beautiful drive, could have been peaceful if I wasn't so amped up over the mystery. I desperately need to find out more about this person. Three hours later I reach my destination and turn onto a private drive. I take note of the telephone pole with electric and phone lines. I check my phone. No cell signal, that explains the land line. This person has chosen to live off the grid and that should make my work easier. I carefully negotiate my way along a long, winding dirt road until I find a suitable spot, a small clearing. I pull off the road and into the woods, settling on a spot behind a few trees. The car should be concealed to all but anyone looking for it. Besides, it will be close to sunset when Kimbra arrives, that will help conceal me as well. I open the GPS tracker on my phone. It's currently out of range, but I'll get an alert when she is close. I get myself comfortable and wait, soon drifting off to sleep.

I awaken in darkness to my phone beeping, the time is 8:35 PM. A green dot on my tracker indicates she's on her way. I follow the blip until two beams of light snake their way up the driveway. I duck down as the car passes by. The tracker stops a short distance up the road, out of sight. I wait a few minutes, then grab my bag, get out, and gently close the door.

It's a good hike up the road to a beautiful log cabin nestled in the woods. I creep into the forest for cover and approach from the side. I notice a doorbell camera on the front door, but see no other outdoor security system. With all the wildlife activity, motion sensors would be going off all the time, that might explain her lack of cameras. She may be relying on security by obscurity. Works well in most situations, that is until someone finds you. This may be easier than I thought.

I see Kimbra and a woman with red hair moving about inside. I open my bag and pull out a listening device, resembling a gun with a cone on the end. I slap on the headphones and point it at the house. The sound is faint, but I can make out most of the conversation through the window. The woman's name is Christina.

They leave the house and I move around back to catch a view of them on an outdoor deck. I direct the listening device at the two of them seated on wicker chairs, sipping coffee. The sound is much clearer now.

Christina: *"What makes you think it's related to the murder of your friend?"*

Kimbra: *"I don't know."*

Christina: *"Where is it specifically that you feel you are being watched?"*

Kimbra: *"Everywhere. When I'm home alone, when I'm out in public, sometimes at work."*

So she suspects, but she isn't sure. Christina moves closer and they hold hands. The woman closes her eyes. What the hell is happening here? I move in closer. *Snap!* A branch breaks under my foot. I freeze in place, hoping no one heard me. I duck down slowly and then stop as Kimbra looks in my direction. Her eyes lock right on me. Can she see me? No, she can't, can she? It's too dark. I remain motionless, like an animal blending in with its surroundings. A moment later she turns back towards the woman, who appears to be in a trance.

Christina: *"Do you have a burgundy, brown and cream area rug in the living room?"*

Wait, what is this? She's describing Kimbra's apartment.

Christina: *"There's something attached to the bottom of the television. An eye of some sort that does not belong there. A camera?"*

How can she know?

Christina: *"You should call the police."*

That bitch! I knew this would not go well. The two women move back inside, Kimbra is on the phone in the kitchen. I point the device back at the house. The sounds are faint but I can make out her end of the conversation.

Kimbra: *"Detective, this is Kimbra Evans. I hate to bother you at this hour, but I have reason to believe someone has bugged my apartment."*

That's it, I have to act on this immediately. This Christina has put a wrench in my plans, but I will not let her ruin everything. I pack my gear and hightail it back to the car. I will deal with Christina soon enough.

# CHAPTER 19

THE OVERNIGHT AT CHRISTINA'S mountain home had been a godsend. It allowed Kimbra time to unwind and prepare for the upcoming chaos. Despite it being Saturday, she was up at the crack of dawn and ready to go. She grabbed a bagel, at Christina's insistence, filled her travel mug with hot coffee and hit the road. The mountain air was crisp and smelled of pine. Early morning shadows retreated as the sun rose in the sky. The closer she got the more anxious she grew. The thought of cameras and microphones recording her every move made her sick. Who was behind it? She gripped the steering wheel tightly as her fear slowly turned to anger.

It was minutes before 9 AM when she pulled into the parking lot. An ominous chill hit her as she approached her apartment building. She pushed her way through the main entrance, up the stairs to the second floor and hesitated at the door, questioning if she should enter or wait for Rizzo. Her anger grew as she waited. She was sick and tired of being intimidated, this was her private space and she was damned if someone was going to take that from her. She unlocked the door and took one step in.

Sensing the eyes of an unknown stalker watching, she moved quickly to locate the first camera. She ran her fingers under the large screen television searching for the small device that Christina had seen placed there. She felt nothing. Getting down on all fours she peered under the set, then the back, and sides. Nothing! She checked the nearby plant for a microphone, rustling through the leaves, digging in the dirt. Again, nothing! She ran into the bedroom and searched the aloe plant. Again, nothing! Could it be Christina was wrong? She began to feel foolish. Rizzo would surely think she was crazy. Maybe he was right.

Something in the back of her mind just struck Kimbra. She rushed back to the living room and stopped cold, now realizing that leaving the front door open was a mistake. A strange man stood in the doorway.

"Sorry, I didn't mean to startle you," a lanky man with a scraggly beard apologized.

"What are you doing here?" she asked him.

He stood motionless, gawking at her. One eye looked off in another direction while the other was fixed directly on her. She was about to repeat herself when he spoke.

"I saw you outside and I came to see if this is yours. I found it in the laundry room."

He held out a single earring. Kimbra examined it from a safe distance.

"I never got your name?" she asked.

"It's Shane, and you're Kimbra, right?"

"No, that's not mine," she said ignoring his question. How the hell did he know her name anyway?

He just stood there holding out the earring, staring at Kimbra. It was an odd behavior. She felt threatened, took a step back and was about to ask him to leave when Rizzo suddenly appeared in the doorway.

"Sorry I'm late," he apologized as he eyed the stranger.

"This is Shane," Kimbra introduced the man to Rizzo.

"I was just leaving," he explained to Rizzo before disappearing down the hallway.

"Who was that?" Rizzo asked.

He lives in an apartment downstairs.

"Friend of yours?"

"No. I see him around and always try to avoid him, he creeps me out."

"What do you mean?"

"I don't know, it's just something about him. He looks like he's strung out on drugs."

"Should I check him out?"

Kimbra wondered why she didn't think of it earlier, he could have grabbed some of her clothing in the laundry room. Could have been by mistake, or maybe not.

"I don't even know his last name," she admitted.

"I can find out."

Rizzo entered the apartment and looked around.

"I couldn't find them," Kimbra said.

He looked at her quizzically.

"The bugs. I couldn't find any of them."

"This was all based on what a psychic said she saw. What did you expect?" he said in an indifferent tone.

She fully expected to find the bugs but now doubted herself. She had no answer.

"Well, now that I'm here, let's have a look."

Rizzo examined the doorway. "No visible sign of forced entry. Could someone have gotten in elsewhere?"

"There's the balcony door," Kimbra pointed out.

Rizzo jiggled the sliding glass door.

"And this was locked? You didn't touch it?"

"No."

Rizzo walked out onto the second floor balcony. The morning air was cool and thick.

"Someone could have easily climbed up here, but there's no sign of entry. You said your friend saw a camera device hidden on the television?"

"Yes."

He returned to the apartment and checked the television, then made a full sweep of the apartment, checking all the locations Christina had mentioned. He found nothing.

"Do you mind?" he asked pointing to a seat at the kitchen table.

Kimbra nodded. "Can I get you something to drink? Coffee or tea?"

Rizzo politely declined and asked Kimbra to take a seat as well. He ran a hand over his shaved head, a fine stubble had grown everywhere except the crown of his head which shined like a cue ball.

"Miss Evans, I get it. This whole thing has got you frightened, and with Mick out on bail it can't be easy. But there is no evidence anyone has broken into your apartment."

Kimbra had nothing to say. He could be right.

"I don't mean to make light of Marie's death, but once the trial is over and Mr. Donnelly is put behind bars, you can put this behind you."

Kimbra nodded, not sure if he was right about that.

"In the meantime, you might want to install a few security cameras," Rizzo suggested. "One with a motion sensor would be best."

Kimbra nodded, wondering who could help with that, maybe Tammy or Daniel. Rizzo was quiet, possibly out of suggestions.

"Well, if there's nothing else, I'd better get going."

"No, thank you."

"Call me if Mr. Donnelly tries to contact you, or if you notice anything suspicious."

Rizzo got up and left, leaving Kimbra alone with her suspicions. There was some measure of comfort knowing he made a sweep of the apartment. But what now? She decided to call Christina.

"Kimbra, what happened? Did they find the cameras?"

"No. I don't know what to feel."

"Let me think. We were certain I saw your apartment?"

"Yes," Kimbra agreed.

"I'm sorry, but I often don't know where or when my visions take place. They usually occur in the past, but since I began the Next Level program, they have changed. My premonition of the plane crash shook me to the core. I can't be certain of anything anymore."

There was silence over the phone. Kimbra could not imagine the horror of experiencing the crash.

"My vision of your apartment was sharp," Christina finally broke the silence. "It could be a future event, but I don't think so. I have a feeling the cameras were removed some time before you got there. I don't know how I know this, it's just a feeling."

The thought of someone getting in Kimbra's apartment so easily, scared the crap out of her.

"If that's the case, this stalker is way ahead of us. What should I do?" she asked.

"I don't know dear. Do you have a gun?"

Kimbra was cuddled up on the sofa with a glass of wine. The sun was setting and her fears were heightening with the approaching darkness. What if he came back in the middle of the night? Maybe she should get a gun as Christina had suggested. She thought about calling Gina, but decided against it. What she needed was a fresh perspective. Someone not caught up in her crazy world. She picked up her phone and dialed a contact.

"Kimbra, how are you doing?" Daniel asked.

"Terrible!"

"Why, what's going on?"

"It's a long story. Can we get together sometime? Sometime soon?"

"Sure, but can you tell me what's going on?"

"I'm not really sure, but it's driving me crazy. I'd rather not talk about it over the phone."

Daniel arrived promptly at 6 PM and Kimbra gave him a desperate hug.

"Thank you for coming," she said.

"No problem. So what's going on? You didn't say much on the phone."

"I'll tell you all about it, but first can I get you something to drink?"

"Sure. Whatever you're drinking is fine," he said nodding at the bottle of wine on the counter.

Kimbra poured Daniel a glass and they sat at the kitchen table. Smokey made an appearance for the event. Kimbra wondered if he had seen a stalker in her apartment. If only he could talk.

"A lot happened yesterday," Kimbra began to explain. "You remember I told you I had a feeling I was being watched?"

"Yes."

"Well, there's this woman at work who had a vision of Marie's murder. She's a psychic who solved a string of murders in the Oregon area."

"Wait, hold on. You said she had a vision of Marie's murder?" Daniel asked.

"Yes."

Daniel was silent, no doubt processing what he just heard. Kimbra continued.

"Anyway, I went to her house yesterday and she had another vision. She described my apartment in detail. She saw someone putting cameras and listening devices in here."

"Did she describe him? Do you know who it was?"

"No. She didn't see him, or whoever. The vision was from the stalker's perspective. I was so creeped out I spent the night at Christina's, that's her name. I called the police and met Detective Rizzo here this morning."

"Did he find any bugs?"

"No."

"Okay, so she was mistaken," Daniel suggested.

"That's a possibility. But I'm not so sure."

"Mind if I take a look around?" Daniel asked. "As a private investigator, I have some experience with surveillance equipment."

"Not at all. Take a look around."

Kimbra explained where the cameras and mics were supposed to be, Daniel checked the place from top to bottom.

"Well, there's nothing here now."

"I know, but I have a strong feeling there was."

Daniel sat down and took a sip of his drink.

"Well, either she was mistaken, or they were removed. Did anyone else know about them?"

Kimbra had to think a minute. "Just Detective Rizzo and Christina."

"You never mentioned your suspicion of bugs here did you?"

"What do you mean?"

"I mean, if you talked about them here, your stalker would know that you knew."

"No. I just found out last night at Christina's."

"What about your ex, Carter?"

"I never mentioned it to him. We haven't talked since the trial."

"Have you changed your locks?"

"Yes. That's what detective Rizzo suggested."

The two sat in silence working on the mystery until Daniel finished his drink and set the glass down.

"Let's go out and get something to eat," he suggested out of the blue. "It'll do you good to get out of here."

"I don't know, this is really freaking me out."

"A change of scenery would do you good, and with a fresh perspective, maybe we can figure something out."

"You're probably right. Okay," Kimbra agreed reluctantly.


It was a short drive downtown. Saturday's were typically busy, but they managed to find a pub with outdoor seating and a short wait. The beer selection was wide and the menu short.

"This was a great idea," Kimbra said after a sip of cold beer served in a frosty mug.

"We got lucky," Daniel agreed. "I've never been here before, but it's nice."

Kimbra tried to clear her mind of the anxiety from the last two days, but she could not. Thoughts raced around her head like steel balls in a pinball machine.

"What would you do, I mean if you were in my shoes?" she asked.

"That's a good question," Daniel took a long drag from his beer, swirled it and looked around. "It's only been, what a month since Marie's death?"

"Just about."

Daniel cleared his throat. "Sure, and you're waiting for the trial. That must be terribly stressful."

"It is."

"I think after the trial, you'll have some closure."

"I don't know. Maybe," Kimbra said. "But right now, I don't feel safe."

Their waitress appeared out of nowhere, "Chicken pesto pizza?"

Daniel nodded as she set a hot pizza on the table between them.

They ordered another round of drinks and dug in. The pizza was delicious.

"So what would you do?" Kimbra asked again between bites of pizza.

Daniel swallowed a mouthful and considered a response.

"I would give it time. Maybe take a little vacation to get away for a while."

"A vacation?" Kimbra bounced the idea around in her head. "Where would you go?"

"Someplace exotic and far away. Maybe Thailand."

"Thailand?"

"Yes."

"That sounds nice," Kimbra said with a wistful smile.

The alcohol and food left Kimbra with a warm buzz, but the anxiety crept back on the drive home. Christina had solved murders and accurately predicted a plane crash. The more she thought about it, the more Kimbra suspected Christina was right about the cameras in her apartment. By the time they reached her apartment she was hyperventilating.

"Kimbra, what's wrong?"

"I don't know. I can't breathe."

"Slow down. Take a deep breath."

Daniel's voice was soothing. He kept talking to distract her, which helped. After a few minutes she was breathing normally again.

"Have you had difficulty breathing before?" he asked.

"No, not really. I'm fine now."

"Do you want me to walk you in? Make sure everything is fine?"

Kimbra nodded, and the two slowly approached the two-story, stucco structure. The night sky was dark as charcoal, outdoor lighting cast ominous shadows as they entered the building and climbed the stairwell. At the top, Kimbra fumbled through her purse and dug out her keys. She unlocked the door and stepped back. Daniel took the cue, disappearing into the apartment while Kimbra remained a safe distance away in the hallway. Minutes seemed like hours as Kimbra waited with jaws clenched. Finally, he returned.

"Everything's fine. I don't believe anyone has been in here."

Kimbra stepped in and looked around.

"I know it's silly, but do you mind staying a while?"

"Not at all, and it's not silly."

They sat together on the sofa, sharing a bottle of wine, listening to soft music. They talked about anything but the stalker. Kimbra could feel Daniel's warm body touching hers. She had not been this close to anyone, since Carter. So close she could smell him. Not a cologne, but a sweet, salty fragrance, the one-of-a-kind scent of a pheromone. Daniel put his arm on the back of the sofa and caressed her hair. Their eyes met. Kimbra felt the blood rush to her face as he moved closer, so close she could smell his warm breath, the ambrosian scent of wine. Their lips met, at first lightly, then passionately, as he pulled her in tight. Kimbra felt a longing in her loins then a sudden fear of rejection. She pulled away, he stared into her eyes trying to read her emotions. She broke eye contact first, took a sip of wine and the moment was over.

They selected a movie to watch and while she could not keep the kiss off her mind, neither of them discussed it. She thought she should explain, but the words never came and with time the tension eased. Between the alcohol and comfortable sofa, they soon drifted off to sleep. When Kimbra awoke, she immediately checked the time and nudged Daniel.

"Daniel. I'm sorry, it's so late. I didn't mean to keep you."

"No problem, I'm enjoying myself. Do you feel better?"

"I do..."

"But you're still worried."

She nodded, "I hate to ask... but would you mind staying tonight? You could sleep on the sofa. I mean you don't have to and I will totally understand if you can't, or don't want to."

"Of course. I don't mind at all. Besides, tomorrow's Sunday and I don't have anything planned."

# CHAPTER 20

EARLY MORNING SUNLIGHT FILTERED INTO THE
BEDROOM. Kimbra awoke refreshed but a bit disoriented. The sweet
aroma of brewed coffee caught her attention and she recalled the
night before. She got up quickly, put on her bathrobe, and stepped
into her slippers. Daniel was sitting at the kitchen table with a mug of
coffee. He looked up and set down his phone.

"I hope you don't mind, I made some coffee."

"No, not at all."

Kimbra worked her way towards the kitchen, a mild headache
lingered from the wine they drank the night before.

"Take a seat. I'll get the coffee," Daniel offered. "Black, right?"

"Yes. Thank you."

"How are you feeling?"

With Daniel there, Kimbra slept like a baby. The wine helped as
well, the hangover being a small price to pay for a good night's sleep.

"Pretty good. Probably drank a little too much though," she
admitted.

"Yeah, me too."

"Thank you for spending the night. I hope the couch wasn't too
uncomfortable."

"You're welcome and it was fine."

The two sat quietly sipping their coffee, Kimbra could not get the
kiss from the night before off her mind. They both drank a lot and she
wondered what was going through his mind at the moment.

"Any plans for today?" he asked, breaking the silence.

"Not really," Kimbra said shaking her head.

"Just a suggestion and I know it may sound a little crazy right now, but how does a nice ride in the mountains and visiting a few wineries sound? Might do us both some good."

Kimbra had to smile at that one. "You mean a little hair of the dog?"

"Absolutely," Daniel agreed.

It was an old expression, short for *hair of the dog that bit you*, referring to the notion of drinking a little alcohol to reduce a hangover. Kimbra had tested the theory before, and it was true.

"Maybe. How about a little breakfast first though?"

Daniel offered, and Kimbra let him cook a breakfast of fried eggs, bacon and toast, Texas style.


Before their day trip they made a quick stop at Daniel's to pick up a few things. He lived in a second floor apartment with retail space below. The building was older and didn't look like much from the outside, but Daniel's apartment was newly remodeled and spacious.

"This is beautiful," Kimbra commented.

"Yeah, I like it here. Lots of room and with the bookstore below, it's pretty quiet."

Daniel gave her a quick tour ending at the office.

"I converted this space to my office. It has a separate entrance to the hallway and I use the extra room as a waiting room."

Furnished with a dark walnut desk, several leather chairs, and a wall of book cases, the room was painted a cool sage green accented by a navy blue area rug.

"Take your time looking around, I'll be just a minute."

Kimbra surveyed the office as he disappeared. She ran her fingers along the many books on the bookshelf. It's been said you can tell a lot about a person by what they read. The books were neatly arranged by topic. She passed over the investigator books and legal stuff stopping at the non-fiction section. Daniel had a fascination with the Civil War, World War II, and the Roman Empire. In the fiction section, she recognized a few classic authors like: Edgar Allan Poe, Ray Bradbury, and Stephen King.

"I got everything. You ready to go?" Daniel popped his head in, startling her.

"Sure, I was just admiring your collection of books."

Daniel smiled, "Yeah, I guess I have a thing for books."


They were on the road by 11:30 AM. Kimbra sat in the passenger seat watching the sun peek through tall pines, the rise in elevation made her ears pop. They didn't speak much, and she was grateful for the silence, it gave her time to clear her head. It was Daniel's idea, and she was happy to let him decide which wineries they would visit. They left route 17 and headed east through the Santa Cruz Mountains.

Before she knew it, they turned onto a winding road. A group of mailboxes and an unobtrusive sign marked the way. Nestled in the trees was an unremarkable, plain looking structure with a metal roof. There were a few cars in the parking lot, along with metal wine barrels. The interior consisted of a bar with stools and an open area in back looking out into a small wooded area, beyond that were the vineyards. Pub style tables were made of slabs of finished wood supported by two wooden wine barrels. Strings of bare light bulbs hung from the rafters, highlighting the eclectic decor.

"Have you been here before?" Kimbra asked.

"Once or twice. This is my favorite spot."

"It's quaint. Nice and quiet, too."

"I try to stay away from the more commercial ones," Daniel said. "You never know when a bus tour of drunks will be stopping by."

They selected their wines and shared a flight. Daniel was driving, and so left most of the tasting to Kimbra. They sampled a Zinfandel, Sauvignon Blanc, and a Pinot Grigio. Kimbra preferred white wines but Daniel introduced her to a nice Pinot Noir, which was wonderful. The owner stopped by and showcased his knowledge and love of wine. After that they viewed the facilities where the wine was made. There were stacks of wooden barrels and stainless steel tanks at various stages of the fermentation process. Metal barrels were used for blends, while the wooden barrels imparted a distinct flavor to the wine. It was an enjoyable lesson for Kimbra, and after purchasing several bottles, they said goodbye and left.

The next stop was a larger winery overlooking the mountains and nearby vineyards. The main attraction was a large farmhouse beautifully restored and embellished. It was crowded, but they were lucky enough to find an empty table out back on the patio. The sun had warmed the air to a pleasant seventy-two degrees, and the view was spectacular. They each ordered a glass of wine and shared a plate of cheeses, fruit, meats, nuts, and chocolates.

"How's your hangover doing?" Daniel asked.

"It's much better, mostly gone. I'm glad we got something to eat, though. The wine was really starting to hit me."

Daniel grabbed a sampling of cheese and fruit and added it to his small plate.

"So what's next?" Kimbra asked.

"I thought we'd hit one more winery before heading down to Santa Cruz. How does that sound?"

"Fantastic!"

Sitting on the northern shore of Monterey Bay, Santa Cruz is a popular tourist destination. They parked the car and walked the crowded beach. Letting her worries evaporate, Kimbra kicked off her sandals, dipped her feet in the ocean, and splashed water on her face and arms. Daniel followed suit, getting his shorts wet. They alternated between laying in the sun and cooling off in the ocean. After an hour of that, they walked the Boardwalk amusement park, rode the Giant Dipper, visited the arcade, and played a round of mini-golf. Sandwiched between all that activity they got an ice cream. The sun was dropping low by the time they returned to the car.

"I'm hungry. How about you?" Daniel asked.

"I really worked up an appetite, I'm ravenous."

They stopped by Abbott Square to grab a bite to eat and walked around the area. There was a cozy bookstore where Kimbra bought a few new reads. Daniel checked his watch as they left the store.

"How about one more stop on the way home?" he asked.

"What did you have in mind?"

"A short hike at Cowell Redwoods. You like hiking don't you?"

Henry Cowell Redwoods State Park was a 40-acre sanctuary of towering old-growth redwoods. The tallest tree was 277 feet and estimated at 1,500 years old.

"Of course. I haven't been there in a while. Sounds like a great idea."

The park was a little out of the way but well worth the stop. They picked a short trail, taking their time to soak it all in. It was a great ending to an amazing day. With all the sun, wine, and walking, Kimbra was exhausted. On the ride home the setting sun flickered through openings in the trees in hypnotic fashion. Her eyes grew heavy and she soon nodded off.

A loud sound startled Kimbra from her sleep. She fumbled through her purse for her phone and struggled to answer it, wishing she had noticed the number first.

"Hello, Kimbra! It's Mick."

Kimbra's body froze. Just like that, the beautiful day was shattered in an instant. She was suddenly struck with the fact that she could never escape the past. Her life's misfortunes returned, like a bad penny. She could run, but she would never escape the misery that life continued to throw her way. Daniel looked her way, sensing something was wrong.

"Yes... Why are you calling me?" she blurted out.

"I'm sorry to bother you. I don't know if you are aware, but my trial is coming up soon."

Kimbra was silent and he continued.

"Well, I want you to know... you must know, I did not kill Marie!"

Kimbra had nothing to say, fear had locked her lips tight. He stole her phone and used it to lure Marie to her death. How could he lie like this?

"I wanted to ask if you have any idea who would have it in for me. I mean I've made a few enemies, but who would do this to me?"

Kimbra looked to Daniel for some guidance.

He mouthed the question, "Who is it?"

"Mick," she whispered.

"Hang up," Daniel spoke firmly.

"Are you there? Did you hear me?" Mick asked.

Kimbra turned her gaze out the window and mustered the courage to speak, "I'm sorry. I can't talk to you."

She hung up the phone, wiped her sweaty palms on her shorts and tried to calm down.

Little was spoken the rest of the way home. Kimbra entered her apartment with Daniel at her heels, opened a can of cat food and fed Smokey. Finally, she burst into tears. Daniel held her tightly as she sobbed.

"I'm sorry. It just hit me all at once. It's hopeless, my entire life has been a mess!"

Daniel guided her to the living area and sat her down on the sofa. After a few moments she began to settle down.

"I can't stay here. Someone has been in my apartment. It's probably Mick, or someone he knows."

"Would it help if I spent another night on the sofa?" Daniel asked.

Kimbra looked up at Daniel with tears streaming down and nodded.

"And how about I stop by tomorrow after work and install a few security cameras for you? Anyone comes near your place and you'll get an alert."

"Thanks, that would be great."

Kimbra swallowed a lump in her throat and spoke, "Do you have a gun?"

"Yes. Why?"

"Can you teach me to shoot?"

# CHAPTER 21

HEADLIGHTS CUT THROUGH THE DARKNESS, as my car careens towards its destination. I am preoccupied with my mission. There is a possibility that the psychic will see me coming. Not in the truest sense of the word, but in a vision, or premonition. She is skilled enough in that regard to have solved several high-profile murders. I studied her, and she could prove to be a worthy adversary, one to be taken seriously. I racked my brain for days searching for a way to gain the upper hand and devised a plan, but I cannot account for the fact that she might sense my presence. Like so many best laid plans, shit happens. I may have to be resourceful and adjust on the fly.

I check the rearview mirror, as far as I can tell no one is following. I turn onto a long, winding dirt driveway and pull over a short distance from the main road. The dim glow from a sliver of moon lights the way as I extract my gear from a gym bag in the trunk and hike back towards the main road, stopping at a utility pole. It looks to be of average height, making it about forty feet tall. I slip my boots into the pole climbers and buckle them tightly, then strap the buck squeeze around my waist. It's been a while since I did any pole climbing, hopefully the training I got in this week will be enough.

I wrap the buck squeeze around the pole and dig the one-and-a-half inch gaff from my right boot snugly into the wooden pole. I proceed to hoist myself up with the squeeze, enough to plant my left gaff into the pole. Timing is everything as I climb the pole, one foot after the other. It's awkward at first but gets better as I continue. With a good deal of effort I finally reach the top. I'm tired and my legs are rubbery, not quite the same as when I was younger. I should have bought better boots, but I had already spent over $1,600 on the pole climbers and squeeze. Anyway, it worked.

I take a moment to enjoy the tree-top view which is quite beautiful in the moonlight. I search for the house but it's too far away and hidden deep within the forest. I pull out my bolt cutters, reach up and cut the telephone line. With no cell coverage here, the land line will be Christina's only option to call for help. That is, if she hasn't already alerted someone.

Climbing down is much easier. Once on solid ground, I allow myself a moment to steady my legs, then I pack up my gear and stow it in the trunk. Back in the car, I am consumed with thoughts of this being a trap. I hesitate for a moment, then slip the car in gear and advance towards the house. Along the way I map an escape route in my head. It would be difficult to turn the car around here, and fleeing on foot would no doubt wind up badly. I reach the area I pulled into last time and turn the car around, leaving it positioned for a fast exit. Back in the trunk I pull out a sheathed knife and attach it to my thigh. I slip on a protective Kevlar vest and strap on the backpack. I pull the 9mm pistol from its holster and chamber a round. Hoping to have the element of surprise, I proceed on foot up the driveway.

Very little moonlight breaks through the tall trees, making it difficult negotiating up the winding driveway. An owl hoots in the distance as I round a turn and see the house. It's time to cut through the woods. Once in position, I holster the gun and remove the backpack, unzipping it carefully. I place the night vision goggles over my head, slide them into position, and study the house. There are no signs of activity inside and no security cameras outside, that's good. My hope is to catch my target sleeping in bed. I grab the cable cutter and approach the house.

I cut the cable to the dish antenna, killing any access to the internet. After stowing the tool in my utility belt, I creep onto the side deck and carefully examine the sliding door. Doesn't appear to be any security sensors, so I jimmy a tool into the door lock. It works most of the time, unless they installed a bar or piece of lumber to block the track. Most people do not bother with that, which is the case here. I slide the door open, take two steps forward, and just like that, I'm in.

I remain motionless, listening intently. I saw no sign of a dog when I cased the place earlier. A cat or two, but no dog. The house is silent. I drop night vision goggles in place to get a better look. A light on the stove provides ample light and my eyes adjust quickly. The main room is clear as I pull out my pistol and move towards the bedrooms cautiously. On my third step the floor creaks. I freeze, hold my breath and listen intently, waiting... Moments later, when I'm sure my presence has not been detected, I inch forward.

Some newer devices are able to see through walls, my stuff will not. I poke a mirror into the first room which appears to be a guest room and is empty. The next room is much larger and well appointed, clearly the master bedroom. I crouch down and approach from a low angle, slowly and quietly. Trigger finger poised to fire several shots, I point the gun at my target, but the bed is empty! Something behind the bed makes a rustling sound. *Boom*! A shot rings out, splintering the door jamb inches from my head. I instinctively return fire repeatedly while scrambling for cover. I stop firing and duck back out. Now I hear the moans of an injured person. I move towards the sound, pointing my gun in that direction until I spot her propped up against the wall, a pistol lies on the floor nearby. I kick the gun out of reach and study her.

The mattress provided her little protection from my bullets. She is bleeding from a gunshot wound to her right shoulder and one in her chest. Her complexion is pale, her breathing labored. Wisps of red hair partially cover her face, but her dark brown eyes lock on me.

"What have you told Kimbra about me?" I ask.

She is silent, but her eyes are fluttering. I begin to feel dizzy...

I find myself suddenly back in the driveway, rocking on my feet! I bend over to catch my balance, clear my head, I feel nauseous. What the hell just happened? Did I somehow imagine all that in the house? I examine my gun closely. It's cool, there is no smell of gun powder. It has *not* been fired! How is this possible? I must be losing my mind. Suddenly, headlights break the darkness, the sound of a roaring engine as a car speeds towards me. Still groggy, I duck into the woods and raise my pistol. The headlights are blinding as I fire in the direction of the light. I continue firing until the car passes, wildly turning around the bend. Then a loud crash! I run to catch up, stumbling along the way. Around the bend I stop cold. The car crashed into a tree, the engine is revving loudly. I carefully approach the shattered front windshield. Christina's head is resting on the blood splattered air bag, her neck and side of her face ripped open from gunshots. Her empty eyes glare at me, as if frozen with her last breath.

# CHAPTER 22

KIMBRA'S SENSES WERE DISTORTED. Her hearing was muted, her peripheral vision restricted, it was all a bit disorienting. The ear protection and goggles made her feel isolated, disconnected from the world, like walking on the moon in a space suit. She could barely hear Daniel bark out instructions as he opened the door to the firing range. Kimbra nearly jumped out of her skin as a loud boom rattled around in her chest. My gosh that's loud, she thought, even with the ear muffs on.

"We've got lane four," Daniel's voice filtered through as if she was in a tunnel, or underwater.

He set a long rifle bag on a table. From a smaller bag he pulled out a pistol and a stack of paper targets.

"You want to shoot the handgun or rifle first?" he asked.

Kimbra shrugged her shoulders, "I don't know. Whatever you think."

Daniel loaded cartridges into a magazine and inserted it into a 9mm Ruger semi-automatic pistol. He stapled the target to the holder and pressed the button, sending it down the range.

"Okay, we'll start with this."

Daniel earlier instructed Kimbra on the basics of gun safety. Rules like always pointing the muzzle in a safe direction and leaving your finger off the trigger until ready to fire. Now, he demonstrated the proper two-handed grip and pointed the gun at the target. Kimbra flinched as he fired off a few rounds.

"Okay, you give it a try," he said setting the pistol down. "Hold it tight, it's got a good kick to it."

Kimbra picked up the gun which felt heavy in her hand. He reached behind her and corrected her grip.

"Take your time," he said as he backed away.

The barrel drifted wildly as she tried to line up the sights on the target. She held her breath and pulled the trigger gently just like she was told. Nothing happened. She squeezed the trigger harder as the barrel continued to move about uncontrollably, then *bang*! She flinched as the shot rang out, the recoil jerked her hands back. She looked down range to see if she hit the target. She did not.

"Go ahead. Keep firing," Daniel encouraged her.

She kept shooting until the magazine was empty, eventually hitting the target twice. Daniel showed her how to load the magazine and she practiced until the gun was empty.

"How does it feel?" he asked.

"I'm not very good."

"You'll get the hang of it, just takes a little practice. Do you want to try the rifle?" he asked.

Kimbra shrugged her shoulders.

"I know you're interested in a pistol, but try it. It's easier to shoot and might help with your aim."

He introduced her to a .22 caliber rifle which she did much better with. By the time they were finished she was feeling a little more comfortable with the weapons. Daniel packed up the guns and they left the shooting range. Kimbra's ears were ringing as they exited the building.

"So, what do you think?" he asked.

"I was a little apprehensive, but it was actually kind of fun."

Kimbra scrolled through her phone as they headed back to the car.

"Hold on a minute, I have a voice message."

Daniel stashed the gear in his trunk and closed the lid. Kimbra's face went pale.

"What's wrong?" he asked.

"That was Detective Rizzo. He and another detective want to talk to me."

"About what?"

"He wouldn't say. But from his tone, I don't think it's good."

* * *

Kimbra sat cradling a hot mug of coffee. She was expecting the visit, but nevertheless jumped when the buzzer rang. Rizzo and another man stood outside her door.

"Thanks for seeing us," Rizzo said. "This is Detective Slater from the Grass Valley Police Department."

Slater had a stocky build and a square face, a thick mop of drab brown hair covered his head. Kimbra showed the two in and sat them at the kitchen table. She offered them something to drink, which they declined. Rizzo waited for Kimbra to take a seat, then wasted no time delivering the bad news.

"I'm sorry to have to inform you, Christina Sullivan's body was found several days ago."

Kimbra froze with her mug held mid-air. Blood drained from her face as the shock settled in. Another person she knew was dead.

Rizzo cleared his voice.

"We were hoping you could help us. Detective Slater is leading the investigation, I'll let him take it from there."

Slater pulled out a small notepad and began.

"We went through Ms. Sullivan's phone records and your name came up as one of the last people she talked to."

"How did she die?" Kimbra interrupted.

Slater glanced at Rizzo, then back at Kimbra. "Her car crashed into a tree. She was shot several times."

Kimbra's body shook, a shaky hand set her coffee down roughly.

"I have to ask you a few questions."

Kimbra nodded, still in shock.

"Can you elaborate on your relationship with Ms. Sullivan?"

Kimbra looked up, than down at her reflection in the black coffee unable to recognize the face staring back.

"Miss Evans!"

"I'm sorry. Can I get you a coffee?" she absentmindedly asked.

"No, thank you. You already offered us some," Rizzo said.

"Oh, sorry. I guess I did."

"What was your relationship with Ms. Sullivan?" Slater repeated.

"We met at work."

"Can you elaborate on that?"

"She was a client of ours," Kimbra explained.

"A client?"

"Yes."

"What kind of work do you do at... Quantum Thunder isn't it?" Slater referred to the notepad in hand.

"Yes, that's right. We are studying paranormal phenomena."

"I'm not familiar with that. Can you tell me more about it?"

"It's not a mainstream area of research. Most of the work we do is under a government contract and confidential."

"Are you aware of Ms. Sullivan's psychic abilities?"

"Yes."

"I see. And Ms. Sullivan's history of solving crimes, was that a factor in her becoming a part of your research?"

"I'm not involved in the selection process for candidates."

"Do you think her being a psychic was part of her being selected?"

"I know they are seeking people with paranormal abilities."

"Do you know if the candidates are paid for their time?" Slater asked.

"I believe they are."

"Can you describe what kind of things Ms. Sullivan was doing there?"

Kimbra cleared her throat and spoke, "I'm sorry I'm not at liberty to say."

"Why is that?"

"I am bound by a non-disclosure agreement. You'll have to ask Dr. Wu, the CEO and owner."

"Of course. We're planning on talking with him."

Kimbra sipped her coffee as Slater studied her. Rizzo asked the next question.

"You called me from Ms. Sullivan's house one week before the body was found. Did you have any contact with her after that?"

"I called her the next day to tell her we didn't find any bugs in my apartment. That was the last time we spoke."

"You may have been the last person she talked to," Slater now spoke. "Can you think of anyone who would want to harm Ms. Sullivan?"

"No, but she may have made some enemies from the murders she helped solve."

"I'm following up on that. Detective Rizzo told me of your connection to another murder victim. Can you think of any connection between you and the deaths of Christina and Marie Sadowski?"

Kimbra's chest tightened. She set down her mug with a clatter, coffee spilled onto the table.

"Why do you ask that? Am I a suspect?"

"Is there something I should know?"

"No."

"Did you know Ms. Sullivan kept a diary?"

"No."

Slater paused to look around the apartment, letting the anticipation build.

"In the diary she mentions a fear that someone is stalking her. Does that sound familiar?"

"What do you mean?" Kimbra asked.

"Detective Rizzo told me you have the same fear. Do you think there could be a connection?"

"It could be the same person, but I don't know who. Isn't that *your* job?"

"Yes, it is."

The silence was killing Kimbra. She was feeling cornered, ganged up on.

"Do I need a lawyer?" she asked looking to Rizzo for help.

Slater responded, "Miss Evans, we are investigating two seemingly unrelated murders. We will find out who is responsible, and to do that I have to consider all the possibilities. Right now the only possible connection seems to be you. Now, you can call your lawyer and I can call you in for questioning. But if you have nothing to hide, I suggest you cooperate."

Kimbra looked Slater straight in his dark brown eyes. He was just doing his job, but nevertheless she resented the insinuation she was involved. She felt a lifetime of being taken advantage of and lashed out.

"Detective Rizzo said Mick killed Marie. You let him out on bail. Why don't you ask him?"

"We already talked to him. He has an alibi and it checked out, so I think we can rule him out as a suspect in Christina's death. I keep coming back to the fact that you wound up in the middle of two murders. Don't you think that's a little unusual?"

Kimbra was feeling more and more like a suspect. Her life felt like a series of mishaps she had no control over. It was not out of the ordinary for her.

"Strange? I don't know. Coincidences happen all the time, don't they? I just wish you two would do your job and catch whoever is behind this, lock them up and never let them out."

Rizzo stood up, looking at his partner who followed suit.

"We'll find whoever is responsible for Ms. Sullivan's death," Rizzo said. "In the meantime, if you think of anything related to the case, don't hesitate to call."

Rizzo turned and headed towards the door, "Oh, I checked out your neighbor, Shane Flannigan. No criminal record. The guy's unemployed at the moment, used to work as a part-time cook. I can dig into it more if he gives you any problems. Let me know."

Kimbra thanked Rizzo. Slater followed Rizzo out, but not before he said one final thing.

"Miss Evans, if I find out you are hiding anything from us, it won't go well for you."

Kimbra's distaste for the man was certainly well founded. She sat alone with her thoughts, worried sick that they suspected she was involved somehow in the murders. Worried sick that whoever was behind all this, was still out there. Was she the next target?

# CHAPTER 23

KIMBRA STOOD OUTSIDE DR. FANG WU'S OFFICE, at the secretary's desk.

"Is he in?"

"Yes, but..."

Kimbra knocked on Fang's door.

"Yes, what is it?"

She opened the door before his secretary could object.

"I'm sorry to barge in, but I have terrible news!"

"Please, shut the door," Fang requested.

Kimbra shut the door, more loudly then intended, and took a seat. It took a moment to compose herself.

"Have you heard about Christina Sullivan?" she asked.

"I just heard yesterday. I was shocked."

Kimbra was filled with conflicting emotions. Was Christina's death related to the Next Level program? Did she have something to do with it? It seemed like everything in her life turned to shit. Maybe her actions somehow caused Christina's death. She fought hard to hold back tears.

Fang offered her a tissue. "I'm sorry, but you didn't know her personally, did you?"

She couldn't hide it anymore, Fang suspected something was up.

"I met her a week before the murder."

Fang's eyes narrowed, his eyebrows crinkled, and his voiced raised an octave.

"You had contact with a client outside of work? That's against our policy. Why would you do that?"

"I'm sorry, but she touched me and... she saw something. She saw Marie's murder!"

"Yes, you told me, but there's no way to be certain it was Marie. Is there something else I should know?"

Kimbra fidgeted in her seat. "I told Christina about my fear of someone stalking me. Someone has been in my apartment!"

"Wait, how do you know that?" Fang asked.

Kimbra stood up and paced back and forth.

"I just know. Anyway I told Christina and she offered to help. She had a vision of someone in my apartment. They planted cameras and listening devices there."

"Did she see who it was?"

"No. The vision was through the stalker's eyes."

Now it was Fang's turn to stand up. He spoke while gazing out the window. It was bright and sunny, people were moving about in the courtyard.

"Did you call the police?"

"I did."

"And what did they say?"

"A detective came and checked my apartment."

"And then what?"

"He didn't find anything."

Fang turned abruptly around to face Kimbra.

"They found nothing?"

Kimbra slumped back into her seat, dejected. Fang sat on the edge of his desk, one leg dangling.

"Are you certain it was your apartment?"

"I'm certain."

"Then the vision was wrong."

That was certainly a logical conclusion, except Kimbra knew otherwise. Fang got up and sat down in his chair, contemplating the matter.

"Kimbra, I'm sorry this is happening to you, and Christina's death is horrible, but there's nothing I can do about it," he said.

"I want to be part of the Next Level research," Kimbra blurted out.


* * *


The coast was clear. Short of security and the maintenance staff, everyone had left the building. Fang sunk into the comfort of his sofa, twilight was falling upon the city outside his office window. This was the day he planned to test his powers and he was hell-bent on success. Fang had been taking the experimental drug, QR-7, for some time, but chose to remain anonymous and out of the research study. Only he and Stanwix knew this, as well as the fact that his test results had sky rocketed. His brain was sharper, his intuition fine tuned, and while he did not personally participate in any telepathy testing, he sometimes *knew* what people were thinking. But for this experiment, Fang was more concerned with consciousness. That, and how it relates to time.

The clock on the shelf displayed 9:17 PM as Fang closed his eyes. He inhaled slowly, held it, and exhaled. He waited before repeating the process. He envisioned himself home earlier that morning, drinking a hot mug of coffee. The early morning sun was setting the mountains ablaze, the television was on, like it was most mornings. The television was airing the news, and a multitude of advertisements; he shut it off, that is, in his mind. Now he burned the peaceful image into his mind, recalling the input from all his senses. The sweet aroma of coffee, the fresh mountain air gently sweeping into the room along with the sounds of chirping birds. Thoughts of the day crept into his mind but he quickly pushed them aside, a task that would have been nearly impossible without the drug. It wasn't easy, but he kept working on it. Breathe in, breathe out, concentrate on the morning. Capture and relive an earlier moment in time.

Fang's mind was locked on the past when he started feeling light-headed. Actually it was his body, it felt somehow lighter, as if gravity was slowly fading away. It's an odd sensation, letting go of the pull of the earth, letting go of reality as we know it. It was both frightening and freeing, as if his soul was leaving his body behind. Fang's head began to spin and he almost fell off the stool. Wait, the stool? Fang opened his eyes. It was dark, but he was quite certain he was back at his house! It was so real, it seemed real, but it couldn't be. It had to be a vision or hallucination.

He checked his watch: 9:07 PM. He was just at the office, and now he was home, in his living room, ten minutes in the past. It could not be real, but what if it was? If it was, what the hell just happened? He stumbled about and turned on the lights. He was only starting to come to the realization that he had just teleported back to his house instantly! But how was that possible?

How do you explain the impossible? According to Einstein, nothing can travel faster than the speed of light, which means teleporting to another location is not possible. Yet there he was. Could it be he was somehow recreated, or materialized out of thin air? Given the amount of energy required to convert energy to matter, that did not seem likely. The only theoretical way to instantly transport from one location and time to another, would be a wormhole. The probability of that would seem just as unlikely. So what happened?

Part of him expected to wake up back at the office, but that never happened. He stepped onto the balcony and breathed in the fresh air; the scent of pine, the cool of night. Whatever the underlying process was, he had done it! He had tried to alter his consciousness to earlier that morning, and in the process had teleported across time and space. This was huge. Never in his wildest dreams did he think their research into telepathy would lead to this.

Fang was elated at his success, but it was more than elation. The whole experience filled him with a euphoria that no other activity or drug could match. Fang had taken a lot of drugs in his life, none of them came close to this. His body was invigorated with the powers of a young man, he felt twenty years younger. It was amazing! He cooked himself a gourmet dinner, drank a well-aged scotch, and pondered the future. That night he slept the best he had in years. In the morning he woke refreshed, feeling like a new man, then took an Uber to work.

# CHAPTER 24

THE SUN DUCKED BEHIND A CLOUD AS THE COFFIN WAS LOWERED INTO THE PIT. Kimbra stood back a distance from the mourners. As the small crowd dispersed, she stood dumbfounded, still trying to make some sense of it. Most of the people took a wide berth from her, except one. A lanky woman with gray hair approached.

"I'm sorry, did you know Christina?"

"I worked with her recently."

The woman's eyebrows tightened.

"You mean the research into her psychic abilities?"

"Yes," Kimbra confirmed, not knowing what the woman knew of the work at Quantum Thunder, not knowing how to read her. Was she angry about Kimbra's presence at the service, or curious?

The woman stood eyeing Kimbra over, her eyes were red and watery.

"I'm sorry, my name is Barb. I'm Christina's sister."

"I'm Kimbra, it's so nice to meet you."

The woman held out her hand which Kimbra grasped. She held onto Kimbra's hand for an eternity. Was she psychic as well?

"She was such a nice person," Kimbra added awkwardly as she let go of the woman's hand.

"How well did you know her?" the woman asked.

"I visited her house once. She was helping me with a problem I'm having. But she never really told me much about herself."

"What kind of problem? If you don't mind my asking."

Kimbra cleared her throat. "Well, there's a lot going on right now, but I have a stalker."

"I see," the woman said. "Well, Christina was a kind soul. She tried to use her unique abilities to help others."

The rest of the crowd was getting in their cars, someone was waving Barb to join her.

"Well, I must be going. You're welcome to join us back at Christina's," she offered.

The obituary mentioned a private gathering after the service.

"Oh, I have to get back to work. But thank you. I really appreciate the offer."

The woman turned to leave as a random thought passed Kimbra's lips.

"Who will take care of her cats?" she blurted out.

Barb turned to reply, a hint of a wistful smile formed around her mouth.

"Ah, Mulder and Scully. That would be Maggie. She's a cat lover. Thanks for asking."

The mourners were leaving and the gravesite was deserted. Kimbra trudged through the grass in her dress shoes and stared into the pit. A knot formed in her stomach as she realized the gravity of her situation. Christina had eagerly listened to Kimbra's problems, she tried to help, and now she was dead. She was gone and Kimbra never really got to know her. Christina never talked much about her family, but the obituary mentioned a large family with four brothers and three sisters. Christina had married once but never had children. Kimbra wondered if that was by choice or circumstance. Twenty-five years later her husband died of cancer at the age of fifty. She never remarried. It could not have been an easy life for her.

Later that night, Kimbra sat at her computer researching psychics. She worked with people with paranormal abilities on a daily basis but never really knew much about psychics. Apparently there was a fine line between mental illness and genius, and that could offer some insight into how the paranormal brain works.

Researchers at Yale School of Medicine were comparing auditory hallucinations, or hearing voices, experienced by schizophrenic patients with others having similar experiences. Eight percent of the general population report hearing voices on a regular basis, and thirteen percent hear them occasionally, yet only one percent of them are diagnosed with schizophrenia. Researchers were able to elicit an auditory hallucination by slowly diminishing a sound. A sound was heard by some subjects when it was gone. Studies revealed that the same part of the brain was activated whether real or non-existent sounds were perceived. Was the brain imagining a sound, or was it real, possibly coming from another place?

How common are psychics? Twenty-two percent of Americans have consulted a fortune-teller, medium, or psychic at some point in their life and forty-one percent believe they are real. So, are the voices that psychics claim to hear real or perceived? As far as a psychic connection or the underlying mechanisms involved, perhaps their research at Quantum Thunder could offer an answer.

# CHAPTER 25

DR. STANWIX SWABBED THE INJECTION SITE WITH ALCOHOL and prepped the serum. An elastic band wrapped around the upper arm insured her vein was plumped and ready.

"Are you certain you want to do this?" Stanwix asked.

Kimbra nodded, "I'm sure."

"You know how I feel. We are proceeding too quickly with the human trials. I wouldn't agree to this if Fang hadn't insisted."

"I know, but I really need to do this."

Stanwix sighed in disapproval.

"All right. This may sting a bit."

Kimbra glanced at the needle entering her vein, then looked away. She had a slight phobia to needles, but was working on it. Besides, she'd be lying if she said there wasn't a little sadistic pleasure that went along with the pain. There was a mild burning sensation which diminished as the needle was removed.

"That's all there is to it," Stanwix said as he applied pressure with a cotton ball to stop any bleeding. "We'll have you wait thirty minutes, just in case there's a reaction."

Possible side effects could be flu-like symptoms. The desired result would be an increased neural count and subsequent increase in telepathic activity. All Kimbra cared about was finding out who killed Christina and who was stalking her.

"You said I could notice some changes as early as 24 - 48 hours?" Kimbra asked.

"I said it's possible, but it will more likely take a week or more."

Stanwix put an adhesive bandage over the injection site and paused, noticing Kimbra's wrist.

"That's an interesting tattoo. Does it have any special meaning?"

Kimbra studied the squiggly black pattern with three dots and a triangular shaped object above and below. It immediately brought her thoughts back to high school, her sophomore year. Mick was a senior with several tattoos, and when he mentioned getting another, Kimbra was intrigued. While her mother had several tattoos, she did not want Kimbra getting one. That was all the reason Kimbra needed. While she was underage at fifteen, Mick took care of that with a phony ID.

"What do you think?" Mick asked pointing to a small four leaf clover design.

"Are you kidding? I'm not Irish and I'm certainly not lucky!"

"All right, well what do you like?"

Kimbra looked over the pages of tiny designs, there were so many it made her choice confusing. She wanted something small and simple, that narrowed it down a bit. One of them caught her eye and she pointed it out.

"What's this?" she asked the tattoo guy, whose name she has long since forgotten.

"That's an ancient Sanskrit symbol."

"Sanskrit?"

"It's an ancient Hindu religious or Indian language."

"What does it mean?" she asked.

"Well, let's see."

The tattoo artist looked up a translation on the back, "Says it means *breathe*. It's a reminder to do what comes naturally. The first thing we do when we come into this world, the last thing when we leave."

It was perfect, just what she was looking for.

"That's the one!" Kimbra declared.

The wrist is an especially sensitive area and generally not a good choice for one's first tattoo. Kimbra didn't care, she wanted it to hurt.

She wanted it to hurt more than the pain she was feeling at the time. The tattoo would be a constant reminder when life became unbearable, to breathe. It helped her carry on, in spite of whatever crap life would throw her way.

She looked up at Stanwix and replied, "Yes. It's very personal."

That night Kimbra was feeling flushed and running a low-grade fever. Wondering if the drug was working, she searched for an object related to Marie in the hopes eliciting some type of paranormal response, a sensation, maybe a vision. She was not gifted with high level paranormal skills like the protocol called for, but there was a chance it could work for her. She picked up a picture of her and Marie from high school and cradled it while recalling their time together. She felt nothing weird or psychic. How would that feel anyway? Next she put on a sweater of Marie's that was given to her. There was no mysterious message from Marie. Finally, hoping to elicit a response from her stalker, she touched the television, plant, clothing; anywhere Christina had seen the stalker touching her things. Again, she felt nothing. It's only been seven hours she thought out-loud. I have to give it time. She took something for the fever and went to bed.

# CHAPTER 26

KIMBRA WAS GIVEN SEVERAL MORE INJECTIONS OF QR-7. Her scores on the paranormal tests went up slightly, but not significantly. The test for synaptic density was up less than hoped for and most important, she sensed no sign of any paranormal insight. If the drug was going to have any effect on her, it should have done so by now. She was seated at a crowded restaurant, feeling down. The din of dinner conversations echoed in her head.

"What's going on?" Daniel asked. "You don't seem yourself tonight... Kimbra!"

She snapped out of her trance. "I'm sorry. What did you say?"

"You seem preoccupied with something. What's going on?"

"I'm sorry, a lot has been going on the past few weeks. It's work related."

"And you can't tell me," Daniel knew her work was confidential and they rarely discussed it.

Kimbra nodded and took a bite of her salad. Daniel put down his fork and lowered his voice.

"We haven't been seeing each other much lately. Is there something wrong? Something about us that I should know?"

"No. There's nothing wrong. It's like I said, there's a lot going on right now," Kimbra tried to explain.

Daniel's eyes narrowed, he was expecting more. Kimbra took a sip of water and set the glass down. She wished she could tell him more.

"Daniel, I'm trying to make some sense of Marie's death. I'm doing everything I can, but it's frustrating."

Daniel paused, she wasn't sure he believed her.

"The trial is coming up soon," he said. "I think you'll be able to put the worry and frustration behind you when it's over."

"Maybe. Did I tell you Detective Rizzo said Mick has an alibi for the night Christina died?"

"No, you didn't. But Mick could be lying."

"Or maybe someone else killed Christina," Kimbra suggested.

"That makes sense, the murders don't have to be related. It sounds like Christina could have made a few enemies."

"Yeah, but they don't have any suspects, at least as far as I know."

"Well there's nothing you can do, except let the police do their job. I'm sure it will sort itself out."

Kimbra wished she could be so confident that would happen.

"And what about the person stalking me?" she asked.

Daniel took her hand and held it firmly.

"Look, we installed security cameras and no one has shown up since. If anyone does, we'll know."

"What if he does show up? Daniel, I'm scared."

"Chances are he won't. If he does, you call the police first, then me. Did you submit your pistol permit application?"

"I did."

"It can take a while. In the meantime, I can get you a rifle if you think that will make you feel safer."

Kimbra considered and dismissed the idea, not really wanting a rifle in her apartment. It was bad enough she had to get a handgun to protect herself. She wasn't crazy about having a gun around, but guessed it would help her sleep better, and if the stalker showed up, it could just save her life.

Back at her apartment, Kimbra felt uneasy.

"Daniel, I'm sorry I haven't been available much lately. I've been too preoccupied with work and Christina's murder."

He turned his attention from the television to face her.

"I understand."

She gave him a hug and they kissed, but it was not the same as the last time, it was not a passionate kiss. They returned to watching the movie, eventually falling asleep on the sofa.

Kimbra woke first and nudged Daniel. He was sound asleep. She pushed him aside, struggling to get up.

"Daniel, it's late. Wake up."

"Ugg, what time is it?" he asked.

"Three in the morning. I'm going to bed."

"Oh, man I'm whipped. Do you mind if I crash on the couch again?"

"Sure... or you can sleep with me," Kimbra offered.

Daniel's jaw dropped. Kimbra got up, and he followed.

"I'm really tired though. I just want to sleep."

Kimbra really liked Daniel, but wasn't sure she was ready for that level of commitment; she had been burned too many times before. She put on some sweats, a top, and climbed in bed. Daniel stripped down to his shorts and t-shirt and climbed in the other side. It had been some time since Kimbra slept with a warm body at her side, and it felt good, it felt safe. They each lay on their backs, staring at the ceiling. Kimbra stole a peek over at Daniel and caught his gaze. They shared a smile, then she rolled on her side, turned out the light, and said goodnight.

Kimbra opened her eyes to darkness as a hot flash washed over her body. Emotions lingered from a dream she could barely remember. She was sad, alone, and desperate. Her eyes fluttered as a dim light came into view, except it wasn't her room, it was the interior of a car.

*She was seated in the front seat. The hands in front of her gripped the steering wheel tightly, they were pale, rough, and hairy. Not her hands, but those of a man. She looked around the darkened garage. The engine was running and the air was thick, the smell of exhaust made her cough. Tears rolled down her cheeks as she was suddenly filled with despair. Depression so deep it hurt, so deep she wanted to die. Bluish smoke drifted in from open car windows. Her eyelids grew heavy and she wanted to sleep, she longed for the pain to end. Her heart rate was slow and heavy as she slumped over in the seat. Bright lights danced around her oxygen deprived brain. Looking up, the rear view mirror was the last thing she noticed before closing her eyes. The reflection in the mirror looked back at her with hopeless, empty eyes. It was the image of her father, Reece.*

A grip on her shoulder shook her to consciousness.

"Kimbra, are you all right? It looked like you were having a bad dream," Daniel said.

Kimbra began to sob.

"I thought I was dying!" she blurted out. "It was so real."

"It was only a dream. You're safe," Daniel reassured her.

She sat up, attempting to sort out the emotions, clear her head of the despair.

"It started as a dream... but I woke up. I was awake, that's when it happened."

"What happened?"

"I was in my father's garage. I saw everything, experienced everything he did. I was there when he died!"

"But it was only a dream. Kimbra, it wasn't real."

"I don't know, this was different. I could see, smell, taste everything. I *was* there!"

"But that's not possible. How did your father die?"

Kimbra buried her head in her hands.

"It's all right if you don't want to talk about it, but it might help," Daniel suggested.

She choked back the tears and gritted her teeth.

"I was twelve at the time it happened. I never really knew him, I was only three when my parents divorced. My memories of him are mostly from pictures and stories from Gina, but she told me he asphyxiated himself in his garage."

"So your mind put it all together in a dream. They can seem very real."

"No. This really happened. It was a vision seen through my father's eyes. Everything I saw and felt was real."

Kimbra staggered into the bathroom with a splitting headache. Gazing into the mirror, a tidal wave of gloom washed over her, all her life's shortcomings became crystal clear. She was doomed to a painful, lonely existence. Anyone close to her either rejected her or died. She opened the medicine cabinet, grabbed a bottle of pain killer and downed two tablets. She was suddenly overcome with thoughts of ending her life. She stared at the bottles of medications wondering if anything there would work. She studied her allergy meds. Diphenhydramine HCL, that was also used as a sleep aid. What would an overdose of that do? She opened the package and counted 19 tablets remaining. Was that enough?

"Kimbra, are you all right?" a voice echoed in her head.

She closed the cabinet, returned to the bedroom and sat on the bed in a daze. Daniel pulled her in close, his body warm and comforting. She gazed up through watery eyes. His dark brown eyes were intoxicating. He wiped a tear from her cheek and moved closer. She did not look away. They were so close she could hear his breaths, feel his heart beat. The space between them narrowed, ever so slowly. Their lips touched softly, and he kissed her.

A wave of emotions washed over her, feelings long since buried rose up. It seemed like years since she shared an embrace, opened herself up to another human being. The walls she built began to crumble, and it frightened her. She paused briefly, recalling past pains. Daniel pulled away, his eyes straining to read her emotions. Kimbra's fears were mixed with a yearning, a hunger she had denied herself for too long. She kissed Daniel gently and before she knew it their bodies were locked tightly together. Primitive animal instincts took over, and she gave in to her desires.

As they lay in darkness, Kimbra let out a sigh of satisfaction. She would not let down her guard, but she would no longer deny herself comfort from the carnal pleasures in life. She looked over at Daniel. His physical appearance was nothing exceptional. He was thin and wiry, but also kind and thoughtful. There was a mysteriousness about him that she found alluring. She did not regret her actions and it would not be the last time they made love together.

# CHAPTER 27

KIMBRA JUST FINISHED DESCRIBING HER VISION TO HAROLD STANWIX.

"So what do you think?" she asked.

"Well, it could have been a vivid dream or hallucination brought on by the drug. On the other hand, it's also possible that you experienced a vision. Ms. Sullivan described enhanced visions she attributed to the drug. If it was a vision, we need some kind of proof. Were you able to verify that any of the events you witnessed are real and not just created from memory?"

"I called my sister and explained a few details that we were never told. We dug deeper, called our mother, and found out they were true."

"That is interesting," Stanwix said.

"But what does it mean? Will I see more, maybe from other people's perspective?"

Stanwix's forehead wrinkled a bit. "You mean from Marie?"

It was widely known at work that Kimbra's best friend had been murdered. Stanwix must have guessed her motive in volunteering for the Next Level program.

"Yes, or from Christina. Could I elicit a vision like that?"

"You mean a vision from someone beyond the grave?" he asked.

"I guess. Is it possible?"

"That I cannot answer. We're making great strides here, but there's so much we don't know."

"But the drug must be working. I never had a vision before."

"It would seem so, but we haven't seen a correlation with your test results. Your earlier tests showed little improvement in paranormal abilities."

"But I've never experienced anything like this before. Something is changing, I can feel it. What about the others? What are they experiencing? Is anybody else having visions?"

"Some subjects have seen a significant improvement in extra-sensory test scores and neural counts and Chad's results are off the charts. But other than Ms. Sullivan, none have reported any visions."

Kimbra squirmed in her seat. Chad had been on the drug longer than herself and he had exceptional paranormal skills to begin with. Wouldn't he be experiencing visions like her or was he hiding something?

"Let's run some more tests," Stanwix gestured for Kimbra to get up. They headed out of his office, into the adjoining lab. She took a seat in the blood collection area. Lab techs were busy performing their tasks, stacks of cages with mice and monkeys lined one wall. Stanwix prepared her arm to draw a blood sample.

"How is Algernon doing?" Kimbra asked referring to the star mouse.

Stanwix lifted his head and gazed off in another direction, then redirected his gaze to the task at hand.

"Algernon is doing well. Sadly, some of the others are regressing."

"Ouch!" Kimbra winced.

"Sorry, I guess I'm a little distracted," Stanwix admitted.

"Others?" Kimbra asked.

"Some of the other mice."

Kimbra sensed Stanwix was hiding something.

"Doctor, are there any other human test subjects I don't know about?"

Stanwix removed the syringe and placed a cotton ball on the small puncture.

"Hold this down. Keep applying pressure," he instructed.

"You're hiding something, I know it. You can tell me, I won't tell anyone else," she pleaded.

Stanwix put the vial of blood aside and applied an adhesive bandage to Kimbra's arm.

"Fang has been acting rather peculiar lately," he offered.

"Is he taking the drug?"

Stanwix's head jerked up, he looked Kimbra in the eye and paused before speaking.

"Yes."

"Is there a problem with the drug?" Kimbra asked.

"I'm not sure. We're all unique, each individual can react to it differently."

Kimbra was beginning to worry.

"Let's try a quick test to see how you are doing," he suggested.

Stanwix led her back to his office where they both sat. He pulled a deck of Zener cards from a desk drawer and held them up.

"Ready to give this a quick try?"

Kimbra sat up straight and nodded. Stanwix flashed the first card. The deck had five distinct cards, each one having a simple black symbol on a white background. Kimbra concentrated, focusing on the back of the card. She ran through each image in her mind attempting to decide which one it was. None of them stood out. She went with her intuition.

"Squiggly lines."

Stanwix held up the remaining cards and she continued to guess.

"How did I do?"

Stanwix's expression told the story. "You actually did worse than average. Let's try again."

The cards were held up three more times, Kimbra did not improve much. She guessed around one-in-five, which was the average.

"I don't get it. What's wrong?" Kimbra asked.

"You are not a psychic my dear. It's important to remember, every individual will react to the drug differently. Let's wait for the other test results."

* * *

Kimbra sat across from Chad, a tall partition blocked their view of each other. She tried in vain to visually break down the partition and see Chad's facial expressions. What he was thinking?

"Are we ready?" Stanwix asked from his position in the rear of the room.

"Ready," Chad announced.

Kimbra's finger probed the back of the head gear, which was pulling at her hair. She clenched her teeth and announced she was ready.

"Fine, then let's get started," Stanwix said. "Trent, if you would like to begin."

Trent was administering the tests while Stanwix collected the data. The first experiment was set up to measure Kimbra's abilities to act as a receiver with Chad being the sender.

"I'm displaying the first image now," Trent announced.

Kimbra closed her eyes and tried to relax, clearing her mind of clutter. Random thoughts popped into her mind: the first time she met Marie in sixth grade; Christina's two cats, Mulder and Scully; Daniel, and their plans for Wednesday night. Would she have anything to tell him? She pushed the thoughts aside and concentrated, focusing on the image being displayed on Chad's monitor. She imagined his soft face, sparse beard and blue eyes, right through the partition. Then something began to happen, she sensed a mild buzz in her head. It was there in a flash, and then disappeared quickly. A sensation along with an image.

"I just got something, more like a feeling," Kimbra announced. "It was warm, no hot. I think it's a fire... a house on fire?"

"Good. Here's the next one," Trent reported.

She had no idea if she was right, and was dying to know, but they couldn't tell her now. Kimbra tried to relax, closed her eyes again and cleared her mind. It happened again, except this time the feeling lingered. A cloud of doom settled over her, wrapping her in its grip. She was smothering in emotions: despair, hunger, and a longing for it to be over, a longing for death. Then an image, a picture devoid of all color, all hope. Half-naked men, emaciated bodies with bones protruding through pale, paper thin skin. The image was gone in an instant, but the emotions remained. It was like a bad dream, but *much* more vivid.

"Kimbra. Do you see anything?" a voice from outside the cloud echoed.

Kimbra's eyes flashed open.

"It was a picture of holocaust survivors."

"Good. This is the last one," Trent announced.

Still stinging from the previous image, Kimbra closed her eyes once more. She tried to purge all thoughts and emotions from her brain, but the horror persisted: man's depravity towards man, the cruelty, the utter lack of humanity. She squeezed her eyes tight and held her breath in an attempt to force it out. Then it came. This one, more terrifying than the previous image, more vivid. A video of a man humping, raping a woman from behind. Kimbra felt violated, terrified, fearing for her life. Suddenly a mouth appeared in her thoughts, then the head, a familiar face. Chad's lips curled into an evil smile... he seemed to be taking great pleasure in something. Was it the rape, or Kimbra's disgust, her fear? The eyes glared, the lips raised upwards, exposing a row of teeth and a chilling laugh. She opened her eyes, ripped off the head gear and bolted straight up.

"I'm sorry! I can't continue."

Kimbra sat on the soft sofa staring vacantly out the window. It was strange how the courtyard outside was always sunny and bright, the office was warm and cozy, yet she felt a coldness down to her soul. Her heart felt a sadness so deep it was difficult to explain. She had just described her test experience to Dr. Malcom Brandenburg. He fit the stereotypical image of a psychologist, with dark rimmed glasses and a full beard. He was seated behind a simple, but tasteful, mahogany desk. His hands clasped, fingers locked tightly around themselves in contemplation. A yellow pad sat on his lap, ready to record highlights of the session.

"I can't get the images off my mind. What does it mean?" Kimbra asked.

Brandenburg's voice broke the common perception, it was higher pitched, definitely not the deep and soothing baritone typically depicted in movies.

"I can't really answer that," he said. "Sounds like you received the images correctly, but your reaction to them was extreme. Which part of your brain receives them and how your mind interprets them, we don't fully understand. I'm more concerned with your condition right now though. Can you tell me what you're feeling?"

"I'm depressed. I've had these feelings before, but this is worse."

"Have you ever had suicidal thoughts?"

Kimbra hesitated, thinking of her father, "I have."

"How often have you had them?"

"I don't know, sometimes several times a week, sometimes less."

Brandenburg jotted down notes as he spoke.

"Do you know when they began?"

"I've always felt the world is somehow out to get me. I guess I first thought about it in middle school, but nothing serious, I mean I never acted on the thoughts."

"We all have startling thoughts at times, and that's perfectly normal. It's when they become an obsession that we need to worry. But it sounds like it's worse now. Have you ever devised a plan to commit suicide?"

Kimbra shifted her position and looked out the window, if she could float off into space and escape the session, she would. Fly off into the future and put this all behind her. Far away from the worry, the sorrow, the death.

"I considered taking pills," she admitted almost as an afterthought, as if someone else were speaking the words.

"Can you think of anything that precipitated those thoughts?"

"Marie's murder hit me hard, and then there was Christina's death. But I think it got much worse after my first vision."

"When was that?"

Kimbra explained the vision of her father's suicide. It felt good to confide in a professional.

"But you've never acted on your suicidal thoughts?"

Kimbra turned her attention to Brandenburg.

"No. But sometimes the pain is so bad I can't take it. I fear there is no way out, that everyone would be better off without me. I need help."

Brandenburg set down his notepad and looked Kimbra in the eye.

"The very fact that you are seeking help is encouraging."

Kimbra caught Brandenburg's stare and turned back to the window. It was uncomfortable reliving her emotions. She wanted to leave the office, head straight home, pour herself a stiff drink and cuddle up with Smokey. Brandenburg was stroking his salt and pepper beard.

"Here's what I'm going to recommend," he finally broke the silence. "I'm going to prescribe several medications for you. One is an anti-depressant, the other should help you sleep. I would like to meet with you several times a week to start. How does that sound?"

Kimbra nodded.

"I'm also recommending you halt any future injections of QR-7."

# CHAPTER 28

KIMBRA SAT IN THE COURTROOM REMEMBERING HER BEST FRIEND and contemplating the past. With all the shit she was dealing with, it's no wonder she had feelings of depression. It was bad, but she was making progress. The anti-depressant drugs and sessions with Dr. Brandenburg were helping. Thoughts of suicide rarely crossed her mind anymore, her feelings of being stalked had subsided, and Daniel had been there for her through it all. Her heart was opening up and though it felt awkward, it was good. And then along came the trial, and with it a whole new level of stress. Kimbra submitted a lengthy statement covering the theft of her phone and friendship with Marie, but she was worried sick about testifying. Dr. Brandenburg stated for the record that he was treating Kimbra and she was not fit to testify at the trial, the District Attorney reluctantly agreed.

Dr. Brandenburg however, suggested it would be good therapy to attend the trial and once told she did not have to testify, Kimbra decided to take his advice. She couldn't take off work for the entire trial, but attending the opening and closing arguments seemed a good compromise. She was staring at the back of Mick's head, the same person she once rode with on the back of his motorcycle. His hair was thinning at the crown, but otherwise he looked much the same as he did in high school. So much had changed since those carefree days of their youth. She hoped the trial would provide some closure and put Mick behind her. It didn't seem possible, but maybe one day she could forgive him for what he did. She turned her gaze to the front rows where Marie's parents were seated. She could not imagine what they were going through.

The district attorney rose from her seat to address the court. Riley O'Connell was an upstart attorney looking to earn valuable points with a win. She had a lithe figure and wore a crisp charcoal business suit with a white blouse. Her raven black hair was neatly tied back with a charcoal ribbon to match. Her eyes were cool-green.

"Ladies and gentlemen of the jury, the people will prove beyond a reasonable doubt that the defendant brutally murdered Marie Sadowski. We will present evidence that was hastily buried on the property where he lives: the murder weapon, along with blood-soaked gloves and the phone used to text her that fateful night. Crucial physical evidence linking the defendant to the crime. "

A shiver ran through Kimbra's body just thinking her ex-boyfriend was capable of killing anyone, let alone her best friend. She was sickened thinking her phone was used to lure Marie to her death. On top of that, Mick had the nerve to call her, proclaiming his innocence. Well, she knew better. Mick Donnelly always was a good liar. How could she ever have loved him? The DA finished her opening statement, saying they would be seeking a guilty verdict of murder in the first degree. Ms. O'Connell sat down and it was now the public defender's turn.

Garrett Briggs had an athletic build and was dressed to the nines in a dark, tailor-fitted suit. He had a neatly trimmed beard and his glowing ebony skin flaunted his youth. Despite his tender age, his presentation was sharp and to the point. He set out to refute the state's evidence claiming it was planted. He claimed the defendant was at a bar drinking with his brother earlier that night and was at his brother's house at the time of the murder. The DA and Kimbra believed that to be a lie.

By the time the prosecution called their first witness, Kimbra began to feel light-headed. The courtroom around her began to spin. Her vision blurred and the whole scene imploded, another scene taking its place.

*Kimbra was seated on a lower bunk bed in a small room covered with old wood paneling. A musty smell, mixed with the stench of urine, permeated the air. The door was shut, a single window looked out into the woods. A chain attached to an anchor on the wooden bunk post, ran down to the floor, ending at her ankle where it was attached with a metal bracket and lock. One overpowering emotion began to fill her head: fear. A vehicle pulled up alongside the cabin and the door slammed shut. Footsteps approached and the front door opened with a bang. A warm glow from outside flickered through the window, like that from a fire. Kimbra began to perspire, her heart pounded. She caught herself shaking violently when a voice startled her.*

"Are you all right?"

Kimbra opened her eyes. An elderly man was gently grasping her shoulder. Several people were staring down at her as if it was some kind of spectacle.

"Miss, are you all right?" the man repeated.

"I'm fine," Kimbra shot back, feeling embarrassed and not really sure what just happened or where she was.

"I'm fine. Thank you," she said in a more conciliatory tone as she got up, brushed herself off, and weaved her way down the row to exit the courtroom.

Kimbra was able to meet with Stanwix first thing the next day. She explained her courtroom episode in detail.

"This is very unusual. Other than Christina, no one else has reported visions," he explained.

"Apparently, not so unusual for me. Do you know what's going on?"

"I have your latest lab results and your neural count is way up, your test scores are above normal as well. I would have to agree, it's related to the QR-7."

"But I've stopped taking the drug."

"Yes, but some of the effects can be long lasting, possibly permanent," he explained. "We just don't know."

"Harold, I have to know if the vision is real. Is it a premonition, am I going to be chained to a bed?"

"It could be from another person's perspective."

"No. It was me. I was there."

"Is the location you saw familiar in any way? Stanwix asked.

"No. It seems like a cabin in the middle of the woods, but I've never seen it before."

"Christina had a premonition, but she was a clairvoyant. It's most likely a hallucination brought on by an active imagination and an overstimulated cortex."

"A hallucination?"

"Yes. They can seem very real. It's really all about perception. Your brain receives a signal and interprets it, but it doesn't always get it right. It doesn't know if it's real or not."

Kimbra played back the words in her mind: all about *perception*. It all seemed pretty damn real to her, and if it was, she didn't know what to do. Was she doomed to be held captive in a cabin in the woods? She did not believe in predestination. The future was not set in stone, we have the freedom to choose, we have free will. Maybe Stanwix was right though, maybe it was an overactive imagination. Whatever it was, she knew three things for sure: (1) Marie was dead, (2) Christina was dead, and (3) Christina's killer was still out there. That was not a hallucination, those were facts.

# CHAPTER 29

THE TRIAL LASTED THREE WEEKS. It took the jury three days to find Mick Donnelly guilty in the murder of Marie Sadowski. Five months had passed since Marie's death, and Kimbra was still numb. Time would ease the pain, that's what people said, but right now she did not see that happening. It was a senseless crime and she could not understand why Mick would do such a thing. The prosecution suggested a deep dislike of the victim and a grudge against his old girlfriend, Kimbra, motivated him to kill. If that was true, Kimbra was responsible... and that she could not live with. There had to be more, something was missing.

Meanwhile, Christina's killer was still out there and as far as Kimbra knew, they had no suspects. She was trying her best to put it all behind her and trust that the police would find the killer soon. She hadn't had another vision, or hallucination as Stanwix suggested, since the opening of Mick's trial and stopping the QR-7 injections. She decided to see if Chad could help. She asked if they could meet outside of work for lunch. It was an unusual request, and against company policy, but he agreed. They settled on the deli close to work. It was fall, but still sunny and warm enough for a table outside in the corner. Kimbra made a feeble attempt to break the awkward silence.

"So, this is nice."

Chad dug into his turkey-pesto wrap and spoke with a mouthful of food.

"Yeah, I've been here before."

Kimbra could not get the picture of his evil face she saw at the last test out of her mind. She had to find out more.

"So, how are you doing? I mean we haven't had a chance to talk since the test."

"I've been good. I was thinking about that test though. Exactly what did you see that bothered you so much?" he asked.

Kimbra wasn't sure how much she wanted to share with Chad.

"I saw the images you were concentrating on. Each one worse than the previous. The holocaust survivor image hit me hard, it came with a flood of emotions. Then the video of the two having sex was too much. I can't explain it but I was overcome with emotions. Fear, anger, but mostly doom. It felt like I had no reason to continue living. It got me so depressed, I couldn't continue."

"I'm sorry about that. But the experiment worked. You received the signals telepathically."

"I certainly did, but I wasn't prepared for the intense emotions that came with it. Did you get that when you received signals from Christina?"

"The emotions?"

"Yes."

Chad took a break from his sandwich and reflected on the question.

"I did, but nothing like what you described."

Kimbra took a sip of her iced tea.

"Chad, have you had any visions?"

"Visions? You mean the images sent to me telepathically? They were kind of blurry, but I got them right."

"No, I mean a vision. Like what Christina experienced."

"No, I didn't. Did you?"

Kimbra took a bite of her sandwich and looked around.

"I did, but it wasn't like Christina's. Chad, have you noticed any changes from the drug?"

"You mean other than my elevated neural count and ability to send and receive signals telepathically?"

"Yes," Kimbra had to admit, what they had accomplished was pretty amazing. "Anything else?"

"Well, my GPA is gonna go up. I've been doing amazing at school. I've even been thinking of taking Organic Chemistry again."

"Anything else?" Kimbra prodded.

"I get headaches."

"Me too. Can you read people's thoughts?" Kimbra asked in a hushed tone.

"No, not really. Can you?"

"No," Kimbra admitted.

It was good comparing her experiences with Chad's, but she wondered if he was holding anything back, and she still had no answer for her visions. The two finished eating and cleared their trays. They left the deli and were out on the street when Kimbra heard a voice from behind.

"Kimbra?"

She turned to face a tall man with a deep voice. His eyes were soft, his beard a dark brown. She recognized him immediately and was momentarily speechless.

"Kimbra Evans! It's been a long time. You look great."

"Jake! What are you doing here? You moved to Colorado didn't you?"

"I'm in town for my sister's wedding."

Jake looked great. They stood on the street gawking at each other, until he turned his gaze to Chad.

"I'm sorry, this is Chad. I work near here and Chad has been participating in our research," Kimbra explained.

The two men shook hands and stepped apart to a comfortable distance.

"Research?" Jake asked.

"It's a long story," Kimbra evaded.

"We should catch up," Jake suggested.

"Yeah, I would like that."

"Hey, you know we have a ten year reunion coming up. Are you gonna go?" Jake asked.

"I don't know. Are you?"

"I was thinking about it. It would be fun."

Jake stepped to the side to allow some people to pass. Chad nudged Kimbra.

"I have to get going."

"Oh, sure. Thanks for meeting with me Chad."

Chad acknowledged it was nice meeting Jake and left the group. Jake took a step closer to Kimbra, his tone turned serious.

"I heard about Marie. I'm really sorry."

"Thanks."

"Mick Donnelly huh, I never would have thought him a killer."

Kimbra had nothing to say, it hurt thinking about it.

"Are you all right?" Jake asked.

"Sure. I'm fine," Kimbra evaded.

Her mind suddenly flashed back to high school. They had just left the prom, she was decked out in her gown and heels when they discovered two flat tires on Jake's car.

"Hey, remember prom night?" Kimbra asked Jake.

"Of course."

"And the slashed tires?"

"How could I forget."

They both suspected Mick at the time. Now it seemed to make complete sense, Jake's silence seemed to indicate he felt the same.

"Have you been in touch with anybody from school?" he asked.

"Not really. Oh, I've been seeing Daniel Visser. Do you remember him?"

"Daniel Visser... Wasn't he going out with that girl that disappeared?"

"I do remember a student that disappeared, but I don't remember them seeing each other."

"Yeah, Lisa Minetti. Pretty sure that's her name. She was in our class."

"Did they ever find her?" Kimbra asked.

"I don't think so."

# CHAPTER 30

IT HAD BEEN ONE MONTH SINCE KIMBRA'S LAST QR-7 INJECTION. Her neural count remained above normal as did her paranormal test scores. Other than the headaches, she felt great. In fact, better than great. Her memory was sharp, she could run calculations in her mind that were not possible before, and her senses were heightened. She sat in an expensive restaurant listening to multiple conversations. Scott and Lindsey were having an argument over his gambling addiction. Lucas and Emily were a young couple in love, if Kimbra was correct, a proposal would be coming soon. Over in the corner there was a particularly interesting conversation. Anthony and Isabella were discussing a big trip, but it was contingent on scoring a big job. Kimbra was pretty sure it involved some sort of illegal activity.

"Kimbra, are you ready to order?" Daniel asked.

She looked up at the waitress who was waiting for a response. Kimbra's new-found skills could also be a distraction.

"Yes, I mean if you are," she lied.

Daniel looked up at the waitress. "Okay. I'll have the London Broil."

"Mashed or baked potato?" the waitress asked.

"Mashed."

"And your dressing?"

Kimbra scanned the menu quickly. Daniel finished his order and the waitress looked her way.

"I'll have the scallops."
Minor catastrophe averted, she turned her attention to Daniel.
"So, are you going to tell me what we're celebrating?" she asked.
"Do you remember that big case I've been working on?"
"Yes, a missing person case, right?"
"One hell of a case, and I just closed it. I found their daughter, and everything is going to work out. I charged a substantial fee, and on top of that I was given a generous bonus."
"That's great Daniel!"
Kimbra held up her wine glass, and they toasted the occasion.

Dinner was served and Kimbra was well into her scallops when she decided to broach the subject. Her research revealed that her high school classmate, Lisa Minetti, was never found. Last seen by her parents the night she went missing, she was reported out with friends, but none of them admitted seeing her that night. Her parents suspected she had seen her boyfriend, Daniel. According to police reports, Daniel stated he was with friends and hadn't seen her that night. Apparently his alibi checked out and the case was never solved, it remains open. Lisa's parents were devastated.
"Oh, you'll never guess who I ran into the other day," Kimbra said.
"Who?" Daniel asked between mouthfuls.
"Jake Campbell. Do you remember him from high school?"
Daniel looked up from his plate, "Not really."
"Well, he remembered you."
Daniel went back to eating his London Broil.
"He mentioned you had a girlfriend in high school that disappeared."
Daniel paused for a moment, then continued eating.
"What else did he say?" he asked.
"That was all. Daniel, I don't want to pry, but how come you never mentioned her?"
Daniel set down his knife and fork. His eyes drilled into her like an eagle focused on its prey.
"Because it's very personal."
"I understand if you don't want to talk about it."

Kimbra took a sip of her drink and tried again, in a more conciliatory tone.

"I just want you to know, if you ever want to talk about it, I'm here."

Daniel's expression softened, "Look, I feel terrible about it. We dated for over a year before we broke up. She was depressed, and I keep thinking the breakup had something to do with her disappearance. I don't know if she's dead or alive."

"I'm sorry. It must have been tough."

Daniel was silent and it was extremely awkward. Kimbra felt guilty for bringing it up, she had to step away for a few minutes.

"I have to use the ladies room. I'll be right back."

She got up to leave, while Daniel remained silent.

In the restroom, Kimbra exited the stall and approached a sink. Another woman was freshening up her lipstick alongside Kimbra. They exchanged a brief smile and the woman left, leaving Kimbra with an uneasy feeling. Was she was getting a bad vibe from the woman, or was it Daniel? Kimbra stared at her image in the mirror. Who was this woman? How much had she changed with the QR-7? She wished she had never volunteered for the program when she began to feel dizzy.

*The room spun around her and evaporated away. In its place was a dark road in the middle of the woods. A familiar road, she had seen before. Then she saw it, hidden off to the side and nestled in the woods was a silver Chevrolet Mailbu. A dark figure was seated in the driver's seat, waiting, lurking. She looked up the gravel road and now she was certain, this was Christina's driveway. Kimbra felt a cold, evil presence as her legs grew wobbly and gave out from under her.*

Kimbra was suddenly back in the ladies room. She stood up straight, still shaking from the vision, and splashed cold water on her face. What should she do? She could call the police, but who would believe her? She should call someone, but who? Dr. Stanwix, Fang... Just then a group of woman entered the restroom.

One of them noticed Kimbra's condition and commented, "Are you all right dear?"

"I'm fine, thank you."

Kimbra dabbed her face with a paper towel and quickly texted her sister:

call me it's urgent

Daniel was finishing his meal as Kimbra returned to the table and sat down. A fresh glass of wine sat beside her plate.

"I ordered another round. Hope you don't mind."

"No, that's fine," Kimbra took a hearty sip of her drink.

"Are you all right? You look like you've seen a ghost."

Kimbra could not get the vision out of her mind. Her head was throbbing, her body cold, she was weak. It felt as if all the blood had been drained from her body.

"No, I'm fine," she lied. "I am full though. I think I'll bring the rest home."

"Sure. So tell me about work. I know you can't share any details, but how are things going?"

"It's going well. There's not much to talk about."

The waitress came by asking if they wanted coffee or dessert. They declined. Kimbra wanted to leave but was apprehensive about leaving with Daniel. Did he suspect she knew something? Why hadn't her sister called? She took another gulp of wine and looked around the room, it seemed a bit hazy. The chatter in the room was now a distant buzz.

"Hey, why don't we get away? Celebrate the case I finished and the trial being over. Go someplace special. What do you think?" he asked.

"Sure, but where?" her voice echoed in her head.

"I don't know. Maybe drive up the coast, find a nice B and B."

"That sounds nice," Kimbra agreed as the room began to spin.

She was beginning to feel relaxed, too relaxed. Something was wrong.

"Are you ready to leave?" Daniel asked.

Kimbra hardly noticed she had finished her wine. She wanted to leave, but had hoped her sister would have called by now. She vaguely remembered leaving the restaurant on a dark night. A cool wind invigorated her, seeing the silver Malibu now felt creepy, but she couldn't remember why. Daniel helped her into the passenger seat. The last thing she recalled was dark scenery flashing past her window.

# PART TWO - THE FIRES OF HELL

# CHAPTER 31

KIMBRA OPENED HER EYES TO A BUNK BED ABOVE. A single window to her side let in soft morning light. She had a strange feeling of déjà vu, something about the place was familiar, but where was she? The door was ajar, revealing a larger room beyond. She peeled back the comforter, noticing she had slept in her jeans and blouse from the night before. She swung her legs over the side of the bed, her bare feet touching the cool wooden floor. Her shoes were placed neatly by the bed. A pleasant coffee aroma filled the air as she tried to recall the night before. She closed her eyes tightly in a failed attempt to clear her memory, then stepped into her shoes, and entered the main living area. Daniel was seated at a wooden kitchen table.

"You're up! Let me get you some coffee."

Kimbra tried to clear her head. Daniel got up and poured her a mug of black coffee.

Kimbra remained silent as he set the mug down on the table. The main room served as both kitchen and living area. An old couch and chair sat in front of a coffee table on one side. On the couch was a pillow and blanket, he must have slept there. A television sat on an old entertainment stand. Kimbra stood dazed, peering down at the steaming mug of coffee.

"What happened last night?" she asked.

"I don't know, you just zonked out. You came out of the restaurant bathroom looking pale and fell asleep in the car. Are you all right?"

"Where are we?"

"Don't you remember?"

"Remember what?" she asked.

"Sit down. Have some coffee, it'll make you feel better. I'll explain."

Kimbra sat down, cradled the mug, and took a sip of hot coffee. It was dark and rich in flavor.

"Better?" he asked.

Kimbra nodded. "So what happened?"

"I suggested we spend a few days at my cabin. You agreed it was a good idea and fell fast asleep. When we got here, you wanted to sleep. How are you feeling?"

Kimbra struggled to recall the night before. She took another gulp of coffee, hoping to clear her head.

"Want something to eat?" Daniel asked.

Kimbra nodded.

"Eggs and sausage all right?"

"Sure," she replied, looking around. "Where are we? I mean, where is this place?"

"This is an old hunting cabin my grandfather built. I added the running water and bathroom. It was pretty rough before I fixed it up."

Kimbra had no memory of how she got there. Her head was foggy, but she knew something wasn't right. She was feeling trapped, something was telling her she had to get away.

"Daniel, I need to go home."

He paused from cooking the eggs, his back to Kimbra.

"Why? What's wrong?"

"I'm not feeling well. I need my meds."

He continued cooking as she tried to replay the night before in her head. She vaguely remembered a trip to the ladies room, and a vision... That's right, she had a vision of Daniel's car at Christina's! She recalled drinking two glasses of wine, but she couldn't have been that drunk. Did he drug her? She held her tongue as he cooked in silence, waiting for her head to clear.

"Daniel, where's my phone?"

"It was out of power so I'm charging it. Won't work here anyway, not a cell tower for miles."

He brought two plates full of eggs, sausage and toast, setting one in front of Kimbra.

"More coffee?"

"Daniel, I'd really like to leave. I'm feeling anxious without my meds."

Daniel looked up from his plate. "We can talk about it later. Eat your breakfast first."

Kimbra had lost her appetite, she ate half her breakfast. She was desperate.

"I'm done. Daniel, I want to go home, now!"

He shot her a look she had not seen before. An icy spirit sunk in, like an evil presence had just been released. Her head began to pound.

"You know, I really want things to work out between us. But you're making it difficult," he said.

"What do you mean? I don't know what you're talking about."

"What happened last night?" he asked.

"What do you mean?"

"When you came out of the restroom, something changed, you changed. Did you have another vision?" he asked.

Kimbra's heart was pounding, her mouth dry. He knew. But how could he?

"You mean like my Dad's suicide?"

"Yeah, like that. What did you see last night?" he demanded.

"Nothing! I didn't see anything," Kimbra lied.

Daniel got up, unhooked her phone from the charger and dropped it on the table in front of her.

"Open it!" he demanded.

Kimbra entered her passcode and gave it to him. He sat down and scrolled through its contents. She began to tremble.

"You sent a text to your sister. What was so urgent?" he asked in a threatening tone.

"I don't know. I can't remember."

"You're lying. Something happened in the ladies room."

"Nothing happened! You have to believe me, nothing happened," she pleaded.

Daniel's mood changed from controlled anger to rage in an instant. He shot up, knocking his chair down, and flew over to Kimbra, grabbing her by the arm.

"Fine! We'll do it your way."

He dragged her by the arm into the bunkroom and slammed the door shut. Minutes later he returned with a heavy chain and some hardware.

"What are you doing?" she pleaded

"Sit down!"

"No!" she refused.

He threw her on the bed and attempted to wrap one end of the chain around her ankle. She resisted, pulling her ankle away and kicking wildly, struggling to get away. One of her kicks caught him in the face. Momentarily stunned, he paused for a second, then slapped her hard across the face, knocking her to the floor. He towered over her with fists clenched, his face beet red, threatening to hit her again. She cowered against the wall as he wrapped the chain around her ankle and locked it tight with a keyed padlock. He secured the other end of the chain to the bedpost with a metal anchor, using a drill and screws.

"I have to go. That'll give you time to think things through. Don't ever lie to me."

He slammed the door shut and drove off. Kimbra remained in shock, the left side of her face stinging from the slap. How could she have so misjudged him? She tugged at the chain on both ends trying to free herself. She looked around the room and now, for the first time, realized this was the room in her vision. How could she have not remembered it earlier? She had a premonition, her mind was warning her. Had she heeded it, she would not be chained to a bed, living a nightmare.

She tried using her new-found intelligence from an increased neural count to plan an escape. She attempted to slip the chain around her heel, that was impossible. She struggled to loosen the screws securing the chain to the bedpost, but without a tool, it was hopeless. Trapped, with no way out, she began to sob, letting out a lifetime of frustration, pain, and feelings of inadequacy. The sun rose and sunk in the sky, and the sobbing subsided, what was the use? She was destined to a life of doom. Chained to a bedpost for hours on end with no access to the bathroom, she wet herself. She held on as long as she could, not knowing when he would return. In the end there was a measure of relief in letting go. Not only her bladder, but her will. She had lost all control of her life and gave up resisting, it was pointless, a waste of energy.

Kimbra was asleep, slumped on the floor next to a puddle of urine when she heard a car approach. Daniel swung the door to the bunkroom open and stood there holding a brown paper bag.

"I brought dinner."

Shaking like a leaf she glanced up, then down at the floor and cried. Never in her life had she been so humiliated and frightened.

"Oh, I'm sorry," he said as he approached and unfastened the chain on her ankle. His voice was soft, almost apologetic.

"I wasn't thinking. Would you like to take a shower?"

Kimbra nodded through her tears and was led to the bathroom and given a towel. She shut the door, sat on the toilet, and sobbed. Who was this man? It was as if he possessed two personalities.

Daniel's voice rang out from the other side of the door.

"I ran into town and picked up a few things for you. I'll leave them on the bed. I hope they fit."

Kimbra forced herself to her feet and ran the shower. She let the steamy hot water warm her trembling body until it stopped shaking, but the fear remained. She gently probed her cheek, it was not tender. She was fortunate he had hit her with an open hand and not a clenched fist. She could not understand how the one person she opened up to, could do this to her. Once again, just as she thought she found a little joy in her life, fate had punched her in the gut. What was she thinking anyway? She would never find true happiness.

She stepped out of the shower, wrapped the towel around herself, and rinsed her underwear and wet pants in the sink. She hung them to dry and opened the door a crack. He was sitting on the sofa drinking a beer. She slipped by him and into the bunkroom. There were two flannel shirts, a tee-shirt, a sweat shirt, black leggings, and a toothbrush on the bed. Fortunately he also bought a few pairs of fresh underwear. She put on the leggings and sweat shirt, none of the clothes fit properly, but they would work. She sat on the bed wondering if she would get out of this alive. Wondering if he had killed before.

"Are you done in there?" he called out from the other room.

Kimbra shook at the sound of his voice. Her throat tightened, she could not speak. He knocked on the door and poked his head in.

"Come join me. Dinner is getting cold," he said.

A few moments later, she got up and sat at the kitchen table. Two plates were laid out with two pints of Chinese food in the center. He set aside the newspaper he was reading.

"Before we eat, I want to hear the truth from you."

She could feel his eyes bore into her as she fixed her gaze on her plain white plate. Her fingernail scratched impulsively into her forearm, an old habit she thought she had gotten over. She dug the nail in deeper, as if the pain would help.

"Look at me," he commanded.

She raised her head slowly. Before today, his eyes were dark and mysterious. Now they were the evil eyes of Charles Manson, a deranged, cold-blooded killer.

"What did you see in the ladies room?"

Kimbra's eye twitched. Her first instinct was to lie, but she was a terrible liar, and if he found out... well, she couldn't think about that now. If she told the truth... if he knew she knew... how could she ever get out of here? She had to decide, his face was contorting in anger.

"I'm waiting..."

Her lips trembled, his black eyes drew the words out.

"I... I saw a car, hidden in the trees."

"And..." he egged her on.

"It was pulled over to the side of a driveway, Christina's driveway."

"And why did that upset you so?" he asked in an almost sarcastic tone.

Kimbra was afraid to speak, but she had to know.

"Was that you? Did you kill her?"

Daniel continued reading the newspaper. Like the flick of a switch, his mood changed in an instant.

"There's a big wildfire in the area. Looks like it's going to get worse before they can contain it."

# CHAPTER 32

THE CALL CAME IN MONDAY AT 1:45 PM.

"Detective Rizzo here."

"This is Detective Liam McKenzie with San José PD. I'm working a missing person case and was hoping you could help."

"Sure, what can I do for you?"

"I made a few calls, and it seems you investigated a murder case in Freemont, the victim being a Marie Sadowski."

"That's correct."

"There seems to be a connection to the missing person. Are you familiar with Kimbra Evans?"

This should be interesting, Rizzo thought. Miss Evans was mixed up in some strange stuff.

"Sure. What's going on?"

"We got a call from her sister that she's been missing since Saturday night. I wanted to see if you knew anything."

"I haven't talked to her in weeks. What makes you think she's missing and not just playing hooky?"

"Her sister received an urgent text on Saturday night to call her. No one has been able to reach her since, and she didn't call in to work today. I checked her apartment and her car is still there. There's no indication she was planning on going anywhere. I tried contacting her boyfriend, Daniel Visser, but couldn't reach him."

"That's interesting. What can I do to help?"

"Is there anything you can tell me to shed some light on this?"

"Are you aware Miss Evans has been a person of interest in a couple of murders in the area?" Rizzo asked.

"You mean in addition to the Sadowski case?"

"There was a murder northeast of Sacramento. The victim was an acquaintance of Miss Evans' and they got together at the victim's home shortly before the murder."

"Do you think it's a coincidence?"

Rizzo filled McKenzie in on what he knew and a few theories he was working on.

"Thanks. I'm waiting for a warrant to obtain her phone records. In the meantime I'm entering her in the National Missing Persons database. I'll let you know of any developments."

Rizzo hung up the phone.

"What was that all about?" Officer Montero asked.

"Remember Kimbra Evans, the one that kept turning up at the homicide here and the one out past Sacramento?"

"Yeah."

"Seems she has gone missing. I'm going to update Slater at Grass Valley PD. There's a chance this could be related to the Christina Sullivan investigation."

"You still think the two are related?" Montero asked.

"I do."

# CHAPTER 33

DAY TWO IN CAPTIVITY. Kimbra sat at the table poking a fork at her breakfast.

"Daniel, what about my cat? Smokey needs food and water."

Daniel finished a mouthful, took a sip of coffee and spoke.

"I have some work to do at the office today. I'll stop by your place, pick up your meds and take care of Smokey for you."

Kimbra was silent, thinking if his absence would give her an opportunity to escape.

"I thought maybe we could go for a hike later. It's really a beautiful spot here, I think you'll like it."

Hiking? What was this a weekend getaway for the happy couple? It all seemed so surreal. She had no choice but to play along.

"In that case, can you grab a pair of sneakers for me?"

Daniel got up from his chair.

"Sure. Listen, I have to get ready. Can you clean up the dishes?"

"Sure, I'll take care of it. You get dressed."

He disappeared into the bunkroom and called out.

"Oh, I wouldn't think about running away. Like I said earlier, there's nothing around here for miles. You'd probably get lost."

Kimbra shot him an innocent look. "Of course not."

The door ajar, his naked body was visible as he dressed. It wasn't like they hadn't been intimate before, but everything had now changed, at least for her. She could not fight back thoughts of fleeing. What if she snuck out right now and ran? Peering down at her flats she wondered how far would she get in those shoes. What if he was right and she got lost? Or worse yet, what if she got caught? He would go mad, but would he be angry enough to kill her? No, this was not the time, she should wait. She cleared the table, glancing down at the newspaper, the Sacramento Bee, then rushed back to wash the dishes. How close to Sacramento were they? Daniel came out ready to leave.

"You can finish the dishes later. Let's get you settled in your room."

It was wishful thinking, but Kimbra had hoped he would trust her enough to leave her unshackled.

"Can I use the bathroom first?"

"Sure."

After relieving herself, Kimbra wandered into the bunkroom. A box of snack bars, a pitcher of water and a glass were sitting on the nightstand. Daniel came in and once again chained her to the bedpost. He left, but ducked back in before leaving.

"I'll try not to be too long but just in case, I had this left over from before I installed the indoor plumbing."

He set a bucket with a toilet seat attached to it on the floor, along with a roll of toilet paper, making sure they were well within reach of the chain. The outside door slammed shut and his car rumbled down the dirt road until out of earshot.

The pounding in Kimbra's chest began to settle down. Her mind, unable to do the same, sought to devise a means of escape. The chain wrapped around her ankle was secured with a padlock. The other end was attached to the bedpost with a metal anchor fastened with screws. Her eyes panned around the room for something within reach that could be fashioned into a screwdriver. She considered breaking the glass into pieces, but the glass was too thick to act as a screwdriver and would not be strong enough. She examined the bed frame and springs. The metal springs were also too thick, as was the frame. Next she tried using her earrings to pry a screw loose, but that was as hopeless as her fingernails. It was no use, she sat on the bed defeated.

Time froze to a standstill as she contemplated her fate. The vision flashed back in her mind: the bunk beds, the window, the bucket for a toilet. Why hadn't she been able to put two-and-two together and figure out it was Daniel? Her ex-boyfriend from high school mentioned Daniel's missing girlfriend. Jake was right in warning her, now it was too late.

Just then, a thought popped into consciousness. She picked up her toothbrush and examined it closely. If she could file one end down thin enough, maybe, just maybe it would work. She sat on the floor and tried scraping it against the metal bed frame. It wasn't quite sharp enough to shave the toothbrush down, but if she worked at it, she could sand it. It was a long, arduous process requiring many breaks, but she was making progress. A small pile of fine, blue dust settled under the bed frame. She was sanding away when she heard a car approaching.

Car doors creaked open and shut. Something was removed from the trunk and footsteps were heard walking away. She feared the worst as she heard the sound of digging and dirt thumping in an imaginary pile. She knew too much. Was her boyfriend a cold-blooded killer? Had he killed Christina? What about his missing girlfriend in high school? How many bodies were buried around the camp? She trembled with fear at the thought of him digging her grave. How would he kill her? She often pondered death, even welcomed it at times. But that was on her terms. Now that is was a real possibility with no control over how or when it would happen, she feared it.

The trunk slammed shut, followed by the slam of a car door, footsteps approached the cabin. Daniel burst into the room, she cowered as he approached with a black, plastic garbage bag in hand.

"I got some clothes for you," he said, dumping the contents of the bag in a pile alongside her on the bed.

Jeans, sweatshirts, underwear, socks, and a pair of blue canvas sneakers, one of which fell off the bed and hit the floor. Kimbra looked at the pile, relieved for the moment.

"Did you take care of Smokey?"

"Yeah, he's fine. I gave him some food and water."

"Did you get my meds?" she asked hoping he forgot.

The drugs helped, but what she really needed was to return to her apartment. He dug a fist into his pocket, pulled out a bottle of pills and tossed it on the bed.

"Yeah, I got them."

He unshackled her ankle and took a step back.

"Get dressed. Let's go for a hike," he said.

Kimbra's relief was short lived as Daniel grabbed a shovel leaning on the outside of the cabin, and off they went. The air was cool and moist, yet beads of perspiration formed on Kimbra's forehead. A thin carpet of leaves softened their steps. Large Douglas-fir, cedar, and spruce trees shielded the sunlight as they hiked in silence, deeper into the woods that seemed to go on forever. They approached a tiny brook, followed it for a while, then veered away and stopped.

"This looks like a good spot," Daniel said, handing Kimbra the shovel. "Dig!"

"What?"

He took a step back, exposing a holstered pistol on his hip. "I said dig!"

Kimbra gripped the handle tightly and raised the blade slightly off the ground. She calculated the time required to raise the shovel and swing it at his head. Odds were he would get a shot or two off before the shovel hit his head.

"Why? Daniel, what are we doing here?" Kimbra pleaded.

"Dig," he repeated.

Kimbra raised the pointed shovel and slammed it into the earth. She stepped on the heel of the blade with her all her weight and drove it into the ground. She bent down, pulled up a load of moist soil, and dropped it to the side.

"Keep going," he said.

When the hole was a few feet deep, he told her to make it wider. Was she digging her own grave? If that was the case, why did he go to her apartment and bring back clothes? Kimbra gripped the handle with sweat dripping off her brow and hands.

"I need some answers, and I need them now," he demanded.

Kimbra stopped digging and looked up.

"Tell me everything you know about the research they're doing at Quantum Thunder."

Exhausted and shaking with fear, Kimbra told him everything, the telepathic research and how it was enhanced by the experimental drug. She mentioned the injections which were responsible for her visions. He told her to keep digging. The hole was now almost three feet deep and four feet wide.

"When I stopped by your place, I just missed a guy snooping around. Had to be a plain clothes cop. What do you know about that?" he asked.

Kimbra stopped digging and hunched over to catch her breath, wondering if she now even had the strength to swing the shovel at him.

"Was it Rizzo?" she asked. "You know I talked to him."

"I don't think so. Who else would be snooping around your apartment?"

"I don't know."

"What about your sister, did she call the cops?"

"I don't know. You saw the texts."

Daniel looked her straight in the eye, studying her intensely.

"What's your sister's full name and address?"

Kimbra felt bile rise up in her throat. She could not involve another innocent person in this.

"I asked you, what is her name and address?"

Kimbra considered her options when her lips quivered out a response.

"Gina Evans. She lives in Colorado."

She prayed he would not ask for more. There must be a thousand Evanses in Colorado. He stood there motionless as she prepared for all hell to break out. Finally he spoke.

"All right. Leave the shovel, let's head back."

Inside, Kimbra let go a sigh of relief. She climbed out of the hole and stuck the shovel in the dirt mound. Daniel picked up the shovel and they hiked back in silence. When they reached the cabin he left the shovel outside and opened the door.

"Sorry I had to put you through that, but I needed to know. You understand don't you?"

Kimbra nodded as the anger inside heated up. What kind of deranged person was she dealing with? She had better figure that out, and figure it out soon, if she wanted to survive.

That night Kimbra cooked dinner, pasta with meat sauce, and they watched a movie together. Just another happy couple spending a quiet night together. Who was this person? They chose the original The Day The Earth Stood Still from his collection of classic movies. Towards the end of the movie he began to nod off. Kimbra's thoughts went to finding a weapon: a knife, his gun, or something to hit him with. She shifted on the sofa, preparing to get up, but he woke.

"How much did I miss?" he asked groggily.

"Not much," she lied.

"No matter. I've seen it so many times."

The movie finished, but not before Klaatu delivered one final message for the people before leaving Earth: "Your choice is simple: join us and live in peace, or pursue your present course and face obliteration."

Daniel got up  from the sofa.

"Sorry, but I have to chain you to the bed."

Daniel had no remorse for what he was putting her through. Perhaps he thought there was nothing wrong with his actions, nothing odd about their relationship. That, or he did not care. Daniel was a riddle that needed to be solved, and soon. If not, Kimbra feared it would cost her, her life.

# CHAPTER 34

DAY THREE OF CAPTIVITY. It was Halloween, All Hallows' Eve, All Saints' Eve or whatever else it has been called over the years. A day to remember the dead, the dearly departed, saints and martyrs. It was also a celebration of the macabre and supernatural. A day that conjured up images of evil spirits and monsters, none of which were any more frightening than Daniel Visser. Kimbra studied her captor as he prepared a breakfast of pancakes and bacon.

"Just like our Sunday mornings together," he said.

Sunday breakfasts at Kimbra's apartment now seemed light years away. How could he compare that to now? What was he thinking, who was this person?

"I figured we could go for a hike this morning," he suggested. "How does that sound?"

"Sure," Kimbra agreed, knowing full well she had no choice. She cringed at the thought of him forcing her to dig another hole. He wouldn't do that again, would he? He seemed in much better spirits now, but then his mood could change in an instant.

"After lunch I'll run into town to pick up a few things for dinner."

"Daniel, what about Smokey? I need to take care of him. His litter box needs to be cleaned. The apartment is going to be a mess."

"Don't worry about Smokey."

"Why not?"

"I took care of it."

"What does that mean?" Thoughts of the worst case scenario ran through her mind.

"I knocked on your neighbor's door and told her you were going to be away a few days. She's gonna take care of Smokey. So you don't need to worry."

Kimbra did worry. She couldn't trust this man and would worry herself sick until she was home safe with Smokey. It had been three days now. She had not shown up at work, she had left an urgent message for her sister. Someone must be looking for her by now, and if Daniel talked to Tammy, then they might ask her where she was and make a connection to Daniel. That is, if he was telling the truth.

* * *

That morning, they hiked a short trail through the woods and it involved no digging. Daniel seemed in good spirits and after lunch he left again. What he described as a short trip into town, turned into several hours. Kimbra spent the time whittling down the end of her toothbrush. The work was exhausting and slow, requiring many periods of rest. On her fifth break she tested it. It was close, but still too fat to be useful as a screwdriver. After another hour of work it was finally ready. She fit it into the slot and attempted to turn the first screw. It would not budge. She tried another screw and this one, moved with a *creak*. As she kept turning it became easier. She did the same with another, and another, loosening them until they each moved freely. Now, back to that stubborn screw, there always seemed to be one. Firmly placing both hands on the makeshift tool she applied more pressure. Still no movement. She wiped her sweaty hands on her leggings and tried again, this time with all her might. *Crack*! The filed down end of the makeshift tool snapped off. All the tears her body could produce would not be enough to wash away the frustration she felt. Exhausted and dejected, she threw herself onto the bed and cried herself to sleep.

A loud *bang* startled Kimbra from her slumber, an orange glow radiated through the window, flickering in intensity. A smoky aroma registered in her brain. The car trunk squeaked open and footsteps quickly approached the cabin. Her pulse quickened, her breathing was rapid. She felt like a dog, her emotions keyed to the mood of her captor, anticipating his every move. She heard Daniel removing stuff from the cabin, making several trips back and forth. What was happening? Suddenly, he burst into the bunkroom holding a black plastic garbage bag. He bent over and removed the chain from her ankle.

"There's a wildfire approaching! We have to get out of here now. Grab your things and get in the car."

He handed her the garbage bag and left. Kimbra sat on the bed in shock. Was she really leaving with him?

"Get moving!" he yelled seeing her still on the bed.

He left the bunkroom and gathered items from the main room. Kimbra gathered her few belongings and stuffed them into the garbage bag.

"Let's go!" he shouted from the other room.

Kimbra quickly removed an earring and left it on the floor next to the wall. She stepped outside the cabin, holding onto her plastic bag and froze at the sight. The sky was dark, with a reddish glow. She coughed as smoke and hot embers swirled high above her. There was a loud crackle in the distance, the sound of limbs breaking. The wind roared, giving the fire a voice; the angry, howling of a creature. She could feel the heat drawing closer as Daniel scurried back and forth from the cabin to the car, stuffing items into the trunk. That's when she saw it.

A shadowy form moved about as if lost. It was faint at first, then it became clearer. It had the shape of a human, dressed in a button down shirt and khakis. She focused on the face with dark, wavy hair and Asian features. It was Fang! He stopped cold, jaw wide open in what seemed to be amazement. They recognized each other at the exact same moment. Kimbra's mouth opened forming the words *Fang* as Daniel approached.

"What are you doing? Let's get going!"

His eyes followed in the same direction as Kimbra's.

"What the hell is..."

His words were cut short as the object slowly faded from view, leaving only the smoky woods in its place. They both stood in wonder for a brief moment in time.

"C'mon, let's get the hell out of here!" he said tugging her arm.

He grabbed her bag of clothes and threw them in the back seat.

"Hop in," he ordered.

Kimbra snapped out of her stupor and climbed into the front seat. Daniel got behind the wheel and stepped on the gas, sending them careening down the dirt road in a cloud of dust. Flames were visible through the thick stand of pines. The crackling roar of the fire was audible through the car windows. They turned the corner onto a gravel road. The smoke dissipated slightly before becoming much thicker. Glowing red embers danced about wildly, pinging off the windshield. They could barely see their way through the dark, swirling mass, it was getting worse.

"There's a turn up ahead, if we can find it," Daniel yelled over the sound of the fire.

The car slowed to a crawl as they searched for a turn through the thick, black fog. Turning on the high beams only made it worse. Kimbra fumbled to close the vents as smoke seeped into the car, it did little to help. She began to cough uncontrollably as it coated her nasal passageways and bit into her throat.

"There it is," Daniel yelled as the car veered left and picked up speed.

A large, flaming limb crashed down up ahead, partially blocking the road.

"Hang on!"

The car swerved around the blockage, onto the shoulder and crashed through burning brush. Boughs of burning pine needles hit the windshield and sizzled as the car veered back onto the road. Daniel turned on the wipers, smearing the windshield with burnt rubber. The wiper arms, now striped of their blades, scraped on the glass as they pushed the debris aside. They continued through thick smoke for another thirty minutes before it finally began to dissipate.

Kimbra's blouse was soaked in sweat and the car reeked of burnt wood. Daniel rolled down his window a crack, then opened it all the way.

"I think we're through the worst of it."

They drove for hours through a dark, remote area. A few signs along the way indicated they were headed north, but where? Kimbra's mind once again feared the worst, then she realized Daniel could have left her chained to the bed to die. Then again, maybe he preferred a more secluded location.

"What you and I saw back there, what was that? Who was that?" he asked.

Kimbra fidgeted in her seat. She was afraid to lie to him. The last time she did, it set him off in a rage.

"I don't know. It looked like my boss, Dr. Fang. I've never seen anything like that before."

Daniel wasn't buying it. He threw her a disbelieving look.

"Your boss? But he disappeared right in front of our eyes. You saw that, right?"

"Yes, I saw it."

"How is that possible?"

"I don't know. I told you all I know about my visions, and Christina's premonition," she pleaded.

"Yeah, but this wasn't a vision, was it? You work there, you must have some idea."

Kimbra searched her mind for a logical explanation. How do you explain the impossible? She remembered something Fang had said.

"Spillover from another dimension. Maybe that's what happened," she almost whispered to herself.

"What did you say? Another dimension? What the hell are you talking about?"

"I don't know, it's something I heard at work."

"You mean from another place, like a ghost?"

"I guess. Yes, something like that."

"You mentioned a drug they were experimenting with the other day. What did you call it?" he asked.

"QR-7."

"And your boss, is he taking the drug?"
"Yes."


It was well after dark when the silver Chevrolet Malibu pulled onto a long and twisting dirt road. At the end of the road they stopped in front a cabin, a single floodlight dimly lit a portico covered wood deck in front.

"I was lucky to find this on such short notice," Daniel said as he turned a cold stare in Kimbra's direction.

"I wanted us to have a nice trip up the coast, but I wasn't sure I could trust you after Saturday night."

Kimbra looked out the passenger window, waiting for the moment to pass.

"C'mon, let's check it out," he finally said.

Daniel pulled out a penlight and illuminated the lockbox by the front door. He entered a combination, extracted a key and unlocked the door, a squeaky hinge announced their presence. A flick of the light switch revealed a rustic interior. The walls were covered with a combination of wood paneling and cedar shingles, the flooring was a dated sheet of linoleum. A metal pendant light fixture hung over a chunky wood table, next to a cozy stone fireplace. The kitchen was homey, with tile countertops, wood cabinets, and mismatched appliances. A block of wood containing a set of knives sat on the countertop, it did not go unnoticed by either of them. Kimbra glanced at the pistol bulging through Daniel's shirt and quickly dispelled any notion of grabbing a knife.

"Looks like we got everything we need here," he said with a look of approval.

A quick tour of the place revealed two bedrooms, one with two single beds, the other a double bed. Daniel left briefly and returned with a cooler, setting it on the counter.

"Why don't you load the fridge and I'll unpack the car," he suggested.

Kimbra imagined grabbing a knife from the butcher block. Daniel returns and she lunges at him with the knife, slashing his throat. He drops to the floor in a pool of blood as she escapes out the door.

Before she knew it, Daniel returned with the last load from the car, ending the daydream. The large chef knife remained in the block of wood, snugly in place alongside the others.

"Are you hungry, I can make a grilled cheese sandwich?" Kimbra offered.

"I'm not really hungry. I don't know about you, but it's late and I'm whipped. Ready to turn in?"

Kimbra nodded, and they headed towards the back of the cabin, stopping at the main bedroom.

"I'd like us to trust each other, like before," he said. "Why don't you grab your things and we can sleep in here."

It didn't sound like a question. The last thing Kimbra wanted to do was sleep with him, but on the other hand, she did not want to displease him. She needed to regain his trust.

"I brought the chain, but I'd rather not deal with that," he added, no doubt sensing her hesitation.

He brought the chain. In all that commotion, he remembered to bring the chain. She quickly recalled the screws she loosened. Did he notice? Was he playing games with her? Kimbra fetched her garbage bag of clothes and entered the master bedroom.

"You can have the top drawer," he offered while tossing a few things in the middle drawer.

He kicked off his shoes and sat on the bed while Kimbra left to wash up. When she returned he was under the covers. She looked around for the gun, it was nowhere in sight. She climbed in under the covers wearing the leggings and tee-shirt he picked up for her in town, wherever that was. She lay on her back, staring at the ceiling. Daniel turned out the light and she rolled over on her side, with her back to him. She was devastated at how her life had changed. Just when she thought she hit rock bottom, it got worse. She should have known better, but Daniel was so nice, he wormed his way into her heart. She wondered, were his delusional affections towards her sincere, or had he been reeling her in all along?

# CHAPTER 35

THREE MEN STOOD OUTSIDE KIMBRA'S APARTMENT. Detective Rizzo knocked, waited briefly, then stepped aside allowing Lou, the apartment manager, to unlock the door. Rizzo and San José Detective Liam McKenzie entered the apartment while Lou remained in the hallway, peeking inside. There was a foul smell of cat urine and feces. A cat meowed, entered the kitchen, and jumped up onto the sink. Rizzo picked up an empty water bowl from the floor and filled it. The cat jumped up, preferring instead to drink from the running faucet. Rizzo recalled his sister's cat having the same odd behavior.

"Doesn't look like the cat has been cared for in days," he said.

Rizzo checked out the living area, running his hand along the television and carefully inspecting the plant and other objects.

"What are you looking for?" McKenzie asked.

"Miss Evans complained someone had bugged her apartment."

"Who?"

"Don't know and I never found any bugs."

They moved deeper into the one-bedroom apartment, checking the balcony, bathroom, and bedroom before returning to the kitchen.

"What do you think?" McKenzie asked.

"No sign of forced entry. Doesn't look like she's slept here in days. Car is parked out front, can't find a purse, and there is no toothbrush in the bathroom. I can't imagine she would leave and forget about the cat."

Rizzo found some dry cat food in a cabinet and filled Smokey's bowl, the cat went for it immediately. They stepped out into the hallway to find the apartment manager talking to a woman.

Lou introduced the neighbor, "This is Tammy, she lives across the hall."

"I'm Detective Rizzo, this is Detective McKenzie. Mind if we ask you a few questions?"

"No, not at all. Is Kimbra all right?"

"When was the last time you saw her?" Rizzo asked.

"Oh, it's been several days. I ran into her last week, Wednesday night I think."

"Have you heard any noise or indication that she was in the apartment since then?"

"Not really. Wait, I thought I heard her door open yesterday."

"What time was that?"

"It was in the afternoon, maybe around two or two-thirty."

Rizzo was surprised to hear that.

"Looks like the cat hasn't been fed in days. The water bowl was dry," he said.

"That's strange," Tammy said. "She usually asks me to take care of Smokey if she will be away. She left me a key."

Tammy offered to take care of Smokey until Kimbra returned, that is if she returned. Rizzo and McKenzie discussed it further, outside by their cars.

"Do you think she returned yesterday?" McKenzie asked.

"I don't think so, she would have taken care of the cat. It's more likely someone else stopped by. No sign of forced entry, so someone with a key?"

McKenzie acknowledged the reference to someone with a key with a raised eyebrow.

"I just got the call records this morning," he said. "There was a text sent to her sister Saturday night, date stamped at 8:24 PM."

"Got a location?" Rizzo asked.

"I've got a location within 500 meters of the nearest cell tower. Her sister mentioned Kimbra often went out to dinner with her boyfriend, so I did a quick search of restaurants in that radius."

Rizzo peered over the list McKenzie held out. There were three restaurants in the area, only two of them served dinner.

"How about I take one, you take the other?" Rizzo offered.

The sign said closed but the front door was unlocked. Rizzo walked in, startling a young man with a dark complexion.

"I'm sorry, we're not open," he said.

Rizzo flashed his badge.

"I just have a few questions. Is the manager or owner available?"

"Let me check. Wait right here."

Rizzo looked around while the man disappeared from the dining area. Rizzo had heard about the place but never ate there. He heard the food was excellent. The decor was contemporary; white walls with modern light fixtures shining from above. Fine glassware and silverware adorned the small tables covered in heavily starched white linen. A large picture window looked onto a courtyard filled with plants and a large fountain. A short man with a round face and full beard appeared from a back room.

"Dante tells me you have some questions. My name is Alfred, I'm the manager. Is there a problem?"

"My name is Detective Rizzo. I'm investigating a missing person who may have been in your restaurant last Saturday."

"How can I help?" the manager asked.

"I'm going to need to see your sales receipts for Saturday night, from 6 PM to closing."

The man's face scrunched up as if he was in pain.

"I'm sorry, but those records are confidential," he said.

Rizzo took a step forward, just inside the man's comfort zone.

"Look, like I said, I'm investigating a missing person and I don't have time to waste. I can get a warrant, but if I do that, it might not go well for you."

"What do you mean?"

"If I were to notice a code violation or some minor infraction, I would be obligated to notify the authorities. I see you have a nice restaurant here. That would not be good for your reputation, they might even shut you down. I'd hate for that to happen to you. Let's just say I would not be able to help you."

The man's expression turned from indignation to worry.

"All right, follow me."

Rizzo followed Alfred into the back office and watched as he typed on the keyboard.

"These are the sales receipts for Saturday night," he pointed out and got up, offering his seat to Rizzo.

Rizzo scrolled down the sheet, scanning for a particular person. Three quarters of the way down a name caught his eye. He scrolled back up. Dinner for two. Payment received at 9:46 PM. The name on the credit card:

Daniel Visser

Rizzo called Mckenzie before reaching his car.

"Rizzo here, I just hit the jackpot. Visser was here Saturday night and he wasn't alone. It was dinner for two. He may be the last person to see her."

Daniel Visser just went from a person of interest, to a prime suspect.

# CHAPTER 36

DAY FOUR OF CAPTIVITY. Sunlight filtered through tall trees, the fall air was crisp. The trail along the coast changed from coastal brush to coniferous forest. Kimbra studied Daniel's back, a bulge from his pistol showed through his button down, chamois shirt. She watched him weave his way through the trail, hating and fearing the man she was once intimate with. That thought of them together now made her queasy.

Just over an hour into the hike they took their first break. The ocean was to the west, but the trees blocked their view.

"Feel like something to eat?" he asked pulling a few snack bars from his backpack.

Not particularly hungry, but also not wanting to upset him, Kimbra accepted one. She had been trying to get a feel for his mood, using her extra sensory abilities the QR-7 drug had given her, but she sensed nothing. She would have to do it the old-fashioned conventional way, and knowing his mood could change like the wind, she chose her words carefully.

"Do you think your cabin survived the fire?"

"Sounds like it stayed to the north, last report said it was 40% under control. I'm hoping we can go back tonight or tomorrow."

He said *we* and that was encouraging. Still, she was worried. In a short while they were back on the trail. They reached a summit and took another break. Few words were spoken, she wondered what he was thinking, but dared not ask. They were out in public, and maybe an opportunity would present itself. They finished their rest and hiked down to the south before turning back towards the ocean.

At the two hour mark they approached a Ranger station, two cars sat in the quiet parking lot. Kimbra considered saying something if they saw a Ranger, but worried how that would turn out. Her heart raced as she ran through several scenarios in her mind, all of which involved someone getting shot. Daniel must have sensed her anxiety for he rested his hand on the pistol. They had not seen a single person on the hike and this area was no different. They worked their way past the station and into a closed campground, stopping for lunch at a wooden picnic table. Ham sandwiches, chips, and apples she packed earlier. She still could not read Daniel's mood but had to uncover something regarding her fate, so she took a chance.

"Daniel, after we check on the cabin, will we be going home?"

He continued chewing his sandwich as if he had not heard a word she spoke. Then he looked her straight in the eye, his face stone cold.

"Well now, that depends on you."

He held his stare, not uttering another word. She was not sure if he expected her to speak. She did not. Finally, he looked away and got up.

"C'mon, we better get going. It'll be dark soon enough."

They walked up the Coastal Highway a short distance and followed a park road west. The dense forest thinned and soon turned back to coastal brush, allowing them a spectacular view of the ocean. They turned onto another trail and were heading north along the coast when they ran into a group of teens. Daniel had the gun and he would use it, if he had to. Kimbra nodded as they passed, hoping her eyes would alert them that something was wrong, but that was probably wishful thinking.

The trail weaved in-and-out along the rugged coastline, high above the ocean. At one spot the coast jutted in towards the trail providing a spectacular overlook. Daniel left the trail and approached the edge, encouraging Kimbra to join him. He looked out over the precipice, waves crashed over rocks a hundred feet below. To the north, a creek spilled over the cliff. The sun was dipping into the roaring sea below, shades of crimson and scarlet splashed over wispy clouds.

Kimbra took a step back, thoughts of her pushing him over the edge flashed through her mind. He straightened up and looked her way as if he had read her mind. Was he thinking of doing the same to her?

"Beautiful, isn't it?" he commented.

"It's spectacular Daniel."

She began to feel dizzy. Fear took over with the realization that something had drawn her closer to the edge. She wanted to turn, but something forced her to stay put. Evil thoughts crept into her mind, more like whispers, telling her to jump. She wondered what it would be like to fly off over the cliff and escape to freedom. She turned her gaze to Daniel, he was admiring the sunset. She looked back over the cliff and took a step back.

"We should get going," Daniel said.

It was twilight and getting darker by the minute. They headed back, the coastal scrub vegetation slowly gave way to trees, the sound of a creek was heard to the north. The temperature had dropped significantly and Kimbra's sweat moistened shirt was now cold, sending a chill through her body. She was filled with apprehension, a premonition of impending doom. Something told her to trust her instincts this time. She had to escape.

"Daniel, I have to pee," she lied.

"It can wait! We're almost to the car."

"No. I have to go now," she cried out.

She stopped, dancing in place, waiting for his approval. He nodded and she hurried off for some privacy. Ducking behind a tree, she dropped her pants, squatted, and quickly ran through her options. She could stay with Daniel and take her chances, or she could run. Both prospects terrified her, but a voice in her head had her spooked, she was in danger and had to act now.

"Got a problem?" Daniel called out from the trail.

"No. Give me a minute."

Time was running out, she had to decide. Too nervous to urinate, she hiked up her pants and took off towards the creek. Daniel yelled out from the distance.

"Kimbra! What's taking you so long?"

The creek glittered in the last vestiges of twilight as Kimbra walked along the bank, following the creek downstream towards the ocean. Daniel's voice was getting louder and she picked up the pace. She stepped down into the creek bed as it dipped below the bank. The cold water soaked through her blue canvas sneakers, rocks and debris from tree limbs slowed her pace.

"Kimbra! C'mon, there's nowhere to go. We have to get back to the car," he yelled out.

A beam of light flashed in the distance. She hopped over a log, fell to the ground and twisted her ankle. She bit her lip as pain shot up her leg. Getting up slowly, she limped to the edge of a waterfall. She could see the sandy beach below, but a logjam of debris blocked her way.

"I'm not going to look for you all night," he yelled out.

Good, please go, she said to herself. The light was now moving her way, illuminating the creek and dancing along the bank. The sound of footsteps above moved closer, she hugged the side of the ravine in an attempt to blend in. She was trapped! If she climbed down the waterfall and slipped, he would hear her. If she stayed, he would find her. She inched her way along the steep wall of the ravine, hoping a bend in the bank would conceal her. Daniel's cellphone light lit up the logjam as it searched from left to right. With one hand, she held on tightly to a small root above. A small rock provided support for one foot, the other hand and foot searched for something to attach to, but found nothing. She was getting tired.

The light scanned both sides of the ravine and her foot slipped, sending a small avalanche of dirt and gravel cascading down the ravine. She quickly regained her footing and held her breath, listening for any movement, hoping the sound of the creek muffled her blunder. The beam of light danced about until it stopped on the spot she had been minutes before. A bead of cold sweat tickled her forehead, catching in her brow; she resisted an incredible urge to scratch it. The ray of light searched frantically as the creek babbled aimlessly.

Finally, mercifully, the light moved in the opposite direction, growing dimmer until it faded into the darkness.

Kimbra wiped her brow with a forearm and shimmied down from the bank. She sat on a log to examine her injuries. Her ankle was swollen and sore to the touch. One knee and elbow were scraped and bruised. She waited by the falls... ten, twenty, thirty minutes. Finally, she stood, put her weight on the foot, and gingerly took a few steps. Pain shot out from the upper ankle, but it was tolerable. She limped her way upstream only to find the ravine growing taller, until it resembled a small gorge. Turning back, she found an opening to climb onto the bank. She gimped to the trail and followed it back to the Coastal Highway, back where Daniel had parked the car. It was gone, but he could still be searching for her, so she stayed in the woods. Daniel would head south to go home, so she followed the highway north. The road wound over the same creek and a short distance later she spotted an opening in the woods. She walked down a winding private drive until she reached a secluded house lit up in the dark.

Her ankle was stiffening and she could barely walk by the time she reached the house and banged on the door. A dog barked and a window drape fluttered, revealing a crack large enough for a person to peer out.

"Please, help me! I was kidnapped and just escaped. Please call the police," she pleaded.

There was a clamoring inside. Muffled voices and the dog continuing to bark. Kimbra waited, blowing warm air into her hands. Finally, the door opened revealing a man with a golden retriever at his side. He spoke through the screen door.

"Do you want me to call the police?"

"Yes, please! I was taken hostage and I just escaped!"

"Margaret, call 911," he told a woman lurking in the background.

The woman placed a call and approached the door.

"George, let the poor girl in! Can't you see she's freezing?"

# CHAPTER 37

DETECTIVES RIZZO AND MACKENZIE QUESTIONED KIMBRA INTO THE NEXT MORNING. She was exhausted, both mentally and physically, but alive. Rizzo escorted her home and an arrest warrant was issued for Daniel Visser. All efforts were now focused on finding her captor. But before her escape, several key events led to breaking the case. The day before, Rizzo received a strange call from Kimbra's boss. That led to an interview at his Quantum Thunder office:

"Dr. Wu, you said you had information on the whereabouts of Ms. Evans on the phone. Can you elaborate on that?" Rizzo asked.

Fang swiveled his leather office chair and gazed out the window. Rizzo was about to repeat the question when Fang spoke.

"I know this will sound crazy, but I saw her and the man she is with, but I can't tell you where."

"Why is that?"

"I was there, but not like you think."

Rizzo thought he had heard it all over the years, but this investigation was one of the strangest. He was also losing his patience.

"What the hell does that mean?" he asked.

Fang swung around to face Rizzo.

"I saw the two of them, and they saw me."

"You mean in some kind of dream or hallucination?" Rizzo asked.

"No, I was there, just as clear as I am here with you now. I could smell the burnt pine, feel the ground under my feet. I was there, and then I wasn't. I can't fully explain it, but I was there!"

Rizzo examined Fang closely. He did not appear to be insane. He owned a large company raking in large sums of money doing government work. Surely, they would know if he was mentally unstable.

"But that's not possible," Rizzo countered.

"That's what I used to think."

Rizzo paused to reflect. Fang was serious, he actually believed he was there. Was he on drugs? What the hell were they doing at Quantum Thunder?

"Does this have anything to do with your work?" Rizzo asked.

Fang crossed his arms and leaned back in his chair. "Yes."

"Look, I know your work is confidential, but surely you can give me some idea of what you're doing."

"It has to do with paranormal research."

"Paranormal research," Rizzo repeated, half believing what he just heard. "You must have some explanation for what happened?"

"Are you familiar with Einstein's theory of spacetime?" Fang replied with a question.

"Not really."

"Well, the passage of time is really a construct of our mind. Time doesn't actually flow, it just is. According to Einstein, time and space exist together as four dimensions. If we think of time that way, then the past and future coexist out there somewhere. I think that's what I experienced. I believe I traveled in time to another location."

Rizzo wasn't buying it, something was fishy. He wanted to get to the bottom of the wild story, and suspected there was something Fang was not telling him.

"Okay, let's say I believe your story. Where is this cabin and when did you see them?"

"I said earlier, I can't tell you where, and I don't really know when this occurred."

"But you were there, you said you were there. You just popped into thin air?"

"Yes."

"And why the cabin?"

"I'm sorry, I don't understand the question," Fang said.

"What made you pop up at the cabin? Why not someplace else, London or Paris?"

Fang seemed anxious. He took a moment to consider the question.

"I don't know. I guess I was thinking about Kimbra..."

"You were thinking about her?"

Fang nodded.

"Dr. Wu, I need to know more about your research."

"I'm sorry, I can't tell you any more than what I have already told you. I've already told you too much."

"Look, Ms. Evans may be in grave danger. This will all come out at some point. I can get a court order, but it may be too late for her. I'm sure you don't want that on your conscience."

"I want to help, but I don't know the man or where she is being held. I *can* tell you they were staying at a cabin in the woods and there was a wildfire surrounding them. They were fleeing the wildfire. That should help you, shouldn't it?"

Rizzo felt his stomach growl, this wasn't getting him anywhere. The clock was ticking, he needed more information and he needed it quickly. He pulled out a photo and handed it to Fang.

"Is this the man?"

"Yes, that's him," Fang confirmed.

The picture he held was of Daniel Visser.

As nutty as the conversation was, it prompted Rizzo to dig deeper into the suspect's background. Given his mother's maiden name of Visser, Daniel never knew his father. His mother, Vivian Hoffmann, left when he was 7, whereabouts unknown, and Daniel was raised by his maternal grandparents, Sophie and Otto Visser. Rizzo checked the property records and as it turned out, Otto Visser owned a hunting cabin. With a little more digging he discovered the property was transferred to Daniel on his grandmother's death. They now had a location that fit Dr. Wu's description of a *cabin in the woods*. Later that night, while Rizzo was waiting for a warrant to search the cabin, he received a call that Kimbra had escaped. The missing person case just turned into a manhunt for the kidnapper.

All that, led Rizzo and McKenzie to a cabin located north-east of San Francisco. The wildfire was contained a safe distance away and had narrowly missed the Visser property. Rizzo and McKenzie pulled over behind two police cruisers. The smell of burnt wood lingered in the air as the men got out and donned their body armor and weapons. Serving arrest warrants was one of the most dangerous tasks for law enforcement and they came prepared. A small cabin with a covered porch stood in the distance. Rizzo and McKenzie followed the police as they approached the structure. Two officers stepped onto the porch while a third stood back with rifle poised. Rizzo and McKenzie took cover, knowing the suspect could be armed and dangerous.

One officer banged on the door, "This is the police! Open the door!"

When no one answered, a battering ram was retrieved. With one big swoop, two officers brought the full force of the heavy object into the door. The door caved in and the jamb splintered with a *crack*! The door was kicked in and three officers stormed into the cabin while Rizzo and McKenzie covered the outside.

After several stressful moments, one officer emerged giving the all clear signal. Rizzo and McKenzie entered the cabin. There were dishes in the sink, shoes and newspapers were strewn on the floor.

"Looks like they left in a hurry," Rizzo commented.

The bunkroom was in disarray with clothes strewn over the floor. Rizzo examined the room closely as he stretched on latex gloves to avoid contaminating the scene. There was no metal anchor attached to the bedpost as Kimbra had described, but on closer examination he saw screw holes where it would have been. He was visualizing a heavy chain secured to Kimbra's ankle when a blue powder on the floor caught his attention. Stooping down he extracted a blue toothbrush from under the bed and slipped it into a plastic bag.

"A hundred bucks says this has Ms. Evans' DNA on it," he said.

McKenzie nodded as he searched through the drawers.

Rizzo stood in place, attempting to visualize the room as Kimbra had described it. A smoky aroma masked a faint odor of urine, a plastic bucket with toilet seat was kicked over in the corner. It all fit with her description of her captivity. A shiny object caught his eye. He bent over and picked up an earring wedged between the floor and the baseboard.

"A breadcrumb she left for us," Rizzo commented as he bagged the tiny piece of evidence.

They searched the premises, inside and out, for about an hour. Kimbra mentioned the possibility of Daniel burying evidence, but the search warrant would not allow digging up the property. That would come later. They did not apprehend the suspect but they had the next best thing, they had evidence connecting Kimbra to the cabin. They would catch Visser soon enough. He could not hide forever.

Rizzo was driving home with McKenzie in the passenger seat when a call came in.

"That's great," McKenzie spoke into his phone.

He made a few more comments before closing the connection. Rizzo took his eyes off the road to glare at McKenzie.

"Well, what's the great news?"

"They just spotted Visser at his office. We've got a team keeping him under surveillance. We'll get him tomorrow morning."

Under California law, unless specified, search warrants can only be served from 7 AM to 10 PM. The reason being to minimize danger to the public. That would give them time to organize and plan for the arrest.

"That's good news," Rizzo said. "Ms. Evans will be happy to hear that."

# CHAPTER 38

KIMBRA WOKE BEFORE DAWN, TERRIFIED. After her interview with the police, Rizzo drove her home. He promised to have an officer keep an eye on her apartment, but that did little to comfort her nerves. First thing she did when she got home was call her sister. She kept the call short, saying she was physically spent and promised to call again later. Then she downed three ibuprofen and climbed into bed, her Sig Sauer P365 pistol lay within easy reach on the nightstand. Daniel had recommended the handgun and helped her buy it. Purchased for protection from an unknown stalker, it sat there lifeless, but ready to use against the very person that trained her to use it. The irony had not escaped her. Her body was exhausted, yet sleep did not come easy that night. She tossed and turned, waking to every little sound. But fatigue eventually set in as it always does, and with it came sleep.

Kimbra was surprised to see the clock displaying 6:32 in red block numerals. She had slept two hours. The sky remained dark and a late fall chill filled her room as she slipped on a bathrobe and stepped into soft slippers. Smokey remained cuddled up on the bed as she picked up the gun and surveyed the bedroom. Rizzo searched her apartment the night before for any signs of an intruder or surveillance devices, but that did little to calm an overactive imagination. Her apartment no longer felt safe, there were eyes watching. Fearful of leaving the bedroom, she paced about like a caged animal. It mattered not whether her suspicions were actual or perceived, the anxiety was real.

But nature is a powerful force and it called to her, momentarily diverting her fear. She relieved herself in the bathroom and shuffled to the kitchen to brew the coffee.

Like an imaginary friend, the pistol followed her from room to room. It sat on the kitchen table, staring at her as she drank hot coffee. Shaking with fear from her four-day ordeal, she wondered how it came to this. All she wanted was to be left alone, but shit kept happening, the way it had her whole life. The one person in the world she trusted, turned out to be a stalker, imagine that! She felt betrayed and isolated, adrift in a sea of calamity, like a castaway stranded on a deserted, remote island. Daniel was the one person she would lean on in times like this. How could she have been such a lousy judge of character? She could not rest until he was captured. She sat watching the clock, waiting for Rizzo to call. Time crept along at a snail's pace, the call never came.

Her stomach growled as her foot nervously tapped an unfamiliar beat. She had to do something. She could call Gina, but she would probably be busy at work. Tammy would be at work as well. Work! That jolted her from her funk. She had lost track of what day it was. It was Thursday and she would normally be at work. Her mind went immediately to the appearance of Fang at the cabin. She had to find out more. She picked up her phone and the secretary put her right through.

"Dr. Wu, I'm back! Are you aware of what happened?"

"Kimbra, where are you?"

"I escaped last night! Rizzo drove me home early this morning. They're looking for my abductor, but until they catch him, I can't feel safe. That's what I'm calling about. I... I have to do something. I'm just sitting here scared to death!"

Kimbra could feel her chest tightening as she spoke. The words hung in her throat.

"Kimbra, take a breath, slow down. Are you in danger?"

She inhaled slowly, then tried to speak slowly.

"Rizzo said there would be an officer watching my apartment, but I don't feel safe."

There was a pause on the other end of the connection.

"Fang, are you there?"

Fang cleared his throat. "Yes, I'm just thinking. Do you think it would be safe for you to drive?"

"I think so, why?"

"I was thinking, you can stay at my house. No one would look for you there. I can get out of work early, or you can let yourself in."

Kimbra was weighing her options. Stay put, scared out of her wits, or drive to Fang's.

"That would be so nice of you but I hate to impose," she said.

"Nonsense, it's the least I can do. Let me touch base with Detective Rizzo. I'll let him know what we're planning and get back to you."

Kimbra felt a measure of relief at the prospect of leaving her apartment. On one hand she was afraid to leave, on the other, she was trapped in an apartment where she had been under the constant watch of hidden cameras. She wondered if it would ever be the same again. She thanked Fang and hung up.

The sun was licking the treetops as Kimbra turned off the winding road and down the driveway. She pulled onto an expensive block paved parking area overlooking Fang's mountain-top retreat. A silver Ferrari sat outside the closed garage. Her red Subaru seemed oddly out of place next to the super expensive sports car. She gathered her belongings: a night bag, and her purse, now heavier than usual with the handgun. What good was it, if not readily available? That's what Daniel had told her, and he was right about that.

A cool breeze and an uneasy feeling met her as she stepped out of the car. She wondered what set her down this dreadful path. Was it taking the job at Quantum Leap, the QR-7 injections, or some other event out of her control? None of that mattered now, people were dead and she had to find answers. She took several steps down and continued along a walkway suspended high above the mountainside, the view was a bit disorienting. The main entrance was tucked into a cranny, sheltered under the roof overhang. The door was plain and modern with no fancy bell, just a simple buzzer which she pressed.

Dressed in a satin smoking jacket and trousers, Fang greeted her with a warm welcome. She was led through the kitchen and into the living area. The interior of the multi-million dollar home was incredible. Full length windows from floor to ceiling covered nearly every inch of wall space, affording an amazing view of the crystal blue sky and pine covered mountains. The back of the house faced west and jutted out over the mountain, an adjoining deck floated over the cliff below. The decor was ultra modern and cool, which suited the rich bachelor's lifestyle. A long marble covered island with padded bar stools separated the kitchen area from the rest of the room. Modern light fixtures and an impressive entertainment center alongside a floor-to-ceiling brick fireplace accented the open space.

"Your home is amazing," Kimbra complimented him.

"Thanks, why don't you have a seat?" Fang offered. "I can show you around later."

Kimbra made herself comfortable on a large wrap-around sofa. The covering was leather, the color a cool white.

"Can I get you a drink? After all you've been through, I'll bet you could use one. Whatever you want."

Kimbra began to get up but Fang insisted she remain seated.

"Sure, that sounds nice. How about a... Moscow mule?"

"Sure, I can do that."

Three simple and modern coffee tables filled the space between them. A collection of magazines were neatly fanned out on the one. The maid must have been by recently, Kimbra thought, that or Fang was a neat freak. Fang handed Kimbra the cool cocktail, garnished with a mint leaf. He sat on the other section of the sofa.

"How about a little music, something mellow and relaxing?"

"Sure, that would be nice," Kimbra agreed.

Fang used a remote device to turn on the system. Soft, jazzy music filled the air from hidden speakers.

"You sounded pretty worried this morning. Are you feeling any better?" Fang asked.

Kimbra gazed out the bank of windows to the west. The sky was now an intoxicating palette of magenta, indigo, and violet. It was a little awkward being at her boss' home, but she had a mission. There was one question she was obsessed with, and she came right out with it.

"I am, thank you. Fang, I have to ask you about the cabin where I was being held."

Fang held up his hand, gesturing her to stop.

"I know. Can that wait a few moments? I promise to tell you everything I know then."

Kimbra held her tongue, and they sipped their drinks quietly, listening to music.

"You must be hungry," Fang said. "Do you like lemon butter chicken with feta and rice?"

Fang cooked over a gas range mounted in the countertop while Kimbra sat on a nearby barstool. The alcohol left Kimbra with a pleasant buzz and the meal was delicious. After dinner, she helped clean up before they retired back to the living room. Twilight was the only light from outside when Kimbra brought it up again.

"I saw you at the cabin."

Fang got up and pulled two glasses from the kitchen cabinet.

"Before we discuss that I need a nightcap. How about a nice cognac?"

"Sure, just a little for me though."

Fang returned with two tumblers and sat next to her, their bodies almost touching. It was a little uncomfortable, but what could she say? He was her boss and he was gracious enough to let her stay there. He swirled his cognac, taking in the aroma before taking a sip.

"Yes, I was there. I discussed it with Dr. Stanwix and we have a few theories."

Kimbra straightened up, "I'm all ears."

"We have proven the existence of telepathic signals and we know that the drug increases neural count, but there is so much more to it than that. We are tapping into consciousness and our perception of time."

"What does that mean?" she asked.

"There are several theories out there, one of which deals with information stored in the vastness of space as electro-magnetic waves and virtual particles. That information may dictate our very reality. I believe the drug is opening our minds to a quantum information field."

"You mean, a database of reality, storing everything we experience?"

"Yes. The essence of a human life. The hopes, dreams, and aspirations of every living being across all of time."

Kimbra shook her head, "But that's not possible?"

"Why not?" Fang countered. "People believe in heaven and an afterlife with absolutely no scientific proof. We now have knowledge of a mechanism that could explain so many things."

Kimbra wasn't convinced of any of his quantum information theories, but she desperately wanted an explanation for what she saw.

"Even if what you say is true, you somehow altered reality. You transported your body to another location!"

"I believe the pathways quantum information takes is a two-way highway, and QR-7 has allowed me to alter it."

Fang went on to explain in great detail how that would work, most of it was over Kimbra's head. He was so wrapped up in the science, she wasn't sure he completely understood the full implications of what he did. Transporting your body across time and space would be the discovery of the century. If this fell into the wrong hands, it would be catastrophic.

"Can you control it? How is it that you suddenly appeared at the cabin?"

Fang took another sip of his cognac.

"I don't really know. I was meditating in an attempt to test my paranormal capabilities. I was thinking about you, perhaps that was the connection."

"Are you still taking the drug?" she asked.

"No, I stopped."

Kimbra took a sip of her drink, which warmed her body. Fang's eyes were locked on her. She wasn't sure it was the alcohol, but her head was spinning. Fang leaned in closer, ever so slowly, and before she knew it, he kissed her. It was over as quickly as it started, as if nothing happened. Pressing a finger to her lips, a salty taste from Fang lingered. What the hell just happened? Kimbra scrunched her eyes tightly and opened them to clear her head. Fang was now on the other section of the sofa! He could not have moved that quickly.

"Is something wrong?" he asked.

"I'm not sure... but I'm feeling woozy. Do you mind if I call it a night?"

"Of course not. I'm sure it's been a rough week for you. There's a guest bedroom downstairs. Grab your things and I'll show you."

Kimbra could not stop thinking about the kiss as she followed Fang down the stairs. The home was built into the mountainside with the back of the structure overlooking the valley below. She took a quick peek at the master bedroom. There were floor to ceiling windows giving it a spacious, open feel. A sliding door walked out onto a patio with a hot tub and a spectacular view of the mountains.

"Your room is towards the front of the house," Fang said.

The guest room was built into the mountain with two small windows, affording it a view with a sunken perspective and a cozy feel. Kimbra set her overnight bag and purse on the bed.

"There is a set of fresh pajamas in the top drawer. Please make yourself comfortable," Fang offered.

Kimbra opened the drawer and examined a beautiful silk pajama set.

"You have woman's pajamas in your guest room?"

"I like to have proper attire available for all my guests, men and women," he explained.

Fang had a reputation of being a ladies' man and this was proof in Kimbra's mind. But she never heard any rumors of sexual harassment at work or elsewhere. Was the drug changing him and what just happened in the living room?

"Thank you, but I brought a comfortable set from home," she said.

Kimbra said good night and got ready for bed. When she finished washing up, she took the gun out of her purse and set it on the nightstand. She turned out the light and lay on her back with arms crossed over her chest. Her head was spinning and the thought of Fang kissing her was creeping her out. She wondered if it had really happened, it now seemed so vague, like a dream. Maybe it was a vision she dreamed up, maybe he had gotten inside her head. She looked at the gun, sparkling from a night light in the bathroom, took several deep breaths and tried to fall asleep. But it was hopeless, she tossed and turned in the bed.

Kimbra's eyes fluttered open, her head was groggy. Something was wrong. As her eyes slowly adjusted to the dark, she noticed a shadowy figure in the hallway float past her door. Wait, she was certain she had closed the door. Was this a dream? She forced her eyes open wide, for if she blinked, she might miss something. Then it appeared again, this time stopping in the doorway, staring in her direction. Her chest tightened as it approached, floating, not walking, to the foot of her bed. Her body remained rigid, like a deer frozen in headlights. Could the figure sense she was awake? Could it see her open eyes? Could she reach for the gun on the nightstand in time? Should she? Her eyes darted to the gun for a brief moment, it was reassuring to know it was still there. When her eyes returned to the anomaly, it was gone.

Kimbra jerked up in bed, heart pounding, breathing heavy. Beads of perspiration formed on her forehead as she frantically looked around the room. The bedroom door was now closed. Was it always closed, had she imagined the whole thing? Was it another vision or a dream? The clock on the nightstand clicked off another minute, now displaying 3:23 AM. Kimbra reached for the pistol and held it tightly against her chest as she tried to make some sense of the nighttime aberration. Her knowledge of Fang's teleporting to the cabin could be dangerous. Would he or someone else try to kill her to hide the revelation? With so much at stake, it was certainly a possibility. She took a deep breath and waited for the break of dawn.

# CHAPTER 39

KIMBRA WOKE IN A PANIC REMEMBERING THE NIGHT BEFORE: the shadowy figure, the gun resting on her chest. Her hands were now empty. Sunlight filtered in through the narrow windows as her eyes searched for the late-night intruder. The room was empty and the handgun back on the nightstand. She did not remember putting it there and shivered at the thought of someone taking it from her hands in the middle of the night. Was it all a nightmare or a vision, and what did it mean? She sat up, trying to make some sense of the bizarre happenings she was experiencing. The aroma of fresh brewed coffee caught her attention. She washed up, grabbed a silk robe from the closet, and stowed the gun in her purse before leaving the guest room.

Fang was seated at the counter and got up.

"Let me get you a coffee," he offered.

Kimbra was struck by the beautiful view. Fang slid a mug of coffee on the counter and she sat beside it.

"How did you sleep?" he asked.

The strange figure in the night flashed into Kimbra's mind. She tried to force it out while attempting to answer a simple question.

"I tossed and turned a bit," she said.

Fang whipped up a gourmet breakfast of pancakes, covered with orange peels and fresh cranberries. He ate quickly, explaining he had to leave for the office.

"You're welcome to stay as long as you like," he offered.

Kimbra thanked him, knowing full well she could not stay another night. Between the bedroom stalker and the kiss, it would not be a wise move. She was uncomfortable staying there, but also terrified to return to her apartment with Daniel still on the loose. She tabled the decision, refilled her mug with hot coffee and stepped out onto the outdoor deck. The sun was fresh and the air crisp as she looked out over the mountains. Something strange was happening here, something strange was happening with Fang. She tried her enhanced paranormal senses to get a clue into his state of mind, but got nothing. She was lost in thought when a familiar sound startled her. Fang stepped out onto the deck.

"You have a call," he said holding her ringing phone.

Kimbra answered the call.

"Miss Evans?"

"Yes."

"This is Detective Rizzo. I wanted to let you know we arrested Daniel Visser."

Kimbra was speechless. The trauma she endured washed over her in a flood of emotions: the cabin, the chain, the humiliation, the absolute fear. She flashed back to digging the hole. Beads of sweat dripping down her forehead as Daniel told her to keep digging. Her sweaty hands working the shovel, the moist, cool dirt in her grave.

"Ms. Evans, are you there?"

She caught herself hyperventilating, took a deep breath, and tried to calm herself. The nightmare faded and she was back on Fang's deck.

"Kimbra, are you all right?"

It took a moment, but she regained her composure.

"Yes, yes I'm fine... That's great news."

"It is. But I don't want you to get any unrealistic expectations. This isn't over. We'll hold him as long as we can, but if the judge sets bail, there's a good chance he could be released in the next twenty-four to forty-eight hours."

Kimbra felt her chest tighten.

"There will be a trial, but the wheels of justice move slowly," Rizzo explained.

Kimbra thanked Rizzo and wandered back inside.

"What was that?" Fang asked, sensing her anxiety.

"They arrested Daniel."

"That's great, right?"

Kimbra's mind was off somewhere else.

"What's wrong?" he asked.

"Fang, I need to get away for a while. Would it be all right if a take a week or more vacation?"

"Sure. Take as long as you need."


Daniel Visser agreed to talk, but on the condition his attorney be present. The kidnapping occurred in San José, and was under Detective McKenzie's jurisdiction, but with Rizzo so closely involved, they conducted the questioning together. The two detectives entered the interrogation room. Kenton Walsh was a young, slick looking attorney associated with a small, obscure law firm. After the formal introductions he spoke.

"My client is willing to cooperate and maintains his innocence."

"We have a witness who claims otherwise," McKenzie began. "She claims she was kidnapped and held against her will for four days."

"Mr. Visser has no knowledge of that. As you are aware, the two have a romantic relationship. The time they spent together in question was as two consenting adults."

"Can you explain in detail what happened on the night of Saturday, October 28th?" Mckenzie asked.

Daniel responded. He was calm and collected, too cool for Rizzo's liking.

"That's the night we had dinner at the Downtown Grill. Not much to tell. We had a nice meal and then left to spend a few days at my cabin."

"We have witnesses claiming Ms. Evans was drunk or drugged."

"She wasn't feeling well, or maybe she drank too much," Daniel explained.

"You didn't drug her?" Rizzo asked.

Walsh grabbed his client's arm, shook his head and whispered, "You don't have to answer that. You're not on trial here."

"That's all right, I'll answer that," Daniel replied before facing Rizzo. "No, I did not."

Rizzo studied the case file in front of him.

"What about the phone call she made to her sister?"

"We are not aware of any phone call. What did she say?" Walsh asked.

"That information will be disclosed after the DA has reviewed it, along with all the other evidence."

The fact that Kimbra was unable to reach her sister or that a text was sent was not mentioned. Walsh once again shook his head, advising his client not to answer the question. Once again, Daniel ignored the advice.

"Look, I don't know what she told her sister or you, but it doesn't matter. Kimbra was not feeling well and mentioned that she was having delusions. She was always a bit unstable mentally. Did you know she was taking experimental drugs at work? I wouldn't take anything she says seriously."

With that Walsh gripped his client by the shoulder and announced the meeting was over. Walsh left and Daniel was returned to lockup.

"What do you think?" McKenzie asked.

"Pretty smug son of a bitch," Rizzo said.

"I got that. Could be pretty smart as well."

"Yeah, he's a real smart ass. Hopefully smart enough to hang himself."

# CHAPTER 40

KIMBRA STEPPED OFF THE PLANE and into the busy terminal hoping the change in scenery would help. She thought of the Jimmy Buffett song, *Changes in Latitudes, Changes in Attitudes*, which made complete sense to her. Denver wasn't exactly an island getaway, but it sure couldn't hurt. With luggage in tow, she dodged several people and worked her way to the side to place a call.

"Hi Gina, we just landed."

"I'm heading to the arrival area now."

Kimbra negotiated her way through the crowds in the massive terminal. The unique tent-like roof looked like of a series of teepees. From the outside they resembled the Rocky Mountains, which inspired the design. She followed the signs, passed the baggage claim area and proceeded straight to the exit.

A sharp breeze slapped her in the face as she exited the terminal. She breathed in the thin mountain air, along with a hint of jet fuel. A black Jeep pulled up to the curb just ahead of a few parked cars. Gina got out and greeted her with a warm hug.

"You're looking good, Sis."

"You too! The mountain air must be good for you."

Kimbra stowed her luggage in back and off they went, wind whipping through the open top. No sooner did they get on the main highway than Gina pulled a joint from her pocket.

"It's gonna be a half hour drive or more, depending on traffic. Interested in lighting up?"

Kimbra examined the tightly packed joint, recalling the many times they smoked pot together as teens. It was a welcome escape from whatever hell was going on in their lives at the time.

"Sure. Why not?"

Kimbra took the lighter from her sister, ducked down to get away from the wind and lit up. She took a toke and exhaled a cloud of smoke which lingered a moment before the wind took it away.

"How about some music?" Gina asked.

"Sure."

Rock tunes from their past filled the air with bands like REM and Radiohead. The scenic ride took them east, past the Rocky Mountain Arsenal National Wildlife Refuge before crossing a river and reaching the more populated community of Welby. There were patches of snow on the ground and before she knew it, they were pulling into a driveway alongside a modest ranch house with a brick facade and small covered porch.

"Well, here we are," Gina announced as they exited the Jeep.

Gina opened the front door and they were immediately greeted by a large Golden Retriever with tail wagging.

"That's Cooper. He loves people," Gina said as the dog sniffed the stranger. "It's not much but we call it home."

"I like it," Kimbra said. "A lot more room then the apartment you were in before."

"Greg, we're here!" Gina called out.

A tall, boyish looking man with sandy colored hair and unshaven face greeted Kimbra with a hug. Kimbra was given a quick tour of the three-bedroom house before they settled in the living area. They listened to music, drank wine, and talked. Kimbra avoided any discussion of home and kept the conversation light. Between the pot, wine, and change in location, she was the most relaxed she had been in months, possibly years.

The hands on the clock leapt forward and Greg was busy grilling burgers. Kimbra watched Gina make the salad and by the time dinner was ready, she was ravenous. She had momentarily left her troubles behind when Gina asked about the kidnapping.

"Do you remember Daniel from high school?" Kimbra asked.

"No, not really."

"Well, we had been dating for some time. Everything was going well, with our relationship I mean. Anyway, I found out later that his girlfriend in high school went missing and was never found. He was questioned but never charged. I asked him about it, and I guess he panicked. Maybe he thought I knew more than I did."

"What did you know?" Gina asked.

"Not much really. But that was enough to set him off."

Kimbra explained the gory details while they listened in shock.

"But why? Why would he do such a thing?"

Kimbra was not ready to reveal Christina's death, the visions, or the experimental drug she took. She wasn't sure she had been making the best decisions lately, and was not proud of that.

"I guess, he must have thought I would go to the police."

It felt good to have someone to confide in, even if she wasn't telling her sister everything. Gina took a moment to process it all.

"Well, you're away from it all now. Plenty of time to sort things out. Will you be comfortable going back to your apartment?"

"I don't know. Daniel could be released on bail."

"Well, it was nice of your boss to let you stay at his place. How long could you stay there?"

"I'm not sure that's a good option."

Kimbra did not tell Gina about what happened there. She wasn't sure anyone would believe her, but Gina sensed something was wrong. It was difficult hiding things from her sister.

"Why not? What's wrong?" Gina asked.

"It's hard to explain. I had a creepy feeling about my boss. It felt like he was watching me in my sleep. I slept with a gun at my side all night."

"A gun!"

"I guess I didn't mention that. Yeah, I got a gun. Daniel helped me get it."

"What! Well, that is scary, I mean your boss *and* Daniel."

"He's been taking an experimental drug, for a research project, and I think it's changing him."

"Who?"

"My boss."

"Changing him? How?" Gina was confused. Kimbra's life had that effect on people.

"I really can't say too much about the program and I can't be certain."

"Kimbra, this sounds suspicious on so many levels. And a gun, do you feel safer with the gun?"

"I do."

"That's good, I guess. You didn't bring it with you did you?"

"Oh, God no. I left it home."

Kimbra didn't think Gina and Greg were comfortable with guns, besides she didn't know how to transport it out of state.

"Well, we'll figure something out," Gina offered.

It was getting late and Greg wandered off to bed, leaving the sisters to reminisce. There were plenty of bad memories, but it's funny how time has a way of softening the edges. They had a tough childhood and leaned on each other heavily, with Kimbra doing most of the leaning. It was comforting knowing her big sister was always there for her, that is until Gina graduated and left home. Gina got up to pour another glass of wine for the two of them.

"I don't know, it's getting late," Kimbra said.

"Nonsense, I don't have to work tomorrow and I'm taking off Monday and Tuesday. We still need to discuss what we're going to do."

Gina set down the drinks, settled back into the sofa and waited for a response.

"There is one thing I would like to do while I'm here," Kimbra offered.

"Oh yeah, what's that?"

"Do you remember Jake Campbell from high school?"

"Of course. What about him?"

"I met him back home a few weeks back and he lives near you. I'd like to look him up."

"So... is he married? Does he have a steady girlfriend?" Gina's voice rose several octaves.

"No, he's not married, and it's nothing like that. We're just friends."

"I wouldn't be so sure about that," Gina said with a grin. "You two were pretty serious in high school."

Kimbra had no idea where a meeting with Jake would lead. Thinking back to her senior year, she thought they had something special, but like everything else in her life, it fell apart.

After her breakup with Mick, Kimbra shut down. She had alienated her best friend, Marie, and had no one to turn to. Mick tried to get back together, but she refused. That wasn't easy, given her low self-esteem. She isolated herself from everyone around her. Her home life sucked: Gina had left, Cody was a sexual predator, and her mom, she just didn't care. Devastated and in such a bad place, she contemplated ending it all. She was consumed with thoughts of suicide: pills, asphyxiation, slitting her wrists. Her life was hopeless.

Then, out of the blue, someone showed an interest. A boy in her science class asked her to the senior prom. It came as a complete shock and it rocked her world. Unfortunately, she was so buried in depression she made up an excuse, a lame excuse, to let him down easy. Unfamiliar with boys showing an interest, she came up with the first thing that came to mind. She couldn't even look him in the eye.

"I'm sorry, I can't. My mom is ill. I can't leave her alone at night."

She could feel Jake's eyes seeing right through her. When he didn't leave, she glanced up quickly. He was tall and lanky, his voice was deep.

"I'm sorry about your break-up with Mick. Look, I understand if my timing is all messed up. If it's too much right now, I get it. You don't have to decide right now. Just do me a favor and think about it. No rush. Can you do that for me?"

It was hard to say no to those soft brown eyes.

"Sure, but it won't change," Kimbra mumbled.

"That's all right, take your time. Hey, it doesn't have to be prom. If you want to hang after school or something, I would like that."

"Sure, maybe some other time," Kimbra said to end the conversation.

Jake stood there until Kimbra looked up again, which she did. His smile was disarming, causing the corners of her mouth to lift.

"That's great. I'll see you around, Kimbra."

Over the next few weeks she would see Jake frequently, waiting for her at her locker. They would get together after class, chat about school, their likes and dislikes, life as they perceived it at the time. In time, the clouds of depression gradually faded. Kimbra opened up and she eventually went to the prom with Jake. They had three beautiful months together. That's when it fell apart. Jake was accepted to Colorado State University and apparently the prospect of a long-term relationship frightened him. They agreed to keep in touch, but Kimbra suspected it would not last, and it didn't. Once again, she was devastated.

# CHAPTER 41

TWO MEN IN BLACK SKI MASKS APPROACHED THE BACK OF A BUILDING. Both were dressed in black, one was tall and lean, the other was of average height and muscular. The time was 3 AM, a cool breeze whistled through the deserted parking lot. A new moon washed away any hint of a shadow, rendering the whole scene akin to a grainy black and white photo. The modern two-story structure had no formal loading dock and deliveries arrived through a garage door. Alongside that, was a metal door. The men approached the door and waited. One man checked his watch several times and shortly later, a light broke the darkness as the door opened.

"You're late!" one of the masked men said.

"Sorry, couldn't be helped. You've got ten minutes," a security guard from inside reported.

The masked men pulled out handguns with silencers attached to the barrels and brushed past the guard. They passed a row of empty offices and used a key card to activate the elevator to the basement. The elevator doors opened to a darkened foyer, dimly lit by security lights. Beams of white light and narrow red lasers shot out from their pistols. The tall man used the key card to open a door. They stepped into a huge rectangular room packed with lab equipment. To their left was a locked door with a window. The shorter man peered in to make sure it was void of any humans.

"Check it out," the taller man ordered.

The shorter man looked back, hesitating before unlocking the door. He moved in cautiously, lighting up animals in cages with his night light. The sight of so many lab animals gave him an uneasy feeling. The animals protested wildly at his presence, jumping about in their cages. He quickly inspected the area and left.

"All clear," he announced as he exited the bedlam, shutting the door behind him.

The taller man was on the other side of the room extracting something from a refrigerator.

"Hurry up. We just hit pay dirt."

The shorter man rushed over, removing his backpack and pulling out a long, cylindrical metal container. Three vials of greenish colored liquid were carefully placed in the chrome container.

"Let's get out of here," the taller one ordered.

They back-tracked to the elevator, past the empty offices and finally to the loading area where they had entered. They slipped out the back and disappeared into the darkness.

The break-in at Quantum Thunder was reported to the authorities as required under the government contract. The news shot up the chain of command to the highest levels and a meeting was set up in the Board Room. Special Agent Baker Manning, from the US Army Criminal Investigation Division (CID), was assigned to investigate the robbery. Physically fit and in his early forties, his clean shaven face glowed an ebony brown, his kinky hair was dark as coal and trimmed short. Attending the meeting were: Dr. Fang Wu, the President and CEO; Dr. Stanwix, the lead molecular biologist; the chief security officer (CSO); and the chief technology officer (CTO). Following the introductions, Manning kicked off the meeting.

"I have received your reports and appreciate your cooperation. I'll be speaking to each of you individually as well as some your staff, but right now I'd like to get an update on our current status. Dr. Wu, can you get everyone up to speed on the internal investigation?"

"I'll let Tom speak to that," Fang deferred.

Tom Holland was their chief security officer and the man responsible for keeping the site secure. He swallowed a lump in his throat and began.

"Two men in ski masks were recorded in the back of the building. The door adjacent to the loading garage was opened from the inside. Normally that would trip an alarm, but an access card was used to open the door from the inside. The card belonged to an employee named Miles Jackson. He reported the card missing one day earlier and was issued a new one."

"Hold on," Baker interrupted. "How are missing cards handled?"

"Lost cards are deactivated and a new one is issued."

"So what happened? Whose card was used in the robbery?"

"It was the card Jackson reported lost."

"Why wasn't it deactivated?" Baker asked.

Holland shifted in his seat, clearly uncomfortable with the line of questioning.

"We're not sure. The security guard responsible for that said it *was* deactivated. Could be a computer glitch."

Manning's eyes narrowed, "A computer glitch?"

"Yes. It can happen," Holland reported, looking sheepish. "IT is looking into it."

"How many people have access to the security card system?" Manning asked.

"That would be most of the IT staff as well as a few key people on our security team."

"Well, someone used Jackson's card. I'll need a full list of all those individuals by the end of day."

Holland nodded.

"I also see in the reports that you are missing some valuable security camera footage. What happened there?"

Holland looked to the Chief Technology Officer, Darius Ming, for an answer. Ming cleared his throat and responded.

"We don't know. It may have been tampered with."

Manning's eyes could have burned a hole in the man's face.

"*May have been tampered with*? What does that mean?"

"We're looking into it. It may take a few days," Ming explained.

Baker looked around the room, opened the file in front of him, and scanned through the contents.

"Well, like I said I'm going to be talking with everyone. What about an IT intrusion? Was any data compromised?"

"We haven't detected a breach but it could take weeks to be sure," Ming said.

Manning had a pained look on his face as he continued through the reports. He spoke without looking up.

"It would be an understatement to say your security has been lacking, this appears to be negligent."

Manning let out a sigh.

"In light of the recent break in, the CIA will be monitoring all operations going forward. Your current civilian security staff will be replaced with our people. There will be additional upgrades coming as well."

Manning looked over the people seated at the table.

"I'd like to get started with the interviews immediately. Just one more question before we finish. Dr. Stanwix, you mentioned in your report three vials of the drug were stolen. What could someone do with that much QR-7?"

Stanwix pushed his glasses up his nose and spoke.

"The drug is highly concentrated, so three vials represents a large amount. They could administer the drug to a small army, enabling each member with enhanced telepathic abilities."

"What kind of telepathic abilities are we talking about? What should we be worried about, worst case scenario?"

Stanwix pondered the question before speaking.

"The full effects of the drug are not yet completely understood, but the potential ramifications are many. They could be empowered with the ability to connect telepathically with others, they could control minds, foresee future events. I'm not a military expert, but an army of soldiers with paranormal powers, would have a huge advantage over conventional soldiers."

# CHAPTER 42

THE WIND TOUSLED HER HAIR AS SHE BARRELLED NORTH ON INTERSTATE 25. Kimbra hoped the hour long drive would give her time to clear her head. She traveled a thousand miles to escape her troubles at home, only to find they followed her all the way to Denver. The morning after she arrived, Daniel posted bail and was out. At Gina's urging she called Jake, and he invited her to visit. So, here she was in Gina's Jeep, on her way to visit an old high school flame living in Fort Collins.

She checked the speedometer and eased her foot off the pedal. The Jeep slowed down and along with it her anxiety. She had mixed emotions about the trip. After her break up with Mick she was gun shy. But Jake persisted, and she fell for him big time. He broke up with her and it hurt. But that was a long time ago. People were not very nice in high school, each one trying to navigate relationships and figure out the opposite sex. Hell, she still hadn't figured that one out. They were different now. She had to let go of any remaining hard feelings she was harboring. They were just a couple of high school classmates catching up.

The black Jeep turned down a long dirt road and parked alongside a white two-story home with a one-story wing to the side. Enormous yellow oak trees hugged the house. A steel-blue pickup truck sat next to a large metal barn. Kimbra followed a block path and knocked on the front door. Jake appeared with a smile and dressed in his forester uniform, a tan shirt and olive pants. An official looking green badge with yellow letters was sewn on his left sleeve. It had a pine tree in the middle with the words *Forest Service* on  top and *Department of Agriculture* wrapped along the bottom.

"Kimbra, good to see you. Any problem finding the place?"

"No, not at all."

"Come in," Jake offered. "Sorry about the work clothes, I didn't have time to change."

Kimbra did not mind at all, there seemed to be something special about a man in uniform. The door opened to a large living area with off-white walls, the rustic hardwood floor had knots in it. Natural finished wooden beams accented the ceilings throughout the first floor. The living room had a masculine feel with a dark brown sectional sofa and a neutral color braided rug. The kitchen flooring matched the living area, the cabinets were white with butcher block countertops.

"The house was built in 1889 and had some major updates done," Jake explained.

"It's beautiful," Kimbra said.

"Let me show you the outside."

They stepped out back onto a cement patio, covered with a sloped roof. The view looked out over a fenced-in area with horses and a spectacular view of mountains in the distance.

"I inherited the horses with the property. The place was owned by several generations of farmers. I'd like to farm it someday, but I don't have the time now."

"The view is amazing!" Kimbra said.

"Yeah, I really like it. Have a seat. Can I get you something to drink?"

Kimbra sat at the patio table, and Jake returned with two glasses of wine.

"Remember the cheap wine we drank in high school?" Kimbra said.

"Oh yeah, I remember. A lot of beer and liquor as well. We were pretty crazy."

Kimbra nodded, remembering the good times. There were plenty of bad times as well, but time has a way of flattening out the highs and lows.

"You wanted to move to the Midwest and work outdoors," Kimbra said. "Did you always know what you wanted to do?"

"Pretty much."

"I wish I had a dream in high school, or now."

Jake seemed to pick up on the melancholy.

"You said you wanted to get out of the house and go to college. You did that."

"I did, but it didn't turn out quite like I thought," Kimbra said.

"Well, life rarely does."

She wondered how different her life would be if they had stayed together. Would she be living in Colorado? Would Marie still be alive? A stiff wind shook Kimbra from her day dream with a shiver.

"You look cold," Jake noticed. "Let's go inside, I'll get dinner started."

Kimbra sat at the kitchen table admiring Jake's simple life.

"You like stuffed peppers?" Jake asked.

"Sure."

"They're prepared. Sorry, I don't have time to cook much. I did pick up a loaf of Italian bread to go with it though."

"That's fine, it sounds delicious."

The dinner was actually quite good. After that, they kicked back in the living room.

"So how is your sister doing?" Jake asked.

"Gina is doing great."

There was an awkward silence for the first time.

"I'm really sorry about Marie," Jake said.

Kimbra nodded and took a sip of her drink.

A hush fell over the room like a dark cloud. Kimbra could not hold back her tears.

"What's wrong? Hey, I'm sorry I brought it up," Jake got up to hand her a tissue.

Kimbra let it all out as she dabbed at the tears.

"No, it's just that everything... has gone to shit. I can't take it anymore."

"What do you mean?"

She explained her ordeal: the days spent in captivity fearing for her life, the escape, Daniel's release from jail just forty-eight hours after his arrest, as well as the feeling that someone was stalking her. It was painful for Kimbra to retell the horror and it was a lot for Jake to process.

"Oh my god, I'm in shock! Why would he do such a thing. I mean, I remember him as strange dude, but wow. What the hell?"

It was brutal reliving the ordeal, especially after just retelling it to her sister and Greg. Jake sat down next to Kimbra and gave her a hug, it was warm and awkward. She accepted it for a moment, then reached for her drink. There was a long silence, neither one knowing what to say next.

"I'm sorry about the way we broke up in high school," Jake blurted out.

That came out of nowhere. Kimbra almost choked on her drink.

"No, I really mean it. I was young and afraid of a long distance relationship. I was afraid of you meeting someone else. I was afraid of being rejected."

That was a revelation to Kimbra. *She* was the one afraid of rejection, she always thought he just wanted to move on.

"I have to admit, I hated you for that," she said. "I was a very angry person and I projected it all onto you."

"That's all right. I deserved it."

Kimbra was relieved at sharing her feelings. Jake helped her get over an abusive relationship with Mick and she would forever be grateful for that. That made the breakup all the more difficult to get over, it crushed her. But, that was then. People change. Still, in many ways she felt like the same vulnerable person she was in high school. She hated herself for that.

"Did it work?" Jake interrupted her thoughts.

"Did what work?"

"Projecting it all onto me."

Kimbra could not hold back a smile, "I guess it did."

"Can I get you some more?" Jake held up his empty glass.

"Sure but just one more, I have an hour drive back to Gina's."

Kimbra watched as Jake left to refill their glasses.

"You always said you wanted a dog. How come you never got a dog?" she called out to the kitchen.

"You're right and I still do. I guess I just haven't found the time for a puppy. I should though."

The conversation grew more comfortable as the time flew by. In some ways it felt like their care-free days dating in high school. Long talks late into the night and the occasional sunrise. Before she knew it, it was 1 AM.

"Oh, my God, I completely lost track of time! Can I get some coffee?" Kimbra asked.

Jake examined her closely with those soft brown eyes.

"Kimbra, you can't drive home this late. Why don't you spend the night? There's a bed in the guest room."

Kimbra's head was spinning and she was tired. It would be so nice to sleep.

"Okay, but I have to get an early start tomorrow. Gina has all kinds of plans for the weekend."

Kimbra woke the next morning to the smell of coffee and a slight hangover. She wandered down the stairs to the kitchen. There was a pot of coffee, a mug, and a note on the counter.

Help yourself to coffee. I'm out back.

She poured filled herself a mug and met Jake behind the house. He was seated at the table with his legs propped up on a chair reading a book. He peered over reading glasses.

"I see you found the coffee."

"Thanks, it's so good."

A grin formed on his face. "How's your head?"

Kimbra sat across from him. "I've had worse."

"I really enjoyed last night," he admitted.

"Me, too."

They both sipped coffee in silence, taking in the fresh mountain air and scenery. Birds chirped away, a horse neighed. Jake was first to disturb the peaceful setting.

"I didn't want to bring it up last night, and forgive me if you don't want to talk about it, but..."

"But what?"

"This whole thing with Daniel. You mentioned you had your suspicions about him, but why did he kidnap you? And Mick's conviction, what did he have against Marie? It doesn't make sense."

"I think I'm connected to all of it in some way," she admitted.

"What do you mean?"

Kimbra set her coffee down, crossed her arms, and stared off into space. A chill ran over her body.

"I didn't tell you about work and what we're doing there, and if I do, you can't tell anyone."

Jake nodded. "I won't. What's going on there?"

"Were doing research into telepathy."

"You mean mind reading, sending messages to someone? But that's not possible, is it?"

"Apparently, it is. But there's more."

Jake sat up straight, his eyes widened with interest. Kimbra hesitated.

"What? You can tell me," he said.

"One of the clients we were working with was murdered. She had visions, some we believe were caused by a drug we are experimenting with."

Jake sat up quickly. "Whoa, Kimbra, that's crazy! Is this legal, what you are doing?"

"It's government sponsored. There are safety protocols in place, but I think it's getting out of control."

"What does that mean?"

"I took the drug."

"You what! Why would you do that?"

Kimbra was feeling faint, her heart beating rapidly. Had Jake lost all confidence in her, did he think she was crazy? She had to push on.

"Like I said, I'm connected to all this. To Marie, Christina, that's the client who was murdered, all of it!"

Kimbra had a hard time breathing, she was feeling nauseous.

"Calm down. Try and relax," Jake said in a slow and deliberate tone.

"I can't! I'm gonna be sick!" Kimbra began to get up.

Jake put a firm grip on her shoulder, guiding her gently back down.

"You're fine. You're having a panic attack. Just do as I say. Close your eyes and listen to my voice. You're going to be fine. Slow down, take a deep breath and hold it."

Kimbra followed his direction. Jake's voice echoed in her head from another place.

"That's it, slow and steady. You're doing great."

Kimbra's head began to clear, her stomach settled down. Beads of sweat dripped down her forehead.

"Let me get you a jacket," Jake offered.

"No. Let me finish," Kimbra let out a sigh and continued.

"I had a vision of Daniel's car in Christina's driveway. I know it was him that killed her."

"Is that why he kidnapped you?"

"I don't know how, but he knew that I knew. I asked about his girlfriend in high school. He must have panicked."

Jake took it all in, it was a lot.

"So what about Marie's murder. Why Mick?" he asked.

"I don't think Mick killed her."

# CHAPTER 43

SPECIAL AGENT BAKER MANNING EXAMINED THE CONTENTS OF A MANILA FOLDER. Across the table was Miles Jackson, a Biochemistry graduate who had been working at Quantum Thunder for several years. Manning raised his head to face the young man.

"Mr. Jackson, where were you on the night of the robbery at approximately 3 AM?"

"I was home, in bed."

"Do you live alone?"

"I share an apartment with a friend."

"Can he vouch for your presence there at or near 3 AM?"

"Yes."

"Did he see you at that time?"

Jackson squirmed in his seat. "Well not exactly, we were both asleep at that time."

"I see..."

Manning turned his attention back to the file, letting Jackson sweat it out. He would verify Jackson's statement with the housemate. Jackson was clearly rattled, which was not uncommon in these situations. Being questioned in a criminal investigation had that effect on most people, innocent or guilty.

"You think I was involved in the robbery?"

Manning ignored the question.

"Why? Is it because I'm black? You should know better," Jackson complained.

Manning put the file down.

"Why should I know better, is it because I'm a brother?" Manning asked.

Jackson nodded slightly, saying nothing.

"Race has nothing to do with this," Manning explained. "These are serious charges, theft of government property and violation of a government contract. You're facing a maximum of ten years in prison and a hefty fine. If you have any knowledge of, or involvement in the robbery you need to tell me now."

"No, I do not! My card was lost or stolen, and I reported it immediately."

Manning went back to studying the file.

"Who did you report the lost card to?"

"Alex Mishkin."

"Who provided you with your replacement card."

"That was Alex as well."

Manning closed the manila folder in front of him and looked Jackson directly in the eye. He would verify everything Jackson said, but he already had his prime suspect.

"That's all for now. You can go," Manning said.

The young man rose to leave.

"Oh, and by the way, don't leave town. I may have some more questions for you."

Alexander Mishkin had too many links to the crime to be a victim of circumstance. He was one of three security guards on patrol that night and the only one in the control room at the time of the robbery. He was also the one who provided Jackson with a replacement access card. He sat across the small table with a worried look on his face. A military police guard was stationed outside the door. Manning began the interrogation.

"Mr. Mishkin, do you know why you're here?"

"I'm being questioned regarding the robbery, like all the other employees."

"Not exactly."

Now that Manning had properly set the mood, he continued.

"I've read your statement and I would like a few things clarified. Where were you at 3 AM on the night of the robbery?"

"I was in the control room."

"You were alone?"

"Yes."

"What are your duties in the control room?"

"I man the phone, handle communications between the security guards, and monitor the surveillance cameras."

"Aren't there security cameras throughout the building, including the lab?"

"There are," Mishkin agreed.

"And what did you see?"

"I didn't notice anything unusual."

"But the robbers entered through the back door and the lab was robbed. How was it that you saw nothing?"

Mishkin's voice was shaky as he tried to explain.

"I'm not sure. The cameras could have been set on a loop... The other guards didn't notice anything either. Did you talk with them?"

It was a feeble attempt to deflect the blame onto others. Manning didn't buy it for a minute.

"I've already talked to them. The cameras were not set on a loop as you suggested, the footage is missing. It was deleted, and you have access to that system."

"So do some other security staff as well as the IT people," he countered.

"You created a new security access card for Miles Jackson," Manning stated.

Mishkin nodded.

"Did you deactivate the lost card?"

"I did," Mishkin said.

Manning fired off several quick questions aimed to intimidate and confuse the subject.

"Then how is it that card was used in the robbery? Isn't the system supposed to lock out access for that card? What happened?"

"I don't know."

"That's not going to cut it. Did you notice the MP stationed outside this office?"

Mishkin nodded as his face went pale.

"I'm going to charge you with theft of government property, punishable with up to ten years in prison! You could go a long way in helping yourself if you tell the truth, now. After today, I can't help you."

Mishkin ran his hands over his face and through his dark, wavy hair.

"I had no choice," he whispered.

"What did you say?"

Mishkin looked around the room before speaking in a hushed tone.

"My family is in danger. I can't help you."

Manning leaned back in his chair and laced his fingers together behind his head, his voice softened.

"You won't be able to help your family in prison. Look, we can protect them. But, you have to trust me. If you can't do that, we're done here."

Mishkin looked up, tears welling in his eyes. Manning was postured to move towards the door.

"How can you protect them?"

"I can have them put under twenty-four hour watch until we catch whoever is behind this. No one will know you told me anything."

Mishkin dragged a sleeve over his eyes.

"All right. I'll tell you what I know."

# CHAPTER 44

CHAD ADDISON WAS NEVER A BIG FOOTBALL FAN, yet there he was at the stadium. The noise from the crowd was annoying and with his enhanced senses it would have been unbearable, that is before he learned to control it. He was able to suppress the raucous fan noise as he entered the crowded stadium. He knew something was up for a while. Emma had been avoiding him. They had been seeing each other for three months and just recently she had become cold as ice. He suspected there was someone else, but he had to see for himself. There was a rumor that Emma would be at the game with a lacrosse player named Jeff, and he intended to settle the matter once and for all.

Chad pushed his way through the crowd and entered a walkway to the stadium seating. Players on the field were dressed in their brightly colored, blue and gold uniforms. The band was playing and the game had started but it was still the first quarter, plenty of time for Emma and her *friend* to be seated. He scanned the crowd, then closed his eyes and concentrated. It's not like he could read the thousands of people's minds attending the game, but he was hoping to hone in on Emma. They were close and shared a special connection, or so he thought. Someone bumped into Chad, breaking his concentration. He leaned against the wall alongside the stands and tried again.

The sun was warm, but the air had a bite to it. The crowd cheered at a big play. A blurry picture began to form in his mind as he sensed her presence, he could see what she saw, sense what she felt. She was seated mid-level, the scoreboard to her right.

"Wait, there could be a penalty," a male voice announced over the public address system.

A lump formed in Chad's throat as he searched for them, anticipating the worst. There, he spotted them! She was snuggled up tight next to a tall guy with blonde hair. The crowd cheered again and they hugged. Chad's fists clenched in rage. How could she be so cruel, so thoughtless? She could have told him, instead of ignoring him and sneaking around. His eyes teared up as he left the stadium.

Chad was not a big drinker, but that day was an exception. After a brief stop at the liquor store, he spent the afternoon drinking himself into a daze. The vodka and orange juice mix did the job, numbing his senses. The pain was still there, but it seemed to belong to another person. Still, Chad could not get the image of Emma at the game out of his mind. He rehashed the good times they had together, the sting of the realization that it was over hit him. Then came the anger, with an intensity he had never felt before. He directed the rage at the two of them, but mostly Emma. Chad didn't know Jeff, there was no bro code violated. But Emma, that was another story. He envisioned himself confronting her:

"I saw you at the game today," he said.
"Yeah, so?"
"Who were you with?"
"A friend, not that it's any of your business. Were you stalking me?"
She was so cavalier about it, and her expression set him off. He grabbed her throat and squeezed with all his might, wanting to wipe that ugly expression off her face.

His head was spinning, his stomach nauseous. Rushing to the bathroom, he vomited an orange concoction into the bowl. He continued to retch until there was nothing left in his stomach, his gut hurt all the way down to his groin. He staggered back to the living room and fell onto the couch. The world was spinning around him and he sat up quickly, feeling the urge to puke again. He fought off the urge and fell onto his side, curled up in a ball.

Chad woke up standing in a strange place. It was dark, but he slowly recognized the single bed with lavender comforter and fluffy pillows, the beat up white dresser. It was *not* his apartment, he was in Emma's bedroom, standing at the foot of her bed! She was sound asleep, the clock on her night stand displayed 3:23. How did he get there? Was it a dream? Last thing he remembered was resisting the urge to vomit and laying down on the couch at home. Emma looked so innocent laying there with her eyes closed, but he knew better. She was seeing someone else, after all they had together. He opened his heart to her and she crushed it. His head was pounding and he inadvertently raised his hands to his head. Emma noticed the movement and her eyes fluttered open. Chad remained motionless as a panicked expression swept over her face.

"Chad? What are you doing here?"

Chad was speechless, not having a clue what he was doing or how he got there.

"How did you get in?"

Emma sat up and turned on the lights, it was blinding at first. She stared at Chad, waiting for a response. Her soft features which once looked so beautiful, were now ugly as they hid her betrayal.

"I thought we were happy together," Chad said.

"What are you talking about?" Her tone was nasty and deceitful.

"Why didn't you tell me you were seeing someone else?"

There was surprise on her face, but no sorrow, no remorse. She got out of bed and approached Chad.

"You need to get out."

Chad stood there in shock. He was confused, did he do something wrong? He was the one that should be angry. Suddenly she shoved him.

"Get out now!" she shouted, pushing him again. "What the hell is wrong with you?"

Something inside snapped and he slapped her across the face. For a second she was stunned, then she punched him hard in the face. He punched back like a man possessed, someone or thing had taken over. He continued punching until he was standing over her on the floor. She screamed. He had to stop the screaming, it felt like a jackhammer taken to his skull.

Chad's hands wrapped around her throat. He squeezed harder. He was somehow enjoying it as her face turned blue, her once beautiful brown eyes bulged out grotesquely, like a fish out of water. A voice inside sounded an alert, something was wrong. He loosened his grip, realizing he may have killed her! That's not him, he was not a violent person. She drove him to this. What now? What should he do? He released his grip and her head dropped to the floor with a *thump*.

He stood over her, exhausted, staring at her limp body. He had loved Emma. What had he done? Suddenly she gasped for air and began coughing violently. He turned and ran.

# CHAPTER 45

THE FLIGHT HOME GAVE KIMBRA PLENTY OF TIME TO REFLECT. Friday night was spent with Gina and Greg, visiting the many local craft breweries along Denver's beer trail. Saturday, she visited the Downtown Aquarium and the Botanic Gardens with her sister. And then there was Jake. Dating him in high school stood out in a time of chaos and uncertainty. The short time spent with Jake was probably the happiest she had ever been. It was great reconnecting with him, though she was a little wistful, thinking of what could have been. They were young and knew so little of life, but they had something special. There's a lot to be said for those wild and innocent days. She wondered what it would be like now, if they stayed together. What if she had tried harder? Can you ever really recapture the glory days? Probably not she thought.

Kimbra opened the door to her apartment and was immediately struck with feelings of gloom. Her privacy was violated in that place, she would never be comfortable there again. Her spirits lifted though, when Smokey appeared to greet her. She picked up the cuddly cat and scratched his ears, he purred in approval. Tammy had taken good care of him, his bowls were full and the litter box clean.

She set Smokey down on her bed and opened the drawer to the nightstand. She breathed a sigh of relief at seeing the safety box. She set the heavy box on the bed and entered the security code. The top sprung open to reveal the semi-automatic 9mm pistol. She cradled the weapon, trying to bring back her motor memory from the firing range. That brought on vivid imagery of Daniel teaching her to shoot, and that brought back memories of the cabin. Her heart raced and her head pounded. She took several deep breaths until the anxiety passed. She ejected the magazine from the pistol, verified it was loaded, and reinserted it with a *snap*. With gun in hand, the entire apartment was carefully examined for any sign of listening devices or cameras. She found none.

Once settled in and feeling reasonably secure, she called Gina.

"Hi Sis. Just calling to let you know I arrived home safely."

"Thanks for letting me know. Is everything all right, I mean being back home?"

"It's a little spooky, but I'm fine. Hey, thanks for everything, I had an amazing time in Denver."

"Well, you have to come back soon."

Kimbra ended the call, feeling sad and alone. She missed Marie. She spent the evening curled up with a book and Smokey at her side. The gun on the nightstand stared back, it would be her constant companion. Thoughts of the stalker at her bedside in Fang's house frightened her and she considered stowing the pistol under the pillow. That's what they did in the movies didn't they? Still, she worried about an accident, didn't most accidents happen in the home? She slept restlessly and would often put her hands under the pillow. Better leave the gun where it was.

The next morning was weird. Returning to work after a vacation was an adjustment, akin to leaving one world and entering another. Kimbra sat at her computer scrolling through the hundreds of emails that had accumulated over the last eight days. She skipped over the older ones, focusing on the more recent. Dr. Stanwix set up a meeting for later that morning, but not before another appointment had been scheduled. She rushed off for the early morning meeting.

Trent's cubicle was cluttered. He brushed a pile of papers and clothing off an extra chair.

"Please, have a seat."

Trent's eyes matched his hazelnut complexion. He spoke with a slight British accent.

"You didn't miss much last week. With Fang out, I had a lot of down time."

"Why was he out?" Kimbra asked.

"I don't know, but there are a few new candidates to evaluate."

They reviewed the new candidates and divvied up the caseload.

"What about Chad? Was he evaluated last week?" Kimbra asked.

"Chad? No, he cancelled his last three appointments."

"Did he give a reason?"

"Not that I'm aware of. Why?"

"Just wondering."

Trent raised his eyes from the papers.

"Okay, there is something else. You will notice an increased security presence, there are military police stationed at all the sensitive areas."

Kimbra took the elevator to the basement and approached the research lab. A barrel-chested soldier blocked her path.

"May I see your badge ma'am?"

Kimbra unclipped her badge and handed it to him.

He examined it closely, then stepped aside. "Sorry Ms. Evans. Haven't seen you before."

"I was away on vacation," she said with a wistful smirk.

She passed several lab workers, spotting Stanwix in back by the exhaust hood. He noticed her approaching and quickly extinguished a cigarette.

"I'm trying to quit, but every now and then I can't resist," he apologized.

Kimbra nodded in acknowledgment.

"How was vacation?"

"Great," Kimbra's thoughts left for Denver.

Stanwix's expression hardened. "I'm so sorry to hear of your ordeal. How are you doing?"

"I'm doing fine. Thank you."

Stanwix must have sensed her reluctance to discuss it, "Yes, well I have something to show you."

He motioned in the direction of the animal lab, Kimbra followed the brilliant molecular biologist. The monkeys howled as they entered the lab, closing the door behind them. They approached the mice section.

"We have a p-problem with Algernon," Stanwix announced in a hushed tone.

The furry white rodent was hard at work spinning the exercise wheel.

"He looks fine to me," Kimbra said.

"I guess, b-but he's not. His behavior has changed, he has become aggressive and an-anti-social."

Stanwix's face contorted in frustration.

"I'm sorry, but I sometimes stutter w-when I am nervous."

Kimbra placed her hand on Stanwix's shoulder, "It's all right. What is Algernon doing?"

Stanwix put on gloves and reached in the cage, stopping the wheel and picking up the mouse. Algernon clawed to get away and bit violently at his handler's gloves. Stanwix put him back in the cage.

"You see. He n-never behaved like this before."

"What do you think happened?"

Stanwix ignored the question. "In an attempt to socialize him, I placed a female in his cage. I came back the next day to find her m-m-mutilated to death."

Kimbra gasped at the thought of the cute little critter mauling its mate.

"There's more," Stanwix said. "One morning I entered the lab to find one cage f-full of mutilated mice, just like Algernon's mate."

"So another mouse is showing the same behavior?"

"That would be a logical conclusion, except all of the mice were killed."

"What! So the aggressive mouse died from the fight."

"I have never witnessed violent behavior like this before. Besides, this was a new batch of mice and none of them were given the drug yet!"

Kimbra's eyes widened. "Wait... and Algernon was not placed in their cage?"

"Of course not."

"Then what happened? What are you thinking?"

Just then a lab worker entered the room, setting the monkeys off once again. The sound was deafening.

"Let's go to my office," Stanwix suggested.

Kimbra sat in Stanwix's office studying the numerous diplomas on the wall, a Doctorate in Molecular Biology and Genetics from Stanford was displayed prominently. His desk was cluttered with papers, a large monitor rose above the rubble. Stanwix leaned forward in his chair and spoke in a whisper.

"I don't have any proof, but I think Algernon teleported into the other cage and killed the mice!"

Kimbra was shocked, though she shouldn't be, Fang had appeared and disappeared at the cabin. She tried to put that out of her mind at the time, writing it off as a shared hallucination, brought on by stress. But Fang admitted to her he teleported to the cabin that day. And this was more proof, or was it?

"Dr. Stanwix, there's something I haven't told you. Back at the cabin where I was being held hostage, when we were escaping the wildfire... I saw Fang there! He just appeared out of thin air, then disappeared."

"Are you sure of what you saw? Are you are certain it was Fang?"

"Yes. We both saw him. Daniel and I both saw him."

Stanwix shook his head, Kimbra wasn't sure what that meant.

"I'm afraid I have more b-bad news," Stanwix said. "Fang has refused to stop taking the QR-7. It's against my recommendation and he is changing."

"What do you mean, *changing*?"

"I'm not entirely sure. He was easily agitated at my suggestions and hasn't been to work last week. He seems to be hiding something."

Kimbra recalled the stalker in her bedroom at his house.

"I stayed at his house one night last week," she blurted out.

"Really," Stanwix raised an eyebrow in anticipation of more.

"I was frightened of staying at my place and he offered."

Stanwix patiently waited for the details.

"Anyway, he seemed fine, except..."

"What is it?"

"I can't be sure if it was a dream, but I saw a shadowy figure in his guest room in the middle of the night. I think it was Fang."

Stanwix paused to process that bit of information. Kimbra did not mention Fang kissing her. She wasn't sure it happened at all. The drug was still in her system, maybe it was playing tricks with her mind. Maybe she was *changing* as well.

"His behavior has been erratic, but I would be surprised if he was a danger to anyone but himself," Stanwix said.

Kimbra wasn't so sure. Her thoughts went back to Algernon and with it came a chill.

"Dr. Stanwix, do you think Algernon can control teleportation?"

"I don't know. What do you think?"

"I think if he could, why go from one cage to another? Why not escape?"

"Yes, that thought occurred to me as well," Stanwix said.

One possibility was that Algernon had enjoyed what he did, Kimbra thought.


If the first day back to work was weird, that evening was shocking. Kimbra had just got off the phone with her grandmother when the phone rang again. Thinking it was her again, she rushed to pick it up.

"Grandma, is that you?" she exclaimed.

There was no reply, only heavy breathing. She noticed an unknown number on her display.

"Who is this?" she asked.

"Kimbra, this is Chad," the voice was out of breath. "I'm sorry to bother you so late, but I need your help."

"Chad, Chad Addison?"

"Yes. I'm sorry, but I did a terrible thing."

"Chad, what are you talking about?"

"I didn't want to do it, it was the drug. I don't know how it happened."

"Chad, you're scaring me! What happened?"

"I almost killed my girlfriend. I was asleep dreaming, and the next thing I know, I'm in her bedroom. I thought it was a dream."

"Are you certain it wasn't a dream?"

"It was real, the police are after me."

If this was anyone else, Kimbra might suspect he was suffering from hallucinations. But he had taken the drug and she was quite certain it was real.

"I have to go," Chad said.

"Wait, let me help!" Kimbra pleaded, but it was too late, the connection was closed.

She called back but there was no answer. Did Chad teleport to his girlfriend's bedroom? It was crazy, but Kimbra had witnessed someone appear and disappear out of thin air in Fang's guest room. She saw Fang do the same at the cabin. Fang's personality was changing, Algernon was a killer. What was happening to Chad? The seemingly mild-mannered kid had become violent. She had no doubt his mind was being altered by the drug. There was no telling how far he would go with the powers he possessed, and that scared the crap out of her.

# CHAPTER 46

IT WAS AN INSATIABLE HATE, A FIRE THAT COULD NOT BE QUENCHED. Chad initially felt sorry for nearly choking Emma to death. But as time passed his remorse changed to a deep-seated hunger for revenge. He loved Emma and she repaid him with betrayal. An overwhelming cloud of doom choked off the very air he breathed. There was only one course of action to take, and it now seemed predestined.

Beads of sweat formed on Chad's forehead as he entered the gun shop. Rows of glass cabinets proudly displayed their wares, a wide array of handguns.

"Can I help you?" a tall man with a dark beard asked.

"I'm looking for a rifle," Chad explained, looking at the rifles mounted on the wall behind the counter.

"Anything in particular?"

Chad had never fired a gun before and outside of the news and movies, knew nothing about them. He decided a local gun dealer would be the logical place to begin except for one thing, he was on the run from the police. Hoping that news of that would fade quickly and that this man knew nothing about it, he took a chance.

"I'm not sure," he answered. "This is my first purchase."

"What are you expecting to do with it?"

Chad imagined himself firing away as Emma screamed in terror. When his thoughts returned to the present, he realized the man was waiting for a response.

"What? I'm sorry can you repeat that?"

"Are you interested in hunting, sport shooting, or personal protection?"

Sport shooting, that's what it was.

"Target practice, I guess."

"Sure, I can help you with that. I'm Bob," the man introduced himself.

Chad replied with his name, and Bob was more than happy to help a newbie, he asked no further questions regarding Chad's intent. Chad studied the military style rifles hanging on the wall. Bob took note of Chad's interest.

"Those are some pretty powerful weapons. You might want to start with something a little smaller."

"How about that one," Chad pointed to one that looked just like the ones he saw in movies.

Bob's eyebrows tightened as he pulled the rifle down and handed it to Chad.

"It's got less recoil than a shotgun, but as I said, it's a lot of gun for your first. You did say you wanted it for target practice, didn't you?"

Chad cradled the rifle and pointed it down the aisle. Bob grabbed the muzzle and pointed it towards the floor.

"Never point a weapon, always treat it as if it were loaded," he explained.

Chad looked Bob in the eye, not liking the contact, and paused, briefly seeing himself shooting the man square in the chest. Where did that thought come from? He pushed the mental image aside and replied.

"Sure, I understand. What is this?"

"It's an AR-15 style featureless rifle, modified to conform to California state requirements."

"I'll take it."

Bob's eyes widened. "All right, sure, if that's what you want."

"So, what's next? Can I bring it home today?"

Bob shook his head. "Unfortunately, there is a 10-day waiting period, a background check, and you'll need an FSC."

"A What?"

"A Firearm Safety Certificate, it's a short written test. I can get you started with the whole process online today."

Anxious to close the sale, Bob waited for a response. Chad could not wait ten days and worse yet, starting the background check could alert the police. There had to be another way. He thanked Bob and left.


That night Chad tossed and turned in his hotel room. On the run from the police with no clear path ahead, he was troubled. He now possessed a superior intellect and paranormal powers, but he wasn't sure how to handle his current dilemma. In his mind he devised alternate scenarios for killing Emma. He preferred a rifle, but it really didn't matter how he did it, he just wanted revenge. He drifted off to sleep thinking of the AR-15 he held in the gun shop.

Chad woke to find himself standing in his boxers in the dark. He looked around, thinking he needed to find the bathroom, when his eyes adjusted to a dim light. Not the night light in his bathroom at home, not the hotel room, but a fire or security system with a red dot of light. He was not in his hotel room, he was at the gun shop! It all seemed like a bizarre dream, except that it happened before. He strongly suspected what he was experiencing, was real. These paranormal powers could be a blessing or a curse. He had to find a way to control them.

He ran his hand across the smooth glass cabinets full of handguns to prove it was real. Next, his eyes went to the AR-15 hanging on the wall. He scurried behind the counter and pulled it down, cradling the powerful weapon. A sense of urgency came over him, a premonition? He set the weapon down and searched for ammunition. What did Bob recommend? Pretty sure it was Winchester 5.56mm cartridges. He grabbed several white boxes of the ammo against the back wall. Now what? How could he get home safely? He looked down at his spindly legs protruding from his boxer shorts, he was not exactly street worthy. He rushed into a back room frantically searching for something to cover up with. An old raincoat was hanging on a hook. What about the rifle, how could he conceal it? He searched through boxes of inventory, rifles, scopes and other accessories, eventually finding rifle covers. He selected a suitably sized cover and grabbed the raincoat on the way out.

Back in the main room, he felt the clock ticking, he had to act. Peering up at the red light, he wondered if it was a security camera or just a fire safety device. If there was a camera, he would not be able to delete any recordings, there wasn't time to mess with that. But it really didn't matter, he was on a one-way mission, one that he did not volunteer for. What he really need was to get out of there, and get out fast. But with no money, no phone, and his hotel room miles away, he needed an escape plan. Chad flung on the raincoat and quickly rifled through the cash register, finding $207.38. He stuffed the bills in a pocket, called a cab from the land line, and rushed out the door.

# CHAPTER 47

KIMBRA WAS PHYSICALLY PRESENT AT THE MEETING, but her mind was elsewhere. She could not get Chad's Monday night call off her mind. He was in trouble and she could not reach him. She tried calling Fang, but he was not answering and had not been seen in weeks. A gruff voice caught her attention. The man was dressed in a blue service uniform.

"I've called this meeting to gather the troops, so to speak. I will be managing the project until Dr. Fang Wu's return."

Colonel William Casey's head was as clean-shaven as his face, his eyes were steel blue. The colonel was part of the CIA Special Activities Center headquartered in Langley, Virginia.

Dr. Stanwix raised a hand, "Do you know when Fang will be returning? I haven't been able to reach him."

Casey cleared his throat, he seemed unaccustomed to the interruption.

"I can't give you an answer to that right now. If you could, save your questions for later, and keep in mind I will be speaking to each of you individually."

Casey took a moment to review the paperwork laid out in front of him.

"It looks like the Next Level project has made significant progress. I see that 74% of subjects are showing some signs of increased paranormal activity. That is remarkable."

Casey reflected for a moment before continuing, "The question is, how can we better understand the mechanics of what is going on to utilize this project to its fullest potential."

He looked out over his reading glasses as if expecting another interruption, there were none.

"Dr. Stanwix, can you elaborate on the latest findings?"

Stanwix looked up from his notes.

"The data shows a connection, but have yet to prove the underlying mechanism between what is going on at the cellular level with what we theorize at the quantum level."

Casey looked around the room as if he expected more.

"That's why we're depending on everyone sitting here. My role will be keeping all of you on track," he explained.

Kimbra was pretty sure the colonel was incapable of providing any of the insight that Fang brought to the project, and that scared her. How could Casey comprehend the inherent dangers involved with what they were doing? On the other hand, in taking the drug, Fang was so deep into the rabbit hole, that he had lost all perspective. Worse yet, his personality was changing. No one was sure who he was anymore.

Stanwix broke Kimbra's chain of thoughts.

"Colonel, have you had a chance to go over my latest report on the problems with the animal trials?"

Casey looked over his notes with a pained look on his face.

"I've looked them over. You and I can discuss that in more detail, later."

Casey went on to mention the status of the current test subjects as well as the newcomers. He explained the new security measures in place. Kimbra worried about the direction the program was headed. Stanwix believed they should stop the human trials and take a step back. That was not the path Casey was taking. They were pushing ahead full throttle. Another thought terrified her. With the military so closely involved, how long would it be until they weaponized the QR-7? That had always been a fear of hers and now with Fang out of the picture, they had lost all control.

Before Kimbra knew it, the meeting was over and she was back in her cubicle reviewing the research data. There were profound changes from the drug, many of which she experienced firsthand. She found them exhilarating at first: heightened senses made her more keenly aware of everything around her, a new intelligence made her see things more clearly, and the ability to foresee events could be of great value. But it also frightened her. The vision of her father's suicide brought on emotions she was unable to cope with, and now with the changes they were seeing in Algernon, Fang, and Chad, she was convinced they should halt the human trials immediately.


Kimbra was relieved to be done for the day and made a quick stop before heading home. Her stomach knotted up as she exited the grocery store. Daniel was in the parking lot, standing alongside his silver Malibu. Their eyes locked. He made a threatening gesture, cutting his throat. Kimbra fumbled in her purse for her keys and dropped the bag of groceries.

She suddenly became nauseous, realizing her gun was out of reach, locked in the car glove box. She fought back the bile rising up in her throat, fixed her gaze on Daniel, and bent down to pick up the grocery bag full of fresh vegetables and a box of pasta. She turned and took an alternate path to her car, looking back frequently. His eyes followed her like a hawk zeroing in on its prey.

Reaching the car she groped in her bag for the key fob, jumped in the car and locked the doors. A shaking hand struggled to unlock the glove box. The pistol seemed much heavier, as if it gained weight with her anxiety. She gripped the gun firmly and considered her next move. He had chosen a position in a clear line of sight of her car and did not move. A grin formed on his face. She set the gun down on the seat beside her, started the car, and raced out the parking lot.

She kept checking the rear view mirror as she drove away. Daniel was nowhere in sight, but that did not mean he was not lurking behind somewhere. Would he follow her home, or be there waiting? She continued driving, constantly checking the traffic behind her, eventually pulling into a parking lot. She cruised around until she was certain he had not followed her, parked the car, and took several deep breaths. There was only person she could think of calling. Thank God the call went through.

"Hello, Detective Rizzo, this is Kimbra, Kimbra Evans!"

"Yes, how can I help."

Kimbra explained her current situation, all the while fearing the silver Malibu would appear.

"Are you safe now? Can you see any sign of him?"

She carefully scanned the parking lot again, "No, I don't see him."

"Okay, good. Did he speak to you or threaten you in any way?"

"He made a threatening gesture, like cutting his throat. But no, he didn't speak to me."

"Did he approach you or come within one-hundred yards?"

"His car was parked several cars from mine. I had to go around him to reach my car."

"That would be in violation of the restraining order, but here's the thing..."

Kimbra braced herself for the *but*, which never preceded anything good.

"He will no doubt claim he parked his car not knowing you were there. Have there been any other encounters with him?"

Kimbra was feeling the hopelessness of it all. No one could help her.

"No."

"I'm afraid there's not much we can do right now. If he has any contact with you or a relative, or appears at your home or place of work, that's a different story."

A dark cloud passed over Kimbra's mood. She would not be safe until Daniel was put behind bars. Her head was ringing from the stress.

"Miss Evans, are you all right?"

"Yes. I guess."

"I'm sorry I can't do more. I'll make a note of this and if he shows up again, let me know."

She ended the call and drove home immediately.

Kimbra was home with a glass of wine to steady her nerves. Dinner was done and the dishes could wait. She was home only three days and already wished she was back in Colorado. She thought about Gina and her sister's hectic, and wonderful, and completely normal life. She thought about Jake. He always seemed grounded in knowing what he wanted to do, and he was doing it. She wondered if she should call him. Was it too soon? If they were dating it would certainly fit into the two to five day window recommended by the social experts. But it wasn't a date. They were ex-lovers and now friends. Or was there something more? Oh, the hell with it, she took a sip of her drink and placed the call.

"Hi Jake, it's Kimbra." The words felt awkward, maybe it wasn't such a good idea.

"Kimbra! It's great hearing from you. Is everything all right?"

There it was. Everyone who knew her, knew her life was a mess. She wanted desperately to have a normal life. Now she was reluctant to mention her encounter with Daniel.

"Everything is fine," she lied. "I was just hanging out and thinking about Colorado. Work has been a drag and I had such a good time last week."

"I did, too," he agreed.

Now the awkward silence. Kimbra sucked at small talk and Jake rescued her.

"So work has been tough?" he asked.

"Our owner and CEO is AWOL and the military has taken over. I mean, they're funding the research, but we seem to have lost all control. It's frustrating."

"That doesn't sound good. Maybe it will get better."

"Maybe..."

There was more silence.

"Is there something else?" Jake asked.

"Well... yes, but I don't want to bother you with all this."

"No, go ahead. Maybe I can help."

She had dumped on Gina too much and Jake was a good listener. Kimbra took a gulp of wine and began to describe the scene in the parking lot with Daniel. It felt good to get it off her chest.

"It sounds like you're doing everything you can. Once the trial is done, you'll feel better."

"I hope so, but getting through that will be hell."

"I can only imagine, but what other choice do you have?" Jake asked.

"You're right. Sorry to dump all this on you."

"No problem. I'm glad you called."

"So what about you? I know it's only been a few days, but anything exciting happening in Colorado?"

The most exciting news for Jake was taking the horses for a ride and enjoying the outdoors. His life was anything but extraordinary and Kimbra loved that. They talked for a total of forty-five minutes, and by the time she hung up, she felt much better. Like Jake said, maybe things would settle down after the trial.

# CHAPTER 48

KIMBRA WAS SEATED IN THE WAITING AREA AS BAKER MANNING APPEARED.

"Miss Evans. Please, follow me."

She was led to a small interview room and asked to take a seat opposite him. He had a youthful, attractive look, but his expression was serious. Kimbra guessed that went with the job.

"I had a conversation with Harold Stanwix and he had some interesting things to say about you."

Manning paused, Kimbra wasn't sure if he expected her to say something. A ringtone broke the silence.

"I'm sorry, I have to take this," he whispered before speaking into his phone.

"Colonel, sorry I couldn't reach you earlier."

Kimbra could make out the colonel's voice, but little of the conversation on the other end.

"That's correct. I have identified our prime suspect, a Russian enforcer named Dimitri Yagodnikov. I'm trying to locate him now."

Manning scanned the laptop computer in front of him as the colonel spoke.

"Yes Colonel, I will be sure to do that."

Manning hung up and let out a sigh, his fingers typed away at the keyboard. He finished and directed his attention back to Kimbra.

"Sorry for the interruption."

"You know who robbed the lab?" she asked.

"I have a suspect, a good one."

He didn't look too pleased. "That's good news, right?" she asked.

"It's a breakthrough. Now, all I have to do is find him. Sometimes that can be difficult, it can take time."

"So, Jackson is in the clear?" she asked.

"Apparently. Do you know him well?"

"I've worked with him for a while. I would never suspect him of robbing the lab."

Manning pushed his laptop to the side.

"Let's get back to our conversation. I understand you were taking the drug, QR-7. Can you tell me more about its effects on you?" he asked.

He had to find out eventually, she thought. After all, it was in the records. Still, it gave her an uneasy feeling.

"I showed an increased neural count and my test results went up," she said.

"No, not so much the data, I have that. I'm more interested in any changes you noticed and how the drug made you feel?"

"Changes?"

"Yes. Cognitive changes, your emotional state. Any new-found paranormal abilities, anything out of the ordinary."

Kimbra shifted in her seat. She wasn't certain she could be a good judge of the changes the drug had caused. Fang and Chad had changed. Had it changed her personality, her perception of reality itself?

"Miss Evans?"

"Yes, sorry. I felt like my brain was sharper, focused, my senses were heightened... I felt alive, I mean more alert than I ever felt before."

"Were you able to read minds?"

"No, not really. But I did receive signals from another test subject."

"Signals?" Manning asked.

"In one of the experiments a sender is shown a picture and asked to send it to a receiver."

"I'm aware of the telepathy experiments. Can you describe what you experienced when you received the signals?"

He didn't seem too interested in the science, Kimbra had to think about it a moment.

"It's hard to describe. It was more than an image, there were strong emotions associated with the image, or it could have been the sender's emotions."

"The report mentions some of the emotions were too much for you. Can you describe that?"

The horrible images and emotions returned in a flash. Her face suddenly flushed, she was uncomfortably hot.

Manning leaned back in his chair.

"Take your time, it's all right," he suggested.

"Some of the pictures were quite graphic, that was the intent, to elicit a strong reaction," she explained. "I felt depression, sadness, and a sense of foreboding doom."

Manning jotted down notes.

"What about the visions?"

Kimbra's eyes moistened as she recalled her father's suicide. This had to stop.

"There were visions, but I'm not going to discuss them. It's deeply personal and much too raw right now."

Manning looked up from his notes with a surprised look, analyzing her facial expressions, her eye movements, the beads of sweat on her brow. He studied her for an uncomfortably long time, it made her feel vulnerable. What was he thinking? Finally, he spoke.

"All right Miss Evans, I understand. There is something else we need to discuss, and I have to insist you tell the truth."

Kimbra nodded, feeling her mouth go dry.

"Dr. Stanwix mentioned an unusual... no let's say an extraordinary event. He said you described Dr. Fang Wu appearing and vanishing while you were held captive. Is that true?"

Kimbra bit her lip. Manning knew just about everything.

"It's true. I can't explain it though, I'm no expert in the field. You'll have to ask him."

"I did. I asked him if he physically transported his body to that cabin in the woods. He said..."

Manning referred back to his notes.

"He said, *our consciousness is locked in the present, but one of the drug's effects is to open your mind to the past or the future.* What do you think he meant by that? Was Fang really there?"

"Oh, he was there. Daniel and I both saw him."

Kimbra wasn't sure Manning believed it. He paused, as if it took time for her last statement to soak in.

"My assignment is to find out who broke into Quantum Thunder and stole the QR-7. I know you're not an expert, but you do have first-hand knowledge of the drug and its effects. So let me ask you, how worried should I be with what the thieves can do with the drug?"

Kimbra looked him straight in the eye.

"The drug was initially intended to help explain paranormal phenomena like intuition or premonitions, but there seems to be much more going on, none of which was accounted for. I'm talking about telepathy, teleportation and God knows what else. I'd be very worried."

# CHAPTER 49

THE SUN WAS SHINING BRIGHTLY as Chad parked his car alongside the student union. He took a deep breath and stepped out with his rifle. He had been buying his time on the run, waiting for the opportune moment. He knew Emma's schedule and the fact that she was usually at the union at this time. It wasn't a foolproof plan, but he felt it had a good chance of success. Part of him wanted no part of this, the rest was compelled by a force he had no control over, the wheels were set in motion and could not be stopped. He was possessed by an evil presence, a force fueled by the pain of rejection and his hatred of Emma.

Several students saw the rifle and ran off as he headed for the south entrance. He entered the union with the muzzle pointed upward. Several students heard the door and looked on, frozen in shock, like a deer in headlights, not knowing whether to stay or run. It didn't take long for the others to realize the threat they were facing. Chad scanned the crowd looking for Emma as several students escaped unnoticed. He was beginning to think Emma was not there, when he spotted her cowering in a corner. Seated at a table with several other students, she began to shake with fear as he approached. There may have been a brief moment in time when she could have escaped, but it was too late now. His rifle was trained on her as he closed the distance. Her mouth dropped open in shock, and he squeezed the trigger, again and again.

The sound was deafening as splintered fragments of the table flew off in all directions. The table was knocked over along with the students seated there. Emma attempted to get up along with the others. For her it was a hopeless endeavor, as several shots had ripped into her body, she fell backwards, toppling over a chair. One or more of the others may have been hit as well. Chad raised his smoking rifle and took in the carnage, the smell of gunpowder filled the room. It was as if he had just witnessed a violent scene in a movie.

Emma lay in a pool of blood. A familiar looking young man was crawling away from the table. The side of his shirt and pant leg were stained with blood, leaving a streak on the floor. It reminded Chad of the moist trail a snail leaves behind when it moves. He pointed his rifle at the student, who turned his head Chad's way. Their eyes met for a second, then he continued to crawl away as if it was just a dream. Chad felt his finger depressing the trigger, waiting for the boom of the weapon, when he stopped, something caught his attention. He looked back at Emma, her breaths were shallow. The room was silent, except for a gurgle emanating from Emma's chest and the snail crawling away ever so slowly. Chad's head was spinning as he looked around the room. He had a sudden urge to get out.

The sun was blinding as he burst outside into the fresh air, the sound of sirens were disturbing the peace. How much time had passed? He had no idea. Suddenly a voice yelled out.

"Put you weapon down or we will shoot!"

Something told him, this scene had played out before, this was his destiny. He turned to face the officer as if we they were both acting out parts in a play. Chad heard the shots a split second after they ripped into his body, sending him back-first onto the pavement. He looked up into the sun, there were blue table umbrellas to his right. He struggled to breath. He heard the sound of his rifle being kicked aside as strange faces peered down at him, blotting out the sun. Only now did he question his actions. Only now did he feel remorse, but it was too late.

* * *

Kimbra was shocked to see the news bulletin reporting live on the mass shooting at San José State University. Four people shot, two were dead including the shooter. No names were released and there was no video of the shooter, but her senses told her it was Chad. She was sure of it. So sure that she had to do something, talk to someone. She could call Jake, but what would he know about it. There was one person who would know, and something told her to call him immediately. When his phone once again went to voicemail, she hopped in her red Subaru and drove the thirty minutes to his house.

Fang had not been seen or heard from since before Colonel Casey took over at Quantum Thunder. Kimbra knew something was wrong, but had no idea what to expect as she pulled into his driveway. Fang's silver Ferrari was parked out front, a good sign he was home. Kimbra stepped down onto the walkway leading to the front door. She listened for any sound of activity before knocking, there was none. She waited, then rang the doorbell. Still no response. She turned the doorknob, expecting it to be locked, but it was not. That was strange, Fang was very obsessive-compulsive about things like that.

She opened the door, cautiously moving through the foyer and into the open kitchen and living area in the back. Fang was slumped over on the sofa. Wavy black hair had grown down to his shoulders, a full growth of beard covered his face. He was thin and looked like he had not changed his clothes in days. The whites of his eyes were visible under drooping eyelids.

"Dr. Wu! Fang can you hear me!" she yelled.

There was no response. He was breathing but unresponsive. She shook his shoulders. No response.

"Fang! Wake up!"

Still no response.

She pulled out her phone and dialed 911.

"911, what's your emergency?"

Kimbra explained Fang's condition.

"Are there any drugs nearby? Do you suspect a drug overdose?"

Kimbra searched the room, then the bathroom and bedroom. She found it hidden in his nightstand. A rubber hose, needle, and vial of QR-7.

# CHAPTER 50

KIMBRA GOT THE CALL FIRST THING IN THE MORNING. Thanksgiving had come and gone, Christmas was around the corner, and Fang's mother reported her son was conscious. Fang had shown little sign of improvement, so this was a major breakthrough. He requested to see Kimbra, and she promised to visit after work.

It was late afternoon when she entered Fang's hospital room, his mother was seated alongside him. Kimbra had met Mrs. Wu once before at the hospital. Her English was broken, but Kimbra was able to gather she visited her son every day, taking the fifty minute drive from her home in San Francisco.

"Miss Evans, so happy you come," she said.

"I'm so happy to see your son is awake!"

Fang acknowledged Kimbra's presence with a wink. He looked exhausted, but alert. His normally dark complexion was pasty, long hair and a beard hid his attractive facial features. Mrs. Wu spoke to her son in Chinese, kissed him on the forehead, and gathered her purse and books. She gently grasped Kimbra's hand and shot her a warm smile on the way out.

"I told her she didn't have to stay any longer today, that you would take good care of me," Fang explained.

His voice was labored, but his mind seemed sharp. Kimbra sat down and held his hand. Seeing him there so helpless, she almost forgot his erratic behavior the night she spent at his house. The kiss and his appearance in the guest room. She thought about Algernon mutilating the other mice.

"You had us all pretty scared," she said.

"You needn't worry. As far as I knew, I was fine. Maybe better while I was asleep."

"What do you mean by that?"

Fang struggled to sit up. His eyes narrowed.

"Just between you and me, I'm not sure this is where I belong."

"You mean at the hospital?"

"No. I mean here, in this world."

He must have sensed Kimbra's confusion, or was he reading her thoughts?

"I have been experiencing two realities. In one, we never began the human trials for QR-7."

Fang's eyes locked on Kimbra.

"You're thinking it must be a hallucination, or a vision, but that's not what happened."

He *was* reading her thoughts.

"You saw me at the cabin, before I vanished," he continued. "This is like that, except it feels like I am inhabiting another person's mind, in another reality. It's like I'm a guest in another body. The thing is, I can't tell which one is real."

Kimbra remained a silent skeptic.

"Look, we are only capable of consciousness in the present moment. QR-7 has allowed me to be conscious of the past and future as well as other realities."

Kimbra shook her head, "Other realities? There's no way to prove what you experienced is not a delusion or side effect from the drug."

"A delusion? You saw me transport my body to another location! I was physically there. Think about it, what is reality other than our brain's interpretation of the world around us?"

He had a point. These were pretty amazing anomalies and she had experienced some of them firsthand. Her vision of her father's suicide felt like she was there, inside his head. She experienced everything he did. But was she really there?

"How is any of this possible?" Kimbra asked.

"Science has been studying paranormal phenomena since the 19th century. QR-7 has expanded those capabilities."

Kimbra interrupted Fang, "Yes, but what's going on? Is there a scientific explanation for it?"

Fang propped himself up on the bed, Kimbra plumped up the pillows for him.

"I think there is a quantum process that can explain the different phenomena we have witnessed for centuries."

Just then a lithe, young nurse walked in with such high spirits. Kimbra could have died with her timing and exuberance.

"Doctor Wu, I see you have company."

Fang introduced Kimbra to the nurse. Linda was her name and she was there to check Fang's vitals. She took Fang's blood pressure, temperature, and would not stop talking. Her eyes widened as she studied Fang, she was clearly flirting with him, and he was well aware of it. Time froze for Kimbra as it often does in painful situations, she wished to get back to her discussion with Fang.

"I'll be by later to wash your hair," Linda offered with an enticing smile.

A foul taste rose up in Kimbra's throat, thankfully the nurse left before she got sick. Kimbra shot Fang a smirk and he picked up where he had left off.

"The latest studies on quantum entanglement may offer an explanation. I believe I mentioned a spillover of energy from another dimension earlier."

Kimbra nodded, wishing he would get to the point.

"We believe that it's not necessarily matter that is being altered across time and space, but information that is being sent."

Kimbra frowned. "Information? What information and how?"

"Information, or state, of an atom or a complete biological being. The information is sent at the speed of light to another location, or time. I can't explain it, but somehow my consciousness was transferred to another place. It's like I'm stuck between two worlds."

Kimbra tried to wrap her head around what he was describing. She had a puzzled look.

"Back in 1998, physicists at the California Institute of Technology successfully teleported a photon about 1 meter, so it has been proven."

Kimbra was skeptical and Fang knew it.

"I know it's difficult to grasp, but you and I have witnessed it. I somehow appeared at the cabin, and you saw me."

Kimbra could not argue that.

"Your brain is struggling between what you have learned your whole life, and what your eyes have seen. I can't fully explain it, but it's real. In the world of quantum physics and entanglement, there may be an explanation."

Kimbra had no idea how any of it was possible, but apparently, it was.

"Now, why don't you catch me up on the last two weeks. What did I miss?" he asked.

Kimbra was ready to tell him about Colonel Casey taking over, but she had more urgent news to share.

"Chad was killed in a mass shooting at San José State University. Four people were shot, two killed. Chad was the shooter!"

Fang's jaw dropped, "I don't understand. None of his psychological profiles indicated any hint of violence."

"QR-7 definitely had something to do with it," Kimbra said. "He called and told me he found himself unexpectedly in his girlfriend's bedroom in the middle of the night. From what he described, it sounded like your experience at the cabin."

"Really."

"What? What are you thinking?" Kimbra asked.

"The drug can play havoc with your emotions, but..."

Kimbra was wondering what the drug had done to Fang's personality. She could feel him in her head, as if a dark presence was lurking there. She quickly pushed those thoughts aside.

"But what?"

"Remember I said it felt like I was inhabiting another body in another reality?"

"Yes."

"Maybe someone was inhabiting his body, controlling him."

Kimbra had thought once or twice about someone in her mind, controlling her thoughts. Was Fang in there now? She could feel the hairs stand up on her neck as she imagined what that would be like. It was a frightening thought.

"But who?" she asked.

"I don't know. I'm just suggesting the possibility."

The thought of sharing your consciousness, your will, with someone else, scared the crap out of Kimbra.

"Fang?"

"Yes."

"Why did you continue taking the drug?"

She felt his hold on her brain let go as he considered her question.

"Initially it was curiosity, I had to know firsthand what we were doing, if it really worked. Later on... I liked the way it made me feel."

"Do you think the drug is addicting?"

Fang's eyes hardened. "If opening your eyes to a new world, seeing things as they are is addicting, then yes."

The thought that the drug could control you as much or more than any sense of control it gave you, was terrifying. The experimenting with QR-7 had gotten way out of hand, it had to be stopped.

# CHAPTER 51

KIMBRA'S EYES FLUTTERED OPEN INTO DARKNESS. It took a moment to regain her senses, she was home in bed. The clock on the nightstand displayed 2:43 AM. She closed her eyes and began to drift back to sleep, but something was wrong. Her heavy eyelids opened again. Had she heard something? She held her breath, listening intently. The only sound was silence. Senses now on high alert, she noticed a shadow at the foot of her bed, a shadow in the shape of a human! Her heart began to pound, beating loudly, so loud she worried whoever was there would hear it. Someone, or something was watching her. Did it know she was awake? Leaving her head locked in place, she slowly moved her eyes to view the nightstand. The gun was gone.

She held her breath again. This time she heard breathing, and it wasn't her!

Fearing she would miss something and too scared to blink, she fixed her gaze on the stationary figure. Her eyes stung as she remained motionless, waiting in silence. Maybe it was a dream, a night terror, she tried to reason. She closed her eyes for a second, scrunching them closed tightly, hoping to blink it away, hoping to wake up alone in her room.

Her eyes opened and suddenly it was on top of her, pinning her arms to the mattress! She could feel the weight, smell the breath, it was warm but not unpleasant. A man's cologne, a familiar scent carried in the air. It was Daniel!

"What do you want?" she wanted to scream, but nothing came out.

His face was inches from hers, the whites of his eyes stood out in the darkness. But the rest of him was oddly translucent, she could see through his face. She could feel his weight on her body lighten. His voice floated in the air, as if whispered in a cave.

"I loved you. But you had to go and ruin everything. You will be sorry for that, I promise you."

Then the form faded, as if it had never existed.

Kimbra bolted up, turned on the lights, and quickly checked the room. She was alone. The gun lay on the floor by the nightstand. She grabbed it and quickly crawled back under the covers. She sat up, knees tucked into her chest, holding the pistol tightly, terrorized but not sure what had just happened. It felt so real, she felt Daniel's weight on top of her. But was it another dream or was it real? If it was real, that meant Daniel was using QR-7, but how did he get his hands on the drug? Kimbra wasn't sure what to think anymore, the drug's long lasting effects were playing havoc with her mind and her head was spinning. The lights remained on the rest of the night and though she did not want to, she eventually succumbed and fell back asleep.

Kimbra woke the next morning exhausted and irritable, having been up most of the night worrying about her late-night visitor. She was tormented by the question: was it real or a nightmare? She had experienced night terrors before and they were terrifying. With all the stress she was dealing with, it should be no surprise she had a nightmare. That's what she now wanted it to be, for if it was real, well that could be too much to handle. She brewed a hot mug of coffee and attempted to put the nightmare behind her.

The new year had come and gone, it had been four months since the kidnapping and Daniel's arrest. The wheels of justice moved slowly, but today was the day Daniel would have to account for his actions. If everything went as planned, today was also the day Kimbra would be called to the witness stand. According to the DA, her testimony was crucial to the case. Having to recount the ordeal in front of a jury of strangers, in front of Daniel... that scared her to death. Nerves frayed from the night before and sleep deprived, she refilled her coffee mug and prepared for the busy day ahead.

Flanked by the US and California flags, Judge Brendon Galloway presided from his perch high atop an elevated bench. The state seal of California was affixed to the wall behind him. The jury sat to the right and the attorney's tables were directly in front of the judge. Daniel was seated with his attorney.

Several rows back, in the gallery, Kimbra peered at the back of Daniel's head. She ducked quickly as he turned to survey the crowd. She sensed he could feel her presence. She closed her eyes, trying to push those thoughts aside. When she opened them, his attention had turned to the District Attorney.

In her mid-thirties, Cynthia Dowd was sharply dressed in a navy blue pant suit and oversized black-rimmed glasses. Her dark auburn hair was tied back in a pony. She stood to deliver the opening statement.

"Ladies and gentlemen of the jury, good morning. It is my pleasure to represent the State of California as prosecutor. The defendant, Daniel Visser, is charged with kidnapping and imprisonment. The State will prove beyond a reasonable doubt that he drugged and kidnapped Miss Kimbra Evans. He held her captive for four frightening days where she was chained and subjected to severe emotional trauma, fearing for her life. Under California law, kidnapping is a felony punishable by up to eight years in prison. We will be seeking the maximum penalty."

Next up was the defense attorney. Kenton Walsh had movie star looks with a square face and a stubble of beard. His dark hair was slicked back, his suit was an Italian made Beroni and expensive. After introducing himself, he proceeded to deny all the allegations.

"Members of the jury, this case had been blown way out of proportion. This is *not* a kidnapping. It's nothing more than a simple misunderstanding between two lovers. We will show that the emotional state of Miss Evans was unstable and her version of the events are distorted."

Walsh went on to deny and make light of the traumatic events the victim had claimed. Kimbra's blood boiled as he spoke, her head pounded, the room began to swirl. She looked down at the floor and took several deep breaths in an attempt to calm herself. Slowly she began to regain her wits. When she looked up, Walsh had finished his opening remarks and the judge called on the State to present their case.

Cynthia Dowd described the kidnapping in detail. She presented witness statements placing the defendant and victim at the Downtown Grill the night of the kidnapping. One witness testified he observed the couple in a heated discussion and Kimbra leaving in a drugged condition. Then came the moment she had been fearing for months.

The DA announced to the jury, "I would like to call Miss Evans to describe to you, in her words, the traumatic events she suffered. Miss Evans, would you please approach the witness stand?"

Kimbra fought back a lump in her throat. Dressed in dark slacks and a modest blouse, her dark hair tied back in a pony, she summoned all the courage she could muster and rose from her seat. She felt Daniel's eyes on her as she stepped forward. Her legs were rubbery as she opened the swinging gate out of the gallery and approached the witness stand. She was sworn in and sat in front of the judge seated several steps above her. Daniel's eyes locked on her, she could feel his hands around her throat tightening. It was difficult to breath.

"Miss Evans, are you all right?" the judge asked in a firm tone.

She began to cough, her face turned beet red.

"Someone please get Miss Evans a glass of water!" the judge demanded.

The court bailiff poured a glass of water and carefully handed it to Kimbra.

"We can take a break if you are not feeling well," the judge offered.

Kimbra's body stiffened as she grabbed the glass, gulped down some water, and coughed.

"No, I'll be fine," she croaked out in a hoarse voice.

The judge gave her several minutes to compose herself, then asked if she was ready. She was.

Cynthia Dowd approached the witness.

"Ms. Evans, can you describe in detail what occurred on the night of Saturday, October twenty-eighth?"

Kimbra recalled the night the painful experience began.

"Sure... I was having dinner with Daniel at the Downtown Grill. He wanted to celebrate a case he recently closed, I wanted to ask him a question that was bothering me. When I asked, he seemed angry, or worried."

"What did you ask him?"

"I asked about a girlfriend of his in high school, Lisa Minetti, who disappeared and was never found. He became agitated, said they broke up before she disappeared. He said he felt guilty but had nothing to do with her disappearance."

"You said she was never found. Was anyone charged in her disappearance?"

"No. Daniel was questioned by the police, but no one was ever charged."

"You said he was agitated with your questions. What happened after that?"

"I got up to go to the ladies room."

Kimbra was uncomfortable describing the vision she experienced in the bathroom, but Dowd decided it was too important to leave out. She described Daniel's silver Malibu in Christina's driveway as well as Christina's crime solving visions.

"That's an incredible story," Dowd said. "What happened when you returned to your table?"

"I was frightened. I mean, I wondered if he had anything to do with Christina's death and the disappearance of Lisa Minetti. I sat down, but I'm sure now that he sensed my suspicions."

"And what happened next?"

"The rest of the night was pretty much a blur. He ordered drinks for us while I was in the ladies room. I believe he drugged my wine."

"Can you recall anything after that?"

"The last thing I remember was sitting in his car. He was talking, but everything was distorted, I mean my hearing and vision, everything was spinning, I could barely keep my eyes open. It felt like a dream. That's it, until I woke up the next day in a strange place."

Kimbra went on to explain her four-day ordeal, in exhausting detail, ending with her escape. It brought with it a flood of emotions. The judge was not untouched by her pain and asked if she would like a recess. Kimbra was desperate for a break, for the District Attorney had told her earlier that the worst was yet to come.

# CHAPTER 52

KENTON WALSH WAS WAITING IN THE WINGS, LIKE A TIGER ready to pounce on its unsuspecting prey. He stood and strutted towards the witness stand. Decked out in his expensive suit, he reminded Kimbra of a peacock, except this one had teeth.

"Miss Evans, can you describe your relationship with the defendant, Daniel Visser?"

Kimbra shifted in her seat, it was as uncomfortable as the question. She thought back to when they first met, how she was uneasy at first but soon grew fond of him, and later relied on him. It was just weeks after Marie's murder, Rizzo had called that morning with news of Mick's arrest. She was feeling betrayed by the world, lost and alone. She bumped into Daniel at a restaurant near work then later at a local grocery store. Was it a just a coincidence, or had he planned it all along?

"Miss Evans!"

Kimbra was jolted back to the present.

"We met last summer... I guess we had been seeing each several months."

"More like five months," Walsh countered.

"Yes, that's right."

"Can you describe your relationship?"

"Describe it how? We were dating."

"Was it a romantic relationship? Did you have sexual relations?"

Kimbra's mind flashed back to Sunday mornings in bed with Daniel, his thin, wiry body that she had become familiar with. She was happy, the sex was great, and everything in the world seemed better.

"Miss Evans!" Walsh startled her back to the present.

"Yes, it was a romantic relationship," she answered.

"Were you in love?"

She didn't have to think long about that one. She was, but there had to be a reason why she was so wrong.

"I don't know. We saw a lot of each other. My best friend was killed. I was lost, I was vulnerable. I think he took advantage of that."

"So it would be safe to assume you were emotionally involved," he continued.

Kimbra wasn't sure if it was a question or a statement. It was as if he heard nothing of what she just said. He shrugged and looked at the jury.

"Miss Evans, isn't it possible you may have misinterpreted the events taking place over the four days you believe you were kidnapped?"

Kimbra's jaw dropped.

"No! Absolutely not!"

"Miss Evans, were you taking any drugs that could have an effect on your state of mind, or your emotions?"

"Objection your honor," Dowd interjected. "The witness is not on trial here."

"Your honor, I'm merely trying to establish the state of mind of the witness. It has a direct bearing on the ability of the witness to interpret the events she experienced."

The judge paused before replying, "I'll allow it."

It seemed like the world had stopped and was gawking at Kimbra. She was confused.

"What was the question?" she asked.

Walsh repeated the question slowly as if she were a child.

"Were you taking any drugs that could have an effect on your state of mind, or your emotions?"

"I was taking some mild anti-depressants," she made no mention of the experimental drug QR-7.

"Mild anti-depressants," Walsh repeated. He looked around the courtroom as if he had just sunk a three-pointer. He turned back to Kimbra.

"I didn't know there was such a thing as a *mild* anti-depressant." He paused again for effect. "And that's it? You weren't taking any other drugs?" he asked.

"That's all my doctor prescribed," Kimbra evaded the question.

Walsh's face contorted as if he had a pebble in his expensive shoes.

"Miss Evans, isn't it true that you were taking an experimental drug at work? And may I remind you, you are under oath."

Kimbra looked to Cynthia Dowd for guidance.

"Objection your honor," Dowd finally spoke. "Her employer works on confidential government contracts. She is not allowed to disclose any details of their work."

"I'm not looking for any disclosure on their work," Walsh explained. "I just want to know if Miss Evans personally took any drugs at work."

The judge carefully considered the objection before ruling, "I will allow it, but only a yes or no answer."

All eyes were on Kimbra. Her heart sank as a lump formed in her throat.

"Miss Evans, please answer the question," the judge said.

She croaked out a response, "Yes."

With a look of surprise, Walsh looked around the room to emphasize the answer he already knew.

Then feeling like he just slam-dunked a basket said, "No further questions your honor."

# CHAPTER 53

IT WAS THE FIRST THING HAROLD STANWIX NOTICED WHEN HE ENTERED THE LAB. He picked up the furry little critter and cradled it in his hands. Stanwix had grown quite fond of Algernon, not unlike one would love a dog or a cat. Algernon was their biggest success, and would now be their biggest disappointment. There was no sign of injury or trauma, an autopsy would have to be performed on the tiny mammal to determine a cause of death. That responsibility fell on Stanwix's shoulders, he felt queasy just thinking about it. For now he placed the body in a sealed bag and put it in the refrigerator. Next he called Fang.

"I'm sorry to bother you at home, but I have some terrible news."

"It's too early for bad news Harry," Fang complained. "I'll be in this afternoon. Can it wait?"

Stanwix did not know how to reply, he was silent.

"All right, just give it to me," Fang said.

"Algernon is d-dead," he blurted out, the stutter returning.

There was a silence over the line, a harbinger of doom. Fang knew full well how much Algernon meant to Stanwix and the program.

"I'm sorry Harry... Do you know the cause of death?"

"No. I will do an autopsy later."

"Well, I'm sorry. He was a super star. Look, I'll see you at the meeting with Manning this afternoon. Are you all right?"

"Fang, we have to stop the program. We have to stop it now," Stanwix pleaded.

"Harry, you know it's out of my hands. Even if I wanted to, I couldn't stop it now."

The human drug trials would continue, new candidates were being evaluated under the supervision of Colonel Casey as they spoke.

Special Agent Baker Manning sat across from Fang and Stanwix. Fang made brief appearances at work and was better, but he was not the same as before the drug overdose. His look was disheveled and he did not appear happy to be there. Manning was wearing a button down shirt, sport coat, and a serious look. An open manila folder and papers were spread out in front of him.

"I need to know more about the capabilities of subjects given QR-7. And just so you know, I am aware of Dr. Wu's appearance at the cabin as well as the reported visions. So let's start with you, Dr. Stanwix, tell me more about the drug."

"I don't have any firsthand experience with the drug," Stanwix explained.

"That's all right, I'm interested in your latest findings," Manning urged.

"Of course. Well, the data confirms a telepathic communication between the test subjects. As far as the mechanism behind it, that remains unclear. There is also Miss Sullivan's premonition of the recent plane crash, but there is no way to confirm if it was related to the drug."

"Is that all?" Manning asked.

"There is something else bothering me... I believe a mouse in the lab teleported to another cage and back, but I can't prove it."

"Wait, what about the mouse?" Manning interrupted.

Stanwix explained how he found a cage full of mutilated mice and believed it was done by Algernon. He also revealed the star mouse had died. The autopsy findings would be forthcoming.

"That is interesting," Manning said. "So to be clear, you mentioned telepathic communication and teleporting. Are we talking about two different things?"

"Yes," Stanwix agreed.

Manning looked confused, Fang attempted to clarify the discussion.

"*Telepathy* is the communication of thoughts or ideas by means other than the known senses. *Teleportation*, is the transfer of matter or energy from one point to another without traversing the physical space between them."

"Yes, but how would that be possible, I mean to transport to another location?" Manning asked.

"To dematerialize and rematerialize in another location would require a large amount of energy. I speculate it's not really a transfer of matter, but a spillover from another dimension."

"What does that mean?"

"I'm not entirely sure, it's just a notion of mine," Fang explained.

Manning squinted, not fully understanding. Fang continued.

"Our notion of time, consciousness, our very perception of reality; I believe they're all stored in a constant state of flux in the quantum universe. The drug has somehow allowed us to tap into that data field and experience other realities."

"You mean, like other dimensions?" Manning asked.

"Think of two sound waves having the same frequency, constantly adjusting in and out of phase. But instead, this happens within the microtubules of our brain at the quantum level."

"And you think you did that? You entered another dimension at the cabin?"

Fang nodded, "Yes. When I appeared at the cabin I became a part of Kimbra's reality."

"Were you able to interact with your surroundings?" Manning asked.

"I didn't try. The whole experience was over quickly."

Manning leaned in closer to Fang.

"Your experience was temporary. Is a permanent transfer possible?" he asked.

"I would suspect that yes, it's possible."

"So, it would be possible to transport to another location and time, is that what you're saying?"

"In theory, I would think yes. And it's teleport."

"Excuse me?"

"I teleported to another location, using the power of my mind. You said *transport*, it's *teleport*."

"Okay, sure. And what about time shifting? I've seen temporal shift mentioned in the reports. Can you *teleport* to any time?"

"When you are ripping open multiple dimensions there are endless possibilities, time becomes less relevant. But yes, I would say it's possible."

Manning pushed his chair back, let out a whistle and swiveled around.

"Relevant or not, that would be quite a tactical advantage."

# CHAPTER 54

THE PROSECUTION RESTED THEIR CASE. Kimbra's testimony painted a clear picture of the trauma she endured and more than one juror was moved to tears. The physical evidence proved Kimbra was at Daniel's cabin. The phone records and eyewitness testimony placed the two of them at the restaurant the night of her abduction. George & Margaret, the couple whose house she stopped at following her escape, described Kimbra's condition that night. Cynthia Dowd, the district attorney, felt it was a solid case. Now it was time for the defense to present theirs.

Under normal circumstances it was not wise to call the defendant to the witness stand. Kenton Walsh decided otherwise, he believed Daniel's testimony was crucial to their case.

Daniel was sworn in under oath to testify. He wore a dark sport coat, a dress white shirt, and an innocent look. After the formal introduction of the defendant to the jury, Walsh began the questioning.

"Mr. Visser, how long had you and Miss Evans been dating?"

"We started seeing each other over the summer, so I guess it's been almost five months."

"Five months," Walsh repeated for the jury. "And in that time, did you ever have a physical altercation?"

"No, sir."

"How about a fight? Did you argue often?"

"No, never," Daniel said.

"What about the night you had dinner at the Downtown Grill? Did you argue that night?"

"No, we were celebrating a case I just closed. Kimbra was acting strange though."

"What do you mean by strange?" Walsh asked.

Daniel's eyes drifted over to Kimbra, there was a message for her in those evil eyes. He was going to win, he was going to crush her.

"She was emotional, acting erratically. I found out recently she was taking an experimental drug at work, and that was changing her state of mind."

"An experimental drug at work," Walsh repeated to drive home how foolish her behavior was. He continued.

"Daniel, I'm going to get right to it and ask you outright. Did you spike Miss Evan's drink that night and abduct her?"

Daniel's face contorted in disbelief, he could have won an Oscar for his performance.

"No! Of course not."

"Then why do you think she would go to all this trouble to accuse you of such terrible things?"

"Well, like I said, she was on drugs. She had herself convinced that I was going to harm her. I think she actually believes everything she has accused me of. She is delusional."

"Objection your honor," Dowd interrupted. "Witness is making a diagnosis he is not qualified to make."

Judge Galloway looked over at the stenographer, "Emily, please strike the comment on *delusional* from the records."

"Let me rephrase," Walsh offered. "In your opinion, simple laymen's terms, did you think Miss Evans had a full grasp of reality?"

"No."

"So, as you stated earlier, she was acting erratically. Why do you think a witness said she looked drunk?"

"We had several glasses of wine, I think she overdid it. But it did seem to calm her down."

Walsh looked over the jury as if he just had a revelation.

"So her account of you drugging her and holding her hostage against her will, it was all made up?"

"Yes. Well, it's not true. I think she believes it."

"Can you explain how you went from a couple having dinner together to her believing she was abducted? When do you think this whole thing started?"

Daniel glanced at the jury, pausing as if the whole experience was an ordeal for him, a puzzle he could not solve.

"I'm not sure exactly. When she came out of the ladies room, she was agitated. She accused me of killing someone back in high school."

Daniel paused as if the entire performance was rehearsed.

"Where did she get that idea from?" Walsh asked as if it was a crazy notion.

"I don't know. I was seeing a girl in high school who later disappeared. Kimbra found out about it and convinced herself I was somehow responsible."

The two went back and forth explaining how Daniel was never charged and had nothing to do with the unfortunate disappearance. He continued explaining Kimbra's odd behavior.

"Then she started to get sleepy. I think the drugs and alcohol had pretty much knocked her out. We drove to my cabin like we had agreed to earlier in the week and she slept there. The next morning she had forgotten most of the night before."

Daniel described the approaching fire and how he single handedly saved their lives. Also, how Kimbra went off the deep end accusing him of abducting her and ran away in the dark when they were hiking. The jury seemed to be buying it hook, line, and sinker.

Kimbra was feeling sick. The thought of her being shackled to the bed, wetting herself, not knowing if he was going to kill her, it was too much to relive. Too painful watching him spew out his lies. She got up and left.

* * *

The DA urged Kimbra to attend the whole trial, but she refused. Daniel was in her head and it was impossible to be there without making a spectacle of herself. How could that be good? She was back at work, while the trial continued in her absence. Funny how life goes on, while the world around you crumbles.

The trial was a big event in San José and was recapped each night on the local news, Kimbra didn't watch. Her mother called occasionally to check on her. Apparently being mentioned on the news made Kimbra a celebrity, now worthy of her mother's attention. Gina also called and that was nice. But burying herself in her work was the only way Kimbra could survive the ordeal, that and a drink or two each evening.

Kimbra sat opposite Harold Stanwix in his office. He called an impromptu meeting out of concerns he was having.

"How are you holding up?" he asked.

Kimbra did not like talking about it, but unlike a lot of others, Stanwix was genuinely concerned for her well-being.

"Okay, I guess."

Stanwix reached into a desk drawer and pulled out a bottle of amber colored bourbon. He held it up, along with his coffee mug and a plastic cup.

"I don't normally do this in the middle of the day, but these are unprecedented times. Care to join me?" he asked in a hushed tone.

"No, thank you," Kimbra declined the offer.

He poured a small amount into his mug and stowed the bottle away, back in the drawer. Then took a swig.

"I have a few concerns I wanted to share with you, actually more than a few," he said as he took another sip.

"Have you seen or heard anything from Fang lately?" he asked.

Kimbra shook her head.

"I'm w-worried. No one has heard from him recently. I'm afraid he may have gone off the deep end again."

"After all that happened, you think he's using the drug again?" Kimbra asked.

"Yes, unless he never really stopped."

Stanwix rolled his chair to the side and looked out into the lab.

"Did you know that they have locked down all the QR-7?"

"No, I didn't. It's all part of the new security measures though, right?"

"So they say. But I think there's a lot more going on. How do you feel about the new test subjects?"

Kimbra had to admit, she was worried.

"I have concerns. There are so many of them and their backgrounds are questionable or missing altogether."

"Exactly. They are ramping up the program for military use," Stanwix suggested.

"Are you sure of that? Wouldn't Fang have something to say about that?"

"I think he is out of the picture."

"But he's the owner and CEO, it's his program. How can that be?"

"Trust me, I'm quite c-certain he's out."

Just then Kimbra's phone rang, startling both of them.

"I'm sorry, it's the DA," Kimbra explained as she opened the connection.

"Miss Evans?" a voice on the other end asked.

"Yes."

"This is Cynthia Dowd. The jury has returned a verdict."

Kimbra felt her heart stop in anticipation, her life hanging in the balance, hanging by a thread. This was her one chance to put it all behind her, the four days of terror she experienced. Twelve strangers would decide her fate. The world around her stopped as she waited for the verdict...

"I'm sorry to have to tell you this... but Daniel Visser was just found innocent on all charges."

# PART THREE - A NEW BEGINNING

# CHAPTER 55

KIMBRA SAT IN THE FANCY RESTAURANT STARING OUT THE WINDOW. A month earlier she hit rock bottom. Once Daniel was found not guilty, he was untouchable. If fact, he became an instant celebrity. Kimbra gained some notoriety as well, except as a drug addicted, crazy woman. She was getting death threats in the mail, vile comments on social media, and angry looks in the street. Daniel was stalking her and there didn't seem to be anything she could do about it, after all he was found innocent, she was the crazy one. Who would believe her now? What judge would issue a restraining order?

Daniel appeared in parking lots, street corners, and called whenever it suited his mood. His behavior alternated from threatening to conciliatory. On one extreme he sought revenge, on the other he wanted her back. It was exhausting, so tiring she began to consider quitting. He would never stop harassing her, he had won. What could she do? It began to feel like he would forever be a part of her life. That's when panic would set in. She would relive the time he held her captive in the cabin: the fear, the hopelessness, never knowing if or when he would explode in a fit of rage and kill her. When the anxiety settled, it was replaced by anger, an anger that gnawed at her gut. She had to put a stop to it before it destroyed her.

There was only one solution she could think of. Out of desperation she quit her job and moved to Colorado, staying with her sister, Gina. It had become unbearable back in San José and she desperately needed a fresh start. With the move and a new phone number, she left her troubles behind. The harassment stopped and she mercifully began to relax. She even found a job. Just a part-time gig at a Starbucks, but it would hold her over until something more permanent came along. For once, her life was looking up.

And then, there was Jake. Their relationship had grown and she was spending most of her weekends at his home in Fort Collins. She sat in the restaurant contemplating her future, a future with Jake. She wasn't ready to move in with him and start a family, but they were getting along great. In some ways, they picked up right where they left off in high school. So when the dark presence filled her mind it took her by surprise. She stopped taking the QR-7 six months ago and most of its effects had diminished, but she still felt more in tune with the world around her, her senses were heightened. So what was the dark, foreboding mood she was feeling? Was it a harbinger of things to come or was she overreacting?

"Kimbra, are you all right?" Jake's voice startled her.

"Yes, I'm fine. Why?"

"You seem distracted. You were staring off into space. What were you thinking?"

Kimbra tried to put it into words, but could not. It was just a feeling, could be a lingering side effect from the drug, a flash back.

"I'm sorry, I guess I was zoning out. Jake, I'm just so happy here in Colorado."

*　*　*

It was a beautiful morning in the Rockies. The air was crisp, the sun pleasantly warm. Everything seemed right in the universe, but somehow wrong at the same time, like a pleasant dream about to be shattered. Why did she keep getting those feelings, couldn't she just accept the fact that her life had changed? She had escaped her rocky past, it was time to leave those skeletons behind. Kimbra cleared her mind and continued hiking along the path when something down low caught her attention. She dropped down on one knee to snap a picture of a grouping of lavender colored flowers, each with a delicate blue and white star-shaped flower in the center. She had an app on her phone that would properly identify them, if she had cell coverage.

"They're beautiful. Do you know what they are?" Kimbra asked.

"Colorado Columbine."

Kimbra stood up with a doubtful look. "Are you sure?"

"Pretty sure. They *are* the state flower."

Kimbra had to give it to Jake, she was new to Colorado and he knew the outdoors. She brushed off her knee and inhaled the fresh mountain air, sweet and dry. There was a hint of an unfamiliar odor. A skunky smell, a little musky.

"Do you smell that?" she asked Jake.

"Smell what?"

"Never mind."

Probably nothing she thought as she took a cool drink from her water bottle and took in the spectacular view. The sun peeked above a rocky rise to her right covered with aspen and pine trees. To her left was the valley below, a vast wilderness untouched by man, covered in a carpet of tall grass and dotted with speckles of yellow and lavender wildflowers.

"Nothing beats springtime in the Rockies," Jake commented after a sip of water.

"It's beautiful," Kimbra had to agree.

The two continued along in silence with Jake a half-step ahead. They rounded a corner when something stopped them cold in their tracks. A black bear cub stood on the trail, some thirty yards ahead. Many times a topic of conversation, a bear was something Kimbra thought she would enjoy seeing in the wild, that is until she actually came across one. She marveled at the sight, but was also aware of the inherent danger. She slowly raised her camera to take a shot, while taking a few steps back.

Suddenly, out of nowhere a dark object flashed by, sending Jake flying over the embankment. Kimbra's body froze in place as an adult bear turned to face her, reared up on its hind legs and roared. Pinned to the rock wall, there was no place for her to hide. She slowly backed away, attempting to put some distance between her and the bear, but it was no use. The bear attacked, it was on her in an instant.

Knocked to the ground hard, she instinctively rolled up into a ball and rolled onto her side. The bear roared again, so close she could feel its warm, moist breath, smell a strong musky scent. Then it came down on her with its full weight, pounding with its paws. Kimbra felt a rib break, her jaw bone cracked with a sickening sound and an intense pain. The bear grabbed onto her shoulder with its powerful jaws and shook violently, snapping her collar bone. She was thrown into the air, some distance down the path.

The intense pain dulled as shock set in. A warm liquid ran down the inside of Kimbra's shirt from her neck to her bosom. She tasted blood and felt a protruding bone inside her mouth. A rib pierced an internal organ as her vision slowly darkened. The bear approached her mangled body and rose back up on its haunches, ready to strike again. She tried crawling towards the embankment with her uninjured arm, but she didn't have the strength. The roar was deafening as consciousness slowly slipped away.

"Kimbra! Are you all right?"

A voice echoed from the distance. The bear shook her body and picked it up again.

"Kimbra!"

Her eyes fluttered open. Where was she? The bear was suddenly gone.

"You were moaning and crying out. Did you just have a bad dream?" Jake asked.

A dream? No it was more than that. She never had a dream so vivid, so real. The only thing that came close was the vision of her father's suicide. That was brought on by the drug, was it still rattling around in her brain? Something was happening, there were changes in her body, in her mind, she could sense it. Something was wrong.

"Are you all right?" Jake asked.

The bed sheets rustled as Kimbra rolled onto on her side to face him.

"I'm fine. It was just a bad dream," she said in her most convincing voice.

Jake's soft brown eyes widened as he locked his gaze on her.

"What?" she asked.

"You know, we have been spending a lot of time together."

Kimbra nodded.

"And you practically live here on weekends..."

"I know. What are you getting at?"

"Why don't you move in with me?" he asked.

Kimbra would be lying if she said she hadn't thought about living with Jake, but was she ready? Jake sensed her hesitation.

"C'mon, you can quit your job at Starbucks and apply at the local coffee shop here."

Kimbra raised an eyebrow.

"Seriously. They're looking for help and I can put in a good word for you."

"You know that's not my dream job," Kimbra joked.

"I know. Just suggesting something temporary. So, what do you say?"

Kimbra stared back at his pouty face, a smirk formed around her mouth.

"I'll think about it."

Jake's expression turned serious as he moved closer, his lips stopping a hair's width from hers. He nuzzled his cheek against her cheek burying his head in her hair. His skin had a sweet, salty scent. Their eyes met again and they kissed. Kimbra's fears were forgotten. The fresh mountain air, the bear and the pain it had brought, all faded away as the two locked in an embrace and gave in to their primal urges.

# CHAPTER 56

**One month later**

KIMBRA MOVED IN WITH JAKE. It was inevitable, right? She was spending every weekend at his home and the relationship was growing, it seemed the natural and logical thing to do. It was that, or find her own place. Gina and Greg were great hosts but Kimbra felt she had overstayed her welcome. It was time to move on.

So, she packed up her things and moved in with Jake. He was not particularly fond of cats, but Smokey had a way of growing on you and Jake quickly warmed up to the gray and white feline. Kimbra had not lived with someone since Carter and it was awkward at first, especially with it being Jake's house. She wished to put a female touch on the place, but also wanted to respect his space. The decor was stark, bold, and lacked color. She added a few curtains, throw pillows and kitchen adornments. Jake liked the additions and it made the house feel more like home.

Kimbra woke up alone to the aroma of fresh coffee. She wandered into the kitchen.

"Good morning. How did you sleep?" Jake asked.

"All right, I guess. I just need a strong cup of coffee."

Kimbra had been having a hard time sleeping. That wasn't entirely true, she could fall asleep but was terrified of getting another nightmare. After the vision of the bear attack, she had several more nightmares and finally got in to see her doctor. He prescribed a sleeping aid along with a mild tranquilizer. Over time the nightmares became less vivid, it was that or she was so dopey she did not remember them. Jake gave her time to enjoy a few sips and clear her head. It was a routine they danced most mornings.

"Are you still up for a hike?" he asked.

"Sure, I will be."

Over morning coffee they decided to pack a lunch and hike the Hewlett Gulch Trail.

It wasn't long before they were on the road. Colorado was so much different than San José and Kimbra never tired of the spectacular scenery. It was a beautiful drive along the Poudre Canyon Highway overlooking the Cache la Poudre River. Before she knew it, they pulled off onto a parking lot and got their gear out of the back of Jake's truck. The air was still cool and the sun warm, perfect conditions for an early hike. The trailhead was clearly marked and they set off in silence. The path led north, winding through a narrow canyon. They crossed several streams before heading uphill to a meadow. Kimbra paused at the sight of yellow and lavender wildflowers dotting the landscape.

"Beautiful, huh," Jake commented.

"Yeah, except..."

"Except what?"

"It reminds me of that nightmare I had, the one with the bear."

Jake's eyebrows tightened, "Kimbra, it was only a dream."

She wondered, was it?


It took nearly four hours to complete the 7.9 mile trail. After that, they stopped for a beer. With over twenty craft breweries, Fort Collins boasted of being the Craft Beer Capital of Colorado. Kimbra took a sip of cold beer from a frosty mug. The pale ale was invigorating after the long hike.

"So Jake, I was wondering if you could take some time off, so we could take a short vacation."

Jake's head rocked back and forth slightly.

"I don't know. It's the beginning of wildfire season and I have a lot of work to get ready. Maybe later, this fall when we have a better handle on things."

Kimbra's eyes drooped. "That's fine. It can wait."

"Did you have something in mind?"

"Nothing really. Maybe a weekend in Telluride."

"We could do that, I mean depending on how the summer goes. How about a ski trip later in the fall? I'd love to take you skiing."

Kimbra had never skied before, but then wasn't that what new relationships were all about: taking chances and trying new things? She imagined herself tumbling down the slope in a cloud of snow dust.

"Sure, that sounds great," she said.


They returned home weary from the busy day, took a nap, ate a light dinner, and settled in for a quiet evening. That's when it happened. Like flicking a switch, it happened in an instant. They were snuggled up, watching a movie together, when Kimbra rose from the sofa. Jake turned his head.

"What are you doing?" he asked.

Kimbra's body moved, but her mind was blank. Jake turned his attention back to the television.

She plodded into the bedroom and sat on the bed, her earlier pleasant mood had turned dour. Filled with an impending doom, the day's earlier activities seemed light years away. She opened a drawer in the nightstand and removed the safe box. She unlocked the box, extracted her pistol, and examined the cartridge, making sure it was filled with at least one round. With a click, it was snapped back it into place.

"Kimbra, do you want me to pause the movie?" Jake called out from the living room.

Kimbra's muscles were activated, but not by her thoughts. Like an involuntary response, she watched her hands pull the slide back and chamber a round as Jake entered the room. His face immediately went pale. Although Jake was inches away, Kimbra felt an isolation so strong it hurt. Her breathing slowed as thoughts of ending the pain invaded her mind in a blitzkrieg.

"Kimbra! What are you doing?"

Kimbra's head turned slightly in his direction, but she barely registered his presence, she no longer controlled her body. Someone, or something had taken control of her mind. It was as if she was a bystander witnessing a tragedy about to unfold. She felt her arm raise the pistol to her temple.

"Kimbra! Stop!"

Jake grabbed her arm, pulling it away from her head, but her muscles resisted. Something inside her bubbled up, an anger like no other, an evil presence. She turned to face Jake with fire in her eyes as they struggled to control the deadly weapon. In an instant, her feelings of dread and hopelessness now turned to rage.

"What are you doing?" Jake grunted as he struggled to wrestle the gun away from her.

The gun moved about wildly, back and forth, pointing at Jake and then Kimbra.

"Kimbra, let go of the gun!"

Jake pulled violently to break her grip, that's when she felt her finger tighten on the trigger, pull back, and then a loud *bang*!

Jake's limp body dropped to the floor. Blood was pooling around his head, a matted tuft of hair and tissue floated in the blood like a ship at sea. The clouds in Kimbra's head cleared. She snapped out of her trance, to find herself kneeling alongside Jake, cradling his head. His eyes fluttered as he drifted in and out of consciousness. Kimbra got up and raced for her phone.

*　*　*

Jake lay unconscious in the hospital bed, his condition critical. He was brought into the emergency department with a gunshot wound to his head, the bullet grazed his skull, leaving behind bone fragments and tissue damage. The surgeons removed as many of the fragments as possible and he was placed in a medically induced coma. Hospital staff closely monitored his brain for swelling. Back in California, his parents, Bob and Mary, and his sister were notified and on their way.

Kimbra sat at the side of his bed, holding his hand. Tears ran down her cheeks as she struggled to make sense of what happened. She told the police it was an accident, but that wasn't entirely true. Something or *someone* had possessed her. She raised the gun to her temple but when Jake intervened, *it* wanted to shoot him. Only three people had that kind of advanced telepathic powers and two of them, Christina and Chad, were dead. That left Fang. He had been acting erratically, and then there was the weird happenings the night she stayed at his house. But why would he want to hurt her, or Jake? Or was it because of what she knew? Did someone want to silence her?

She suspected the police did not believe it was an accident. I mean, what was she doing handling a loaded gun in the bedroom anyway? They released her, but she worried that the results of the investigation could lead to a charge of some sort. What were the charges typically mentioned on television: assault with a deadly weapon, criminal negligence, or both? She should probably look for an attorney, maybe Carter could help with that. Something had forced her to pull the trigger, but deep down her conscience told her she was responsible. Anyway, none of it really mattered for she could not tell the truth. Who would believe that a telepath, hundreds of miles away, took control of her mind and made her shoot Jake?

So there she sat with Jake, dreading the arrival of his parents. How could she face them knowing she was responsible? She would remain at Jake's side until they arrived, then she would leave and never return. What else could she do? She was a danger to Jake and everyone around her.

Bob and Mary Campbell entered the hospital, luggage in tow. A woman at the front desk directed them to Jake's room. Kimbra got up and stepped aside as they rushed to Jake's side, their faces were pale as a fresh fallen snow. Kimbra recognized them from her days in high school. They had aged some, but the years had treated them well. Tears flowed down Mary's cheeks as she kissed her son's forehead and held his hand.

"Oh, my poor Jake. What happened?" she whispered to herself.

Bob noticed Kimbra and greeted her.

"Hello Kimbra. It's been a long time."

"Hello Mr. Campbell. I'm sorry we have to meet under such terrible circumstances."

"What happened?" Mary directed her question at Kimbra, her tone was sharp. "The police told us there was an accident."

Kimbra shrunk into the corner and began to shake. She would have given anything to have faded away at that moment, just like Fang did at the cabin.

"I don't know. I'm sorry Mrs. Campbell..."

How could she tell them an evil presence forced her to get her gun and shoot their son? That would certainly not make this any easier on them. It was her fault and no explanation would ease their pain. Like everyone else around her, she had sucked Jake into the catastrophe that was her life.

"It was an accident," she muttered feebly.

"An accident!" Mary said tersely.

Bob moved a chair alongside Jake's bed and coaxed his wife to take a seat.

Kimbra stood there enduring their questions, enduring their cold stares. She was relieved when the doctor mercifully appeared. While he was explaining Jake's prognosis, she ducked out quietly.

# CHAPTER 57

GUILT STRICKEN AND FILLED WITH GRIEF, Kimbra could not possibly live in the same house with Jake's parents. She gave her key to the Campbells and moved back in with Gina. She toyed with the idea of leaving Colorado, but she could not leave Jake, not like this. So she drove an hour each day to visit Jake, only to leave if his parents were there. She spent her days wandering aimlessly about Fort Collins, frequently stopping at a coffee shop near the hospital. Then she would take the long drive home if Jake's mother spent the night at the hospital. For the first week that's just what Mary did, but as time wore on she would occasionally sleep at Jake's house to regain her strength. That's when Kimbra would spend the night, if the hospital staff allowed it. She wasn't family, but she got to know a few nurses who were kind enough to let her stay.

"Jake, I'm so sorry," Kimbra would whisper. Tears ran down her cheeks as she held his hand in the darkened room.

"I don't know how that happened. I should have never taken that drug."

A familiar nurse appeared to check on Jake.

"Are you all right dear?" she asked Kimbra.

"Yes, I'm fine. Thank you."

The nurse checked Jake's vitals and left. Kimbra remained there until the nurses on morning shift arrived.

Kimbra kept her part-time job at the Fort Collins coffee shop, mostly to be near Jake, but she also needed the money. Over time Jake improved and his condition was upgraded to stable. They weaned him off the drugs, but he remained in a coma. In most cases patients wake from a coma in a few days or a couple weeks, but it could last months, years, or forever. As far as Jake's long-term prognosis, the doctors would not commit. Recovering from a traumatic brain injury could take years and many times there were long term effects. Right now they focused on the coma. While coma patients cannot move and are unresponsive, they are sometimes conscious. Kimbra would talk and read to Jake each night, sensing he was in there somewhere listening. The nights she spent alone with Jake, she would bleed her heart out, apologizing for everything. She could never forgive herself, but she hoped some small part of Jake would understand and be able to forgive her one day.

Back at Gina's, Kimbra sat with a mug of black coffee, staring at a blank television screen. She spent the day in Fort Collins only to be kicked out of the hospital that night. A nurse in a bad mood decided to take it out on her. She missed spending the night with Jake, but was enjoying the solitude that came with the darkness of twilight. Gina and Greg were out on a *date* as they called it. Her mind was drifting when she was suddenly aroused by a knock on the door. She got up and peeked out the front window. It was a delivery man with a package in hand. The knock came again. He probably needed a signature as that would explain his persistence. Kimbra turned on a light and opened the door a crack.

The door pushed opened until she stopped it. Before she could register who it was, a man's boot stepped into the threshold. She looked up in shock.

"Daniel! What are you doing here?" she croaked out.

"I stopped by to see how you're doing."

Kimbra attempted to push the door shut but his foot remained firmly in place, blocking the door. Her mind quickly went to her pistol that was confiscated in Colorado. She had only her words to protect her now.

"Please, I just want to talk. I promise I'll leave. Just give me a minute to explain," he pleaded.

"Go ahead, explain," Kimbra held the door firmly against his foot.

"Can I come inside?"

"No. Say what you have to, and leave," she demanded.

"C'mon Kimbra," he pleaded. Then his tone changed, "You're starting to piss me off."

Kimbra pushed hard on the door, but it would not budge.

"Please leave. Gina and Greg will be back soon, I'm going to call the police."

His eyes were as dark as the night sky.

"No, they won't. Now just let me in, please."

Kimbra kept all her weight on the door. Then it burst open, sending her backward, her socked feet sliding on the wood floor.

"I just want to talk," he yelled as he entered the house, slamming the door shut behind him.

Kimbra backed into the living room, moving towards her phone.

"Sit down," he commanded.

She sat on the sofa, hoping he would not notice her phone on the end table. He sat down opposite her on a chair.

"I came all this way to see you and this is how you treat me?"

"What do you want?"

"I want us to get back together again. I want us to go back to where we were before."

"I can't do that," Kimbra tried to explain.

"Why not? Don't you love me anymore?"

"I don't," she said.

Daniel looked around the room. Did he notice the phone?

"Well, I don't believe you. Anyway it doesn't matter. Over time you'll change your mind. You'll see."

"No, I won't! Daniel, can't you see it's over, you and me? Why can't you just accept it and move on?"

That seemed to be the wrong thing to say. He rose up, fists clenched, hovering over her.

"No, you will accept that we are meant to be together. You see, if you don't, I will hurt everyone you love. Gina, Jake, everyone. You know I will."

Kimbra did not doubt him. Not wanting to anger him further, she remained silent. She only wanted him to leave.

"I'm different now," he said. "I can see things I never saw before, my senses are exceptional, and I'm growing stronger. You and I are a team. Besides, what choice do you have?"

There didn't seem to be anything she could do. No matter how hard she tried to have some semblance of a normal life, it always unraveled into chaos. It was hopeless. Maybe she should just give in and move back to San José before anyone else got hurt.

Daniel reached for Kimbra's phone and handed it to her.

"You've changed your number. Call me so I have it."

Kimbra did as he said, he updated her number and put his phone away.

"I'll be sticking around for a few days. I'll come get you, and we can go home together."

Kimbra sat there dumbfounded. This could not actually be happening. He approached her and bent over as if he was going to kiss her. She turned her cheek, he stopped and stood straight up.

"Don't disappoint me Kimbra," he said before turning to leave.

And then he was gone, leaving Kimbra in shock. She thought about what he said, everything he knew. He said he was *different now*. He *saw things he never saw before*, his *senses were exceptional*, and he was growing stronger. All those things, Kimbra could have used them to describe how she felt while using the drug. Did he somehow get his hands on QR-7? Was he involved in the theft at Quantum Thunder?

Gina and Greg returned home late, giddy from a rare night out, to find Kimbra awake and drinking wine.

"Kimbra, is everything all right?" Gina asked.

"Yes, I'm fine."

"You don't seem fine. You look frightened."

Kimbra wanted badly to tell her sister about Daniel's visit, but she couldn't, she could not endanger anyone else. They had been so kind to take her in, and then take her back after the shooting. No, she couldn't put Gina through any more grief.

"No, really. I'm fine," she lied.

Kimbra would make arrangements in the morning to move back to San José.

# CHAPTER 58

THE NEXT MORNING BROUGHT WITH IT MORE BAD NEWS. Gina caught Kimbra in the kitchen filling a mug of coffee.

"Mom called this morning."

Kimbra finished pouring her coffee and listened for more, expecting some kind of drama from their mother.

"Grandpa died suddenly!" Gina announced.

Kimbra's heart sank into her chest. She had been very close to her grandparents. They were getting along in years but were still in relatively good health. The news came as a shock.

"Oh my gosh! What happened?"

"They think it was a heart attack. Mom said the funeral will be Thursday."

Kimbra booked a flight for the next day. Gina was skeptical when she caught Kimbra packing all her belongings later that night.

"Looks like you're packing everything. What's going on?" Gina asked.

Kimbra looked up from her suitcase. "After the funeral, I'm moving back to San José."

"What, why? I thought you liked it here. What about Jake?"

Gina deserved an explanation, but Kimbra could not tell her about Daniel appearing at their house.

"I can't stay here. Jake's parents are here to take care of him and..."

"And what?" Gina prodded.

"I just can't. It's all my fault and my staying here only makes it worse."

Gina sat on Kimbra's bed alongside the luggage.

"What do you mean by that? You're not making things worse."

"Yes, I am. My whole life, all I've done is hurt everyone around me, I've ruined everything."

"No, you haven't. You've had some rough times, we both have. But that will change, just give it time."

Kimbra didn't believe that for a minute, but she didn't want to argue with her sister. She sat down next to Gina and looked her in the eye.

"We've both had hard times, I know. But you have to trust me, I need to do this."

"You know I'm always here for you," Gina's eyes moistened.

"I know."

Gina gave her sister a big hug and left.


The plane touched down in Pendleton, Oregon early the next morning. Kimbra headed directly to the baggage claim area, picked up her luggage and stepped outside. The sky was a bright blue and the air a cool 65 degrees, not exactly in sync with her mood. But her spirits picked up when a brown sedan pulled over and a balding man in his seventies stepped out.

"Uncle Vinny! Thanks for picking me up," Kimbra shouted with excitement, and to make sure he heard her.

The man wrapped her in a warm embrace. It was just what Kimbra needed. The Rossinis were huggers and Uncle Vinny was no different. His facial features and mannerisms resembled her grandfather in so many ways. In some way, his presence kept her grandfather alive, part of her grandfather lived in his brother, Vincent.

"How is Granny doing?" she asked.

Her uncle kept his eyes on the road. Her grandfather and he came from a large family, four boys and two girls. She wondered what it would be like, being part of a large family.

"It was sudden," he said. "When you've been together for so many years... it's a shock. At least he didn't suffer."

A lump formed in Kimbra's throat at the thought of her grandfather suffering. She cringed at the thought of Marie suffering as well. Kimbra had seen far too much death lately. Her eyes moistened as she revisited her grief, opening old wounds like picking at a scab. The two continued in silence, her uncle was saddened as well.

They arrived at their destination after a short ride, and seeing the house brought back a flood of memories. She recalled her childhood summers spent with her grandparents. The frequent outings for ice cream and to the local toy store, playing in the backyard pool and sandbox with the neighborhood kids, the bedtime stories and being tucked in after a calming back rub. They were indulged and spoiled a bit and it was just what she needed, a warm and loving environment, a refuge from the storm of her home life. The time she spent there was priceless.

They worked their way to the kitchen to find Nora seated at the table with a cup of black coffee, no doubt laced with a shot of sweet anisette liqueur. Her face brightened when she saw her granddaughter. Kimbra leaned over and gave her a hug.

"Grandma, it's so good to see you."

Nora got up and offered them something to drink, which Kimbra finally accepted. Knowing better than to offer to make it herself, she watched her grandmother brew a fresh pot of coffee. It wasn't long before Kimbra was sipping coffee, recalling the card and board games they played so often on that kitchen table.

"So how is everything in Colorado?" her grandmother asked. "We haven't talked in a while."

Kimbra hadn't called her grandmother in a while and she felt bad about that. But what could she tell her? She didn't need to hear all the shit that was going on in Kimbra's life.

"It was great seeing Gina. We did a lot of sightseeing and caught up on our lives."

"I'm so glad you stay in touch with your sister. You know, when your mother and I are gone, it will be just the two of you."

Kimbra's eyes drooped. Her grandmother must have sensed her reluctance to dwell on that.

"When is your sister getting here?" she asked.

Kimbra was happy to avoid discussing her chaotic life, she filled her grandmother in on Gina and Greg's arrival the next day.

"So how are *you* doing?" Kimbra asked.

Nora took a moment to reflect.

"I don't know. I guess it hasn't fully hit me, I mean there's an emptiness words cannot describe. You spend your entire life with someone, and then, in the blink of an eye, they're gone. The grief comes in waves, hits me the hardest when I'm alone with my thoughts... But what can I do? I'm just trying to get by, taking it one day at a time."

Vinny's tired eyes wandered in Kimbra's direction, "Aunt Anna offered to stay here with your grandma, but she refused."

"Oh, I'm fine. I don't want to put anyone out," Nora interjected.

Kimbra focused her gaze on her grandmother.

"Well, you don't have to be alone now. I'm going to stay here as long as you like."


The hours passed peacefully at her grandmother's, it was a gentle reprieve from Kimbra's personal hell. Gina and Greg arrived the next day, abruptly ending the peace and quiet. Her mother arrived the day after that, on the morning of the funeral. It didn't take long for Heather to bring up old skeletons and say something hurtful.

"So I hear you moved in with your sister," she commented to Kimbra.

"Yes," Kimbra was not going to give her mother anything more.

"Boyfriend problems in California? You always did have difficulty with relationships."

Kimbra glared at her mother. Knowing she had a way of pushing her buttons, she wanted to avoid a confrontation, still...

"That Mick was a loser," Heather continued. "And what happened with you and that fellow from LA, Chuck wasn't it?"

It was Carter, but what did it matter? It was useless trying to reason with her mother. Her mother continued. Like a prize fighter jabbing away, she was relentless.

"I do remember one nice one from high school. Jake wasn't it? But then you went and ruined that one too."

That was it, Kimbra's face turned a crimson red as she exploded in a fit of rage.

"As if *you* would know anything about men! *You* drove my dad to suicide, *you* drove Tim away, and that loser Cody, did you know he molested Gina and me?"

Kimbra regretting the words as soon as they left her mouth. Heather's jaw dropped, for the moment silenced. Gina, Greg and her grandmother were there to witness the ugly exchange. After several awkward moments, Gina stepped in and grabbed her sister, directing her to another room.

"You shouldn't let her get to you," Gina said. "You know what she's like."

"I know, but I just couldn't take it again. Not now."

Gina gave her sister a hug. She knew.


Kimbra had been to funerals before, but this was different, this was her Papa. Her grandparents were a lifeline for her in a time of turbulence. She would miss him dearly. It was difficult, but mostly for Nora. The calling hours, funeral service, and graveside burial were painful and slow. The family gathering was an opportunity to reminisce and catch up with long lost relatives, a mix of grief and nostalgia. Time has a way of washing away your past. They say blood is thicker than water, yet this was family you would never see again, until the next funeral or wedding.

The large group gathering helped to keep Nora's mind off the inevitable, which arrived too quickly. Life moves on, in spite of our best efforts to hold those nearest and dearest to us close. The out of town family left, leaving Nora with the grim realization that John, her husband of 54 years, was gone. Kimbra and her grandmother were once again alone in the house. They sat in silence watching a game show on the old television set.

"Kimbra dear, is something bothering you?" her grandmother asked.

"No, I'm fine. Just the usual stuff," Kimbra lied.

Nora stared her down, knowing something was wrong.

"You know you shouldn't let your mother get to you like that."

"I know, but sometimes I just can't take it anymore."

Nora fumbled with the remote and muted the volume on the television, catching Kimbra's full attention.

"She's my daughter and I love her, but your mother has always been a problem. She's like the wind, always drifting, searching for the next best thing, never happy with what she's got."

Nora paused to reflect.

"You my dear are different, you're nothing like your mother. You have met adversity head on, and dealt with it."

Nora clenched her fist for emphasis and continued.

"You're a fighter. The wind may blow and howl, but you are stronger. You have a strong heart and it will guide you through all the shit that life will dish out and believe me, it will dish out plenty."

Tears rolled down Kimbra's cheeks, "Thank you Grandma!"

A smile came to her face. Her grandmother always knew what to say, she was also surprised to hear her say *shit*.

Nora turned the volume back up and nothing more was said about it.


Kimbra was packing her bags again, saddened that her time with her grandmother was nearly done. The time had come to deal with her life, to meet adversity head on like Granny had said, she just wasn't sure how to do that. She was thinking about what her grandmother said when her phone rang. It was Daniel.

"How was the funeral?" he asked, as if they had some semblance of a normal relationship.

Kimbra felt a presence over the distance. Was he reading her mind?

"Are you there?"

"Yes, I'm here. What do you want?" she snapped.

"Just checking on you. When are you coming home? You are coming home aren't you?"

Kimbra clenched her jaw. She wanted nothing more than to remain in Oregon, start anew and leave everything behind. But she couldn't, for he would find her. She didn't know where it was going, but her life was moving ahead, out of her control, towards an inevitable destiny.

"I'm coming home, but I need time to adjust."

"What does that mean?"

"I'm going to stay in a motel for a while. You need to give me this."

There was a silence over the airwaves, as if he was probing her mind.

"Okay. I'll give you that."

# CHAPTER 59

KIMBRA WAS BACK IN SAN JOSÉ, ANXIOUSLY WAITING when a light knock came on the door. She got up and opened the door a crack, leaving the chain attached. Two owl-like eyes peered through thick lens eyeglasses. She unchained the door, allowing the man to enter her cramped motel room. He took a seat near the desk, a dark briefcase rested on his lap.

"I'm glad you called," Stanwix said.

Kimbra sat down on a bed, "Have you seen Fang?"

"No, no one has. But a lot has happened since you left, it's gotten worse. Casey and his thugs are moving the whole operation."

"But it's Fang's company, it's his research," Kimbra countered.

"I don't think it matters to them. Besides, like I said, he hasn't been seen, there's no one to object. And to make matters worse, Casey is stepping up the human trials. I think they're planning on assembling a paranormal army."

Kimbra's jaw dropped as Stanwix sat there fiddling with his briefcase.

"An army? What do you think they're planning?" she asked.

"I don't know, but it can't be good. They know about Fang teleporting, that could be their greatest weapon."

"I know I saw Fang at the cabin, but how is it possible to physically transport your body somewhere?"

Stanwix scratched his head. "It should not be possible, but it happened. We can only speculate as to how."

Kimbra's eyebrows arched upward as she anxiously awaited an explanation for the impossible.

"Fang discussed it with me. He suggested a quantum connection to a primordial black hole."

"Primordial black holes?"

"They are hypothetical black holes formed soon after the Big Bang. A miniature wormhole could offer an explanation for the mechanics behind the transfer of matter or whatever is happening."

The physics was over Kimbra's head. She only knew she was in danger and any talk of a paranormal army terrified her. What if she was a target for knowing what she did?

"So what did you call about?" Stanwix asked.

Things had gotten worse than Kimbra imagined. Still, she had her own problems to deal with.

"A lot has happened to me as well. I was hoping you could help, I need your advice."

Kimbra updated Stanwix on everything, including shooting Jake, Daniel's phone call, and the vision of the bear attack.

"So, you think Daniel is taking QR-7 and stalking you?"

"He's in my head, he must have the drug. How else could he be doing this?"

"Have you told Agent Manning?"

"No. I mean, I don't have any real evidence."

"Doesn't matter, you should let him know Daniel is a potential suspect in the theft."

Kimbra nodded, he was right. Stanwix sat there, fingers tapping on his briefcase. He was contemplating something.

"Now, back to your stalking problem. I may have a way to help, but it could be dangerous."

Kimbra's eyes widened as he opened his briefcase and pulled out a vial of greenish liquid.

"Is that what I think it is?" she asked.

"The drug is locked down tighter than Fort Knox right now. Fang has a personal supply he secured before the military took over, and I decided to pilfer a small amount for myself."

"What are you going to do with it?"

Kimbra peered into the briefcase, seeing a syringe and needles.

"Well I wasn't sure, until now. I think you may need this more than me."

"What do you mean?" Kimbra asked.

Stanwix's eyes narrowed. "You have a stalker who is using the drug. This may be the only way to defend yourself."

Kimbra recalled the vision of her father's suicide, the emotions, the pain, all the result of QR-7.

"I don't know. What about the side effects? What about Chad and Fang?"

"I have been experimenting with smaller doses."

"What do you mean, *experimenting*? Are you taking the drug?" Kimbra asked.

"No. What I'm doing is short dosing some of the new subjects and keeping the rest for myself. I've found that smaller doses can produce the desired result without any apparent side effects. It might work for you."

Images flashed through Kimbra's mind: She imagined Chad being shot dead in a hail of gunfire from the police, she recalled Fang lying comatose in the hospital bed.

"Kimbra, are you all right?"

"Harold, I had another concern."

Stanwix leaned on top of the open briefcase, listening intently, "What is it?"

"When Fang came out of the coma, there was something he said."

Kimbra searched for the exact words.

"He said he didn't belong here. He said he was *stuck between two worlds*. Does that make any sense to you?"

Stanwix leaned back in his chair and pondered the remark.

"We have seen the drug alter a subject's personality, and perception of reality. But we also know it has given them paranormal abilities beyond our wildest dreams. We know he teleported at least once and who's to say he hasn't done it again."

Stanwix reflexively pulled out a pack of cigarettes, as if his subconscious took over.

"I know. I shouldn't smoke in here and I'm trying to quit," he stuffed the pack back in his pocket and continued.

"Fang and I discussed telepathy as well as entering another person's mind. We were concerned with what happens to your consciousness. Are you in one body or the other, or both? I don't know the answer, but maybe he does?"

Another thought just crossed Kimbra's mind.

"Fang also mentioned someone could have occupied Chad's mind. What do you think he meant by that?"

"There may be a fine line between sending your *thoughts* to another person and sending your *consciousness*. But for the latter, the question is how much of you and how much of the host is in there? Whose consciousness is it?"

These were questions that only Fang could answer but Kimbra was desperate, maybe taking the drug would provide some answers. Maybe it would help protect her from Daniel. With her gun held by the police back in Colorado, she had nothing to defend herself with. She was torn, the drug could be a way out of the mess she was in, but at what cost?

Stanwix checked his watch, he seemed nervous.

"Let me show you how to inject it. That way, you'll be prepared if you decide to use it."

Kimbra nodded. Daniel would be calling soon, demanding her return to him. Not having a clear plan for her future, it would be wise to keep her options open.

Stanwix tied a tourniquet around her arm and swabbed the injection site with an alcohol wipe. He drew the desired dosage into the syringe, then held the needle up and squirted out a tiny amount to insure there was no air trapped in the syringe.

"This is the correct dosage, but I'm using a saline solution for our demonstration."

Stanwix instructed her on inserting the needle at a 15 to 45 degree angle. Kimbra winced as he pierced the skin and drew up a tiny bit of blood to insure he was in the vein. Then he pushed the plunger down and removed the needle slowly.

"That's all there is to it. Do you think you can do that yourself?"

Kimbra was more than a little queasy about self-injecting. Drug addicts did it all the time, but...

"I don't know... I guess if I really had to."

"Fine. Then I'll leave this with you?"

Stanwix packed the drug and all the supplies in a black ziplock travel bag and gave it to her. Kimbra stopped him at the door.

"Harold, what are you going to do now?"

"I'm not sure, but they have to be stopped. Good luck my dear."

Stanwix shot her a crooked smile and left.

Kimbra was laying on the bed watching Law & Order SVU on the television. Her eyes darted over to the travel bag on the nightstand. What if Stanwix was right? The drug could be a way out, offer her some protection, warn her of danger. At the very least, it would level the playing field. On the other hand, she was well aware of the inherent dangers. She decided to table any decision for now, wait and see if there were any other options. She was attempting to put those thoughts aside for the moment, watching a dramatic scene play out on the crime show when a loud *knock* came at the door. She jumped off the bed and hid the travel bag under a pillow. Her worst fears were confirmed when she opened the door. Dark eyes peered through the opening held secure by the chain.

"Daniel, why are you here?"

"What's wrong? You're not happy to see me? Remove the chain," he demanded.

"I thought you were going to give me a little more time."

"Kimbra..." A smirk formed on his face as he spoke. "I've given you all kinds of time. Enough of these childish games, it's time to pack your things and come with me. Now, remove the chain!"

Kimbra hesitated and in that instant he slammed the door into the chain. Kimbra stood back. Once, twice, and on the third try the chain broke free. The door swung open, along with the attached bracket and a loud bang and a clatter. He entered the room, slamming the door closed behind him.

Kimbra worried he would find the drugs under her pillow. She had to act quickly.

"I'm coming, but you don't have to wait for me. Let me pack my things and I'll meet you back at your place."

Daniel studied her closely, probing her thoughts. He looked around the room. She resisted looking in the direction of the travel bag under the pillow. Stop thinking about it she willed herself.

"No, we're leaving now. I want to make sure you have time to settle in," he insisted.

"But what about my car?"

"We can pick it up tomorrow. C'mon let's get going."

"No. I'm staying here to pack and I'll meet you later."

Kimbra regretted the words immediately. He was on her in an instant, like a bomb just went off. He grabbed her by the hair and dragged her close to him. His lips curled.

"No! We're going NOW!"

He loosened his grip on her hair only to punch her in the face. Kimbra hit the bed, her face exploding in pain, the taste of blood in her mouth. He threw her luggage on the bed and began to empty the contents of the drawers into the bag, then zipped it shut and yanked her up by the hair.

"Let's go!"

Daniel exited the motel room with Kimbra and her luggage in tow. A large man outside, noticed the encounter and approached cautiously. He was older than Daniel, probably in his forties, and muscular.

"What are you looking at?" Daniel shouted at the man.

The man looked at Kimbra, seeing her bruised face.

"I don't think she wants to go with you," he said.

"Really! Well, it's none of your business, so why don't you fuck off!" Daniel shot back.

"What did you say?"

"You heard me, fuck off!" Daniel repeated.

That was the wrong thing to say. The man looked at Kimbra, reading the fear in her eyes, then stepped up and punched Daniel square in the face. Daniel flew backwards barely regaining his footing, blood dripping from his mouth. The man stood his ground next to Kimbra ready to go at it again. Daniel wiped his bloody mouth on his forearm. He stood hunched over staring up at the man, like a wounded animal. The world around them froze as the two adversaries eyed each other over. A car suddenly came to a stop nearby and a couple stepped out, gawking at the standoff.

Daniel spit out blood, stood up straight and growled at Kimbra, "I'll be back!"

He got in his car and drove off.

The man turned to Kimbra, "Are you all right?"

Kimbra thanked the good Samaritan and returned to her room. With no idea what her future would hold, she put ice on her face and plopped down on the bed.

# CHAPTER 60

SPECIAL AGENT BAKER MANNING SAT ACROSS THE TABLE FROM A HULK OF A MAN. Known on the streets as a low level enforcer, Dimitri Yagodnikov had a shaved head, pudgy face, and no neck. The robbery at Quantum Thunder was aided by security guard Alex Mishkin, who later admitted Dimitri blackmailed and threatened him into helping the robbers. Manning placed a manila folder and a pack of cigarettes on the table.

"Cigarette?" he asked.

The man nodded, Manning passed the pack and lit one for him.

"We had a hard time locating you," Manning admitted.

The man shrugged, seemingly unconcerned.

"What were you doing in Kansas City?"

Dimitri took a drag from the cigarette, exhaled a cloud of smoke upwards, and ignored the question.

"Any idea why you're here?"

"Not really," Dimitri's voice was deep, his tone calm.

"I have a witness who claims you threatened his wife and family, blackmailed him to assist in a robbery at Quantum Thunder. I don't suppose you know anything about that?"

"I don't know anything about that."

"Leaving Oakland was a violation of your parole and with all the evidence against you, this is not going to end well for you."

"Sorry, but I can't help you."

Manning leaned in and looked Dimitri in the eye.

"Look, I'll be straight with you. I'm more interested in the people who orchestrated the robbery than what you did. I've got bigger fish to fry, but you're the one that got caught and you're the one that's going to pay for it. I need answers and if you cooperate, I'll see to it you get a deal."

"A deal?"

"Yeah, a deal. Without it you're going back to prison for a long time. I can make sure they go easy on you, maybe even drop the charges."

Dimitri uncrossed his arms. He was opening up.

"Even if I wanted to, I couldn't help you," he said.

"What does that mean?"

"If I knew someone, it would be by nickname only."

Manning opened the folder and placed six photos across the table.

"Recognize any of these gentlemen?"

Dimitri's eyes darted over the photos, then widened before he looked away and shook his head. Manning knew he was hiding something.

"No deal if you can't help me. Why don't you take another look?"

Dimitri took another drag on his cigarette and examined the photos more closely. He pushed one aside.

"That's the dude that hired me to rough up Mishkin. I never got a name though, he called himself the *Shadow*."

Manning picked up the photo and studied it carefully. Daniel Visser was never a suspect until Kimbra Evans called with her suspicions. He wasn't able to identify the thieves yet, but he now suspected Visser was the mastermind behind the robbery and could lead them straight to the missing drug. He could also be using the drug, as Miss Evans suggested. That could make him dangerous. He would notify Colonel Casey immediately.

Late that night, Dr. Harold Stanwix was putting in extra hours. He waited until the last shift of workers left, all that remained were security personnel. He had been pilfering small amounts of QR-7 for some time, collecting it for some unknown use in the future. Now that he had given it all to Kimbra, there was one last task to perform. The military was moving the operation off-site to a more secure facility. More and more subjects were being injected with the drug and judging from the candidates' backgrounds, Stanwix believed they were creating a paranormal army. He wasn't sure he could stop them, but he might be able set them back, possibly years.

The stockpile of QR-7 was being depleted rapidly, he had to prevent them from producing any more. The production process began with DNA modified human cells locked in a refrigerator. The main cell bank was stored in the freezer while the working cells were in the refrigerator section. He had the key, but could not get in there without being detected by the live cameras. He had a plan, but it would be risky. If caught, this would surely land him in prison for many years. That, or something worse. After all, he was dealing with a covert branch of the government that operated clandestine missions all over the world. Who knew what extreme measures they would take to protect the drug and its secrets?

Stanwix put on his jacket and hat with shaky hands before turning out the lights and leaving the lab. Working his way towards the elevator, he stopped at a utility closet. He opened the door and pulled out a penlight, shining it on an electrical box in the back. He opened the panel door, flashing the light up and down the circuits. There it was, clearly labeled, *fridge & lab lights*. He flicked the breaker off, shut the panel door and wiped down everything he touched with a handkerchief. He did the same with the utility room door knob before leaving. He was in and out in five minutes.

He took the elevator to the main floor and passed a security guard at the exit.

"Late night Doc?" the man asked.

"Just some r-reports to catch up on."

"Well, good night."

"Thank you. You have a good night as well."

The human cell lines required a narrow temperature and humidity range to survive. Thawing the cells required a very precise process. If the freezer remained off long enough, the frozen cells would thaw too slowly and they would be rendered useless. The cells in the fridge would warm up and die.

# CHAPTER 61

IT HAPPENED AGAIN. Kimbra woke in darkness to see a shadow at the side of her bed, watching her, waiting for her to wake. Before her eyes could adjust it was on top of her, choking her. She tried to scream but his hands were clamped down on her throat, it felt like her windpipe was about to crush.

"You had to go and screw it all up," he grunted as he struggled to hold her down.

She tried to kick, but the sheets were wrapped too tightly around her legs.

"We had something special, but you wouldn't listen to me."

The bed was creaking as Kimbra continued kicking and flailing wildly from side to side to escape his stranglehold.

"Only now do you see, it was hopeless to resist me. But now it's too late."

Kimbra was growing weaker by the moment. She was seeing stars as her oxygen deprived brain was losing consciousness, her muscles were growing limp. The room around her faded as she focused on his eyes. Those mysterious brown eyes were now evil, the eyes of a cold-blooded killer. This was how her crazy life was going to end, and he was enjoying it.

Suddenly, her one leg broke free from the sheets and she kicked with all her strength, landing one square shot to his groin. His grip around her throat loosened for a moment, and she turned to her side coughing. He let go, groaning in pain as she jumped off the bed, stubbed her toe on the nightstand and tripped.

"Help! Help me," she cried out in a raspy voice that no one would hear.

Dizzy and nauseous, she struggled to get up. Before she could regain her wits he was back, throwing her against the wall. Kimbra screamed again for help the best she could. She dove onto the floor, crawling under the bed for safety, pulling her legs in and coiling up in a ball. He laughed as she fought to survive.

"It's no use. Don't you see?" he taunted.

Daniel pulled at her legs and dragged her out kicking. She sat up against the side of the bed as he pulled out a knife.

"All the things I did for you, and for what? I thought you were different, but you're just like the others, an ungrateful bitch!"

"What did you do for me Daniel, what did you do?" Kimbra croaked out along with a cough.

He grabbed her by the hair and flashed the knife in front of her face.

"I killed Marie and framed your high school boyfriend for it."

She tried to keep him talking. Every minute he talked was another minute to live, a chance to survive. Tears welled up in her eyes.

"Why would you do that? She never bothered you!"

"She hated me. She would have broken us up. Don't you see?"

"And what about Christina? Did you kill her too?"

"She knew what I was doing, she knew I was watching you. She had to be stopped."

He paused for a moment. Could he be talked out of this?

"She alerted me to the visions," he explained. "And that led me to the experimental drug. But it was your boss appearing at the cabin that convinced me. How else would anyone believe the crazy things being done there?"

Kimbra bit her lip. She couldn't get her mind off him killing Marie, and it was her fault. Her crazy life had brought Daniel into the mix. She had to keep him talking, hoping someone heard the struggle and called the police.

"You never told me about Linda, the missing girl in high school. Did you kill her, too?"

Daniel paused, and turned his head. Kimbra thought she heard a car door closing outside.

"Did you kill her, too?" she asked again.

"Linda was not the right girl. I was young, it took me a while to see that."

Daniel turned again as the sound of footsteps approached. Kimbra took the opportunity to crawl back under the bed. There was a loud knock on the door.

"Police!"

Daniel grabbed at Kimbra's kicking legs.

"Police! Open up!" The knock came harder now.

Daniel had hold of one leg and dragged her out from under the bed. He held the knife up high, ready to slash at her. She kicked hard, landing her heel square in his face as pain shot through her leg. He let go, stood up, and disappeared. The bathroom door slammed shut as Kimbra got up and rushed to the door.

"I'm coming," she called out to the police in a hoarse voice.

With gun drawn, a uniformed officer stepped in and examined the room.

"Are you all right, Miss? We had a report of a disturbance."

"I was attacked, he's in the bathroom."

The officer looked down at her injured foot, she was standing in a puddle of blood. His eyes followed bloody footprints to the bathroom.

"You say he's in the bathroom?"

"Yes."

"Does he have a weapon?"

"He has a knife," Kimbra said.

"Stand over there," the officer motioned her to a safe corner as he approached the bathroom.

Standing to the side, he knocked on the bathroom door.

"Come out now with your hands up!"

The officer repeated the command. Hearing no response, he turned the knob slowly and pushed the door open. With gun held out in front, he disappeared into the bathroom. Kimbra cowered in the corner, waiting. Moments later the officer reappeared.

"There's no one in there!"

# CHAPTER 62

RIZZO RETURNED TO HIS DESK WITH A HOT MUG OF COFFEE. He took a gulp and chased it with an antacid tablet.

"Rough morning?" his coworker asked.

"You could say that. I've been trying to tie up a few loose ends on the Sadowski case."

Montero swung her chair over to Rizzo's desk, "I thought you said that case was closed."

Rizzo ran a hand over the stubble of growth on his head. He left the Los Angeles Police to get away from the rat race and back log of murder investigations. Now, here he was in Freemont, snooping around where he didn't belong. They had their killer, the file was closed.

"It is," he admitted.

Liz Montero's dark brown eyes widened, expecting more. "So what are you doing?"

"Daniel Visser seems to have skipped town."

"Visser? Who's he?"

"Could be the guy that killed Marie Sadowski *and* Christine Sullivan."

Montero's jaw dropped. "What makes you think that?"

"Remember Marie's friend, Kimbra Evans and her connection to both of the victims?"

"Yeah..."

"Miss Evans mentioned an ex-boyfriend, Daniel Visser, as a suspect in both murders. She's convinced he's guilty."

"Based on what evidence?" Montero asked.

"She says he confessed to both murders."

Montero leaned in and lowered her voice, "He confessed! So, are you going to bring him in? Did you tell the captain?"

Rizzo crossed his arms and leaned back in his chair.

"Well like I said, he skipped town. But there's one problem. Police arrived on the scene shortly after Miss Evans stated that Visser beat her and confessed."

"So what's the problem? Did they let him go?"

"Not exactly."

Montero, a type A personality and not one for keeping secrets, was way past impatient.

"Now what the hell does that mean?"

"Daniel Visser somehow disappeared. He apparently vanished into thin air from a bathroom with no exit."

"So she imagined the whole thing."

"Yeah, except that several eye witnesses heard two people fighting in the hotel room, and she had wounds from a fight. Bruises and a nasty cut on her foot."

Montero sat there rolling her eyes. "Look, you said the whole thing was weird, with psychics and visions and such. She's a nut, right?"

"Maybe, but there's more."

"Okay, nothing will surprise me after that last one."

Rizzo rubbed his tired eyes and tried to explain.

"I just got back from one of the stores I checked earlier to see if Mick Donnelly purchased the murder weapon there."

Montero sat in silence.

"This time I looked for another name and guess what?"

"Oh dear lord, what?"

"Daniel Visser purchased the exact type of knife we recovered on Donnelly's property and identified as the murder weapon."

"Okay, but his prints were not on the murder weapon, right?"

Rizzo shook his head and opened a pack of gum, offering Montero a stick, which she refused. He popped one in his mouth and spoke.

"Any prints were wiped clean. I dug deeper into Visser's background and discovered he was connected with a missing person. His high school girlfriend, Lisa Minetti, was never found. He was questioned by Oakdale and Stanislaus County Sheriff's Office but never charged."

"That's interesting but it's all circumstantial," Montero pointed out.

"I also found out he served in the Army in Afghanistan, working as a communications specialist. That would give him the skills to climb the pole and knock out the phone line at Christina Sullivan's house."

Rizzo wasn't sure that warranted reopening the case, but he was convinced they had convicted the wrong guy in Marie's murder. Montero took a moment to think it through, then spoke.

"So what are you going to do? I'm not sure the captain will think it's enough."

"I don't know but I think Mick Donnelly is innocent, and we may have a serial killer here."

# CHAPTER 63

BAKER MANNING SAT ACROSS THE TABLE FROM THE COLONEL.

"So you think this Daniel Visser is behind the robbery?" Colonel Casey asked.

"I'm sure of it."

"And what about his disappearance from the motel room? Do you believe Miss Evans, do you think he teleported out of there?"

"I do. It all fits. We know Fang was taking the drug and he teleported to the cabin where she was held. If Visser stole the drug, it's logical to assume he is using it."

Casey's steel blue eyes narrowed.

"It's all based on Miss Evans' statements though," he noted.

"It's been corroborated by others. I think we have enough on Visser to bring him in and press charges," Manning offered.

"Hold on, not just yet," Casey said.

"Why, what are we waiting for?"

"I have other plans for Mr. Visser," Casey said.

Manning wasn't sure he liked that, but wouldn't dare say otherwise to the colonel.

"What about Fang? He's involved in this somehow as well."

"Let me worry about Fang," the colonel replied.

Casey was part of the CIA Special Activities Center which oversaw covert operations. Manning couldn't be certain, but he suspected a military action was being planned in response to the theft. Manning's job was to report his findings to the colonel and the CID Director. His involvement ended there. After that, all he could do was let them handle it.

"That brings us to the destruction of the QR-7 stockpile. Have you made any progress on that?" Casey asked.

"Some of the stockpile was saved, but the main bank was destroyed and it will have to be rebuilt from scratch. That will set the program back months, maybe longer."

Casey's face reddened.

"I know a few people that will not be happy with that. So what happened?"

"There isn't any proof the circuit box was tampered with, but forensics is working on it. Stanwix was working late and I questioned him."

"And?" the colonel asked.

"He was extremely anxious. He's hiding something, I'm sure of it. But, he's denying any involvement and like I said, we're waiting on forensics for more."

Casey laced his fingers together in contemplation.

"All right Baker, keep me posted."

* * *

## Six months later

Daniel Visser's second floor apartment was dark, most everyone short of the incurable insomniac had long since turned in for the night. The bookstore below was closed along with the other retail stores on the first floor. A strange vibration filled the living room as subatomic particles in the room became energized. A tiny wormhole formed, grew, and an object became visible where seconds ago there was none. The translucent object phased in and out of existence before slowly appearing in the shape of a human, a man in full tactical gear, who had just traversed hundreds of miles in a matter of seconds.

The soldier scanned the room with night vision goggles. He aimed a laser sighted rifle fitted with a noise suppressor. A narrow, red beam of light danced around the room searching for its target. Nothing was found, the main living area and kitchen were clear. He moved towards the office in back, again searching for any signs of life, but found none. The bedroom was next. Gripping the rifle tightly, he approached carefully. The bed was unmade and empty. Down on one knee he peered under the bed, but found nothing. Next, he opened the closet door and found it empty. Only one place remained. He slowly approached the bathroom, the only hiding place remaining was the shower. With the end of the rifle he quickly slid the shower curtain open. The curtain holders clanged along the shower rod, but the shower was empty.

The assassin lifted the goggles and let his eyes adjust. His attention was drawn to the mirror as he fumbled for the light switch. Now it was clear to see, a note written in red on the mirror.

Catch me if you can!

He pointed his rifle down and sighed. Perhaps they had underestimated this man.

# CHAPTER 64

**One year later**

KIMBRA GOT OFF THE TRAIN AT THE HALSTED STREET STATION. It was a short walk home. The air was a crisp 59 degrees, a typical spring day in Chicago. She stopped at a local bakery along the way, picking up a few muffins to go with her morning coffee. Back on the street, she snaked her way through the neighborhood, turned onto West 19th Street, past a preschool, and shortly later reached her destination. She had been lucky to find a nice, affordable condo in Pilsen. The Lower West Side used to be one of the most dangerous areas in Chicago. Today, it was home to a vibrant community with local coffee shops, cafes, art galleries and studios. Kimbra climbed the stoop and took the stairs to the second floor.

Painted in neutral tones of gray and beige, the two-bedroom condo was updated and clean. The kitchen had white cabinets and stainless steel appliances, the floors were a dark brown, wood laminate. Kimbra left her keys on the counter and looked around. Sure enough, Smokey was soaking up the warmth in his favorite sunspot by the window. After stroking his ears, Kimbra kicked off her shoes and relaxed on the couch.

A lot had happened over the last year, all of it for the better. Kimbra was working in a clinic for troubled youth and going to school for her master's degree. Stanwix did his undergrad work in Chicago and helped her get accepted there. So life was good, but it wasn't always like that. She picked up an old notebook on the end table and flipped through the tattered pages, each one represented a slice of time from her past. Drowning in depression, she wrote poetry back then as an escape. She stopped at a short poem, recalling how some days it was impossible to muster the energy to get out of bed. She ran her fingers over the text and whispered the words out loud. It was a simple thing she called Morning Lament:

> *I lie in bed, unable to move*
> *So tired, so heavy, unwilling to bend*
> *There is no light, only gray*
> *A struggle played out, again and again*

At the time, it helped to put into words what she felt. There were only two people in the whole world she shared that notebook with: Mick and Marie. Both had been an anchor in troubled waters, an escape from the reality that was her life. But like most good things in her life, they came to an ugly end. Mick proved himself a liar and a cheat and Marie, she was gone. But why? Why was Kimbra's past such a catastrophe? What she should be doing, was place the blame on Daniel, because that's where it really began to spiral out of control. Only now did she realize that while he never approached her, he was stalking her back in high school. His twisted longings for her had hurt everyone around her: He killed Marie and pinned it on Mick; he killed Christina; Carter was convicted for a crime he did not commit; and Jake was shot. All because of Daniel! He was to blame for everything.

But since she moved to Chicago, her life had changed, it was good. The nightmares were gone, for the most part, and she had stopped taking the sleeping medication and tranquilizer. Had she finally put Daniel behind her, or would it all crumble away at some point? Right then her phone rang. She set down the notebook and answered the call.

"Hey sis!"

"Kimbra, it's been a while since we talked. So, how is everything going?" Gina asked.

"Everything is good. I'm actually happy here in Chicago," the word *happy* seemed strangely out of place coming from her lips.

"And how is school going?"

"It's not easy, you know me and school never got along. But I'm really working at it and I like my courses, well most of them."

"I'm so glad it's all working out for you. It was a very courageous thing you did, moving to Chicago all on your own."

"Thanks, Gina. How are things in Welby?"

Gina was doing great and there was talk of starting a family. That did not ever seem possible for Kimbra. She was happy for her sister, but things were different now, she could never trust someone again, not after Daniel. Kimbra was lost in  thought when the conversation turned back her way.

"So what about San José?" Gina asked. "Any developments since we last talked?"

"Let me think. Did I tell you about my boss?"

"No. What happened?"

"Well, Harold called. Remember Dr. Stanwix?"

"Oh yeah, the molecular biologist."

"He stopped by Fang's house and found him unconscious. He's in a vegetative state with no brain activity."

"That's terrible. What happened?"

"No one knows for sure, but they suspect it was drug induced."

"You mean that drug you said he was taking?" Gina asked.

"Yes."

Though a drug overdose was reported to the public, Kimbra was not sure it was the QR-7 that killed him. Fang knew too much, and so did she.

"So what happened to the project you were working on?"

"They shut the doors. Stanwix said they moved the whole operation to a secure military facility."

The whole experience sounded so dark and sinister, like a science fiction thriller. But it had happened, it was all true.

"And Daniel? He killed Marie and the others?"

"Yes, he admitted it all to me."

"But they can't prove it, can they?"

"I don't know."

That was the million dollar question. Would they ever prove Daniel had killed any of them? But, none of that mattered if they couldn't find him. Detective Rizzo reported Daniel had disappeared. Kimbra grew nauseous just thinking about the cabin, his attempt to kill her, and all the pain and suffering he put her through.

"Kimbra, are you there?"

"Yeah, sorry. Just thinking."

"Well, I hope they find him and put him away for life."

"Me too."

Kimbra wondered if that would ever happen.

"How is Jake doing?" Gina asked.

It was still raw thinking about Jake. Daniel had gotten into her head, but *she* pulled the trigger. There was no denying that.

"Kimbra?"

"He's doing fine, I guess the best you could expect."

Kimbra visited Jake a couple weeks ago. He finished physical therapy and was getting along fine, he was even back to work. But there could be long-term effects from the injury. Memory loss, mood swings, loss of balance, headaches, seizures; they were all possible down the road. Victims of traumatic brain injuries also had shorter lives. Kimbra did not mention any of that to Gina.

"Do you think you two will ever get together again?" Gina asked.

Kimbra had fallen in love with Jake's easy going lifestyle, she once thought it possible for them to have a life together. But that was before Daniel had gotten into her head, causing the accident. She knew now, that would never happen.

"No, I don't think it would work. Too much has happened, we changed. We're two different people now."

Kimbra closed the connection, turned her attention back to the notebook and reflected on her life. She flipped through to the last page, to a poem with no title:

*Breathe in, breathe out, each second a gift;*
*One conscious thought, a grain of sand on the beach;*
*But with it comes power, to do evil or good;*

DARK PRESENCE

*To lie and cheat, or enlighten and teach;*
*For in the end, I came and I went;*
*My only hope being, that my life was well-spent;*

 She picked up her pen and scribbled a simple two-word title:

*My Life*

# CHAPTER 65

FANG'S EYES FLUTTERED OPEN, ALLOWING A GLIMMER OF LIGHT IN, THEN CLOSED AGAIN. His thoughts were fuzzy, like having just regained consciousness when awakening. He tried lifting his heavy eyelids open again. A room slowly came into view, a hospital room. His eyes darted around but his body was frozen. He tried speaking but couldn't. A nurse glanced in his room and hurried to his side.

"You're awake! Let me get the doctor."

She returned with a small army of hospital staff. A dark-skinned doctor of Indian descent shined a penlight in Fang's eyes. Her long dark hair was tied back with shorter bangs in front covering her eyebrows.

"Mr. Kai, can you understand me?"

Fang nodded as he reached for his throat.

"Pupils are equal and reactive to light," the doctor reported to the group.

"Mr. Kai, you're on a machine to help you breath. I'm going to begin weaning you off it. When we do that, we can remove the tube. How does that sound?"

Fang nodded again.

The doctor directed the nurse to elevate the head of his bed while another member of the team adjusted the breathing machine.

"I'll be back to check on your progress," the doctor said.

Fang overheard the doctor talking in the hall to the staff. She was shaking her head as she spoke in a hushed tone.

"I never thought he would come back, there was no brain activity. I don't know what happened, but it is truly miraculous!"

Hospital staff came and went as Fang tried to make sense of his new surroundings. He looked down at his thin frame. He remembered nothing of what landed him in the hospital, but he was familiar with this person, the mind he was now part of, for he had been here before. Fang struggled to recall what happened before, but he grew sleepy. He fought to stay awake, fearing he would return to his other existence. But it was no use and he fell fast asleep.

"Mr. Kai, we're ready to remove the breathing tube. Do you feel you're up to that?"

Fang slowly woke to see a group of people surrounding him. He nodded.

"Your girlfriend is here," the doctor said.

Fang looked over at a beautiful girl with long dark hair and a silky complexion.

The nurse raised the head of his bed all the way and carefully removed tape holding the tube to his face. The doctor took over and examined the tube running down his throat.

"I'm going to pull the tube out. Are you ready?"

Fang nodded.

"Okay, take a deep breath and let it out."

Fang inhaled and as he exhaled, the tube was removed. The doctor told him to cough but he did that naturally. The staff cleaned up the area and moved the breathing machine out of the way.

"Your vitals are good," the doctor reported. "Rest up and I'll check on you later."

The young woman referred to as his *girlfriend*, bent over and gave Fang a kiss.

"Oh Yin! I knew you'd come back."

Fang could not remember her name, but deep down in this new mind, he had feelings for her. She pulled a chair over and held his hand, a trickle of tears ran down her cheeks.

"How long?" Fang croaked out in a hoarse voice.

"Two months! You were unconscious for two months. But, I knew you would come back."

"What happened?"

"You were in a car accident, don't you remember?"

Fang shook his head.

"It doesn't matter, don't worry about that now. Save your voice and rest. The doctor said you may have some difficulty remembering. For now, just sleep. I'm here and I'm not going anywhere."

It was reassuring to know she would be there for him and deep down, he yearned to be there for her. These were new emotions for Fang, he wondered if they were truly his. No matter, he liked the way he felt. It was like he was reborn, given a second chance.

Fang closed his eyes and tried to remember. He recalled having been here before, for a short time before the accident. He was experimenting with teleporting his thoughts elsewhere. Somehow that landed him here, in this body. The body of a young man named Yin Kai, not unlike Fang in his youth. Except this man had nothing to do with neuroscience, physics, or QR-7. This man was still finding his way in a world Fang was unfamiliar with. Fang yearned to learn more, but his experiment was short lived and he soon found himself back in his mountain-top home. So he tried again, raising the dosage of QR-7 and here he was. Except this time he would stay. Wherever *this* was, he wished to remain here for the rest of his life.

# CHAPTER 66

KIMBRA LEFT THE CLASSROOM ALONG WITH THE OTHER STUDENTS. Night classes at UIC were sometimes a drag, especially after a full day's work. Social Policy 420, not being the most interesting, didn't help. She left the classroom with another a girl, her name was Dakota.

"Interested in joining me and a few others at the Ratskeller?" she asked.

"Oh thanks, but I can't tonight."

Kimbra had no other plans, and tomorrow was Friday, but she was just too tired. She just wanted to head home, put on her PJs and relax.

"Maybe some other night then?" Dakota offered.

"Yeah, that would be nice."

Kimbra left Dakota outside. There was a fall chill to the air as she pulled up the collar on her jacket and headed home on foot. She enjoyed the solitude and loved the sounds and smell of the city. A car honked in the distance as she passed the recreation fields covered in darkness, the scent of moist grass in the air. A couple of guys were drinking on the bleachers, probably local high school kids. She left the campus behind and worked her way through a series of brick apartment buildings. As she stepped onto a curb, a man appeared out of nowhere, startling her. He was older, dressed in a shabby overcoat and was most definitely not a student.

"Where ya goin, miss?"

Kimbra kept walking, careful to keep him in her sights while trying to ignore him.

"I said, where ya going?" he repeated, this time louder.

"What?" Kimbra looked in his direction while continuing to walk away from him.

"Want some company?"

Kimbra picked up her pace, trying not to look frightened. He picked up his pace and pulled up alongside her. She began to trot, that's when he sprinted to catch up and put a hand on her shoulder. She instinctively shoved his hand away.

"What the hell. Don't touch me!" she snapped back before turning away.

He was slightly out of breath and grabbed her from behind, wrapping her in a bear hug. She tried to escape, but he dragged her to a stop. Kimbra turned and kicked, aiming for a shin or right between the legs, but she missed. There was a struggle and before she knew it, she hit the pavement hard and he was on top of her. She pushed but he was too heavy, he pinned her shoulders to the ground and worked his legs between hers. She smelled the foul odor of his cigarette and alcohol laden breath, she could feel him getting aroused.

"Get off me! Help!" she yelled.

He slapped her in the face hard, so hard she blacked out for a second. He came at her trying to kiss her, she turned away and he slobbered over her cheek. That's when her mind went blank, her head began to spin, and a vision began to form. She was on a grass field with another young woman. The woman was beaten badly, unable to resist, her clothes ripped. It was him, she knew it. She was inside his mind, seeing what he saw, feeling his sadistic thoughts as he raped the poor woman. There was no pity, no remorse for his victim, only his dominance over someone weaker. That and his perverted desires. She knew the same fate was planned for her, but not tonight, not ever again.

Kimbra took control of the rapist's mind. She sifted through the filth, searching for a weakness, all the while knowing he was on top of her, pawing at her body. She found it in a distant memory, a prostitute mother with live-in boyfriend who beat him, a history of sadistic, antisocial behavior. She climbed into the limbic system of his brain and hit him with the deepest emotions, pulling them up from the deepest, darkest corners of his mind. Feelings she had experienced firsthand: despair, hopelessness, a complete lack of self-worth. The man rose up on his knees. Kimbra took the opportunity to slide out from under him and crawl away.

The man remained on his knees motionless, his eyes fluttered. Kimbra could get up and run away, but something stopped her. She knew this man had raped before, she knew he would do it again. Her thoughts turned to Daniel and how he tormented her in the cabin, tried to kill her. In that instant she redirected all her rage at Daniel towards the rapist. She had to do something before this man hurt another woman. She rose to her feet and concentrated, directing her thoughts outward. The man pulled out a gun from his overcoat and pointed it at his head. The gun wobbled in his shaky hand, not certain of its next move. Then his grip tightened and the gun steadied itself. For a moment, his eyes stopped fluttering and cleared. In that split second of time, he recognized his victim, he knew it was she who was controlling his mind, but it was hopeless to resist. Then it was over, his eyes rolled back in his head and fluttered. A single tear rolled down his cheek as he pulled the trigger.

Blood and brain matter splattered over the sidewalk as the lifeless body keeled over. Kimbra turned and vomited at the sight. She dragged a sleeve across her mouth and hurried back to her apartment, running most of the way. She locked herself inside, kicked off her shoes and tossed her overcoat on a chair. Shaking like a dried up leaf in an autumn breeze, she poured herself a brandy and sunk into the sofa with a warm blanket. Sipping brandy, isn't that what people did when they celebrated a milestone or marked a major event in their life? That's what Carter would do. She took a large gulp, thinking she had just crossed a line. A line most people never cross, and for good reason. She had just killed someone!

Frayed nerves began to settle and she contemplated her actions. She could have walked away. That's what most people would have done. That's what she would have done before. But she had changed and she knew it. Life had changed her, Daniel had changed her, and the drug... that had changed her as well. She took another sip of the sweet liquor, letting it warm her inside, relax her mind. Her thinking, senses, and reactions, they were heightened now. She was a different person, the drug had transformed her. At first she was afraid it would make her violent, turn her suicidal like Chad. But Stanwix was right, and in time she learned that lower doses given less frequently, enhanced her abilities without those terrible side effects. She would have to make the drug last, but was beginning to suspect some of the changes were now permanent.

As the brandy kicked in, she began to unwind and open her mind. For a clear mind could listen, a clear mind would be receptive to telepathic signals from far away. She felt a presence, a dark connection she would forever be linked to. Whether she liked it or not, he was out there somewhere, waiting, lurking. She sensed Daniel would be looking for her. But the next time, she would be ready.

# EPILOGUE

A FRESH START, A NEW BEGINNING, THAT'S WHAT I NEEDED. With enough money and the right contacts you can do anything. I changed my name and created a new identity, I am a new man. Still, I have to wonder what it would be like if things had happened differently. What if I hadn't bumped into Marie that fateful day she met Kimbra outside for lunch? I panicked, thinking I had to kill Marie before she told Kimbra about me. But if I didn't act quickly, she would have ruined everything. Marie never liked me and suspected I killed her friend Linda in high school. She absolutely would have told Kimbra. I had to do something.

Regardless, I did it all for Kimbra. Why couldn't she see that? I loved her and how did she repay me? She called the cops, reported me to Fang or whoever was running that program, and now the *paranormal army* is after me. I can sense them probing my mind, searching for a weakness. But they will never catch me, they can't. Not as long as I have the QR-7, and I have enough to last a long time. But they will try. They wish to kill me: either for what I know, or what I can do with the drug. Maybe I can somehow use that against them. I'm not yet sure what I will do about that, but I have to be careful. I will have to forever remain vigilant. Yes, my past will always haunt me.

So here I am in the Midwest, enjoying the small town life. The people are so nice and welcoming. I could settle here, start an investigation business, maybe open a little bookstore. Yeah, that would be nice. There are plenty of outdoor events in the summer, plenty of places to meet people, plenty of pretty girls as well. In the winter there are dances and bingo. Right now I'm in the stands enjoying the local rodeo. I had my eye on this one girl in particular. She has a button nose and long dark hair covering her soft shoulders. Her dark brown eyes are entrancing, her lashes enticing. I had been observing Mandy for a while and when the time was right, I introduced myself. Oh, she's back.

"Derek, they're all out of your favorite beer so I got you a Bud. Hope it's all right?" she asked.

"Thanks, that's fine."

Mandy snuggles up close to me, I feel the soft warmth of her body.

"I just love the rodeo, don't you?" she asks in that innocent, sweet voice of hers.

"They really grow on you. I guess I do."

Mandy flashes me a big smile, and I almost melt. She has really got a lot going for her.

There is a lot to be said for starting a new relationship. I mean, don't get me wrong, there is nothing like a long-term relationship, the comfort of knowing each other's every wants and needs. But when you first meet, you just can't match the excitement, curiosity, and pure adrenalin rush from a new lover. I want this one to last, I do. I hope Mandy does not disappoint me like the others. All the others changed over time, but I'm not going to worry about that now. I'm going to enjoy every moment. I will use all my enhanced powers to make it last.

But, as I sit here in the warmth of the sun, watching Mandy enjoying the bronc riding, thoughts creep into my mind. I sense another presence, a person that will always be a part of me. I knew that from the first time I laid eyes on her in high school. Two lovers inextricably joined for life, forever changed. I owe everything I am today, to her. I will one day make her mine again and if not, I will make sure no one else has her. She broke my heart and for that, I will seek revenge, but not today. I will bide my time and wait for the perfect opportunity, when she least expects it. She has telepathic powers, I know this. Not as refined as mine, but I have to be careful.

So, as I sit here enjoying this beautiful thing I have going with Mandy, I realize there is another who will always have my utmost attention. Kimbra is special, unlike any of the others. Sure, she's beautiful and we have shared so much, but there's more. She has the one thing none of the others had. Kimbra is the one that got away.

# Also By

Three people united under extraordinary circumstances. A brutal murder alters history, a time device opens a world of possibilities. Look for all three stand-alone novels in the time travel trilogy, Project Eight Ball:

FLASH BACK
EXTREME PERIL
PAST PARADOX

To get more on future promotions and the latest book releases, subscribe to the mailing list at:  jturiano.com/author.htm

If you like what you've read, consider leaving a short review on your favorite online book seller's website. It's a great way to help independently self-published authors like John. Your interest and support is greatly appreciated.

# About the Author

JOHN TURIANO is the author of the time travel trilogy, Project Eight Ball, which began with his debut novel, *Flash Back*. He followed the trilogy with the psychological thriller, *Dark Presence*.

John lives where he grew up in western New York with his wife, Sue. Living nearby are their two adult children. When not writing he can be found camping, hiking and biking.

Visit John Turiano at:  jturiano.com/author.htm